Selected praise for

JENNIFER BLAKE

"Each of her carefully researched novels
evokes a long-ago time so beautifully that you are
swept into every detail of her memorable story."
—*RT Book Reviews*

"Blake…has rightly earned the admiration and
respect of her readers. They know there is a world of
enjoyment waiting within the pages of her books."
—*A Romance Review*

"Beguiling, sexy heroes… Well done, Ms. Blake!"
—*The Romance Reader's Connection*

"Jennifer Blake is a beloved writer of romance—
the pride and care she takes
in her creations shines through."
—*Romance Reviews Today*

"*Guarded Heart* is a boundlessly exciting and
adventuresome tale…sure to be one of the best
historical romances I will read this year."
—*Romance Junkies*

"Blake's anticipated return to historical romance
proves to be well worth the wait."
—*A Romance Review* on *Challenge to Honor*

JENNIFER BLAKE

By Grace Possessed

MIRA®

MIRA®

Recycling programs
for this product may
not exist in your area.

ISBN-13: 978-0-7783-1254-3

BY GRACE POSSESSED

Copyright © 2011 by Patricia Maxwell

For questions and comments about the quality of this book please contact us at
Customer_eCare@Harlequin.ca.

www.MIRABooks.com

Printed in U.S.A.

Gerard C. Faucheux
1967–2010

For the music and the memories.

1

England
December, 1486

She could not bear to be present for the kill.

It was not that Lady Catherine Milton was unduly squeamish, only that she could not stand to see such a noble stag pulled down by the hounds. He had given them a gallant run through open meadows and into the thick growth of the king's ancient hunting preserve known as the New Forest, eluding the hunt with cunning and bursts of supreme power. Now he was flagging. Soon the king and his courtiers would close in for the coup de grâce.

Cate reined in her palfrey to a walk, allowing the others to pull away in their crashing pursuit along the narrow animal track. She had been at the laggard end of the crowd of courtiers, peers and their ladies for most of the afternoon. She could give the need to rest her mount as an excuse for dropping back. With luck, the worst of the bloody business would be over by the time she rejoined them.

She'd rather have avoided hunting altogether today,

would have except for the king's invitation, which was as good as a command. Henry VII liked company during his efforts to supply venison for the hundreds that flocked to his tables, and had need of extra meat for the Christmas season, which was upon them. More than that, he was particularly concerned that the heiresses summoned to his court display themselves on horseback to prospective suitors. He had overcome the dread curse of the Three Graces to make an advantageous marriage this past summer for Cate's older sister, Isabel, and was determined to repeat the triumph twice more. Isabel was in the north of England with her husband and six-month-old Madeleine, King Henry's love child entrusted to their care, but their younger sibling rode with the others somewhere ahead. Marguerite would not be overly concerned if she noticed Cate had gone missing. This wasn't the first time she had fallen back at the end of a hunt.

The afternoon was drawing in, growing dark with lowering clouds. The feel of snow was sharp in the air. Cate would much have preferred to be sitting before a fireplace with embroidery in hand and a beaker of mulled cider close by. Though her upper body was warm enough under her ermine-lined cloak, the tip of her nose was half-frozen, and her feet and gloved fingers had little feeling. At least the end of the chase meant the return to Winchester Castle where, please God, a roaring fire and a hot meal awaited.

Abruptly, her gray mare threw up her head and curveted to the side. Cate tightened her knee on the horn of her sidesaddle, controlling the palfrey even as she glanced around. Fair Rosamond, dubbed Rosie within an hour after she was named, was not usually of a nervous habit. She must have sensed something she didn't like.

Nothing moved beyond the stirring of a light wind among the bare limbs of the great oaks, beeches and alders that meshed above the forest track. The thudding hoofbeats, calling voices and horns of the hunt that faded into the distance left behind an unnatural quiet. The scent of leaf mold, disturbed by their passage, shifted in the air along with a hint of damp moss and lichen.

Something else drifted toward Cate, as well, something rank, familiar and malodorous.

The boar burst from the underbrush. Squealing with rage at the invasion of its territory, it came straight at them. It kicked up dried leaves and dirt as its sharp hooves found purchase. Its small black eyes were narrowed and its snout lowered, while the gray evening light caught wicked gleams from the knife-sharp points of its curving tusks.

The mare whinnied in fright, rearing up on her haunches. The instant Rosie came down she leaped into a gallop and plunged into the deep woods.

The boar gave chase.

Cate could hear it snuffling and snorting behind them. Once, it gave a piercing squeal of pain or rage. She had no time to look back, but gripped the reins in one hand while leaning to grasp the mare's mane with the other. She let Rosie run, trusting her to escape the danger at their heels. Behind them, the thudding sounds of pursuit made the boar seem a veritable monster.

Limbs slapped at Cate, ripping her flowing skirt, snatching the hood from her head, catching her veil and tearing it free. She almost left the saddle a dozen times as Rosie leaped fallen logs, dodged around thickets, splashed twice through the same winding stream. Clinging like a burr to the mare, Cate ducked and weaved, heart pounding as she prayed in breathless phrases.

Her prayer seemed answered as they struck a beaten pathway and Rosie turned down it. It had some width, as if it might be used by foresters gathering wood for the king, or gamekeepers en route to the castle. The palfrey slowed, blowing, jolting into a trot.

Cate glanced back as she tried to catch her breath. The boar was not there, could no longer be seen or heard. They had cleared its part of the forest, or else it had lost interest and abandoned them. She closed her eyes an instant in thankfulness before facing forward again.

Her relief was short-lived. As the forest track curved, a large brush pile appeared ahead of her, barring the way. It stretched between two great oaks whose thick limbs overhung it.

Cate pulled up, frowning in consternation at the untidy heap of rotted logs and dead limbs. She'd half formed the intention of following the pathway in hope it would join the track taken by the hunt. To go over the brush pile seemed impossible; it was too high, wide and deep. She might go around it if she made a wide enough circuit, but would have to pick her way with care so she did not lose the pathway she was following. The New Forest belonged to the king, an expanse of many uncharted leagues where no one was allowed to live and few ventured except on royal business. Those who became lost in it were sometimes found too late, if at all.

A rustling noise overhead drew her attention. Directly above her, a man rose from where he had been lying along the thick width of a limb. Rough-haired, garbed in odds and ends of once fine raiment, he gave her a gap-toothed leer. Then he grasped a limb and dropped to the ground, landing on his feet in front of her. As Rosie backed and whinnied, trying to rear, he sprang to grab the mare's bridle and pull her head down.

Sick dread burgeoned inside Cate as she controlled Rosie to prevent more pressure on her tender mouth. Never go into the wood alone, she had been told again and again. Fearsome beings lived there, trolls and beasts with the faces of men who feasted on tender flesh. Or if not these, then lawless scoundrels who lived by their wits and what they could take from others.

From women, they wanted one thing. That was, of course, after they had taken everything else of value.

Cate wore a gold cross that had belonged to her mother, a ring of gold set with a ruby that had been a gift from Isabel, and, at her waist, an Italian poniard given to her by her first love, with silver filigree on its ebony hilt and a finely pointed steel blade. She would surrender no single treasure without a fight. Slipping her right hand inside her cloak, she grasped the hilt of the small knife, where it hung from her leather hunting girdle.

"Well, now. What have we here?"

The man's voice was layered with equal amounts of insolence and anticipation. He stood with his legs spread and gloating triumph beneath the grime that coated his face. From his accent, Cate judged him to be some petty noble, mayhap one removed from his holdings during the endless wars of recent years, or else a renegade from the defeated army of Richard III. He was no mere villein or cottager turned forest outlaw; he was too cocksure for that.

His purpose could not be good. Still, it would be foolish to show her alarm.

"Well met, sir," she said, her heart threatening to choke her even as she gave him her best smile. "I was with the king's hunt, but lost my way through misadventure. Could you direct me how best to rejoin it?"

"The king, is it?" he said, an avid gleam in his eyes as he stepped forward. "No doubt you are a favorite of Henry's, a lady sure to be missed."

His voice carried snide suggestion, as if she must be on terms of intimacy with the king. Cate cared no more for it than did Rosie, who blew through her nostrils as she tried to sidle away from the man's stench. Or no, it may have been from his followers, a dozen or more in number, who slipped from among the encroaching trees. They eased forward with weapons in hand, a few bows and arrows, the knives carried by all for eating and a scattering of age-blackened swords.

Who had they meant to take in this crude ambuscade? The king, mayhap, had he chanced to come this way? It would have been a dangerous undertaking, for Henry made no move without his yeoman guard. No, their quarry would have been any straggler.

Gathering her reins with a firmer one-handed grip, Cate lifted her chin. "A favorite of the queen, rather," she said in tart reproof. "Can you or can you not direct me?"

"I can do many a thing for you, milady, and better than

any king, I'll warrant. Get you down and I'll be pleased to show you."

A shudder of revulsion moved down her spine at the loose-lipped grins and chuckles of the men who crowded closer around her. "I must not linger or I'll be caught by darkness," she answered in tones as icy as the clouds that hung low above the treetops.

"So you will, now. Too bad."

The threat and raw suggestion in his colorless eyes were mixed with overweening confidence. He thought she was cowed, his for the taking. His hand was lax on Rosie's bridle. His gaze rested on Cate's breasts beneath her cloak, giving her a squirming sensation like worms crawling over her skin.

If she was going to get away, it must be now.

Cate gave a high-pitched yell, tugging Rosie's head around. She prodded the mare with an urgent heel.

The outlaw leader lost his hold, but jumped up to fasten a hand on Cate's arm. She clung to her sidesaddle with thigh muscles clamped around its horn as Rosie backed and whinnied. A second outlaw ran forward to catch the bridle on the other side. The outlaw leader scrabbled with his feet in the dirt of the track, jerking at her, using his weight to bend her toward him.

It was too much. Cate gave a cry of angry despair as she felt her saddle girth slip, felt her knee slide free of its anchor.

Pain burst through her as she struck the ground. Her breath left her in a gasp so sharp it seemed to slice into her lungs. A red mist appeared at the edge of her vision.

The palfrey reared in terror, then broke the hold on her bridle and danced out of reach. Whinnying, shaking her head, she kicked up her heels and raced away, back down the track. The outlaw leader paid no heed, but leaned to catch Cate's arm in a numbing grip. He hauled her upright so fast she staggered, almost fell against him.

Her chest ached with the sudden return of air to her lungs. White-hot rage flashed over her. She did not pause to think or plan, but grasped her poniard's hilt again, snatching it from its scabbard. She threw back the edge of her cloak and struck with all her might.

The blade ripped through tattered velvet and soiled linen, found flesh and bone. Her assailant howled and reeled away, even as the knife point struck a rib, then tore free. Cate, sick yet exultant, skipped backward with her skirts trailing over the half-frozen ground.

The outlaw clapped a hand to his chest, lifted it to stare at the blood that stained it. His face twisted as he clenched his fingers into a fist and started after her. Two of his dirty band fell in behind him, followed by more, and yet more.

It was then that a great shout rang through the forest. Savage, full-throated and deep, it rose to a battle cry that lifted the hair on the back of Cate's neck and sent a chill spiraling through her. Wild-eyed and with her poniard still in her fist, she swung in the direction from whence it came.

He rode toward them at a hard, flying gallop, his plaid of blue and green shot with red billowing in the wind of his passage. His long dark hair rippled with waves beneath his bonnet and his face was set in deadly determination. The hilt of a great sword loomed at one shoulder, and the thighs that gripped his mount's sides were bare above knee boots crisscrossed by leather thongs. His mouth was open with a cry that sang of retribution, justice and the fierce, steel-hard joy of battle.

The Scotsman, Ross Dunbar.

Cate recognized the rider with a sudden, amazed acceleration of her heart.

All at court knew of the man, though none claimed to know him well. Women sighed as he passed with his plaid swinging against strong, well-formed legs, his bonnet at a proud angle on his head, broad shoulders squared in defiance, and his eyes, blue as the lochs of his native land, set straight ahead. Men gave him a wide berth, for he had a coldly effective temper, little patience with fools and bleak disdain for Henry's court. There only as a pledge for the goodwill of his father, an irascible old border laird too fond of raiding across the line between Scotland and England, Ross Dunbar despised his enforced attendance upon Henry VII. He scorned to drink and dice with most of those he called Sassenachs, and named none among them friend. Few were willing to meet him on the practice yard, for when he unlimbered his great sword with its silver chasing, someone always suffered.

He had been with the hunt, Cate knew, for she had marked him among its leaders. How he had come to be on this track she could not think. Nor could she see what he, one man, hoped to do against outlaws armed to the teeth and careless of lives that were worth nothing if they were caught by the king's men.

* * *

Ross was barely aware of the figures that ranged themselves behind the outlaw leader. All he saw was the blood on the man's filthy doublet and the knife in Lady Catherine's small, white fist. She was no match for the man she had injured or his overweening pride that would demand she suffer for it. Regardless, Ross had never seen so fierce a warrior queen. She was magnificent in her defiance, valiant beyond hope of any man's equal as she faced them with only her courage and small blade as weapons.

She had been insulted, manhandled, brought to earth like the most hunted of vixens; he had seen it happen. Regardless, she would not be taken. He would see her safe or die in the attempt.

The power of the hunter he rode was in his favor. The great steed with its flashing hooves scattered the forest scum in all directions. Before they could gather their wits, he was among them, sliding from horseback, drawing his sword before he hit the ground. The long blade flashed silver fire as he whirled to face an attacker similarly armed. A single blow of his heavier weapon, and the other man's rust-pitted sword broke in half. As its owner threw it down and turned to run, Ross helped him along with a boot to the backside. Whirling then, he slashed and hacked, kicked, feinted and plunged to face two attackers, three, four, sending them into headlong flight. It was a brutal and dirty business without finesse, but then little was required. His foes had scant honor and no restraint; else they would never have laid hands on the lady.

Their leader had circled behind him to take her again. Seeing his men defeated, the outlaw used her as a living shield, backing away as Ross rounded upon him. His eyes were feral and he held a dirty knife against the fine white skin of her throat.

For a single instant, Ross allowed his attention to stray to Lady Catherine. One arm was twisted behind her back, and her knife, a poniard, now lay on the ground at her feet. Yet she met his gaze, her eyes bright blue and steady, shadowed by knowledge of her danger, yet without defeat. Her valiance touched some fastness inside him with such sudden fierce need that he tightened his grasp on his sword, stepped forward with hard purpose.

The outlaw's eyes widened. He ran his tongue over his white lips. With a vicious oath, then, he shoved Lady Catherine from him so she stumbled forward, arms outflung.

Ross whipped his sword aside barely in time to keep from impaling her on it. Reaching with hard muscles well-oiled from the fight, he caught her with one arm, snatching her against him. Face set, heart pounding with terror for what he had almost done, almost been forced to do, he swung back upon the outlaw leader.

He was almost upon him, his long knife raised to strike. A swift, backhanded slice, singing with its hard purpose, sent the man stumbling back. He crouched, clutching a long gash in his belly that might well be the end of him.

With Lady Catherine firm in the curve of his arm and his sword in a hard grasp, Ross paced forward. The outlaw paled, looked around, saw that he was completely

alone. Being no fool, he turned and fled at a staggering run.

In less than a heartbeat, the forest track was empty.
The wood around them crackled with retreating footsteps, and then was silent.

To let the pack of merciless brigands get away went
against the grain. Had Ross been alone, he would have
pursued them, laid at least one or two by the heels and
seen them hung. The first to have his neck stretched
would have been their leader. He deserved that and more.

Ross couldn't afford it. For one thing, the retreat was
possibly an attempt to draw him to where he could be
surrounded and taken down. Added to that, he was en-
cumbered by the lady, who would become a liability if
he had to move fast or fight off a surprise attack. The
value of silence while tracking could also be an unfa-
miliar concept for her.

Come to think of it, she was not making much noise
now.

She was making no noise at all.

Ross frowned down at the woman pressed against his
side. Her face was pale, her lips bloodless, and her eyes,
though the pure blue of the Madonna's robe, were stark
and wide. Tremors shook her from the fine, springing
blond tendrils that hung around her face to her long,
white fingers that clutched his hard arm at her waist.
Even the hem of her skirt fluttered, rattling the leaves
where it swept the ground.

"What is it?" he demanded, the words rougher than
he intended. "Are you hurt?"

She lifted her chin a fraction. "N-no. I just...I don't know."

Comprehension struck him. He had seen the like before in street brawls and on the field of battle, where men who fought like devils incarnate while it was needful, then shook until their teeth rattled afterward. He'd just never seen it in a female.

Releasing his hold with some reluctance, supporting her with a hand around her upper arm, he leaned to scoop up the cloak that had been torn from her shoulders. "Wrap this around you," he said as he draped it into place. "Getting warm again should help."

"Yes." She ducked her head as if to avoid his gaze as she tried to fasten the torn cords meant to hold her cloak. "I should...should thank you for...for..."

"Nay, not at all. In God's truth, 'twas a pleasure." Bending, he picked up the small knife she'd dropped, returning it to the scabbard that hung from a chain on her girdle.

Her pale lips trembled into a smile as if she understood his intent to make her feel safer by the return of her weapon. The valor of that effort, in spite of her shivering, sent a peculiar pain through him. Brushing her hands away from her cloak cords, he made a hard knot of what was left of them.

"Nevertheless, you have my gratitude."

Her voice was stronger, he noted as he glanced at her from under his brows. A hint of pink crept across her cheekbones, mayhap from resentment at his presumption in touching her. It seemed progress that should be aided, one way or another. It was certainly better than dragging her into his arms and holding her so tightly against him that neither of them could breathe.

"What I fail to see," he added as if she had not spoken, "is why rescue was necessary. Had you stayed with the hunt as you should—"

"What makes you think I left it of my own will?" she interrupted, meeting his gaze for the barest of moments before lowering her lashes again.

"You dropped back and let it go on without you, for I saw you." He allowed a corner of his mouth to curl. "The question is why. Were you about nature's business, or did you expect to meet a lover in some thicket?"

"As if I would do such a thing!"

That was better. Hot rose color had returned to her cheekbones and her lips were not so pale. "Many English lasses would, or so I've found. And most men are glad to tarry if a woman is halfway presentable."

"If you followed me because…"

"Nay," Ross said in hard disavowal. He'd not have her think him as bad as the scum he had vanquished. Not that he wasn't well and truly aware of her womanly charms; he could still feel the imprint of her curves along his side, had her scent of lavender, warm velvet and well-bathed, gently reared female in his nostrils.

"Yet you are here," she said with a small frown. "You must have a reason."

She was quick, in spite of the shock of what she'd been through; he had to give her that. He had indeed followed her. He'd been far too aware of where she was and what she was doing all this long day, though that was something he preferred to keep to himself. His main regret was that he had not fallen back in time to prevent what had happened. Yes, and that she had been manhandled while he dispatched the boar that frightened her mare, and then paused long enough to discover exactly what he faced from her attackers.

"'Twas diplomacy," he answered in irony laced with self-protection. "To show up the king by killing his stag for him would be more than a thought unwise. Besides, I heard the boar that fair scared the wits out of your mare, and thought to add his tough hams to Henry's larder."

She gave Ross a sharp look that showed more than a little doubt, but did not challenge his statement. It was a moment before she spoke again. "Now Rosie is gone. You might give thought to how we are to return to the hunt without her or your mount."

She was right. His hunter had disappeared in company with the outlaws, and there was no sign of her palfrey.

Ross cursed in blistering Gaelic phrases as he turned in a circle to scan the encroaching wood. He would not have been laggard in noticing their loss if not distracted by the lady. Still, that was no excuse. He should have noticed, should have prevented it.

He considered plunging after his own beast, chasing down those who had taken him. His reason for not doing so was unchanged, however. He could not drag Lady Catherine with him any more than he could before, nor could he leave her alone in case the outlaws circled back.

The hunter was as fine a piece of horseflesh as Ross had ever straddled, and he hated to see him go. At least he need not mourn the poor beast too much, as he had been borrowed from Henry's stables.

Lady Catherine sighed and then drew away from him, turning toward the track along which they had come. "I suppose we had best start walking."

"Nay," he said with a slow frown. "I think not."

"No? But surely…"

He lifted a shoulder, readjusted his plaid, which had slipped from it. "It will soon be full dark. To find our way back through the wood in broad daylight and on horseback would be hard enough, but afoot in the night is too great a risk."

She stared at him as if he had gone mad. "We can't stay here!"

"It's better than wandering in circles until we're lost, or freezing to death while we're at it." He did not think her able to make the long trek just now, though he would not say so.

"Oh, but—"

"Besides, the king should have sent out searchers for you. We have wood here for a beacon fire that will surely bring them to us." It would also serve to help warm her, as would constructing a shelter. But mentioning either need was another thing that seemed unwise at the moment.

"And if it doesn't, if we are not found before morning?"

"Then it will be later," he said with finality.

"You may be satisfied with that, but I, sir, am not!"

He cocked his head, frowning at her as she stood facing him with blue fire in her eyes and the bearing of an injured queen. "Meaning?"

"We will be expected to marry. Had you not considered that point, or is it that you anticipate taking an heiress to wife?"

Anger stirred Ross's blood to a slow simmer. "You think I would keep you here of a purpose, to force you to the altar?"

"It's been done before." She glanced at him and then away again.

"Not by me," he countered in hard deliberation. "I've no use for a Sassenach bride."

More hot color flared in her face for his plain speaking, and her chin came up. "Excellent," she said in clear disdain, "because I have no use for a Scots husband. No, nor any other kind."

"None at all?" He could not keep the surprise from his voice. To be unmarried was an odd ambition in a woman, or so was his experience.

"I'll not be the death of a man."

She was so certain in her pronouncement, and so grim withal. He couldn't prevent the salacious grin that curled one corner of his mouth. "His death, is it? And from what cause might that be?"

"Not what you may suppose!" she answered with fierce ire and another flood of rose-red in her face. "Have you not heard of the accursed Three Graces of Graydon?"

"Oh, aye, that."

Her eyes narrowed. "You may treat it as a jest, but I assure you it is real."

"Sisters who may be married for no reason except love, is it? And who can cause the death of any man who betroths himself to them without it? It's a tale bandied about the court. I heed it not."

"So you would accept whatever consequences may befall."

He watched her, enjoying the stiff disdain on her features, glad of that show of temper compared to her earlier pallor. "I see little reason to get in a bother. No one can force us to marry. The scandal may affect your marriage prospects, but that hardly matters if you don't expect to wed."

"You are forgetting King Henry."

"And what has he to say to it?"

"A great deal, as I am a royal ward by his grace. He has been contemplating the best match for me for some few weeks now. Suppose he should decide an alliance with the son of a Scots laird would suit him well?"

Unease spread through Ross. God's blood, but she might be right again.

He had been left behind in England after James III of Scotland made peace with the Sassenach back in the summer, pledged as a hostage to keep his father in check. That randy old goat took savage delight in feuding with his English neighbors, raiding across the border any time boredom moved him. The results did nothing to ease border tensions. Ross had endured five months of enforced English hospitality, had supped at Henry Tudor's table and become a boon companion of the solemn-faced conqueror of the last Plantagenet king. Henry could easily decide to attach him permanently to his court with a marriage tie. That was, if he had no better match for the lady.

"I am of Scotland and answer to King James alone,"

Ross said in harsh reply. "Never will I bow to the will of an English king."

She stared at him, her eyes darkly blue. It was as if she weighed him, not just his outward appearance but what he was inside. An icy trickle moved down his spine that was very like a warning.

"Do you swear it?" she asked.

Ignoring the presentiment, he raised his clenched fist and thumped it upon his chest above his heart. "You have my word."

Her smile was as wintry as the evening sky. "And will remember it, as I have no defense of my own against Henry's intentions. See that you do the same."

It was then, as they stood facing each other with the determination to avoid marriage standing like a drawn sword between them, that the first flakes of snow began to fall. They drifted down, swirling around, over and between them like the ashes of a Samhain fire.

2

The fire crackled, leaping toward the lower limbs of the great oak overhead. Sparks flew up to mingle with the branches before being extinguished by falling snow. The dancing flames gilded the hands of the man who had built it as he held them out to the warmth, outlining their hard strength in orange and blue light, glancing over myriad white nicks and scars. Above them, the planes of his face were sculpted in fire glow and shadow, with a raptor's nose and guarded eyes set in a handsome, yet masklike visage that appeared hard and distant, impervious to the emotions that plagued other men.

He seemed dangerous. That was not at all a comforting observation for Cate, given that she was about to spend the night alone in his company. That it must happen grew ever more certain as the minutes passed. Darkness had fallen more than an hour ago, and there was no sign of a search party. It gave her an odd feeling in the pit of her stomach, one that spread deep into her lower body as it grew more intense.

She stirred uncomfortably on the log where she sat, just inside the small lean-to he had formed by propping logs against the oak's wide trunk and weaving boughs through them. "Do you think the outlaws will return?" she asked with a brief glance beyond the fire's glow. "I mean, now that it's dark."

"Might." He reached for a twig and began breaking bits from it, tossing them into the flames.

"Mean you to sit up all night to guard against it, then?"

"I do."

"It's my belief they are cowards, as they ran away so easily rather than face you."

"Nay, milady. Only men who have discovered it's better to retreat than die for no reason."

"For no reason?" They had expected to take her, after all. Was she not worth some little effort as a prize?

"None at all." He gave her his attention for a flickering instant. "The poor fools saw there was no hope of keeping you, so abandoned the effort for easier prey tomorrow."

"There being no shame in retreat for a brigand? I pray they stay away." She shivered under her cloak.

"Mayhap they'll be happy with the hunter as reward."

"At least my palfrey made her escape. Last I saw of her, she was galloping down the track. She may not stop until she reaches her stall at Winchester Castle."

"Aye," Ross said in laconic agreement, "but I don't depend upon it."

The palfrey showing up at the stable without her would suggest something had befallen her. Whether the stable master would take notice, or be concerned enough to discover if she had returned with the others, were different questions altogether.

She sighed. "No."

She opened her mouth to ask what he would do if the men came back, after all, but then closed it again. There could be only one answer. He would fight as he had before.

"That's why you made such a great fire, isn't it," she said instead, "so you can see them before they get to us. You don't really think the king's men will be guided by it."

"No way to tell."

"The hunting party either failed to notice my absence or thought I went back ahead of them. Surely they know by now that I'm missing."

"To send out searchers in the dark would be foolish. The snow has covered all sign of tracks."

"Yes, but still…"

"Then they'll have noticed, not being blind, that I'm also among the missing."

She frowned at him. "You believe that will relieve their minds?"

He tossed a piece of his stick into the fire, speaking without meeting her eyes. "Or set them smirking, if they have any imagination."

Cate's heart sank inside her as she saw his point. Henry would surely be torn between worry that she might be alone and exposed to danger, and annoyance that she was in the Scotsman's company. She could not think his plans for her future had ever included such a misalliance. "I'm sorry to be the cause of concern," she said with a frown. "Henry has enough to plague him at the moment."

"You're thinking of the whispers that a son of Edward IV still lives? That tale has been around since Bosworth. He can't credit it."

"Can he not?" The two young sons of the late King Edward IV had been heirs to the throne before they were declared illegitimate and confined to the Tower by their uncle, Richard III, so he might snatch the crown upon his brother Edward's death three years ago. After Richard was killed at Bosworth Field, the Tower had been searched most diligently. No sign of the two boys had been uncovered. The countryside had been scoured high and low, but the princes, brothers to Henry's queen, Elizabeth of York, seemed to have vanished as if they had never lived.

Cate had never met Edward's sons, as she had arrived at court only a year ago, after Henry's coronation. She had seen miniatures of them, however. They had been so fair, so young and proud in their sturdy strength. What fate other than vicious murder could have caused them to disappear so completely? Though it would have sparked more strife and bloodshed between York and Lancaster factions had they emerged from captivity, their deaths were still a horror beyond words.

"The Thames runs close by the Tower," Ross Dunbar said without inflection, answering her thought, "and has carried many a soul out to sea."

"Some whisper that Henry's supporters did away with the boys in secret, to clear his way to the crown."

"While Richard had them in his charge, watched day and night against just such a trick? Don't be daft. The warders of the castle might be corrupt on occasion, but not when they could hang for it."

"They even say Henry's mother might have seen to it."

Ross snorted, breaking another twig and tossing it into the fire. "Yon duchess of Richmond and Derby is an officious little busybody, I'll grant you, with more to say about Henry's business than most men would allow. She busied herself with putting her son on the throne, right enough. Yet she's so godly a woman that I'd as soon suspect the Holy Mother."

"I suppose," Cate said in agreement. Lady Margaret was well known for devotion to the church, her good works and the black gown she often wore like the habit of a nun.

"More than that, rumors of the boys being done away with came to Scotland scant months into Richard's short reign."

"Indeed?" It was odd how relieved she was to hear it. Though she placed little credence in court gossip, it was worrisome all the same.

"The diplomats clacked back and forth about it, so I heard tell, from England to Spain, Spain to France, France to Scotland and back to England like a whirligig."

"You don't think Richard could have spirited them away to keep them out of Lancaster clutches."

"Or Yorkist, mayhap, as those who supported the older boy as Edward V were a far greater threat just then? Nay, where would he have put them that no whisper of it has been heard?"

"Unless this new threat might be that whisper," she said almost under her breath.

"And wouldn't that be convenient, a young prince as the rallying point for a push to be rid of Henry." The Scotsman hunched a broad shoulder. "Not that it's any worry of mine. The more Sassenachs kill off each other, the better."

"So Scotland might take advantage of any rebellion by invading," she said, "another worry for Henry."

"The very thing the treaty between England and Scotland is supposed to prevent."

"But will it? Know you anything of what King James will do if rebellion breaks out?"

"How should I, being stuck here as Henry's unwilling guest?" he returned, scowling at the fire.

That was reasonable enough, Cate thought as she joined him in watching the flames. They wavered in the wind, grasping at the snowflakes that swirled into their clutches. Beyond where she sat, white billows of snow swayed like bed linen hung out to dry. From the corner of her eye, she saw her rescuer tuck his plaid closer to his neck.

"You could keep watch from the shelter, could you not?" she suggested. "There's more than enough room."

He gave her a quick, unfathomable glance. "Here is fine."

"You'll soon be covered with snow. Will you not be soaked?"

"Belike, it won't melt."

The ironic humor in his voice was unexpected. It was

also appealing in some odd fashion. Watching the way his mouth curled at the corner, she forgot to answer.

"Any road, it's a mistake to get too comfortable," he added with barely a pause.

"Meaning you might fall asleep? 'Tis no great haven of warmth in here." She indicated her shelter with the twitch of a shoulder, then drew her fur-lined cloak closer around her as a chill draft found its way down the back of her neck. "You should be as uncomfortable as a body could desire."

His smile was crooked. "You think I like being cold and miserable?"

"You're doing little to prevent it."

"So you are inviting me to share your chamber. Is that the way of it then?"

She looked away, made suddenly uncomfortable by the flash of something intent yet secretive in the blue depths of his eyes. The faintest herbal scent came from him, possibly from the sprig of dried heather stuck in his bonnet. Mingled with it were the smells of fire-warmed wool, leather, horse and clean male. The combination made her stomach muscles tighten into knots.

"I'd hardly call it mine," she said in irritation. "You did build it, after all."

"For you, being you aren't used to sleeping in the weather."

"And you are."

He made a sound somewhere between a grunt and laugh. "Snow falls fair often in Scotland."

No doubt that was also why he kept a tinderbox in his sporran, the small bag with its silver emblem that draped across his lower belly. It seemed an excellent habit, one she applauded just now with every ounce of her being. "And you, a lord's son, are used to it? Somehow that seems unlikely."

"The word is *laird*," he corrected, "and has little that's lordly or noble about it. It means only that my father is a landowner of manifold responsibilities and goes, betimes, to attend Jamie's parliament."

"But you will inherit that one day?"

"Aye, as I've no brothers or sisters, or at least no legitimate ones." His smile had a fierce edge. "Well, and if the old warhorse doesn't decide I'm too soft."

She laughed; she couldn't help it. "You, soft?"

His gaze met hers for a long, intent moment that sent a quiver deep into her lower body before he looked away again. "I think too much to suit my father. He acts first and worries about it afterward, if at all. And he'd as soon ride out on a cattle raid in a rattling snowstorm as not—never mind that he's likely to lose half the cows before he gets them home. In fact, he'd rather ride in bad weather, as he'd be more likely to catch our enemies sleeping."

"Your enemies, the English." The thought was disturbing, though why, she could not say.

"Sassenach with more cows than sense, though usually 'tis Trilborn cattle."

"Trilborn?"

The Scotsman inclined his head. When he spoke, his voice was hard. "The same as we rode with this day."

Winston Dangerfield, Lord Trilborn, had been with the hunt. His estates were in the north, as she recalled.

"I can't imagine his family allows the theft without retaliation."

"Nay, nor his father and grandfather before him."

Cate met his gaze between tongues of leaping flames. "You sound as if there's bad feeling between you."

"A blood feud of long years standing that involves more than cows." Ross Dunbar shrugged. "Though a raid on his herd is more satisfying than on any other."

The last was meant to distract her from the enmity between him and Trilborn, she thought. It seemed just as well to allow it. "So you do steal other cattle?"

"On both sides of the border," he said with a low laugh.

"Both sides...you don't mean your father steals the cows of his neighbors?"

"Oh, aye. 'Tis a game of sorts, do you see, a wee bit of competition."

"It sounds dangerous."

"'Tis that which makes it worthwhile. Though the poor beasts have been chased back and forth on so many moonlit nights, have mingled and bred so often, it's near impossible to say who owns any cow."

Cate tilted her head as she watched snowflakes settle on his bonnet and the dark waves of his hair, turning all gray-white. "At least your presence here prevents your father from raiding across the border now. I believe that's the purpose of it?"

"In part," he said, inclining his head so snowflakes shifted onto his knees. "Fair ruined his fun, it has. No more rapine and pillage of his sworn foes."

She lifted a brow. "Rapine and pillage?"

"Ah, well, there may be less of it than he remembers, but he does like the old tales."

The tales weren't that old, she was almost certain. The border Scots, descended from Vikings who had once raided those northern shores, were known for their bellicose natures. Some named them Steel Bonnets for the helmets they wore on their lightning forays into English territory. It seemed reasonable that Ross Dunbar was of that warlike tribe, given the dark Nordic blue of his eyes.

There was a lulling quality to his voice, with its soft vowels that turned the word *cows* into "coos." There was also a barely concealed smile in it, as if he had enjoyed his forays into cattle theft, or at least taken pleasure in the skill and daring of the moonlit chase. Yes, and in tweaking the noses of his hereditary enemies.

Cate's mouth curved a little as she watched him. Leaning forward, she rested her elbow on her knee while holding her chin in the palm of her hand. "And what do you do with these 'coos' when you bring them in from a raid on such a snowy night?" she asked, as much to hear him talk as from the need to know.

"Put them in with our others in the cow byre, and guard them against being taken back."

She sighed, shivering a little as the icy wind lifted the hood of her cloak. It was a moment before she went on. "I wish I knew Rosie was safe in a cow byre this night, if she didn't return to her stable."

"Your palfrey, you mean?"

"I can't help thinking she might have come across the boar again." It was a legitimate fear, as a boar's tusks could open the soft underbelly of a horse in an instant.

"She didn't. She couldn't have, as I gutted the beast, and will send after him tomorrow."

Cate straightened. "You…you killed him."

"It seemed necessary at the moment, though I'd have done better to ride on when it turned on me as I came upon it."

"But…I was sure I heard him right behind me."

"For some small distance only. Is that why you didn't turn back? I thought your Rosie had run away with you, being you got so far ahead of me."

"Not…entirely." She had been so certain the boar was behind her, though the noise of her passage through the forest made it difficult to be sure.

"Too bad. All this could have been prevented, otherwise." He gestured at the brush pile that had become their wood yard, the fire, the woodland beyond, where the outlaws had disappeared.

"What, depriving me of the opportunity to sleep out in the weather?" she said with an attempt at lightness. "Heaven forbid."

He snorted but made no answer. With a glance at the snow that was falling thicker out of the night sky, he caught the drape of his plaid and unwrapped it from his shoulders, exposing the simple leather jerkin he wore under a short coat of darkest green wool and over a shirt of cream linen so brightly colored it was almost saffron. Shaking the white flakes from his head like a dog shaking off water, he lifted the wool length over it as a covering before wrapping the rest of it around him like a blanket.

His movements were so swift and unstudied, yet rife

with masculine grace, that they stopped the breath in Cate's throat. His hair was black silk, falling in waves to his shoulders, his jawline square and firm. His shoulders were broad enough that he had dislodged sheaves of snow from them. The movement of his plaid, as he drew it higher, exposed a length of thigh that was brown, hard and corded with muscle.

The sensation that seized her was heated and virulent, an exhilaration in the blood. She had never been private with a man before, never been close to one in quite the same way. Oh, she had been seated next to admirers at table on occasion, had walked in the cloisters at their side. There had always been other people about, however— her sisters, the king's guards, stewards and sentries—to prevent any untoward familiarity.

There was no one here except her and the Scotsman. He could do whatever he pleased to her with no one to gainsay him. All she had to depend upon was his sworn word that he had no desire to take her to wife.

That said nothing of what else he might desire of her. Her strength was no match for his, no matter how hard she might fight him. She would be at his mercy. And why that thought made her ache with emptiness deep inside instead of terrifying her, she could not have said.

Silence stretched around them, broken only by the whine of snow-laden wind in the limbs overhead and the flutter and snap of the fire. The cold air, scented with wood smoke and snow, hurt the back of Cate's nose and threatened to freeze her lungs. She was miserable and not precisely secure in her mind. And yet she could have been worse off, she knew, much worse.

"It was good of you to follow upon my trail after killing the boar," she said with some difficulty. "I am truly thankful. If…if you had not come, I don't know what might have happened."

His eyes glinted with a blue steel edge as he glanced at her. "Don't you?"

"You think they would have…" She shook her head. "I'd have been worth more if held for ransom."

"Oh, they'd have thought of that, too, I don't doubt. But rapine and abduction have the same penalty, and a man can hang only once."

She swallowed, clasping her hands together. "Then I'm even more in your debt."

"Don't think of it," he said. "It didn't happen."

"No, but I wish there was some way—"

"And you'd be wise to keep that wish behind your teeth," he interrupted, "unless you would invite me under your cloak as well as into your shelter."

Hot chagrin flooded her face, burning its way to her cheekbones, and then receded so quickly that she felt light-headed. "I didn't mean it that way, and you know it well."

A grunt shook him. "So much for gratitude."

"And neither did you mean it." She narrowed her eyes in sudden discovery. "You wanted to silence me."

"If so, it didn't serve."

"I can be quiet enough," she said with precision, and turned her shoulder to him. Frowning, she stared out into the falling curtain of white that blended from gray to black beyond the firelight.

* * *

Ross missed the music of Lady Catherine's voice when she stopped speaking. He also missed her pointed questions and even her prying into what was none of her concern. He missed her warm and human company even more after she scooted deeper into the lean-to he had made, turned her back and lay down wrapped in her fur-lined cloak.

He told himself he was better off without the distraction. He could concentrate more on what was around him, on what might be watching from the woods that whispered around him with the falling snow.

Of course, her resolve to be silent would not last beyond the first idle thought to cross her mind. She would sit up again, give him one of her penetrating stares and begin talking of nothing. It was a rare woman, in his experience, who could or would hold her tongue. Curiosity and the dislike for having no one to share their thoughts would not allow it.

He was wrong.

An hour passed, the snow sifted relentlessly down, wind clattered the icy tree branches together, and still she said nothing. She was a stubborn wench. Or rather a stubborn lady—he could not call a female who wore a gold ring and velvet habit under an ermine-lined cloak by a less exalted title.

She was also as hardy and uncomplaining as any cottager's drab. Who had taught her to retreat into herself, to accept what came and endure it? She had been through enough in one evening to throw most gently bred ladies into strong hysterics, yet she was able to overcome it, to smile and take interest in someone else.

Not that he had noticed her smiles all that much, of course.

He had barely been aware of the glow of firelight on her pale skin, or the way it turned the tresses spread over her cloak into spun gold. Nay, hardly at all. It had only come to him half a dozen times that he was the only man other than her future husband who would ever see the shining length of it in such casual disarray, without the cover of a veil. Yes, and somewhere deep inside he was loath to think even her husband should have that right. How dim-witted could he be?

She was an Englishwoman. She wanted no part of him and he none of her, and he'd best not forget it.

Except that was a bald-faced lie. He'd take all of her he could get but for the small matter of binding himself to her as a husband. She was fair to look on and lovely to touch, and she stirred his blood as no female had since he was three and ten, and saw his first naked woman, his sister's nursemaid, in her bath. He fair ached to see Lady Catherine in the same state of nature, clothed in nothing except the shining cape of her hair.

Not that it meant twopence. The need for coupling was like any other appetite for him, satisfied when the means was at hand, controlled when it was not.

The old laird, his esteemed father, was rabid in his dislike of the Sassenach; only his hatred of those who went by the name of Trilborn went deeper. He'd go off in an apoplexy if his firstborn son dared bring an Englishwoman home to Scotland. That was if he did not disown him for even thinking of such a betrayal.

Not that he was, Ross assured himself, as he traced with his gaze the sweet curves of Lady Catherine's backside for the thousandth time. His thoughts were wandering only because there was nothing to occupy them, nothing to be seen in this interminable night except clouds of snow, the gray ghosts of trees and the orange heart of the fire in front of him. He was half-blind with watching them, half-frozen from the back of his neck to his rump, half-roasted on his front from sitting so still. Yet he dared not shift his position except to shove another section of log into the flames, throw another broken branch into their maw. Once erect and moving, there was no telling what he might do.

A quiet clicking sound came to him. He glanced around quickly before pinpointing the noise inside the shelter, which he'd positioned so its opening took advantage of whatever warmth there might be from the fire. Lady Catherine's teeth were chattering where she lay huddled on the hard ground. She was no more asleep than he was, and her position put her farther from the fire.

He could ease inside with her, slip under her cloak while throwing his plaid over both of them for extra warmth. He could pull her close and turn her so her fine, firm bottom pressed against the hard rod of him, and his arm clasped her waist. He could bury his face in her hair, pressing his lips to the tender curve of her neck at the vulnerable nape as he had first wanted when he saw her trembling with shock. Mayhap they would both be warm then.

Mayhap he was a half-wit.

He had no pretence to sainthood, so could not trust his hands not to stray where they did not belong. She might scream, then, fighting away from him. Or worse, she might not. She might turn to him with soft murmurs, sweet kisses and sighs, urging him to the one place certain to hold the sweet heat of paradise. And he would go there, blindly willing, strutted in rampant desire. He would enter her in heart-pounding fervor, taking her wet softness, her clinging, pulsing comfort, in such mindless rut that he'd care not a whit what came on the morrow.

It was a trap, that comfort, one that could close them both in its stranglehold and never let them go. A single step in the lady's direction now and their fates were set. Conscience as well an English king would demand it.

He had given his word that he would never marry her.

Rising so abruptly that his knees cracked and he dumped snow from his back and shoulders with a slithering crash, Ross moved to drag another log onto the fire, then another, and another. He piled the timber high until the flames spat and crackled like demons, lighting the night for a dozen yards around, spreading heat like a benediction. He laid on more until he was sure it would warm the lady, yes, and do it more safely, for all its fiery danger, than he could.

Wrapping himself in his plaid once more, then, he squatted well back from the great, bright conflagration. Face set, eyes hooded, he endured.

3

Cate stood waiting as the horsemen rounded the bend in the track. She'd heard them coming from some distance away, a full score of gentlemen and men-at-arms, making a great clatter on the frozen track. The watery sun overhead reflected on helms and sword hilts with a dull sheen, and their horses blew white plumes into the icy air. They had come from the king, for they rode under his banner.

She should have been overjoyed at their arrival. Instead, her chest was tight with apprehension.

The snow had stopped by the time she woke an hour ago, and the world was hushed under its smothering layer of white. The only thing that moved was a bird or two, flitting among branches that clicked and clacked with ice. Her skirt and cloak had been wet near the knee where snow had drifted into her shelter and melted with the heat of Ross's fire. That burned still, a great, leaping pyre that sent a plume of gray-blue smoke skyward. It was, without doubt, what had brought their rescuers to them.

Ross stood a few yards away, where he had been

breaking more limbs to thrust into the flames. A bleak expression lay in his eyes, and his mouth was set in a grim line. He made no move to step forward or lift a hand in greeting, but only waited for the horsemen to come to him.

Nor did Cate move from where she had taken a stance with her back to the fire to allow her skirts to dry. She recognized the cavalcade's leader as Winston Dangerfield, Lord of Trilborn, and was in no hurry to acknowledge him. She would as soon someone else, anyone else at all, had arrived as its head.

What chance that his presence was a coincidence, she thought, when she and his sworn enemy had been lost from the hunt at the same time? What chance, when he had made her the object of his cautious gallantry since the early autumn?

Trilborn was of medium height, well-made, and far too satisfied withal. On this dreary day, he wore a black surcoat edged in silver braid over his mail, both covered by a heavy black cloak that was lined with beaver and held on his shoulders by a multitude of silver chains. His hat was of beaver, as well, and stuck with a great white plume that curled over the brim to lie on his shoulder. He was pleasing enough in his features, though his peat-brown eyes were a little close together and his chin made to appear needle-sharp by his pointed black beard.

"Lady Catherine, by all the saints!" He slowed his mount to a walk, throwing up a hand with more force than necessary to halt the men behind him while he came closer to the fire. "We had nigh given up hope."

"Milord," she said with the barest of curtsies.

He swung down, swept off his hat and fanned the snow at her feet into a white whirl as he made his bow. "The others were for turning back an hour ago, but I would not have it. You would be found, so I told them, found safe and well." His eyes were tense at the corners, as if he had doubts about the last.

The smile she gave him was brief. "As you see, though for the last I am indebted to Henry's Scots guest. I believe you are acquainted with Ross Dunbar?"

Contempt flickered over Trilborn's face as he nodded in Ross's direction. "I would ask how he came here before us, but he has ever had the devil's luck."

She could have allowed it to be assumed that the Scotsman had come upon her only that morn. Common sense dictated the polite lie. Her conscience would not allow it.

"The good fortune was mine in this instance," she said in clear tones. "Had he not been here, I might have been taken by forest outlaws or died from the cold during the night."

The men who had pulled up behind Trilborn exchanged glances, muttering among themselves. The earl stiffened and his hand went to the hilt of his sword, which swung from its scabbard worn low on one hip. "He has been here with you all this time?"

"Of a certainty," she answered in disdain. She would not be affected by the suspicion she could see being levied against her. No, not at all.

"You might have done better, I should think, to take your chances with the outlaws."

"Sir!"

Ross moved with negligent, muscular grace to take a stance at her side. "What he means to say, Lady Catherine," he drawled, "is that he would have preferred it. No gentleman enjoys knowing that his enemy has been overnight in company with his lady."

The glance Cate shot the Scotsman was scathing. "I am not his lady, nor am I likely to be."

"Through no fault of his own, I'll be bound," Ross replied for her alone. "Don't tell me here's another man you would save from the curse of the Graces?"

"Have you no idea who this man is?" Trilborn demanded, slapping his hat against his well-hosed lower leg. "His family has been the scourge of the Scots march that borders Trilborn lands for a hundred years or more, Scots vermin who dare to abduct Trilborn women, steal away Trilborn villeins, Trilborn cattle."

"Aye, and can nay persuade them to go back home again," Ross said, grim humor lacing his exaggerated Scots burr.

Trilborn clenched his hand on his sword hilt as if he meant to draw it. The Scotsman merely swung out his arm, showing his sword already in his fist, its tip resting on the ground, while half its length was revealed from behind the skirt of his plaid.

"Your grandsire kidnapped my grandmother," Trilborn declared in a growl.

"Indeed he did, to ransom ten young girls your own grandsire carried off after burning their village."

"He put his bastard get in her belly." Trilborn shook his hat at Ross.

"That he did, as he found her winsome and easy to

love. He'd not have given her up except for the pleas of his people, who longed to see their girl children. Yet he kept her until the child was born so your grandsire could not kill the babe. And a good thing it was, too, for he certainly killed its mother when she was returned." Ross glanced at Cate. "My own grandmother had died years before, you know. My grandfather so regretted giving up the Trilborn lady, mourned her death so deeply, that he never took another woman."

"Certainly not another Trilborn," the English lord declared.

Ross snorted in hard contempt. "Nay, though two Dunbar wives were then kidnapped in retaliation and returned in such desperate shape that one drowned herself and the other entered a convent."

"What of the child?" Cate asked, because she could not help herself.

"Brought up with my father, like his own brother. He was shot in the back from ambush, though not before he sired a son, my cousin Liam."

"Shot during a cattle raid," Trilborn said with a sniff.

The Scotsman's hard gaze did not waver. "Oh, aye, being as daft for reiving as my father. But enough. Lady Catherine is weary, hungry and half-frozen, and grows more so while we stand here nattering. Do you have a mount for her, or must she walk back to the castle?"

It was a point Cate would have been glad to have made herself, had she not been transfixed by what she had learned. Border feuds were notorious for their violence, but this one seemed more vicious than most. She had never before seen Trilborn in a rage; he was usually all smiles and studied pleasantries. The glances he divided between her and the Scotsman were murderous. Either his interest in her was greater than she had known, or it had been sharpened by discovering her with Ross Dunbar. Well, and perhaps by the knowledge that a forced marriage was the usual result.

He could not know that she and the Scotsman had vowed between them to see that no such sacrifice was necessary. Let him discover it when he would. That was soon enough.

Accordingly, she summoned her most wan smile, looking as fatigued as she was able. Trilborn offered his arm and she took it, ignoring Ross's dry laugh as she allowed the nobleman to lead her to a sturdy gray rouncy.

She paused, reaching to allow the horse to sniff her hand, and then rubbing its soft muzzle. The rouncy was more suitable for a man, or else for transporting a body, she saw with a small shiver. "Is this the only extra mount?" she asked over her shoulder.

"We knew not what we might find, so prepared for the worst," Trilborn said with an air of haughty defense. "Dunbar can run along behind us, or else wait until another horse is brought back for him."

It was purest insult, that suggestion that the Scotsman run along behind them like a serf. "Or I can ride pillion behind him," she pointed out. "The saddle is a man's, after all."

"If that's your preference, then you shall ride with me," Trilborn said at once.

His arrogance was incredible. She was possibly more tired than she knew, for it made her contrary. "I would not dream of subjecting your stallion to such an indignity," she said before turning to the Scotsman. "Sir, if you would be so kind as to mount and then allow me to settle behind you?"

Ross came forward, his gaze considering as it rested on her face. He did not answer, however, but only vaulted to the saddle with such swift ease that the ends of his plaid flew wide. Once seated, he held his hand down to her.

Cate met the rich blue of his eyes for endless seconds while an unaccountable impression of safety settled deep inside her. She stretched high to clasp his arm above the wrist, then, while he did the same to hers. A brief heave with iron-hard muscles, and she was seated behind him with her arms locked about his waist.

Trilborn was displeased, but could hardly order a guest of Henry's unhorsed. He stalked to his stallion, snatched the reins from the man-at-arms who held them and accepted a leg up into the saddle. With an imperious gesture, he detailed two men to put out the fire and then swept around, leading the troop from the small clearing, making for the castle.

Cate looked back, imprinting the fire and the snow-covered shelter that lay behind it on her mind, while an odd sense of loss made her chest ache. For a few short hours, she had been free. No one had cared how she looked, what she wore or how she stood, walked, sat, ate or prayed. She had not been expected to dip curtsies like a duck bobbing for river weed, had not been required to recall obscure titles and who took precedence over whom. She'd had no need to watch every word for fear of offending or having something she said repeated to the king. She had been herself without let or hindrance, something she might never be permitted again. She had enjoyed the company of a man who did not simper, posture or attempt to take advantage of her.

She did not turn away until that small clearing, with its ring of mud where the heat of a great bonfire had melted the snow, vanished behind the track's wide bend.

Ross devoured two servings of beef, a loaf of bread soaked in the meat's juices and a currant cake, all washed down with a hot posset and most of a butt of ale. With these as well as a hot, herb-scented bath and change of clothing, he began to feel less like a chunk of ice. He was returned to normal, except for the undoubted fact that he could not go more than a pair of breaths without thinking about Lady Catherine.

Had she ordered a hot bath to warm her chilled flesh? What he would not give to have seen her in it. Had a serving woman bathed her? He'd have been more than pleased to perform that service, could think of many ways to make it pleasurable for her. To dry her with slow care seemed a magnificent way to while away an hour, and one not without promise of reward. To apply a brush to the pale golden glory of her hair, holding its warm, silken weight in his hands, was a fine fantasy. Sharing a meal with her in the privacy of some chamber seemed more than enticing. They could feed each other bits of this and that while whetting other appetites.

God's blood, but what ailed him? He was no mooncalf reduced to standing and staring at his beloved's window in hope of glimpsing her shadow. He was a grown man with duties and obligations that left no room for lusting after an English lady, be she ever so beauteous and daring. The incident in the forest had been a few hours out of his life, a mere snippet taken from a pattern woven before he was born. No place existed in it for a female of English blood.

He needed to put the episode behind him. Other matters were far more important, such as judging the strength of any force Henry might be able to put into the field, plus the loyalty of those around the king and how they might react if it were to be tested. He would attend to that without further ado. Aye, he would indeed, as soon as he assured himself that Lady Catherine had suffered no ill effects from her night spent in his company.

She was not in her chamber, one of the cramped rooms allotted even to the nobility in this ancient castle built for defense rather than comfort, its only luxury being a small, glowing brazier that made it barely less frigid than the corridor it opened upon. Her serving maid stood barring the door, a woman of early middle age who had, from all appearances, been clearing away after her mistress's bath. She eyed him with disfavor, he thought, looking him up and down with all the doubtful care of a housewife appraising a pig at market. He did not flinch under it, even as the tops of his ears burned. Nor did he show her the least reaction when he learned Lady Catherine had been summoned by the king.

It was not an official audience, as it turned out. On gaining the castle's great hall, Ross saw her, a bright beacon in the smoke-hazed gloom, where she perched on a low stool at the foot of Henry's great armchair. The king's canopied throne sat on a dais along with the castle's famous round table, which some said had once been used by King Arthur of distant legend. No one encroached upon this private colloquy; none appeared to notice it taking place in their midst.

Men talked in groups, played at knucklebones or chess, or watched the antics of the fool who juggled and told jokes for their amusement. The place smelled of wood ash, sweaty men who had been to horse, dogs, shattered green rushes and the ghosts of bread, beef and ale from the recent morning's repast. The fitful sunlight falling on the snow outside penetrated the high, narrow windows with faint gray light, leaving the space in gloom except for the bright islands of standing oil lamps.

Ross found an unoccupied bench and flung himself down upon it, using the wall behind it as a backrest. He watched the king with Lady Catherine in brooding displeasure. He did not care for the way Henry leaned toward her, speaking in measured phrases while tapping the arm of his chair for emphasis. He looked displeased, or else more interested in her welfare than was seemly in a king not yet thirty years old, one with a wife of only a year, and a two-month-old son.

The king's intentions toward the lady were no concern of his, of course, Ross assured himself with a scowl. It was only that talk about her would be vicious enough without Henry adding to it.

Ross would give much to know what was being said between them. At King James's court, he might have walked up to them to discover it. Such lack of ceremony did not apply here. As with most newly minted kings, Henry was a stickler for the ceremony that reinforced his position.

"Milord Dunbar?"

So intent had Ross been on the pair he watched that he failed to notice the approach of a manservant until he stood bowing at his elbow. It was a startling bit of inattention compared to his normal vigilance.

"Aye?"

"The king requests your presence. Come with me, sir, and it please you."

It was a command for all its politeness. He must go, Ross knew, regardless of whether it pleased him. Though mayhap it did, at that. Shoving himself to his feet, he threaded his way through the murmuring crowd, following so close on the menial's heels that he almost stepped on them.

Henry VII acknowledged his kneeling presence with a grave and regal nod, but did not suggest that he rise or be seated, not even on a stool at a lower level. Ross barely noticed that studied sign of royal disfavor. Resting his arm on his bent knee, he fingered the soft bonnet of green wool he'd doffed, waiting to hear the purpose of his summons. Though he suspected what it might be, it was as well to be certain.

"Lady Catherine has told us of your timely appearance in her hour of need," Henry said with easy use of the royal plural, "also of your daring attack against these forest brigands. We are grateful that you were close by."

"'Twas naught, only what any man would have done." Ross glanced at the lady. Her eyes were shadowed with warning. She seemed intent on communicating something to him, though he knew not what.

She was a vision of rich color in that drab hall with its banners and ensigns so smoke begrimed that it was impossible to make out their crests, its stag horns strung with spiderwebs and moth-riddled boar's heads. Her arms and breast were molded in vivid burgundy velvet that was edged at neckline and wrist in gold lace, and her hair confined in gold netting attached to a headpiece like an upturned goblet, from which hung a many-layered veil of *couleur rose*. Her gold cross on its chain graced her throat, her gold-and-ruby ring was on her finger and she had such brightness about her that no other female in the room warranted a second look.

Her curves outlined in soft and luminous cloth were so enticing that Ross felt his mouth twitch with the need to trace them with tongue and lips. It was the first time he'd had leisure to observe them at close range; he'd seen her only from a distance before last evening, and she had been wrapped from neck to ankle in her cloak from beginning to end of their time in the king's forest. Still, he knew them with an intimacy that burned like a knot in his lower abdomen, had felt them pressed against his back every miserable league of the ride homeward this morning. He hardly needed sight to confirm what was engraved on his soul.

"The fact remains that you accomplished it," Henry said, dragging Ross's attention back to the matter at hand. "Touching on what occurred afterward..."

"I have explained that nothing occurred," the lady said quickly. "That you made a fire and also a small shelter from the snow. I remained inside it while you kept watch outside throughout the night, with no contact whatever between us."

Ross inclined his head but made no answer. There were times when it was best for a man to keep a still tongue in his head.

"Admirable," the king said with some irony. "Even so, we are concerned with the effect upon Lady Catherine's good name. You both surely understand that there will be talk. People are ever ready to put the worst possible construction upon events."

Henry should know that well enough, Ross thought somewhat distractedly. The king's son and heir had been born a scant eight months after his wedding. Speculation was not only that he had anticipated his nuptials, but that he had made certain of the fertility of his future queen before committing himself to the marriage.

The unions of kings were a cold-blooded business, poor sods. Sympathy did not require Ross to put his head into that same matrimonial noose.

Regardless, this seemed to be the point where he was expected to guard the lady's reputation by offering his hand. He had no such intention, particularly after his solitary vigil the night before. He was due some consideration for his misery, self-imposed though it might have been.

"Nothing happened, I give you my word," he said with deliberation.

"And we would be pleased to accept it, were not so much at stake." Henry made a brief gesture. "The lady has expressed her willingness to accept you as a husband."

Ross glanced quickly to Lady Catherine. The resigned look in her eyes was testimony enough to her feelings, also to her inability to gainsay her king. She was depending on him to do his part by declaring that he would not be wed at Henry's command.

Instead, all he could think of was that he could have her. A single word, two at the most, and she would be his before the New Year. The instant the betrothal documents were signed, he could take her to bed, could strip away her fine clothing until he reached the warm and naked female underneath. He could mold her curves with his hands, touch every inch of her skin and invade her hot depths until he found plunging release from this torment that she cast him into on sight.

He could have her. He could have her and…and his father would disown him. He would be cast out of his homeland and his clan, left to kick his heels at Henry's court forever and a day, instead of only a year or two. He would be forever a bastard Sassenach.

"I have no wish to be ungallant," he said, with strain beneath the quiet certainty of his voice, "but you will recall that I am nay here of my own will. I am of Scotland, and answer only to James, king of the Scots."

Henry frowned, tapping his chair arm. He stopped. "And if your king should order it?"

"I must still have my father's consent and his blessing as laird of our clan."

"Natural enough, we must suppose. And has he no concern for Scotland's welfare?"

Aye, the old laird did that, Ross thought in grim humor, when it ran alongside his own. "What welfare might that be?"

"Insurrection is a contagion that can easily spread across borders. Every king has enemies ready to pull him down, waiting only for the right time, the right excuse."

"You are thinking, mayhap, of this business of one of the vanished princes returning," Ross ventured. Cate had suggested it might have some bearing, though he could barely credit it. He glanced at her in time to see approval flash across her face.

"My agents report a child in the fair and blue-eyed Plantagenet mold being referred to as the son and heir of Edward IV. The truth remains to be seen. We've never set eyes on the boy or his brother, but any number of people did in the days before the two were consigned to the Tower. Witnesses can easily be brought forward to prove the claim false."

"The dowager queen, or Queen Elizabeth?" The first was the widow of Edward IV, mother of the boy who had briefly been hailed as Edward V, while the second was her daughter, Henry's queen, and the boy's eldest sister. If anyone could say with authority that this youngster was a pretender, it would be these two.

Not a flicker of emotion crossed the king's face. "We prefer to reserve that as a final resort. It can only be distressing for either of them."

That much could not be denied, Ross thought. What would they do, the dowager queen dependent on Henry's goodwill for her daily bread, or his wife, mother of his son and the Lancaster heir apparent, if the boy should turn out to be the rightful Yorkist king?

"And you expect proving the boy an imposter to serve?" he asked.

The king inclined his head with an air of weary assent. "For a short while, at least. Yet a Plantagenet prince is required as proxy for Yorkist ambitions. They will have one if they must fashion him of whole cloth."

"Well enough, but what has Scotland to do with it?" The question was blunt, but Ross let it stand.

"Those who plot and plan must have a safe base from which to launch their attack. If not Scotland, then it will be Wales or Ireland. We would prefer it was the last named, as the Irish are less likely to have strength of arms. Wales is also weaker than your homeland."

Henry should know this well, as his own plan of invasion had been hatched in Brittany and set in motion from the Welsh coast. "You believe King James might aid them?"

"Or be drawn into the rebellion, one way or another, if care is not taken."

"I hardly see how my father can affect that," Ross said.

"It only requires that he refrain from lending men and arms to the enterprise. Well, and persuades his neighbors to do likewise."

"If it's a matter of exchanging one English king for another, the laird of Dunbar is more likely to sit on the border laughing at the show," Ross said plainly. "Should King James seize on this chance to invade in force, he will certainly ride with him."

"We understand and applaud such loyalty. Still. It is our hope your father would counsel against invasion for fear the holdings of his son could become a battle-ground."

A trickle of apprehension moved down the back of Ross's neck. "You can't mean my holdings, for I have none, will have none until my father leaves this earth."

The king's smile was grimly amused. "Lady Catherine's older sister is married to Braesford, a loyal subject who fought at Bosworth and received a barony for his service to us. He has a pele tower keep and manse on the northern coast. A sizable estate, known as Grimes Hall, lies no great distance away and is in our hands. It would be a worthy wedding gift."

"But, Your Majesty—"

"Then there is Lady Catherine's dowry derived from the estate of her father. As he left no living sons, his property was divided between her and her two sisters. Lady Catherine's portion comprises a castle, a manse and some seven or eight villages with extensive lands."

Ross looked again to the lady, wondering what she thought of this blithe gifting to him of her inheritance. The tender curves of her mouth were set in a straight line, but her frown was not directed his way. He faced forward again.

"A bribe?" he asked in quiet derision.

"We prefer to call it a reward for loyalty."

"My father would name it treason to kith and kin, much less to the name I hold."

"So he may. We can at least present the formal proposal under our royal seal."

That official badge was one his father sneered at as belonging to an upstart with little more claim to it than any petty nobleman, as it came through Henry's mother's line rather than direct descent from his father. The laird was hardly likely to be impressed.

"If you must," Ross answered.

"Meanwhile, we consider the alliance as pending until such time as permission for the marriage arrives."

"Sire!" Cate exclaimed with alarm in her voice. "The curse, you must recall—"

The king waved her objection aside as he might a fly. "Yes, yes, we will deal with that when the time comes."

"Or not," Ross said. "I should tell you there is no hope in heaven my father will agree." In fact, the old man would let him rot in hell before extending permission to add an Englishwoman to the Clan Dunbar.

"He may see reason if the prospect is presented to him in suitable terms. We are prepared to make a generous settlement upon your father for the sake of peace on our northern border."

A generous settlement for the old laird. If there was one thing that might influence him, it was the prospect of acquiring Sassenach gold. He could always use it, as who in Scotland could not when there were so many mouths to be fed? Yet it was outwitting the English, driving a bargain to their disfavor, that would tempt his father most sorely.

Not that he could be depended on to honor any pledge made to the English. Such a thing would scarce count, to his way of thinking. Henry should at least be warned of that possibility.

"You'll want to take care," Ross said with caution as he met the king's pale blue eyes. "Any agreement made by man can be broken."

"We have had ample proof of that in recent years," Henry said with a chilly smile. "Nevertheless."

Ross met Cate's gaze for an endless time, seeing the shadow of fear that lay in its depths. She turned from him then, looking back to the king. "Sire," she said, her voice not quite even, "you can't mean, can't expect…"

"Indeed we do, Lady Catherine," Henry VII said with stern benevolence. "A betrothal is hereby decreed. It shall be proclaimed the instant we have Laird Dunbar's agreement."

4

Cate said not a word as she made her curtsy and backed from the royal presence, then turned to walk with dignity at Ross's side. Her jaws ached with the effort to contain her refusal to wed, but one did not defy a king.

That did not mean she intended to be married at Henry's command. She yet hoped to find a way out of this contretemps. If she could not do it alone, then the man at her side must and would aid her. He was surely no more ready than she to give up his freedom.

"Well, sir," she said in low agitation when they had descended from the dais and were beyond range of the king's hearing, and other curious ears, as well. "What is to be done?"

"Done?"

"About this betrothal that's been foisted upon us, of course," she said with scarcely contained patience. "I have no wish to be your wife, and you have less to be my husband. You were supposed to refuse outright. What became of that?"

"I did refuse."

"For a moment only! Henry scarcely acknowledged it. You must be as enraged as I am."

The Scotsman gazed down at her without answering, his eyes glimmers of blue between narrowed lids, faithfully reflecting the main color of his plaid, which was held across one shoulder by a silver pin shaped like a small dagger. His face was set in stern lines, though his manner seemed distracted.

He was, she saw with sudden clarity, a man of devastating attraction as well as consummate power. Despite his cold and sleepless night, his gaze was clear and alert. His wind-burned features were arranged in rugged planes and angles that pleased the eye; his brows were thick and dark, and his lashes of more than enough length to shield his expression. Strolling beside her, he seemed taller and wider than she remembered, with shoulders that pulled the sleeves of his shirt taut across their musculature as he gestured, and calves sculpted in corded muscle beneath the swing of his plaid's lower fullness.

Much of the female interest directed toward them in the crowded hall, Cate was sure, was composed of envy allied to curiosity about how she had gained the aloof Scotsman's attention. If they but knew she had merely needed to be menaced in the wood, half of them would become lost from the king's next hunt.

That she was actually betrothed to Ross Dunbar was beyond belief.

"Well?" she demanded, while a choking sensation invaded her chest. "Aren't you?"

A wry smile curved his mouth. "Enraged, you mean?

Oh, aye. Still, you must admit the thing will offer protection from insult."

"Protection for me, you mean, because of our night together. I don't regard what people may say, I promise you."

Across the hall, Cate noticed the gleam of her younger sister's light brown hair with its shades of gold like captured sunlight, and the flicker of her ale-brown eyes. Marguerite was watching with concern upon her piquant features. She had not been in the chamber they shared when Cate returned earlier, and there had been no time to speak to her before the king's summons. She would be wondering what had befallen her, and what was behind Henry's particular attention.

She was not the only one watching, Cate saw with a twist of acute trepidation. Small knots of courtiers, diplomats, nobles and their ladies stared and nodded in their direction while whispering behind their hands.

Beside her, Ross sent a hard stare toward one grinning jackanapes, returning no answer to her comment until the man turned purple to his eyebrows and looked away. When he finally spoke, his voice was brusque. "It's damnable that you should be the target of clacking tongues."

"My sisters and I have provided fodder for the gossips these many years due to our ill luck with betrothals. It has brought us no harm."

"Always a first time."

"What form should it take, pray? Are we to be attacked for discouraging suitors? No matter. I am still no more inclined to wed an unknown than you!"

He favored her with a serious glance. "You've no thought to have a child one day?"

"No hope of it, rather, as it requires a living husband." She stared straight ahead, though she could feel the heat rising into her face.

He made an impatient sound through his nose. "It's all nonsense, this dread curse."

"Tell that to the suitors who have died since matches began to be made for us while we were in our cradles," she answered in exasperation.

"Have there been so many?"

"A goodly few, yes. To the four who expired after being promised to my older sister, Isabel, you may add for me an earl's youngest son who succumbed to a fever, an elderly banker from Bruges lost at sea and a youth related to the once mighty Woodvilles taken by blood poisoning after being stabbed in a drunken brawl. And that says nothing to the list credited to my younger sister."

"Such things happen when the wedding must wait for the bride to gain the required thirteen or fourteen years."

"So it does, and I will admit that Isabel first spoke of the curse as a jest. But let death arrive before the wedding often enough, and men grow wary. Few are willing to chance a betrothal now."

"Nevertheless, I am bidden to it by royal decree."

"I'm sorry for it, but I did try to warn you," she said, with a stricken sensation inside her.

"Don't upset yourself," he answered, his voice even. "Henry may command as he pleases, but no priest will hear our vows unless we both consent."

The supreme confidence in his bearing and his face

served to calm a portion of her agitation. She drew a deep breath and released it in a sigh. "Yes, I suppose."

"Though 'tis a shame, in all truth. Any child of yours would be a beautiful babe."

It was an oblique, almost impersonal compliment, yet she valued it for that reason. And it was good of him to be concerned, as he had nothing to do with what had sent her careening deep into the New Forest in the first place.

He was no mere courtier, this Scotsman, all polished courtesies and glib phrases. He was a trained soldier, one hardened in a hundred skirmishes and cattle raids. Still, even he could be laid low by fever or accident, disease or deliberate murder. That was if the curse of the Three Graces should be invoked against him.

Even as these thoughts, fretted with anguish, ran like quicksilver through her mind, she realized he awaited her reply. "I will become a wife and mother only if a man will have me for love alone," she said with precision. "What chance of that, think you, when all who don't quake with fear require to know the size of a woman's dowry before wondering if she has teeth or toenails?"

"Love," he said with a wry shake of his head. "It's a thing for milkmaids and kitchen scullions, those with no property or hope of having any."

They had paraded down one side of the great hall and across the end, passing the screened corridor that led to the buttery, where butts of ale and wine were broached, the pantry, where bread loaves were sliced open, and also the kitchens. Savory smells of roasting meat basted with herbs and spices, simmering broths and fresh-baked trenchers wafted from it, along with the yeasty scent of ale. They skirted the outside entrance where cold drafts stirred the front hem of Cate's gown and burrowed beneath its train. She shivered as they reached her hose-clad ankles.

"Cold, are you?" he said, bending his head toward her. "Would you care to take a seat by the fire?"

It was unlikely they could locate two places together. He would leave her then, and she was oddly reluctant to brave the great hall without his wide shoulders between her and the crowd. There were matters that still needed to be made clear between them, as well. "I'm warm enough as long as we keep moving," she said, with a shake of her head that sent her veil shifting around her shoulders. "Meanwhile, I don't believe you answered my question."

"Which one might that be?" he asked in dry inquiry.

"As to what we are to do now."

"We wait, I think."

"Wait?" She gave him a quick look to be certain he was not teasing her again.

"Upon my father's answer. We may trust him for a swift refusal. Yes, and probably a blasphemous one, as well."

"He may be as profane as he pleases, so long as he is definite," she answered with fervor.

"Aye," Ross agreed without inflection.

She twitched the long train of her gown from under the feet of a manservant who darted past with a sloshing jug of wine, then walked on for a few steps while curiosity dogged her. "So," she said after a moment. "You don't believe love is possible for the higher orders."

"It happens, but not often."

"You have no expectation of it when you are wed, care nothing for how your lady may look or what she may feel for you or you for her?"

He twisted his neck as if easing its tightness. "My father will consult with me, I make no doubt, or I with him, and the lady will be comely enough. But the deed will unite our holdings with those of some neighbor or distant kinsman."

"And this will content you."

"It's the way of the world."

"I see," she said, disappointed in some manner she could not name. "You will get a quiverful of sons on this comely female, while buying ribbons and other frippery for…for milkmaids."

He laughed, a deep, rich sound. "A quiverful, is it? Your faith in my prowess flatters me."

"No such thing!" She refused to meet his gaze. "I meant only to say that you would look elsewhere for love."

"I don't know that I'd call it by such a name, though you may be right. It is, as I said…"

"The way of our world. Yes, I know."

"You would marry for love, and to the devil with property, security, and a father for your children who has your same rank?"

"Yes."

One brow rose until it almost touched the bonnet he had donned again as he left the king. "You seem very sure."

"It can be no other way, being ordained so by the

curse. Any man who attempts to wed me or my two sisters without love will surely die."

"But there is that caveat, the one way to avoid the curse's dire consequences."

"If you care to call it so."

"I am to accept that this dread fate awaiting your betrothed is the only reason Henry is being so generous with the marriage settlement."

Cate gave the Scot a cool stare, affronted by some small change she heard in his voice. "What other purpose could there be?"

"I don't know," he answered, his concentrated gaze scanning the crowded hall much as he had scanned the forest around them last night. "Mayhap you'll enlighten me."

Shock surged over her, only to be routed by anger. "You think that I... No, and no again! I must tell you that however gently reared females may behave in Scotland, sir, they do not play at dalliance in England!"

He turned his gray-blue eyes upon her in heated assessment. "Not even with a king?"

Dunbar's audacity robbed her of speech. Lifting her train out of the way with a hand that trembled with the need to strike him, she swung about to leave him.

"Hold." His voice was low yet firm as he reached out to catch her arm in a loose clasp. "I was wrong to speak so. It's just that Henry seems uncommonly concerned for your welfare."

Her arm burned where he touched, setting off a melting feeling inside her. She drew it swiftly away, holding it against her side. "If he is concerned, it's from gratitude and obligation, because my older sister helped prevent injury to his heir and his queen not long ago, as well as to Henry himself. There is nothing personal in it whatever."

"I did hear whispers of an attempt on his life during the summer," Ross allowed.

"You may have done, though the details are known to few. I was not there myself, and Isabel refuses to speak of it."

"Isabel is your sister married to this Braesford that Henry mentioned?"

Cate tipped her head a fraction. "A fine knight and great favorite. Know you of him?"

"The name is familiar, though I don't believe he's among the border lords my father counts as enemies."

"You may thank God for it, as he is a dangerous foe. He has not had time to make many enemies, however, as he received his lands from Henry after Bosworth."

"That would explain it." The Scotsman paused, and then went on in quite a different tone. "Shall I make my amends now or later?"

"Amends?"

"For my insult."

"Later would be…"

Cate stopped, unable to go on for the hard knot that formed in her throat. That he accepted her word without further explanation was so unexpected that she knew not what to say or where to look. Her late stepbrother, who had been guardian to her and her two sisters until his death, had never been particularly reasonable.

"Later it is," he said quietly. "Meanwhile, on the subject of what we should do now, I have another suggestion."

"Yes?"

"We could dance."

"Dance," she repeated, not quite certain she had heard him correctly. Though someone played on a lute, it was not a tune suitable for such exercise. Moreover, a shadow of amusement lay in his eyes despite the gravity of his features.

"During the coming evening. If we lift our feet to music, it may appear we are light of heart and obedient to Henry's commands for the time being."

"Surely there is something else."

"Or we could sing."

"I am more inclined to wait." She laughed a little as she spoke, in spite of herself. She had no real wish to forget his suspicion or be distracted from it by his nonsense.

"As you will. We may sing while making merry at the approach of Christmas. We can hum with the monks in their chorals, whistle with the serving maids and trill with the jongleurs. No one will ever suspect we are plotting treason."

"Treason?" she exclaimed. "Not I!"

"Aye, you, as flaunting the will of a king can be a hanging offense."

"Be serious, please! Are we to pretend to happiness at this betrothal, then, as if we long for the wedding date? Must we act as if it is real?"

"Have I not just said so?" He reached to take her hand, lifting it to his mouth, brushing his smooth, warm lips across the backs of her fingers while holding her gaze with the dark blue of his own.

Cate drew a swift breath as the muscles of her arm jerked in uncontrollable spasm. "Don't!"

"I fear I may have to do more, though not at the moment." He smiled down at her, his eyes heavy lidded, almost sleepy. "Try a bemused and adoring look, Lady Catherine, if you can manage it. It may be helpful just now, since Trilborn seems to be panting to know what passes between us."

It was an instant before she caught the meaning of his last, softly murmured phrase, and glimpsed Trilborn scowling at them from where he leaned on a support post. Her reaction then had more to do with instinct than conscious thought. With the lift of her chin, she stepped closer and laid her hand upon the daring Scotsman's wrist.

"Yes, I do see what you mean," she murmured. "Shall we walk again? If we do not, I may be forced to sing, after all, and I promise you won't like it."

To act a part went against the grain, Ross thought, as he stared out over the snow-covered town and the chalk hills beyond, watching as the king's falconer set his charge to coursing after hares in the open fields beyond the castle walls. He liked matters to be simple, preferred to state his views and intentions and stand by them come what may. That he could not do that in the matter of Lady Catherine was unsettling.

He had remained with her through the noon meal. They had enjoyed a place near the king's table, and been honored by choice dishes sent down to them. The mark of Henry's favor had not gone unnoticed. Only a blind man could have failed to guess that a betrothal was in the offing, particularly with the tale of their night spent together in the New Forest spreading through the room like a bad odor.

Lady Catherine had smiled and played the blushing bride-to-be to perfection. Her hands had been like ice, however, and she ate almost nothing. Ross pressed tidbits upon her while seeing that her wineglass was kept filled. Afterward, he'd accepted her excuse of a headache and escorted her to the door of the hall, where her sister awaited her.

God knew she had reason enough to make an escape; he felt the strong need of solitude himself. That his strongest inclination was to take her away to a place where they could be alone again together was maddening in its lack of logic.

Worse still was the welter of emotions that beset him whenever he looked at her. She fired his blood beyond imagining; the need to have her made his body ache until his eyes watered. Her grace and courage, the way she smiled, moved, tilted her bright head—everything about her fascinated him. Yet he was the son of a contentious laird who despised everything English, and she the ward of an English king. To tie himself to her, to act the part of pawn in the game Henry played, would cut Ross off from his family and his homeland. He had sworn he would not wed her, and she depended on him to keep his word.

Trilborn wanted her and her dowry; that much was

clear. Ross resented the simplicity of the Englishman's desire, and was determined he should not gain it. Ross wanted to think this was for Lady Catherine's sake, because she intended to remain forever a maiden, but feared it was purest dog-in-the-manger spite. To see Trilborn gratified in any manner was anathema, but particularly when it involved so lovely a prize.

Ross had sworn not to wed Lady Catherine, but had not foresworn bedding her. He had sworn not to bow to an English king's will, yet had said nothing of combating his own will in the matter. These facts had reared their ugly heads in those first moments after their audience with the king. They troubled him still.

Did Lady Catherine realize the self-serving distinctions a man could make in order to satisfy his desires? She was an intriguing blend of innocence and sophistication, no doubt the result of her months at court, where she was free to enjoy the licentious atmosphere while under strict royal protection. She recognized the base motives of those around her, but was somehow above them.

"Dunbar!"

Ross pushed away from the battlement's crenellated wall. He turned without surprise to see his old enemy bearing down on him with his cloak flapping at his heels and a petulant glare on his smooth, aristocratic face.

"Trilborn," he said with scant politeness. Dealing with the arrogant fool was the last thing he needed. The sight of him, still wearing the black and silver he'd had on early that morning, set Ross's teeth on edge.

"Who would dream you'd be up here? I'd think you'd have had your fill of cold wind."

"What do you want?"

If the bluntness of the question registered with Trilborn, there was no sign of it. "Precisely what you'd expect, I'm sure. I want to know how matters stand between you and Lady Catherine. Is there to be a wedding?"

He should concede nothing, Ross knew. The temptation to tweak his enemy's pointed beard, at least in a manner of speaking, was just impossible to resist. "The king sends to discover if the laird of the Clan Dunbar can be persuaded."

Trilborn eyed him with disfavor. "And you are overjoyed."

"Why not, given so lovely a lady?"

"So wealthy, too, though there is always the curse to consider. Come, Dunbar. You can't mean to accept this arrangement. What will you do about it?"

Ross allowed a small smile to curl one corner of his mouth. "What would you? I wait on my father."

"You could take a horse and ride out of Winchester. No one is likely to stop you. They'll scarce even notice you've gone."

"I make no doubt you would supply mount and escort."

The man's eyes narrowed to conceal their glint of triumph. "Why, yes, if you like."

"It grieves me to disappoint you, but I must decline. I gave my parole, and cannot go back on my sworn word."

"What do you care, when it was given to an English king?"

In that was an echo of his thoughts about his father's

word, Ross saw with an internal grimace. "What matters is that I gave it of my will."

"At the behest of others, for matters of state that would not touch you otherwise."

"The reasons make not a whit of difference." That was also true of his betrothal to Lady Catherine, he saw with inescapable clarity. He had vowed not to marry her, and must now abide by that promise.

If simplicity was what he craved, he should be well pleased. Odd, how little that was so.

"So you would take a Sassenach wife, no matter what your father answers."

Ross turned his head to study Trilborn. "Instead of leaving her to you, you mean? You think with me gone, Henry may give her to you?"

The Englishman fastened upon him a look of purest detestation. "It was discussed between us. He would have agreed to it soon enough, but for your interference."

"If you think Henry is swayed by anything other than what may benefit the crown, you don't know him."

"So you think he'll push Cate—that is, Lady Catherine—into your arms for the sake of a tie with Scotland? The conceit of it beggars the imagination."

Cate. Ross tested the shortened name in his mind. It suited her. Even as the thought occurred, however, another arrived full blown in his mind.

"My interference?" he inquired without inflection.

"The honor of rescuing her should have been mine!" Trilborn said in savage indignation.

He was not talking about his arrival this morning, for that was scarce a rescue at all. Was it possible Trilborn had known Lady Catherine would fall behind the hunt? Had his old enemy, just possibly, intended an abduction, followed by a night in his company and a wedding shortly thereafter?

It was feasible. Everyone knew she was reluctant to be present at the kill.

So what had prevented him from carrying out his intent?

The boar. Yes, of course. Trilborn had not counted on the beast sending Lady Catherine's palfrey careening into the deeper forest. Neither could he have guessed she would stumble upon the ambuscade built by forest outlaws to catch wayward members of the king's hunt.

"Except that I happened to gain the honor," Ross said quietly. "Your loss, I fear."

"Or not," Trilborn answered, his black eyes hard with promise. "You are unlikely to live long enough to take Lady Catherine to wife."

He swung away with a jerk that sent his cloak flapping like the wings of a bird of prey. His strides were long and powered by rage as he took himself out of sight.

Ross watched him go, listened to his footsteps echoing on stone, listened to the hollow echo of his threat as it bounced back and forth in Ross's head. And he marveled that he was more fraught at the idea of never having Lady Catherine than he was at meeting his promised death.

5

"Have you not heard? Henry intends that we leave here tomorrow morn, making our way to Greenwich Palace. 'Tis time, else Christmas will be a sad affair."

Marguerite's breath fogged in the air as she spoke, drifting behind her in the frigid corridor as she and Cate made their way from the great hall to their small chamber. Cate thought her sister's voice had a disgruntled edge as she trudged along with her hands burrowed into her wide sleeves for warmth. The glance she gave from under straight dark brows was also less than pleased.

"You are anxious to go?" Cate asked with the lift of a brow.

"I would go if I had to crawl," Marguerite declared. "I weary of this progress of Henry's that makes little progress. I despise being cold and am sick unto death of hunting. Why Henry could not abide in London with Elizabeth and his heir is more than I can see."

"I believe he removed to allow the queen to recover in peace from her coronation."

"I daresay, or because he was galled by it." Cate's younger sister, just sixteen, gave a brief shake of her head. "Men have such egos, do they not? So the cheers for Elizabeth, a princess of the house of York, were louder than those raised for him when he was crowned last year, what of it? She has lived among these people all her life, while he has spent fifteen of his near thirty years in exile, but he must be more lauded because nature put him above her."

Cate waited to speak until a trio of serving women, coming toward them with baskets of linens to be loaded for the move, had passed. "Take care, my dear. We are dependent on his goodwill and needs must keep it."

Her sister's glance was sharp with ill humor. "Yes, well, it was ridiculous of him to leave Elizabeth to rest while Christmas preparations for upward of two thousand must be made at Greenwich. Fine rest that will be for her!"

"He is at least thinking of the holiday, my dear," Cate said. "We are to transport a Yule log from the New Forest, along with enough holly, bay and mistletoe to deck a dozen castles."

"Which only means more work for Elizabeth and her ladies. I'd like to tell him a thing or two."

"Are you sure it isn't me you would take to task?" Cate said with warm irony. "If you want to know what occurred with Ross Dunbar last night and the king this morning, you have only to ask."

"What occurred?"

The look that went with that question was stolid, as if her sister thought the answer must be unpleasant. It was all Cate could do not to smile. "Nothing happened."

Marguerite gave a tired sigh. "I knew you wouldn't tell me."

"It's the truth, or at least in so far as my time with the Scotsman is concerned." Cate went on to explain, making as light of her rescue as possible.

"By all the saints, Cate, how can you be so calm? To be mauled and threatened with rapine, rescued by a northern barbarian and then forced to spend the night in his company while surviving a blizzard? You should be laid up in bed with a hot posset instead of strolling about the great hall just now with your...your—"

"My betrothed?"

"Oh, Cate! No!"

"Yes, at Henry's behest, though it is not yet official."

Marguerite shook her hands free of her sleeves, then slid an arm around Cate for a quick hug. "And I am being disagreeable because you didn't come at once to confide in me. You must be so dazed that you can barely think, or else ready to weep with vexation."

"A little of both, I suppose."

"Ah, well. Your Scotsman seems too hardy for a fever to take him off, and there is little prospect of a battle where he may fall, yet some disaster will put an end to him. A pity, but he brought it on himself."

An odd numbness seized Cate's chest. "No, no, surely it won't come to that!"

Marguerite lifted her head from where she'd rested it on Cate's shoulder. Her brows almost met above her nose as she scowled. "It sounds as if you might care what happens to him."

"Of course I care. He is a decent man who went to

great ends to save me, Marguerite, and did nothing untoward afterward. We have made it up between us to
avoid the king's command, and so we shall."

"You did what?" her sister asked, her eyes widening
with shock.

It was necessary to present every detail. By the time
Cate was done, she and Marguerite had reached their
chamber, kicked off their slippers and settled in comfort
upon the featherbed. Gwynne, the serving woman who
attended to their needs, was absent upon some task, so
they need not watch their words.

Her sister stared at her in frowning concentration
where she rested her back against one of the bedposts.
"You think intentions matter where the curse is concerned? You believe your Scotsman will be safe as long
as he doesn't agree to marry you?"

"Something like that, though I wish you would cease
calling him my Scotsman."

Marguerite waved that objection away. "But, Cate,
that's wonderful. You may enjoy Dunbar's company
without troubling over whether he's courting death as
he courts you."

"May I, indeed?"

"Only consider! When has any one of us had the freedom to walk with a man, talk with him or simply be with
him without fearing he will seal his doom by deciding
to take us to wife?"

"Why, never," Cate said in dawning discovery.

"Dunbar has not only given you his word, but knows
his father will never consent to a marriage."

"Just so."

"You need feel not a whit of guilt, no matter what may come to pass between you."

Cate narrowed her eyes in sudden suspicion. "What are you saying?"

"Why, only that— Well, aren't you curious, Cate? Do you never wonder what it might be like to meet a man in a garden as in the *Roman de la Rose,* to allow him the caresses that may lead to…to exploration of soft petals and warm centers? Love like that between Isabel and Braesford is so rare. If we are never to have husbands because love is denied, well then?"

"Marguerite!"

Her sister's face turned mutinous. She took a corner of her veil, nibbling at its hem. "Don't try to tell me you haven't thought of it, for I won't believe you."

"Well, if I hadn't, then I will now that you've put the idea into my head!"

"What is wrong with that, pray? Are we to be denied such joy of the flesh because of a stupid curse? Life is uncertain, Cate. We have so little time to gather memories before we dwindle into old age, like the forgotten women in nunneries."

"Oh, Marguerite," Cate whispered, leaning to put her hand on her sister's bent knee. She had not known her younger sister felt so passionately about what the curse foretold for their futures. "We may be denied the boon of being wives and mothers, but we have also been saved from the grief of being wed to men twice our age, men who will get a babe upon us every year without the least care for whether we live or die. We have avoided brutal men like our stepbrother, who would give us bruises rather than kisses or caresses."

"So you suppose, but how can we be sure? Who can say we might not have found love among the men-at-arms who serve our husbands, once we had provided him a son or two to secure their lines? It happens to other women, Cate. It happens."

"Yes, and young girls die from bearing that son or two while they are still children themselves. Meeting a man in a garden could lead to the same thing."

"It would almost be worth it to have the mystery understood at last, to lie in a man's arm, to feel the kisses and caresses."

"Or it could be a vast disappointment." Cate managed a wan smile. "But I do see what you are saying, Marguerite, and I have thought of it. Oh, yes, I've thought of it."

"Well, then?"

"I don't know," she answered with strain in her voice. "I can hardly go to Ross Dunbar and say, 'Please, kind sir, make love to me so I may know what it's like just once in my life.' What if he laughed? What if he refused because he thought it was a trap to make marriage necessary? What if he had no desire to take me into his arms, much less his bed?"

"What if he did?"

What if he did.

The thought was a fire in the blood, a mystery of mysteries, a rare and wild unicorn of the heart. Cate felt it settle inside her, within the small, tight fence of her mind. How she would be rid of it, she did not know, or if that was even possible. She feared it might be with her until set free with the aid of the Scotsman.

The following morning brought a great hustle and bustle in the castle as the king's retinue prepared to take to the road. Several carts laden with bedding, foodstuffs and other comforts left ahead of the rest, additions for whatever preparation might be made by the household of the nobleman they would descend upon come nightfall. Cold beef and bread would be their fare during the day's ride, but they could expect more sumptuous viands at day's end. The Feast of Saint Nicholas had passed while they tarried at Winchester, ushering in the Christmas season which would not end until Epiphany or even Candlemas. Doubtless there would be rich and warming stews and soups this evening, along with roast goose, bacon with lashings of mustard, venison, frumenty and a hundred other things.

Once the main column left the town of Winchester, Cate rode with Marguerite and one or two other heiresses ordered to attend upon Henry. They ambled along at a pace not much faster than the slowest cart, with Marguerite on a bay gelding and Cate on her palfrey. It was a pleasure to be mounted upon Rosie again, just as it had been a joy to discover her safe in her stall. The gray mare seemed none the worse for her run through the wood, beyond a few welts from limbs and a briar scratch on one fetlock. Cate leaned forward often to smooth her fingers over Rosie's neck or run them through her mane.

The king rode at the head of the winding procession for the most part, but coursed up and down its length every hour or so. He was a meticulous man who left little to his minions, but seemed compelled to make certain all was well with the march.

Ross Dunbar rode with Henry, both while in the lead and for his inspections. Cate caught the gleam of his ebony hair under his tilted Scots bonnet, was able to compare the width of his shoulders to those of the king who, though a tall man, was less square and broad even with the aid of his flowing cloak. Still, the two were a fair sight in their mature strength, both being of an age. Cate's gaze strayed in their direction more often than she liked.

It was a fine day, with the sun glistening in eye-stinging brightness on the melting snow, and a hint of something near warmth in the wind. Bird calls could be heard above the rattle of hooves and squeal of axles. Spirits mounted as the morning passed. After a while, someone began to sing. Others took up the old rondel about the holly and the ivy. Beneath its innocent verses lay an older paean to love in which the holly was a pagan man and the ivy his woman.

Cate, laughing with Marguerite over the suggestive lines, failed to notice Ross Dunbar's approach until he thundered up beside her. She turned sharply, her heart battering against her breastbone as she controlled Rosie's efforts to shy away.

"Good day to you, milady," he said with a smile. "Your mare looks in fair trim after her adventure, as do you."

"We both thank you," she said with a wry smile, but could think of nothing at all to add.

"You gave me to understand that you could not sing, but I see it was mere modesty."

"By no means!"

"I disagree. And we were to sing, you and I. Shall we?"

"This?" The verse that came next, she blushed to recall, was about the growing, swelling fervor of the holly caused by the ivy's embrace.

"What better?"

Merry challenge lay in the dark blue depths of his eyes. How was she to refuse it? With a smile and half despairing shake of her head, she took up the refrain.

Ross joined her in a baritone as deep and full as it was true. Their voices soared, rising above the rest. That was until Marguerite joined them in an alto that matched well in counterpoint, so they were not quite so conspicuous.

So they rode, the pacing of their horses well matched, Ross's knee brushing Cate's thigh now and then, sending shafts of tremulous awareness to the center of her being. And they sang as if nothing momentous pended between them, as though nothing mattered except the melody and Henry's slow yet certain pace toward London.

It was on the third day of the progress, after a morning spent slogging through mud churned to the consistency of butter, that Ross was finally able to secure a few moments alone with Lady Catherine. She had left the cavalcade, riding to the top of a brown knoll. She sat her palfrey, watching the long procession wind past below her while a light wind stirred the mud-spattered hem of her habit and lifted the linen layers of her veiling like angel wings behind her. She appeared pensive and in low spirits, he thought. Without conscious intention, he kicked his mount into a canter and rode out to join her.

"Weary?" he asked, circling her position to draw up at her side.

Her smile was slow in coming. "No more than anyone else."

"A seat in one of the carts can be arranged, if you like."

She shook her head. "I'd as soon ride horseback as have the teeth jarred from my head."

He could hardly argue, as he felt the same. "We won't be that much longer on the road. With luck and good weather, you'll be back in some chamber at Greenwich by tomorrow night."

She looked at him then, a curious glance. "And you, where will you sleep?"

"Oh, I'll find a rat hole somewhere." The words acknowledged his odd position at court, neither as high as the English nobles nor as low as their lackeys, neither courtier nor court fool. He had slept in high places and low in his months with Henry; not that it signified either way. He had endured worse in Scotland, as well as enjoying better.

"I expect the serving woman who travels with us can arrange something. Gwynne is a genius at finding the best of what's available."

"For you and your sister, doubtless. She'll not be troubling herself for the likes of me."

A smile flitted across Lady Catherine's face. "Oh, I don't know. Gwynne has an eye for a fine-looking man."

"Does she now?" he drawled, more intrigued and,

yes, pleased than he wanted to admit by the oblique compliment.

The lady colored and looked away from him. He had not meant to embarrass her. In a swift change of subject, he said, "While rubbing elbows with Henry, I learned he sent a messenger bearing the betrothal agreement to my father. The man was instructed to continue to Holyrood to gain the approval of King James."

"Already?"

"He wastes no time, does Henry."

She took a deep breath, released it with a sigh. "I had thought he might wait until he was established at Greenwich Palace."

"Or even after the Christmas season." Ross lifted a shoulder covered by the long tail of his plaid. "He was apparently not so inclined."

"Think you…" she began, before trailing to a stop.

"What?"

"That your King James will agree? I mean…"

"Could be. Jamie is of a mind to form an alliance between our two countries, as witness the treaty. He almost married his son to Elizabeth's sister, Cecily, some years back, so may look with favor on another such tie."

"I feared as much, particularly after such haste to arrange it."

"As to that, Henry sends couriers in every direction during the present uncertainty, but especially to the north, where any landing by an invasion force is to be expected. He doesn't intend to be caught napping like Richard III."

"Is that likely?"

"Who can say? I hear tell Margaret of Burgundy may contribute equal amounts of gold and spite to the plot involving the Yorkist pretender."

"It's natural enough, I suppose. Margaret was close to her brothers, both Richard and Edward."

"I'll hardly argue against invading with revenge for a reason, not being a hypocrite." He shifted in the saddle to stretch a tight muscle. "But I only meant to point out that Henry had no need to send a special messenger north to the border, as he had one headed in that direction already."

"How long do you think before he can have an answer?" she asked, her gaze clouded with uneasiness.

"With my father, it's hard to say. He may not answer at all."

"If he considers the proposal beneath contempt, you mean."

"Or in the nature of an insult," Ross said in wry agreement. "At least he won't send the messenger back minus his head. I trust not, anyway, as I am in Henry's hands."

She looked at Ross askance. "Surely you don't believe Henry would execute you in retaliation?"

"Maybe, maybe not, though he would be justified."

"What of King James? How long before we hear from him?"

"A month or two, even three, as he'll want to turn the question up, down and sideways, searching for a trick."

Her smile for his drollery was brief. "And if he decides in favor?"

"Who? Jamie or my father? Or is it that you fear they'll both betray us?"

She swallowed, a movement in the line of her white throat that made his belly clench. "Yes, both."

"Trilborn believes I should break my parole and return to Scotland."

"Unwise, I would think. Your king may take it in bad part if you avoid a wedding he considers politic."

"Possibly."

She searched his face, singling out the doubt he could feel there. "Or not, if it should be a ruse, and James intent upon taking advantage of Henry's distraction during any invasion."

"He is not so underhanded," Ross said in stiff rejection. "He will keep to the treaty he signed last spring. Besides, it would be cannier for him to wait and see who wins. As for fighting, I will follow my king when I can, though I'm not much disposed to kill men I've been drinking with these many months."

"Not even Trilborn?" she asked in dry tones.

"An exception might be made in his case." Ross paused, and then went on in a different tone. "He was entertaining you earlier."

"If you care to call it that. He's difficult to discourage, without simply riding off and leaving him."

"Your sister remained beside you, I noticed."

"It seemed best."

Grim humor surfaced inside him. "She does have a forbidding way of looking at a man, not that it seemed to trouble Trilborn."

A gust of wind blew Lady Catherine's veiling across her mouth. She lifted a hand to draw it away before she spoke. "He left soon enough. I take no particular gratification from his company, as you must realize, but though he is your enemy, that does not make him mine."

Sudden tightness invaded the lower part of Ross's body as his gaze was drawn to her moist and enticing lips, emphasized as the veiling was moved away from them. It sounded in his voice as he spoke. "He wants you and means to have you. He made that much plain when he warned me off a few days ago. I almost think…"

"What?"

Ross looked away toward the tail end of the column, which was approaching. "You'll think it Dunbar mistrust, or even lunacy."

"Or I may not."

"Think on this then. You are a good horsewoman. You aren't fearful of being alone in the wood. You often fall back at the end of the hunt."

Her gaze sharpened. "I'm not sure how you come by the knowledge, but what of it?"

"Those who hunt with Henry are well used to you removing yourself from among them for half an hour or so at the time of the kill, then showing up again. They barely notice when it happens, as you saw in the New Forest. If you had been carried off and held overnight, it would have been no different."

"You are saying…" She stopped as if unwilling to put the perfidy of it into words.

"I am saying," he continued, his voice gruff, "that you should have a care for your person. Be aware of what is taking place around you. Avoid going anywhere alone, and know always where the nearest palace guard is stationed."

She sighèd with a slow shake of her head. "Foolish man."

Irritation surged through him at the lack of alarm in her voice, and the note of pity. He could feel his face set in hard lines. "My lady?"

"Oh, not you," she answered, with a flashing glance in his direction. "I was thinking of Trilborn. He had best be glad he failed, if abduction was indeed his scheme. He might be dead by now, otherwise."

"You would have killed him." Ross thought he kept the skepticism out of his voice, but could not be sure of it.

"The boar would have attacked and killed him, he'd have been unhorsed in chasing after me, and broken his neck, or the outlaws would have murdered him for his purse. Any number of things might have happened, but he would be dead all the same."

"You speak of the curse." Ross's voice was flat in his attempt to control his annoyance.

She inclined her head while still holding her veil back from her face.

"I'm not sure the thing would have been so obliging, or acted so fast."

"Mayhap not, but he would have contracted an inflammation of the lungs at the very least."

"After you suffered at his hands."

A dark look passed over her fine, pale features. "That is possible."

"You will have a care then, if only to prevent him from achieving that much."

She sat her horse, her gaze steady upon his face,

while the wind flipped her palfrey's mane and threatened to take the bonnet from his head. Reaching up, Ross snatched off his headgear and then slapped it on again, pulling it snugly forward and to one side. His mount stirred restively, and was controlled by him with more firmness than was strictly needed.

"Why?" she asked finally. "What do you care what happens to an Englishwoman you barely know?"

"Why should I not? You've done nothing untoward, yet may be married out of hand because I elected to remain in the wood that evening instead of trying to find the hunt."

"It was the right decision at the time."

He was grateful to hear her say it, more so than he expected. "Nevertheless, I am responsible for what happened afterward. If I am not to offer the recompense of marriage, then you must allow me to keep you safe in other ways."

"Safe from Trilborn."

"And those like him who would take advantage of your fall from grace. Some men think nothing of bedding by force a woman they feel is fair game. There are worse things, milady, than being married against your will."

Ross waited after he fell silent, waited to see if he needed to speak more plainly. He would not descend to crude and pithy description unless forced to it, yet neither would he stand like a stone-carved saint, letting her risk what she might not understand.

"Yes," she said in stiff acknowledgment, "I am aware."

He let out a breath of relief. Though doubtless more innocent than she thought herself to be, she was not ignorant of what could happen to a woman. "Excellent. I don't mind carving a hole or two in Trilborn's hide, but would be loath to sully the floor of Henry's palace with his blood."

Her eyes narrowed a fraction as she searched his face. "You despise him that much."

Ross tipped his head, his smile without warmth.

"Because of the feud he spoke of, and the Trilborn wife stolen away across the border by your grandfather, but…"

"He didn't tell you of more recent abductions, including the Dunbar lass he made off with himself just last year, and only returned when he knew she was carrying his child."

"A Dunbar lass."

"My cousin, who was but thirteen at the time, fourteen when she died in childbirth. So yes, I would kill him with pleasure, might have already except for being sworn to peace while at Henry's court."

"You think his pursuit of me now has an element of personal retaliation due to the feud between your families."

Ross lifted a shoulder. "There is also your inheritance. Court life is expensive, and his estates have been so neglected they return little." He failed to mention her lovely face and form, though it required stringent effort.

"He may try his worst," she said with a wintry smile.

"You think he fears your curse."

"Many at court are superstitious, much though they might deny it," she said in oblique agreement.

Ross thought it more likely Trilborn feared the man whose ward she was, Henry VII, or had until a great Scots oaf had spent the night with the lady without being sent to the Tower. "If he tries it again, he'll be a dead man, with or without its help."

"You would break your oath of peace while in England?"

"Oh, aye, a hundred times over, rather than let him take you into his bed."

God's blood, he was daft for saying such a thing, he knew with instant disgust. Though he meant every word of it, and would not withdraw a single one.

6

"Lady Catherine, a moment of your time!"

Cate started as Trilborn stepped from an alcove in the empty antechamber she was passing through, and grimaced privately before she swung to face him. She had evaded his every attempt to speak to her alone since their return from Winchester. It was ill luck that he had caught her now as she came from an hour with the queen.

How he had known where to find her was more than Cate could see, unless he had followed her earlier. She had not known herself that Elizabeth would send for her, desiring to be told the latest on her peculiar betrothal.

"I am in haste, sir," she said with the briefest of smiles. "My sister awaits, and I must join her in good time for the midday meal."

"In truth, I am amazed to see her absent from your side." He strolled closer, sweeping off his plumed hat for his elaborate bow. His attire was in the latest mode and his signature colors, being an extremely short doublet in black velvet with slashed sleeves that revealed a linen shirt embroidered in silver. His manly parts were covered by close-fitting black hose, but were emphasized rather than concealed by the few inches of skirt that extended below the doublet's belted waist. The low boots he wore were of soft black leather, with toes of such length they curled backward and were attached to the boot tops by silver cords.

"Marguerite was not summoned to the queen's chamber," Cate replied with equanimity. She kept her gaze fastened on his face, being wary indeed of showing any interest in what stirred beneath the front of his hose. The scent that came to her from him was not quite as pristine as his clothing, being composed of stale sweat and ale mingled with a strong odor of cloves.

"Allow me to accompany you, if you will," he said, holding out his arm. "I have missed passing the time of day with you."

To refuse could lead to the very confrontation she hoped to avoid. Though she well recalled the warning Ross Dunbar had given her, she was no great distance from the queen's apartments with its guards, and the great hall was not far away.

Greenwich Palace, fast becoming a favored residence of the king and queen, was a great rambling manse with one large square tower and several of lesser size. Located in what had once been a fishing village, it had been enlarged and refurbished by Edward IV as a retreat for his queen, Elizabeth Woodville. Henry had improved it as well, with any number of Flemish tapestries, French cabinets and Saracen carpets. It had a splendid array of glazed windows that filled it with bright light and gave pleasing views of the Thames. It was also composed of numberless, echoing rooms that opened one into the other, with only a handful of corridors leading from one section to the next.

Cate was not at all sure she trusted Trilborn to guide her where she wished to go, but neither did she want him trailing along behind her if she should lose her way.

"As you wish," she said without enthusiasm, and laid her fingers upon his sleeve with as light a touch as she could manage.

"You found the queen well?" he asked as they began to walk.

"Very well indeed." He would like to know why she had been in private with Elizabeth of York, but Cate was in no mood to satisfy his curiosity.

"And the new prince, young Arthur?"

"The babe grows plump and fine."

"You and Henry's Elizabeth are of an age, I believe. You must have much in common."

"She takes an interest in all the ladies around her, both those officially in waiting upon her and those who are not." It was a banal thing to say, but better than being drawn into particulars that might be repeated.

Trilborn closed his free hand into a fist and placed it behind his back as he walked, the only sign of his annoyance with her. "What of your health?" he continued. "You suffered no ill effects from your night in a snowstorm?"

A smile curled one corner of her mouth. "None whatever. It may not appear so, but I have the constitution of an ox."

"That must gratify your bridegroom, as the Scots place great store upon rude health."

"He is not displeased." Cate had no idea if that was true, but thought it sounded well enough.

"And where is Dunbar this day?"

She sent the man a brief glance from under her lashes, noting the careful smoothness of his hair, the pleated frill of his shirt at the neck and sleeves. Even the king did not dress with such particularity. It was clear he had been nowhere near the exercise yard, where Ross had been disporting himself when last she saw him.

"I have no idea," she answered, "though he will appear in time to eat, I feel sure."

"His appetite is prodigious, I do agree. But nothing has been heard from Scotland? The betrothal does not progress?"

How everyone knew the details of her private affairs, she could not imagine, but so it seemed. Her deepest suspicion was that the king himself had informed all and sundry as a form of coercion. "It's early days yet."

"You can't be happy in it."

Her lips twisted for an instant. "Happy or unhappy, I must bow to Henry's will."

"So obedient, though you might escape the business with a little resolution."

"You think so," she said in droll disbelief.

"It would please me beyond my ability to express to have you as my wife, Lady Catherine. The king favors you and your sisters to an extraordinary degree. I'm sure he would listen, should you declare your preference for me above the Scotsman."

"You are supposing I would actually prefer you."

Trilborn swung his head to give her a narrow stare

before his features smoothed again. "You are pleased to jest. By my faith, I am quite serious."

His arm beneath her fingers had grown rigid with his displeasure, in spite of his attempt to pass it off. It would be best if she stepped lightly. "The king has a purpose in this, as in most things. I am not likely to sway him from it."

"You sound unwilling to try, if I may say so. Something took place between you and the Scotsman in the New Forest, did it not? Was it so satisfactory that you pant to enjoy it again?"

"You are offensive, sir." She lifted her hand from his arm at once.

"But am I right?"

"Nothing took place, nothing!"

"Dunbar says the same, and has bludgeoned half a dozen men to insensibility with fists, cudgel and the flat of his sword over it. Still, the king moved with amazing swiftness to mend your good name."

"An affair of state rather than a necessity, I do assure you." That Ross had been forced to defend her honor with physical prowess was disturbing. She'd had no idea of it until this moment. Certainly, he'd said nothing to her.

"How so?"

She remained silent as Trilborn held open the door to a short and windowless corridor that led to another series of chambers. Only when she had passed through ahead of him did she answer over her shoulder. "I believe Henry sees the alliance as a way to decrease border tensions."

"It seems more likely to fan them. Surely he knows of the bad blood between my family and Dunbar's?"

"I should be surprised to know Henry gave the feud a single thought." She hesitated a moment, then went on. "Is it of such moment that he should heed it? Can it not be mended?"

"My lady, you must know better."

"How did it start? What dread deed made it necessary to continue these many years?"

Confusion rippled across Trilborn's face before he lifted a shoulder. "I hardly know, if truth be told. I was brought up on bedtime stories of the dread Dunbars, shook with nightmares of being dragged from my sleep and hanged in my little nightshirt, or having my head chopped off like a young cockerel ready for the pot."

"They did nothing of the kind to children, surely!" She could almost be sorry for him, or at least for the boy who had been steeped in such a frightening legacy.

"Who can say?" he answered, his face grim. "They did enough."

"As did your family, from what I heard."

"Yet we are never quite even."

"What will that take, the death of all Dunbars?"

"Or their defeat and dishonor, so my father and grandfather would say," Trilborn allowed with a snorting laugh. "That Henry would overlook the business is hard to credit when he is well versed in all else that takes place, keeps his thumb on the country's pulse through his cadre of agents and paid informants." The courtier shook his head. "He plays a deeper game. I wish I knew what it was."

"You are mistaken if you think I can tell you." That was true only in part, as Cate had gained some small insight during the audience at Winchester. Still, it would be the height of conceit to presume her betrothal played a major role in the matter.

"You don't have to understand it to become his pawn."

Pawns were often sacrificed in order to save more valuable pieces. Cate felt hollow inside as that thought struck her.

"So," Trilborn said, reclaiming her regard, "you will not speak to Henry?"

"He would never listen. How many times must I tell you?"

"Those who venture nothing also gain nothing," he declared.

"A maxim for the battlefield, as I recall. This is my life we are discussing."

"Which you will spend in Scotland, if you don't have a care. I should think an English husband would suit you better. I could give you as much satisfaction as any Scots oaf, I'll warrant."

"I am promised. Can we not leave it at that until it proves otherwise?"

"Promised to Dunbar, of all men," Trilborn said, ignoring her plea. "By all the saints, I believe it's what you want!"

"All I want, sir, is to be left alone!"

She picked up her skirts, preparing to leave him. It was to be a fine, indignant exit with the trainlike hem of her gown frothing in her wake.

She was snatched up short as he wrapped hard fingers about her upper arm and whirled her against the nearest wall. Her head thudded against the stone, so hard that lightning flashed behind her eyes. Trilborn came up against her before she could move, slamming his body into hers, flattening her so she could barely draw breath, grinding against her from chest to thighs. He caught her wrists, squeezing until they creaked as he jerked them above her head. Holding them on either side of her head-dress, he tried to claim her mouth.

She twisted, whipped her head aside, ducking away from his wet, seeking lips. "Let me go," she cried, shuddering in revulsion.

"Are you sure that's what you want?" he demanded with harsh satisfaction in his voice. "Are you?"

She could feel the ridge of hardness he pressed against her, with only fine hose fabric between it and her abdomen. Shifting her weight, she tried to bring her knee up. He turned so she grazed his thigh, then he slid his leg between hers, bending his knee to rub against her. Catching both wrists in one hand, he reached for her breast, squeezing, kneading it in paroxysms, pinching the nipple through the cloth.

Cate heaved with rage and disgust. So wrenching was the experience that she snapped her head forward and sank her teeth into his neck.

He cursed, jerking away. For a single instant, she could breathe, was close to freedom.

Trilborn put a hand to his neck, brought it away again to stare at the blood on his fingers. He curled them into a fist while the disbelief in his face turned to fury. Drawing back his arm, he struck her, putting so much force behind it that she spun away from him, falling in a tangle of skirts. Her elbow and hip struck the floor with such jarring agony it brought tears to her eyes.

Behind her, Trilborn gave a guttural cry. Cate expected him to be upon her in an instant. She heaved up, struggling to her knees.

Through the blue gauze shimmer of her veil, which had fallen over her face, she saw two figures rolling over the carpets that stretched down the very center of the corridor. It was Ross and Trilborn, locked in vicious combat loud with oaths, grunts and the smack of flesh against flesh.

Abruptly, there was a flash of steel. Trilborn broke free then and staggered to his feet with a red-stained blade in his hand. He slewed around, his face wild as he looked at Cate. He'd lost his hat, his straw-colored hair hung in his face, his nose dripped blood and a purple-red splotch marred his neck.

Ross sprang up with his dirk grasped in a hard fist. Trilborn, pale and sweating, backed away. He swung around and plunged into a run. His thumping footsteps faded as he fled through an end door.

Cate flung her veil behind her shoulders as Ross came toward her. He was white around the mouth and none too steady on his feet, she saw, and his hand was clamped to his side. Still, he reached his free hand down to her, pulling her up when she took it.

"Are you all right?" he asked, his gaze on her cheekbone, which throbbed with every beat of her heart.

"Never mind me. What of you?"

He didn't bother to lower his gaze to where blood seeped between his fingers, made no answer at all to what she'd asked. Releasing her hand, he trailed a gentle fingertip over the curve of her cheek. "I should have killed him while I had the chance."

"Instead, he nearly killed you."

"My fault. Like the greenest chucklehead, I was nay thinking. I expected the devil's spawn to send footpads after me in some dark alley, but didn't credit him with the nerve to draw knife himself, and inside the palace walls."

Dunbar's Scots burr, always present to some degree, had thickened under duress. He must be more injured than he wanted her to know. "I am grateful you were near, all the same. But something must be done for your side. Can your manservant bind it? Shall I send for him?"

"Servant have I none," he said with a quirk of humor at one corner of his mouth. "I'm nay such a strutting cock as yon Trilborn, needing aid with my dressing like a babe in swaddling, nay, nor with anything else. I can strap it up my own self."

"So you might, if you don't drip so much gore on Henry's silk carpets that you pass out between here and your chamber."

"Henry's carpets are no worry of mine," he drawled. "As you have such a care for them, you'd best see to it."

He thought her reluctance to see a stag brought down meant she'd no stomach for dealing with a bloody wound. He was sure she would refuse and send him on his way; she could see it in his face. How little he knew her.

"So I shall, but not here." She touched his sleeve, indicated the corridor that stretched ahead of them. "There will be cloths for cleaning and binding in my chamber. It's not far."

He drew back. "That I can't do, and well you know it."

"Because I'm a maiden? No one believes that except you, as Trilborn made abundantly clear."

"The man's a fool. If others are not ready to accept it, it's for their own ends."

"Or else they think the worst because it's so often true," she said in dry correction. "But what is the point of enduring ill beliefs if I am not to have the advantage of it? Come, this way."

He took a step, then stopped. He raked back his hair with an impatient gesture, exposing a black scowl. "You would not prove them right out of anger?"

"What, wallow in sin because I've lost my shiny halo? My pride is greater than that. Besides, Gwynne, my serving woman, will be there."

"Well enough, but if I am seen going into your chamber, all the holy angels may not bring back that halo's polish."

"No, but the wound from Trilborn's knife may turn putrid, so prove the curse of the Three Graces yet again. I would see that doesn't happen."

Rueful humor gleamed in his eyes. "You think the feud will do me in because of this curse? Belike it's Trilborn who will die of blood poisoning after you set upon him with your sharp, white teeth."

"It was all I could do." Her voice was curt and she did her best to disregard the heat in her face as she urged him toward her chamber.

"And a fine thing it was, for all it drove him fair mad. Belike, he'll be the victim of this dread prophecy, as he tried to claim you."

"Pray God. Yet you are the more injured."

"I've also sworn not to wed you, so how am I to fall victim?"

"Don't mock it!"

"Nay, but you must see it makes little sense."

She shook her head, a movement heavy with concern. "We are as good as betrothed, like it or not. Come with me now, before you bleed to death from it."

He should refuse; Ross knew that well. It would be far better if he made whatever bow he could manage, and walked away while Lady Catherine was still talking. The slash halfway across his belly was irksome, but not deep. Certainly, it was nothing he had not dealt with before. A few strips torn from an old shirt, a stitch or two with good Highland wool, and none would be the wiser.

He didn't do it. Meek as a newly dropped shoat, he followed where Lady Catherine led. He walked into her chamber behind the intriguing sway of her hips, side-stepped the sweep of her trailing hem as she came to a sudden halt, then waited to see what she would do next.

The chamber was simple, containing only a curtained bed with a chest at its foot, a table with bowl and ewer, a low stool, and a carpet instead of rushes on the floor. It was warmer than the outside corridor by grace of coals that glowed in the brazier on a three-legged stand. Yet what struck him like a clout to the head was its scents of perfume, spice and warm, indefinably feminine linen.

His reaction was immediate and all too predictable. There were times when the front-and-center placement of his sporran—called a cache-sexe by Scotland's

French allies for obvious reasons—was most useful. It was Ross's personal belief other men at Henry's court would do better with one instead of the useless codpieces they sported now and again.

"Oh, I forgot," Lady Catherine said with an air of confusion. "Gwynne is washing linens this morning. If you will be seated on the stool, I'll send to the laundry yard—"

"Nay, 'tis not worth the trouble or the time, as you'll be needing to arrange yourself before you leave here again."

She reached up at once to feel for the placement of her veil. Which was more than a little off-kilter. "Am I that bad? I didn't think—"

"Don't fuss, that wasn't my thought at all. I'll just take myself off to my own chamber."

"Indeed, not. I can see to your wound as well as Gwynne, if you won't mind my ministrations."

The serving woman who had been with her and her sister on the progression was an older woman with a no-nonsense manner and skill in divers things. The only advantage Ross saw in having her tend him was that he would have no difficulty whatever in keeping his hands off her.

"You should not be called upon for such," he said, in a last attempt at reason.

The look Lady Catherine gave him held two parts regret and one part impatience as she indicated the room's squat stool. "You should not need it, but that can't be remedied. If you sit, this will be easier for both of us."

He failed to see the logic. The difficulty that lay ahead

was obvious, but he moved deeper into that feminine fastness and dropped down onto the stool.

She bustled around, stirring the coals in the brazier and tipping in a few more from a scuttle that sat beneath it. As smoke rose in a thin column toward the low haze that lingered near the high ceiling, she moved to take up a small basin. "I must fetch water. Mayhap you'll remove your shirt while I'm gone."

"My lady…"

"Now what? I refuse to believe you are shy."

His laugh was low and rather breathless. "Nay, but to strip off the shirt, I'll have to remove my belt and sporran."

"Do so then."

"If I remove my belt, there will be nothing to hold my plaid. And I should point out that we Scots have no great liking for yon braises Englishmen wear to cover their private parts."

She opened her mouth to speak, standing there halfway to the door with the basin in her hand. Then she closed it with a snap as rich color moved from her neck to her hairline. "Well, then, wrap your great coverlet of a plaid about you. It appears you'll be no more naked under it then than you are now."

It hurt to laugh, but he couldn't help it. He'd thought to see her rattled. Aye, and so he had, though not for long. She was no milk-and-water English milady. For all her cool blond coloring, she had fire inside her. She might keep it tamped down, as doubtless she'd been taught, but it flared up now and then, burning so bright Ross longed to warm himself in its glow. And he would, naked and shameless withal, in this brief time heaven had provided.

Reaching up with his free hand, he began to unfasten the lacing that closed his shirt's slit of a neck opening. Lady Catherine's gaze rested for long moments on the movements of his fingers. As he exposed the dark and curling hair that pelted his chest, however, she drew a sharp breath and whirled, whisking from the room.

By the time she returned, Ross sat naked to the waist, but with the rest of him decently wrapped in yards of woven wool. She stopped just inside the door, sloshing a little water from her basin so it streaked down the skirt of her gown. Sensing her gaze on his shoulders like the brush of butterfly wings, he felt a rash of goose bumps spread across them. In sheer reflex, he pressed the wadded shirt he held against his wound so hard he feared he had caused more damage.

Averting her gaze, she came on almost at once. Like the busiest of serving maids, she drew the small table near and placed the basin on it, then went to pull a ragged linen shift from the box at the foot of the bed. She tore it into strips with a few quick jerks. Face set, she returned to his side.

Ross eyed the bruise on her cheek. It was bluer now than moments before. Murderous rage surged in his chest. The need to smash Trilborn's face instead of just his nose, to pound it with his fists, was so strong Ross ached with it. The fingers of his left hand curled into a fist.

Lady Catherine seemed unaware of her disfigure-ment. Her gaze rested on his chest and shoulders. The absorption that lay in the blue depths of her eyes pleased him so mightily that he felt the flat, dark rounds of his nipples bead with it. It was a moment before he realized her interest was not caught by his manly physique but by the white streaks of old scars, a four-day-old sword cut on his upper arm and sundry bruises picked up in recent fights.

Her gaze lifted to his face. "You are cold. Shall I drape my cloak around you?"

"I'm not cold." The words came out as a growl.

"No?" She looked away without arguing. "I'll bind the wound as quickly as I can, anyway. Here, let me see the damage."

She took hold of the shirt he held wadded against the slash, peeling it away with slow care. The cut gaped, oozing, but was not the freshet it had been before. Ross watched her face, waiting for the sick disgust that would have been expressed by many. All he saw was calm appraisal.

"The edges need to be pulled together," she said quietly, "else it will take forever to heal."

"Do it then."

"Gwynne would be better at it."

"Don't tell me you are no hand with a needle. I see your work there." He nodded toward a basket that sat on the seat beneath the room's single window, and the piece of embroidered silk that spilled from it, showing flowers in jewel colors.

"It isn't the same." The words were laconic.

"Nay, it should be easier, as I have no need for daisies stitched round my navel."

The corner of her mouth twitched. She turned away then, speaking over her shoulder as she moved back to the boxlike trunk at the bed's foot. "On your head be it."

He was busy dabbing at the ooze from the cut and did not see what she took from the box. It was brought to his notice as she cast a handful of white powder into the water she had fetched, and stirred a piece of linen cloth in it, which she then pressed to his side.

"God's blood!" he swore, coming up off the stool as the sting of a thousand ants bit into him. His plaid began to slip and he caught it in haste, holding it in front of him. "What is that stuff?"

"Salt. It's only a salt-water wash. Gwynne swears by it."

"So might I, if I were a piece of boar meat needing preserving," he declared, subsiding back onto the stool.

"What prevents flesh from putrefying in the cask does the same for it on the body. Can you not be still?"

Thus abjured, he sat like stone. He required distraction from the pull and throb of his side, however. It was found, somewhat, in his close view of her curves under the deep rose silk of her outer tunic. At the center bodice, and again on either side at the level of her knees, this tunic had sizable slits with bound edges that spread open to reveal the vinelike tracery of embroidery on the pale pink gown it covered. The small cap that held her veil had the same color and embroidered design.

Strands of her hair had become enmeshed with the gold threads during her struggle with Trilborn, Ross saw. His fingers tingled at the tips with the need to set them free, to smooth them back into the heavy braid that shifted between her shoulder blades, under the semi-concealment of her veil. The fine fabric of her bodice molded to her shape with utmost fidelity, outlining the gentle globe of her breast. He could see where the areola made a flower shape around the tiny peak that was, most likely, a close match in color to the silk that covered it.

Trilborn had laid hands on her there. Ross knew a sudden ferocious need to wipe away that touch by cradling both her breasts in his hands, brushing the crests into sweet berries that he might taste, tease, gently suckle. He yearned to help her forget.

It was a part of the blood feud, it must be, this deep need to obliterate the very memory of his enemy from her mind. There was nothing more in it. No, not even if his yearning extended to greater liberties, to testing her soft heat and womanly fragrance while she lay naked in his arms.

He needed to think of something else, anything else.

"You have had difficulty with Trilborn before? He makes a habit of accosting you in quiet corners?"

"Not at all. I've managed to avoid him since our return," she replied, explaining in a few words how she had been accosted. While she spoke, she finished cleaning around his wound, and then moved to where her sewing basket sat, bringing back a needle threaded with black silk.

"Deliberate, then, of a certainty."

She appeared to consider that while she patted his wound dry with a soft cloth. Dropping it on the table, she knelt at his side, then reached to take up the needle. "I suppose it must have been."

"He meant to force himself on you if you failed to see reason. It seems to me he could have chosen a better place for it, though he may have only…seized the moment." Ross's breath hissed between his teeth as she caught the edge of the slash and pierced his flesh without warning.

"It was fortunate he did not choose differently, else you might not have come upon us."

Though her words were prosaic enough, a small shudder ran over her. "Nothing of chance was in it," he said deliberately. "I saw Marguerite, who let fall that you'd been summoned to the queen. I was on my way to meet you, and make certain all was well, when I saw Trilborn intercept you. I thought to discover his intention before I joined you. I almost left it too late." He sucked in a breath as she pushed her needle through his skin again, but was too intent on how she would answer to give the stinging pain his full attention.

"Not quite," she said.

"He hurt you." He reached to brush a knuckle over her cheek as he had before, unable to resist the urge. Her skin was as soft as apple blossom petals. To see it damaged pained him in some way he could not explain.

"Not as much as he hurt you," she answered, with her attention on what she was doing. "Nor as you are likely to be hurt if you continue to fight every man who speaks an incautious word concerning our time in the New Forest."

Her features were grave, her voice severe. That she spoke of preventing pain for him while thrusting a needle into him was a wonderment, though he said nothing of it. "Would you have me ignore them?" he asked instead.

"To make much of what they say lends credence to

our odd betrothal. It will be more difficult to renounce it at some future date."

"To let it pass would have it appear I have no care for your good name, or mine."

"Courting death merely because my mare ran away with me seems beyond foolish."

"'Twas not my plan." He held up his hand as she opened her lips to speak again. "It's a conundrum, agreed, but what would you? I must act the part of a man about to be married, or else appear the coward. After the seven or eight I've made eat their words, mayhap fewer will hunger to face me."

Her eyes widened, turning a darker blue as they met his. "Trilborn said a half dozen."

"He is behind time," Ross said shortly. Dropping poison wherever he went was both habit and pleasure for his old enemy.

She pressed her lips together before she spoke. "It's too much."

"Even if 'tis said I took advantage of you? I'll not stand for that."

"I'm to believe you fought for that reason, am I?"

Many women would have, if only because it absolved them of blame. He should have known Lady Catherine would be different. "I am pleased to be your champion," he said, his voice resounding deep in his chest, "as I can be nothing else."

Her eyes held his, twin wells of dark blue, for endless moments before she spoke. "You feel I require one then."

"Aye," he said, inclining his head, "that I do."

She gave a small shake of her own head, turning her

attention to her stitching as she released a sigh. "You may be right."

She finished the task in short order, and tied off the last stitch with a small, flat knot. So surprised was he that she was done, he barely felt the tug as she leaned to bite the thread just above it, freeing the needle. Or mayhap it was the sight of her veiled head so near his lap, the brush of her lips against the skin of his abdomen, the press of her breast against his bare thigh. Aye, and the knowledge that he was near naked made no difference, that all he need do to take her was throw off his plaid and pull her down to the floor with him.

His body hardened with a drawing agony so strong he felt his eyes water. It took his breath, destroyed reason, so he was left with nothing but impulse and desperate need. Unable to move without reaching out for her, he sat as still as death while she got to her feet and, oblivious to his state, began to dress his wound.

She compressed her lips so tightly they almost disappeared while she concentrated. He had noticed it before, but now he wanted to follow that tucked line, to coax them free, tease and stroke until they were soft, full and moist as she opened to him. He wanted to cup her face in his hands while he trailed a thousand healing kisses over her bruised skin. He longed to remove her veil and free her hair, to comb his fingers through it until it spread over her back and shoulders in a shining cape. He yearned to remove the yards of stifling fabric she wore, unfastening hooks and ties, saluting the flesh he uncovered until she was naked and pliant in his arms.

Unaware, she made a pad of linen and pressed it to

his side, held it down with another strip while she passed her arms around him to the back, crossed the ends and drew them forward again. She was close, so close that he caught the lavender-and-rose scent she wore, the warm fragrance of her hair. He held his breath while she wrapped his waist with the all too brief embrace of her arms, wrapped it again and then began to tie a small square knot.

Something in his stillness must have communicated itself to her. She glanced up, met the heat of his eyes, searched the set expression on his face.

For long seconds, she did not move. In the sudden quiet, the sound of ash falling away from the coals in the brazier was a slithering whisper. By slow degrees, her eyes turned as dark as the sky before a summer storm. A small tremor passed through her hands, which rested upon him.

Her lips parted at last, at last, and he was lost. He was lost, and feared it might be forever.

7

She was close, so close to the Scotsman. She could see the individual lashes that sprang thick and black from his eyelids, could see the shards of silver that spiraled around the pupils of his eyes against the background of dark blue irises. She was aware of the thin scar that bisected one eyebrow and the blue shadow of his beard stubble beneath the skin. The firm curves of his mouth were peculiarly enticing; she could almost feel their heat, their smoothness. The herbal scent that was his own, mayhap from some Scots soap, surrounded her. She sensed with an instinct beyond her understanding the power he held under restraint, and the price he paid for it.

She should step back, should move away while saying something commonplace. It would be the wisest course, the best thing for both of them.

She couldn't do it. Her muscles would not respond to her will. Her mind was blank except for the treacherous memory of Marguerite's voice murmuring in perilous reason: *"Do you never wonder what it might be like...to allow those caresses that may lead to...to exploration of soft petals and warm centers?"*

This was no garden, yet was an opportunity that might never come again. She had dreamed of such a time, just as she had told Marguerite. Oh, yes, she had dreamed.

Added to that, she was far more conscious than she wanted to be of Ross Dunbar's unclothed virility there in the virginal chamber she shared with Marguerite. He was so large, so masculine in the sculpting of the muscles that formed his body, catching the warm bronze glow from the brazier in their firm strength. The whorls of his ears, the slope of his neck, the way his hair grew were all a fascination. The soft feathering of hair across his chest made her want to run her fingertips through it, to spread her palms over it for the silken friction, to follow the narrowing tail of it as it arrowed down beneath the folds of his plaid.

She didn't move, didn't lift her eyes from the firm shape of his mouth. Her heart thudded against her ribs, shuddering under her bodice. Her hands trembled as she pulled the ends of the bandaging she held into a flat, tight knot. She may have leaned a fraction, may have sighed. She did not close her eyes, however, not until his features moved nearer and his mouth touched hers.

He was so warm. Heat radiated from him, surrounding her so she shivered with reaction. His mouth was hot against the coolness of her lips, branding her so her internal warmth surged up to meet his. Her lips tingled, setting off minute vibrations that shifted through her, settling in the lower part of her body. The skin of his arms and shoulders was like velvet over warm marble as she slid her palms over them. She felt the hard, possessive strength of him as he circled her waist with his arm and drew her against him, felt the slide of his free hand over the silk of her gown, pausing at the turn of her waist before capturing her breast with his fingers.

A low moan, half protest, half surrender, sounded in her throat. How different was his touch from Trilborn's earlier. Ross's hand cradled her, making her shiver as her flesh swelled to fill it. She smoothed her palm over his bare shoulder, then threaded her own fingers through his hair. The silken strands clung, catching in the spaces between them, rousing her to an awareness of him so acute it was almost painful.

The taste of his mouth was as sweet and heady as the finest wine. She was enraptured by the gentle abrasion of his tongue, which ignited a fire deep inside her, and by the hard wall of his chest against her breasts, the strong throbbing of his heart. She felt, too, in wonder and excitement, the firmness of him against her thigh, so different from the punishing jab of Trilborn's stiffness.

She was on fire, burning with desire so elemental it felt like compulsion. The slow brush of his thumb across the tip of her breast, the inexorable tightening of his hold, were incendiary beyond her imagining. The need to be closer to him, to feel him against her bare skin had such urgency that she moaned again.

"Ah, lass," he whispered against her lips, his warm breath a caress against their sensitized surfaces. And hearing the question in it, she hardly noticed the sudden draft as the door opened, or the footsteps that scuffed over the threshold in felt slippers before coming to an abrupt halt.

"Saints preserve us!"

Gwynne. It was Gwynne.

Cate gasped, coming so suddenly to her senses that she felt disoriented for endless seconds. Disentangling herself from Ross's arms, she stepped back, righted her veil, which had somehow loosened again.

"There…there you are, Gwynne," she said hurriedly. "The gentleman was injured and had need of aid."

"Aye, mistress, so I see," the serving woman said, setting her hands on her wide hips, "and you were giving it to him."

Cate lifted a brow, sought for authority. "You were not here to do it. Now…now he requires fresh linen, for his shirt is torn and bloodied, as you can see, and he can't leave in his nakedness. Go you and find something for him to wear."

"Where I am to find this linen?"

"In my chamber," Ross answered, as Cate hesitated, at a loss. "I give you leave to search my belongings and bring back what is needed."

If he was chagrined at all by being found three-quarters naked in a lady's chamber, nothing of it was present on his face, nor did he appear the least embarrassed at being discovered with her in his arms. Mayhap he was used to such events, or else cared nothing for what a serving woman might think of him.

Cate could not be quite so sanguine. Gwynne had been maid to her mother from the day she was wed, and also nursemaid to Cate and her sisters. Gwynne was the only mother left to them when their own died while they were still children. She had seen them through a hundred illnesses and upsets, had shielded them from the wrath of their stepfather and stepbrother before those two died, had shared their sorrows and their joys. She was family.

"Please, Gwynne," she said in fraught supplication. "I will explain, but not now."

The woman searched her eyes, her faded gaze disturbed but not unsympathetic. After an instant, she gave a short nod. "Aye," she said, "though I'll not be long about it."

It was a warning, if such were needed. It was not. The moment, so fraught with unnamable dangers, was past. When the door closed behind Gwynne, Cate moved to where she had dropped Ross's shirt. She picked it up, shook it out for inspection, aware as she did so of its width across the shoulders, and of the dark shade of the blood that soaked it.

"The stain may come out if it's put in water," she said, her voice tight and not completely even. "If so, I—or Gwynne—could mend the tear for you."

"Leave it," Ross answered. "Some things are beyond mending."

She glanced at him and away again, alerted by some undercurrent in his voice that said more than his words. "You have to try, often enough, before you can be certain of it."

"Not always. Betimes, the damage is obvious."

She pressed her lips together, busied herself folding the shirt and placing it firmly in the red-tinted water that remained in the basin. "And what then?"

"Then you make what accommodation you can. You vow to do without, or else begin anew."

She could feel the heavy beat of her heart, the fullness

in the lower part of her body, the weight in her mind. Something momentous was being decided here, and she could not be certain what it was or what the consequences of it might be. When she spoke again, the words were a mere thread of sound.

"And which shall it be for us?"

"Ah, you know, Cate. You've known from the first."

She feared she did. She feared it greatly.

Ross's wound became inflamed. It was no great surprise, in spite of Cate's salt water, as it had been Trilborn's dirty blade that sliced him. He kept to his chamber, tossing and shivering with fever, sleeping much, eating nothing. On the second day, Cate's serving woman bustled into his room with a tray holding bread, chicken broth and a water jug. She clacked at him about his failure to appear in the great hall, bullied him, forced him to eat a little and drink much, changed his sweaty linens and left him far more comfortable. She came again on the third day, and the fourth. Sometimes she came at night, as well, though then she sometimes looked amazingly like her mistress, and her long fair hair sometimes brushed over his fevered skin like a hundred tiny fingers as she sponged him with water like that from a snow-fed loch. Her hands were gentle, yet made his skin pebble in reaction as she changed his bandage, brushed his hair free of tangles, smoothed a cloth over his face.

By the fifth day, he was restless, irritable, thrown into a temper by every stray noise as his fever climbed each evening. When two idiots in the chamber next to his started an argument over a dent in a helmet, he rose from his bed, knocked their heads together and, weak as watery porridge from the exertion, went back to his chamber. Within moments, he was drenched with sweat, but calm enough that he slept from prime to vespers.

On waking in the middle of the sixth night, he had a fierce longing to throw on his plaid, saddle a horse and leave this self-imposed prison. He wanted, needed, to ride out and pit both wit and strength against a foe. It mattered little whether that meant keeping Dunbar cattle safe from theft or stealing the beasts of his neighbors, so long as he was moving, out in the open night air on this last day or two of the raiding season. Soon enough the nights would grow too short, forage for horses too scant and the cattle too weak for rough herding. The reiving would be over until spring.

As he lay staring into darkness lit only by the guttering stub of a tallow candle, he thought it doubtful he would ever ride out again with friends and the male members of his family to wreak havoc on those who stood against them. They would go without him, as they must have done during these many weeks since Michaelmas. He would be stuck here in England forever and a day, forgotten by all he knew.

A part of his melancholy came from loss of that close companionship of his youth and the surety of blood ties, another part from isolation and weakness due to lying abed. Adding to his gloom, however, was recognition of the great gulf that existed between him and Lady Catherine Milton.

He had let her know there was no future for them. It was idiocy, then, to bemoan her failure to appear. True, she had sent her serving woman, which could be seen as a display of concern, but she had not come to soothe his brow or relieve his boredom.

She could not have stayed, of course. He would have sent her away at once. Still, she might have made the attempt.

He was being unreasonable and knew it. They were both aware there could be nothing between them, had agreed upon it twice over. For her to be seen anywhere near his chamber could have disastrous consequences for them both. News of it would fly about the court more wildly than a sparrow lost among the flags and banners that draped the great hall's ceiling. They would be wed before cockcrow.

The only thing worse would be if he was caught slipping into her chamber in the dark of night. In that case, he could wind up clamped in irons.

Still, he had considered it, particularly when half crazed with fever. Would she welcome him, all gentle smiles and soft, enclosing arms, or scream the palace down around his ears? Only the knowledge that she slept with her sister prevented him from sliding from his bed to find out. Yon Marguerite would not hesitate a second before calling for the guard. That was, if she didn't brain him with a fire iron instead. And wasn't he beyond hope that he could think to entice Cate from her bed while Marguerite slept beside her?

He needed a woman. That was what ailed him; he'd been celibate too long. Between scorning the blandishments of the court ladies, who looked upon him as a barbarian who might show them his rough ardor, and avoiding the drabs who sold their wares in tavern attics and alleyways, he had gone without. He could barely remember his last encounter, but thought it was with Sadie, the blacksmith's daughter, who had smelled of hot metal polish, heather and the wind off Solway. They went at each other fast and hard that day in the bracken, two bodies grasping, holding, pounding together with no pretence of anything other than seizing the moment. When it was over, Sadie had walked away, skirts swishing, flinging a satisfied smile over her shoulder.

In his drifting daytime fantasies and midnight dreams, too, it was Cate who smiled and swung her skirts. She left him lying there in the grass as naked as he was born, wishing she would remain to sleep in his arms. Her kiss haunted his nighttime hours, returning to him with such tenderness, such untutored sweetness and gentle sighs, that he woke groaning aloud with the need for more.

In the evening of the eighth day, or perhaps it was the ninth, a messenger arrived at his chamber. Ross rolled out of bed as the hammering came on his door, then grabbed for the post, cursing, until his head cleared. The man outside was his cousin Liam, tall and burly, with hair the color of rusty armor and a grin that took up half his face. He buffeted Ross on the shoulder so hard he almost floored him in his weakened state, then grabbed him and set him on the bed.

"Ye look like cat vomit on a dung heap, mon," he declared with typical diplomacy. "What've they been doing to you?"

The catching up took some little time. At the end of it Liam shook his craggy head. "A bad business, all around.

Yon Trilborn is no the most canny creature under God's heaven, but sly enough to make up for it. Think you he meant to gut you?"

"Oh, aye, though he could not know I'd come upon him with Lady Catherine," Ross allowed. "He just meant to do as much harm as possible while he had the chance, would have done more had I not blocked it with my dirk."

"Being that fearful of ye."

"Or that determined to have the lady."

"To spite a Dunbar then."

"Or because he not only pants after her but has need of her dowered lands and their revenue."

Liam looked wise. "And you've no notion of letting him have her."

"I never said that."

"Ye didn't have to, for 'twas in your face. But it won't do. 'Twill never do."

Ross had known as much, though a slow anger simmered inside him at hearing it plainly spoken. "You've come to tell me so, I suppose."

"The laird was fit to be tied when he got yon King Henry's message. Raved up and down like a madman, he did, threatening to horsewhip you for getting yourself entangled with an Englishwoman. The upshot was a fine vow that you'd be no son of his should you dare give her the Dunbar name. Said you could get all the bastards you pleased upon her while Henry's guest, but you are no to stand with her at the church door."

Ross snorted in disgust. "Disowned, is it?"

"Wed her and you may as well call yourself a Sassenach. In fact, the laird said as how he'll see you dead if you show yourself on Dunbar land."

The old man had been on a rant, sure enough, or else he meant to make certain his will was obeyed. "You brought Henry this refusal of permission?"

Liam chuckled and slapped his knee. "Nay, not I. What the auld laird had to say to him went by the king's messenger betimes. And what he said was that he'd have to think on it longer, seeing as our Jamie considers it such a fine match."

"King James gave it his blessing?"

"Aye, being that content with the treaty signed between him and England's Henry as to favor anything that may aid it."

"So he's kept the door open, the wily old devil, while making sure I'll not step through it on my own."

"Something like," Liam agreed.

"Odd that I've heard nothing of it from Henry."

"Ye wouldn't, now would ye, if he still thinks to persuade ye? Well, or allow the lady to try? Though I can't think what manner of female she must be that he's so bent on handing her over to a dastardly Scotsman."

"A sorceress, or something like it."

Liam drew back, his eyes wide. "Never say so!"

"A jest only," Ross said, giving his cousin a thump upside the head. "Henry plays a deep game, I think, with an eye toward a likely rebellion."

"Because of this talk of a prince nay so dead as all thought? We've heard of it, across the border, along with stirrings in York, which was dead King Richard's home ground. Just what's needful, another little skirmish between white rose and red, followed by another row of lopped off heads stuck on posts to feed ravens."

"As long as they aren't Scots heads."

"Oh, aye."

"There's no indication our King James intends to meddle in the business then."

"None I've heard, him being that busy worrying over a braw little rebellion all his own."

Liam lingered only long enough to give news of the Dunbar clan—who had been born, married, sickened, died or killed. He complained of the boredom of being idle under the laird's promise of good behavior—though he also laughed over a fine jest played on the Johnstones wherein a half-dozen Dunbars had dressed in sheepskins on a foggy night and made away with enough cattle for a fine feast.

When his cousin had taken himself off to find food and drink after his long journey, Ross sat staring at the four walls of his chamber, turning over in his mind all that had been said.

He had known how his father would react, so there was scant surprise there. The lack of an outright, damn-your-eyes refusal to Henry was more about taking the time to study all the angles than concern for his son. He'd figure Ross could take care of himself, and so he could, right enough. Why, then, was his first impulse to defy the laird of Dunbar? What maggot of perversity made him want to say to hell with his father's orders and threats, and do what he wanted?

What he wanted...

Cursing, Ross shoved himself off the bed. Splashing and slopping the cold water that sat in his basin, he scrubbed away the stink of sweat from skin and hair while routing the stupor of illness. He bound fresh linen over the slash in his side that was still an angry red line set with neat stitches in black embroidery. Pulling on his thigh-length linen shirt, he pleated his plaid about him in folds to his knees, threw on his belt and sporran over it and topped the whole with his leather jerkin. Moments later, he slammed from the chamber on his way to the great hall.

The fresh smell of greenery assailed him as he entered, along with the smoke and brightness of a great crackling fire. Glancing at the enormous Yule log that blazed on the hearth, Ross realized it must be the eve of Christ's Mass, that the holiday had crept in upon them all while he lay abed. Mingled with the unusual saplike fragrances were the aromas of roast meats, hot bread and ale.

For an instant he felt light-headed, almost ill, then realized it was because he was hungry enough to fight the dogs for the bones under the table. Striding to the end of the nearest bench, he made a place for himself and snagged the shirt of the boy moving past with large slabs of warm and crusty trenchers.

It was afterward, when the tables had been cleared and their tops and trestles stacked against the wall, that Ross was joined by Lady Marguerite. He glanced behind her for Cate, but his betrothed seemed to be waiting upon the queen at present, holding a bowl of spiced water while the royal lady dabbled her fingers in it to clean them. The younger sister seemed at loose ends without her sibling nearby, with an air about her that said his company was as good as any other.

Ross was not fooled. The lady had something on her mind, though he wasn't certain he was ready to hear it.

"So you have deigned to join us again," she said as she came to a halt where he leaned against one of the support posts that marched in pairs down the center of the hall. "We were of two minds whether to send a priest for last rites or alert the guard of your escape."

"But you did neither."

"Both seemed premature, given Gwynne's report of your ill humor. You threw a boot at her head last evening."

"She wanted to bathe me."

"If so, I expect you needed it."

Cate's little sister had an intelligent face and large brown eyes dark enough to hide all manner of secrets. Her fine, golden-brown hair was several shades darker than Cate's fair locks and she was not so tall. She seemed a bit fey, almost mysterious somehow, an impression heightened on this evening by a Christmas gown of sea-blue velvet worn under a tunic of lavender blue that was sewn with tiny suns and moons in gold and silver and drops of jewel-colored glass. She was, in addition, so self-possessed and unaffected by whatever he might say that Ross could not resist the urge to shake her from it.

"Or just preferred a different female wield the cloth," he said in his best Scots burr. "Unfortunately, no other was nigh."

"My sister, you mean."

"If she should be willing."

"To resist was a great strain for her, I've no doubt," Cate's sister said placidly, "but she managed it with aid from the Holy Mother."

Ross felt the back of his neck burn at the suggestion that Cate might have wished to be with him. That was before he saw the glint in the eyes of her sister, which told him he was transparent to her. "Little witch."

Marguerite paled. "Don't say that!"

Surprised at her distress, he put out a calming hand. "I didn't mean…"

"Never say it, not even in jest, I beg you," she said earnestly. "There are those who have no sense of humor at all where such things are concerned."

She was right, of course. And he was not glad, after all, to see her so shaken. "I crave pardon."

"Truth to tell, I fear Trilborn sees me in that light, just as he does Cate. He is superstitious, you know, otherwise he'd have had my sister long ago. If she is ever forced to marry him, a charge of witchcraft will be a convenient way to be rid of her."

"While holding on to her estates, of course."

Marguerite gazed at him a long moment, a small frown marring her piquant features. Ross had the uncomfortable feeling that he was being weighed in the balance. Something else hovered there, an odd speculation that he didn't care for at all.

"What of you?" she asked, finally. "Would you cherish Cate or be rid of her as soon as she has provided you an heir or two?"

The rage that hovered inside him rose to the surface with a growl. "What kind of question is that?"

She didn't flinch, which suggested courage might be hereditary in their family. "One requiring a simple answer."

"If I could marry her, I would not release her, not ever."

"And if you came upon her in a rose garden at dusk?"

She could not be asking what he thought. But what if she was? "We…would brave the thorns together."

"So you could be in love with her, if you really tried."

He gave a short laugh. "For what purpose, when she is a Sassenach with the title of lady before her name and I a common border reiver?"

"Not so common." Marguerite watched him a moment, taking a corner of her veil, biting down on it, then dropping it again before she added, "Your father is the laird, and so will you be when he dies. That is, if you live."

"If?"

"You stand in danger, though it's interesting that the chance came for you to die and you did not."

"Was I meant to?" he asked in blunt suspicion.

"Most have, those who sought to make brides of us before you."

"You're talking about this ridiculous curse." He had thought for a moment that she meant the knife slash, and Trilborn's need to be rid of him.

"But of course. I'd thought…but no matter." She heaved a sigh. "It's really too bad." Turning, she wandered away from him as if he no longer held her interest.

Ross, watching Cate's sister go, feared he had been consigned to an early grave. It was a hasty verdict. He was not so easily done to death.

A creeping sensation on the back of his neck made him turn then—just in time to avoid the direct jab of an elbow to his injured side. The glancing blow was enough to take his breath, however, and send his senses whirling for an instant.

"Well, Dunbar," Trilborn said, as he swung to a halt at much too close a range for comfort, "what a surprise to see you abroad. We were sure your next appearance would be in winding sheets."

8

Cate was aware of Ross the instant he passed through the entrance to the great hall. Though he appeared drawn and pale under the weathered bronze of his skin, no one else had his air of command or ability to dominate his surroundings. No one possessed his casual grace or darkly handsome features. Of course, few others wore a plaid, either, though there were a handful of other Scots at court as pledges for the treaty with Henry.

Her heart stuttered in her chest, doubling its beat. She tracked him with her gaze until he was lost from view somewhere in the far end of the vast hall. Suddenly, the holiday evening seemed twice as bright.

The windows and doors of the hall were hung with swags of red-berried holly, bay and ivy interspersed with thick sprigs of mistletoe and other evergreen boughs that released their scent into the warm air. More garlands draped the front edge of the dais where stood the high table, and framed the king's arms on the wall behind it. Pomanders made of apples stuck with cloves were heaped in bowls along the high table's length, while wide ribbons made swaths of color between them. Behind these,

Henry and his queen, with his attendants to his right and her ladies to her left, sipped their wine and waited to be entertained.

Cate, along with several of the other ladies invited by the queen, had directed the hanging of the greenery, and made the pomanders. The decorations were meant to remain in place for the six weeks between now and Candlemas. The meal took so long, however, that she began to wonder if they would last out the evening.

At last the cheese and nuts were removed and lower tables broken down and set against the walls. The pantomime to be presented by a traveling troupe was about to begin. After it would come dancing to harp, lute and vielle, beginning with a carol dance. Other merrymaking would fill the time until the midnight Angel's or Christ's Mass, which glorified the arrival of the light of salvation at the darkest hour of the darkest date in the depth of winter.

Pantomime had never been a favorite of Cate's; she had not missed it after it was banned following a horrific *Danse Macabre* put on by Henry's master of revels at Westminster a few months before. It was surprising that the mummers had been allowed into the palace this evening. She supposed the tradition of their presence during the Christmas season was too strong to be denied, or else the king meant to replace old memories with new. As the men with white powdered faces and rich costumes came forward, she turned away in search of Ross's tall figure.

There he was, with one shoulder propped against the support post nearest the entrance. Marguerite must have been talking to him, for she was just walking away. Her shoulders had a defeated droop that made Cate frown as she wondered what had been discussed between them. She must ask her sister when they were alone.

An abrupt movement at the edge of Cate's vision brought her head around again. Ross had been joined by three men. She took a swift step forward as she saw one of them jab at his side and the Scotsman wrench away. Fury gripped her and she narrowed her gaze upon the black doublet of the man who had tried to prod Ross's injury. Though he stood with his back to her, she would have known him anywhere.

What could he hope to gain, unless it was to goad Ross into stepping outside to cross swords while he was less than fit? That was, just possibly, the reason Trilborn had friends with him.

Cate made no decision to move. One moment she stood in ladylike composure, and the next she was striding toward the trio surrounding Ross. She stepped among them in a flurry of crimson velvet and veiling edged with gold braid, her smile cold as she swept them with contempt.

Ross rested his hand on his dirk, she saw. He must not be allowed to draw it, for that could be taken as an insult requiring redress.

"Ross, my dear sir, how laggard you are," she said, allowing her voice and her gaze to soften as she reached to take his arm. "You promised that we would dance, if you recall. 'Twas at Winchester."

"Oh, aye. And?"

Drollery lurked in the mountain-blue of his eyes. He knew what she was doing and thought it comical in some fashion. So it might be, though she would not give over because of it. "If you will not come to me, then I must come to you, for I intend to hold you to your word. A carol dance will follow the mummery, so you may sing to me as we caper."

"But, Lady Catherine," Trilborn exclaimed.

"My lord?"

This was the first time she had seen the earl since the incident in the corridor; he'd apparently nursed his own wounds in solitude this past week. His nose was still discolored and a little crooked from where Ross's blow had broken it, and he wore a high collar to his chin to cover the site where she had bitten him.

The anger that leaped to her gaze seemed to give him pause, for he lowered his head with the pretence of a humble bow. "Your pardon, but I'd meant to ask you to step out onto the floor."

"I must refuse," she answered at once.

"Because of the small misunderstanding between us? I was hasty, I will admit, my feelings too strong. I hoped for an opportunity to beg forgiveness."

Cate gave that suggestion the answer it deserved, which was none at all. Turning her back upon Trilborn, settling her gaze on Ross's face, she asked, "Shall we, sir?"

"We're to caper, is it?" The Scotsman smiled down at her, tucking her hand into the crook of his arm so she was aware of the hard bunch of muscles there that showed his readiness for action in case of need.

"Merrily, as 'tis the season." Her heart beat a wild tattoo against her ribs and the warmth in her cheeks seemed to heat the air around her. Her greatest fear was that Trilborn would lay hands upon her, or upon Ross. Though she knew the Scotsman would fight like a demon, in either case, she was not certain he could survive it.

"I was speaking to the lady, Dunbar!"

"Her wishes must take precedence, Trilborn, especially as she is one of the incomparable Graces of Graydon."

"By God's beard, I'll not be passed over this way!"

"You have your friends about you," Ross said over his shoulder as he led her from among them. "Mayhap one of them will partner you in the dance."

The wrath that dawned on Trilborn's face was most satisfying. Head high, looking neither right nor left at the audience that had gathered, Cate walked with Ross Dunbar to the edge of the cleared space before the high table. And if her heart was attempting to tear its way from under the silk of her bodice, only she knew it.

"Tit for tat, one rescue for another," Ross said, his voice deep and low near her ear as they waited for the mummery to end. "We should be equal now."

"Hardly, sir. You have rendered two to my one." She kept a cordial smile upon her face and her gaze on one of the mimes, who seemed in acute distress over the fate of the actor costumed as a white mouse.

"I count it differently. You not only sewed up my belly, but came of a night to rout my fever."

"To tend your wound was the least I could do. For the other, you are mistaken. 'Twas Gwynne."

Ross's smile was wry. "I'll admit I thought it a dream until now, when I am with you again."

"I don't know what you mean."

"Half-mad with delirium I might have been, but scent and touch do not lie. Nor was I so far gone, now I think back on it, as to miss the rare colors of a most glorious black eye."

"Oh!" She clapped a hand to her face, covering where her cheek had indeed been so bruised by Trilborn's blow that color from it seeped upward to give her eye all the shades of the rainbow. For some few days after the meeting with Trilborn she had resorted to paints of the sort used by Spanish ladies, and had only ceased that morning.

"Not," Ross added with great magnanimity, "that it appears so now. No, and I was never so addled in the head as to mistake old for young or plain for fair."

"Fie, sir!" Cate railed with heat rising under her skin. "Is that any way to speak of the woman who bathed and dressed you as if—how was that you put it?—oh, yes, as if you were a babe in swaddling?"

"I cry foul, milady. Words spoken in the heat of the moment should not be used against a man. But if you will not have it even between us, then I've no objection to being saved yet again."

She glanced up at him, searching his face. "Some men would."

"Aye, and some come nigh to slicing their own throats while shaving, but it doesn't make them wiser for it. Take yon Trilborn, for instance."

"You take him, as I have no use for his fine self." Her

answer was stiff in her annoyance at the turn of subject. She would far rather have spoken of what was between the two of them alone.

The Scotsman ignored her ill humor. "He intends to have you to wife, and minds not at all if he earns your hate in the process."

"So you've pointed out before, and I told you—"

"You place your confidence in the protection of your curse, though it's done little to prevent two attacks so far."

"It sent you to stop them, did it not?"

"You may think so if it pleases you. But I believe you would be wiser to look around you for another husband, as you've no wish to warm Trilborn's bed."

"What? Seek out a third prospective husband to fend off, when I have two already? I may as well choose a few more for an even dozen."

"Now there's a thought," he said with an affable nod, "being there's safety in a crowd."

"I'd sooner go into a nunnery!"

He scowled down at her. "You never mean it."

"At least it would be quiet and free of strife," she said with a toss of her head. "I'm sure Henry's mother, half a nun herself, could arrange it."

"Mayhap, but would she go against the king's will?"

"She might if convinced I have a true vocation."

"Ah, well, in that case," he said, taking her hand and leading her forward as the dance began to form. "But it would still be a tragedy."

Cate was barely aware of the circle of dancers or the start of the music for the carol dance, paid scant attention to the first line sung that must be repeated by each pair of dancers as they added their own line to the carol. "Why a tragedy?" she demanded. "Many women dedicate their lives to the service of God."

"Those without a prayer otherwise." He made his bow, his smile irreverent and lacking in apology for the punning quip.

"You are mistaken. My sisters and I were placed with the nuns for our education, and spent many happy hours tending herbs and vegetables, bees and sheep. Many women had taken refuge there from the ills of marriage."

"And a fine thing, if they were content. But it might have been better had they chosen a man who'd not use them ill in the first place."

"Fine talk, when you must know few choose at all."

If she sounded bitter, she could not help it. There had been too many betrothals foisted upon her and her sisters, arrangements that might have ended in tragedy of a different kind had the men involved not died.

Ross stared down at her averted face a long moment as they circled each other with arms akimbo. When he answered, his voice was abrupt. "I spoke without thought. But I will not be put off by this wandering from where we started. Why will you not admit you came—"

"Hush," she said, with a quick glance around her. "And make ready, for it's almost our turn to sing."

It was upon them within the instant, a list of nine items brought from a peddler's pack as gifts for the New Year, each of them more fanciful than the first. Cate expected that she would be required to carry the burden of remembering their sequence, but it was not so. Ross's fine baritone rang out in perfect measure and progression, adding ten silver bells as their contribution even as he moved with smooth grace around the circle, turning, twisting, taking her hand and walking around her, then moving down the line.

She was loath to be separated from him. She followed him with her gaze while she slipped through the intricate winding of couples. Men stepped warily around him, or so it appeared. Women smiled and gave him their hands all too readily, while brushing against him in the turns. Not that Ross noticed any of it, she thought. Features grim, and favoring his left side, he worked his way purposefully from one partner to the next until he was before her once more.

"Does your wound pain you?" she asked in concern as they swept together and then apart again with a flourishing bow of greeting. "Would you prefer to sit this out?"

"And break the circle? I'd not think of it."

His breathing was less strained than hers, his smile just as easy as when they began. He was stronger than she might have expected, given his ordeal. Another day or two and no one would guess he had been close to death.

"You were there, admit it."

The demand came from behind her as he circled her once more and then danced to the fore again. He was relentless in his will. He would not stop until he had his answer.

"Oh, very well!" she exclaimed, with a swift glance toward their neighboring partners. "I was there. What of it?"

"Why would you deny it? Did it please you to make me think I dreamed you beside my bed?"

"I was not meant to be there," she said in a strained whisper as she danced close and away again. "If anyone knew…"

"It was a grave risk."

"I am aware, believe me." She gave him a fulminating glance, thinking of how she had traversed the cold corridors of the palace in one of Gwynne's loose day robes and with a thick peasant's kerchief covering her hair. More than once while traipsing back and forth, she had been forced to step into a storeroom, doorway or the darker shadows to avoid meeting those she knew.

"Why would you chance it?"

"You ventured more for me, and suffered more."

"Nothing that might affect my future."

Her glance was scathing. "I should think being killed an almighty affect!"

"Mayhap keeping you safe from Trilborn is my purpose in being allowed to live," he suggested with a whimsical smile.

"Henry has had a bellyful of wrangling nobles, every one of them thinking himself the equal of a king. He will brook no meeting with sword or lance that he has not specifically decreed."

"That isn't my intention. At least, not unless I'm forced to it."

What was he saying? Surely not what it sounded? "What else?" she asked with more than a little wariness.

"A husband acceptable to Henry, one who would not misuse you, should solve your dilemma. Add to that the joy of snatching the bride he wants from Trilborn's grasp, and the thing begins to have merit."

"You swore you would not agree!" she reminded to him in sibilant undertones. "If this is the way you repay my efforts to lower your fever, then I am sorry I bothered!"

"Are ye, now?"

No, it was not true. He had been so near perfect a specimen of manhood as he lay sprawled on his bed. She had taken guilty pleasure in running a cool cloth over the muscled expanse of his chest, along his arms, down the long, firm length of his thighs. And if she had lifted a corner of the sheet that covered him while Gwynne's back was turned, who was to know? Unless it was he? Unless his suggestion came from some awareness of that heart-stopping instant of intimacy that gained her the knowledge of just how well, how bountifully, he was made?

"That was before I knew your danger," he was saying.

"Yes, and before you saw how I could be used to spite your old enemy."

"You would rather be wed to him? It may come to that if you refuse. I don't see Henry handing over your share of your father's estates to a nunnery, as he must if you escape behind its walls."

Dread caught her by the throat, squeezing slowly so she felt the full pain of it. "It isn't that, you know it isn't."

"Because you think I may die then? The reaper comes for all of us, soon or late. We do what we are allowed, betimes."

"But don't you see the feud with Trilborn may be your

death? The vengeance and betrayal are there waiting, have always been there. They could overtake you if you defy the curse."

"They may do it, any road. I might as well make what goes before count for something."

"You can't!"

"No?"

He watched her as he asked it, his eyes dark with unnamable impulses. She held his gaze, regardless, because she must. "No, not...not ever."

"Ah, well," he said with a smile that did not light his eyes, "as you will, milady."

"You must promise me you will not change," she insisted.

He shook his head. "Whist, now, lass. It's time for us to sing again."

The Yule log, tall as a man and so large four could not reach around it so it might burn the entire twelve days of Christmas, made the great hall insufferably hot. When Cate and her sister left to don cloaks and gloves for the midnight mass, Ross made his way outside. Greenwich Palace overlooked the Thames, and the deeper basin of a shipyard in a long curve of the river some distance away. It was a fair prospect during the day, though only pinpricks of light from stern lanterns could be seen in the darkness. Nearer at hand, the river was quiet and nearly empty of traffic.

Ross took a well-worn path that led downhill, winding through a copse of leafless horse chestnuts and beside a stone wall before ending at the riverside. The quiet rush and gurgle of the water drew him to the edge. A pair of black swans approached, silent and almost invisible in the night, their eyes reflecting small pinpoints of light from the dimly glowing palace. He squatted and held out his hand to them, but they floated away when they saw he had nothing to feed them. Chuckling, he remained there on his haunches.

The weather had turned somewhat warmer but was still cool and damp. The breeze off the water felt so good on Ross's flushed face that he was barely aware of the smell of mud, decaying vegetation, and human and animal waste. Plucking a dried reed that grew at the river's edge, he fashioned a rough flute and piped an air that had often sent men marching into battle with their plaids swinging and their swords weighty on their backs.

It had scarce been two hours since he'd eaten, but he was hungry again. No doubt he would be until he was fit once more. Tomorrow would see a great feast at Henry's expense. The boar Ross had killed in the New Forest would play its part. It most likely lay in salt somewhere in the bowels of the palace, after being dragged from the wood on his instructions and transported with the carts that had come from Winchester. He looked forward to sinking his teeth into it.

He'd saved the beast's tusks. One day they would grace the hall of his home, when his father had gone to a reiver's reward. They would be a souvenir of a miserable yet magical night.

For this evening of dancing and singing, and of looking into Cate's face, flushed with effort and firelight, he required no reminder. It would live in the deepest part of his mind for many a long year, mayhap forever.

By all the saints, but she was bonny, brave and true, a woman in a thousand.

But not for him, never for him. If he told himself so often enough, he might one day come to accept it.

Not that he felt anything beyond the concern any man might have for her plight. It was no fault of his that she had been lost in the wood or come under his protection. That Trilborn was sniffing around her was Henry's problem, though Ross was certain his old enemy's interest had sharpened once he saw she might be awarded to a Dunbar. If the man had never panted after her before, he would have conceived a sudden passion. It was how he was made.

A dull thump, followed by a creaking sound, floated over the dark surface of the river. Hard upon it came a whispered reprimand. Ross lifted his head, quartering the shimmering flow with narrowed eyes.

Just beyond where he hunkered in the reeds, a boat eased downriver, drifting with the outgoing tide until it turned toward the palace. Had it not been so silent, Ross might have shrugged it off as some nobleman returning from a carouse in freer surroundings than Henry's staid court. The oars were muffled, however, and the occupants swathed in cloaks and wearing broad-brimmed hats that left their faces in shadow.

Ross eased flat with the same slow care he'd have used if stalking a herd of nervous cattle. As he watched, the boat landed well above the stone dock that served the palace. Two men leaped ashore and made their way swiftly along the outer wall. They paused at a rustic gate, one from which kitchen refuse was taken away or slops emptied into the river. It swung open, and the two night visitors vanished within.

As it began to close again, it seemed to stick. The man stationed at the gate stepped forward to give it a hard pull. Light from somewhere inside glittered upon silver braid outlining a black tunic, winked over silver chains that held a black cloak. The way the man moved, the way he looked back over his shoulder before the gate thudded shut, made the hair on Ross's neck stand up like a dog's ruff.

Trilborn, by the bones of Saint Peter.

Trilborn had admitted the newcomers, though what he could be about was more than Ross could guess. Whatever it was, it was unlikely to be good.

Ross sprang to his feet, brushed mud from his plaid with a quick gesture while keeping watch for more visitors, departing guests or sentries. A guard appeared on the wall high above his head, too far away to be a concern. Whistling a little, trying to act as if he'd been attending to an urgent call of nature in the open air, Ross strolled in the general direction of the gate where the men had disappeared.

Guards, a pair of them, came to attention as he approached. Where they had been moments before, he could not guess, but they were certainly on watch now. To be admitted presented no difficulty, however; there was more than one advantage in being among the few known for wearing a plaid at Henry's court. Either that, or the men on duty could not conceive of anyone asking entry at such a noisome back passage unless he belonged inside the palace.

Ross made his way across the muck-littered space between the gate and a heavy door in the stone wall. Easing inside, he paused in the square entrance. Seeing nothing, hearing nothing to the right except the distant clatter as Henry's kitchen staff labored over a feast for several thousand to be served on the morrow, he turned swiftly in the opposite direction.

He had taken only a few steps when the bells began to peal from the king's chapel. Matins, the midnight hour. It was time for the first mass of Christmastide. Hardly a soul in the whole palace would fail to head to the chapel, there to kneel with tightly closed eyes for the holiest of all celebrations. Trilborn had chosen well for his clandestine meeting, if that was what he had in hand.

Ross thought he had lost the men for long moments as the rough corridor he traveled filled with serving staff hurrying toward the chapel. Carried along with them, he entered a series of public rooms leading one into the other. These in their turn were crowded with men-at-arms, minstrels, members of Henry's yeoman guard, lords and their ladies hurrying with cloaks lifting behind their shoulders, and nuns in flying wimples. He dodged among them, protecting his side as best he might while using his height to see above their heads.

It was in an antechamber that he spied his quarry again, a square room with a wooden floor that rumbled and squeaked with every footstep, and tapestries that shuddered in the draft that wafted from where its doors stood open to allow free passage. The men, three in number with Trilborn, had diverged from the main herd to enter a connecting chamber to what seemed to be a series of cabinet rooms. Ross forged after them, cleaving his way at a diagonal through the bustling throng while keeping his eye on the flash of silver braid. He did not try to close the distance, until the trio disappeared through a door at the far end.

Before he reached it, a cloaked figure hurried to catch the heavy door panel before it closed. His face was concealed by a hood, but its width, as if it covered a headdress in the latest horned style, indicated a female. The light of a lamp, burning with a trio of wicks in its shallow bowl on a corner tripod, picked out the device embroidered upon the flowing velvet cloak she wore. It was that of the dowager queen, Elizabeth Woodville, wife of the late Edward IV and mother to Henry's queen of the same given name.

Elizabeth Woodville despised her son-in-law, so it was said, naming him a usurper with little royal blood in his veins, and that from the wrong side of the blanket and in his mother's line. That was true as far as it went. Edward IV and Richard III had both descended from the eldest son of Edward III, while Henry's line derived from the third son, John of Gaunt, and his mistress, Katherine Swynford. John of Gaunt had married the woman when he was able, and their offspring were made legitimate by royal order, but that hardly mattered in the Yorkist view. It was only the removal of all other Lancaster claimants to the throne, during the internecine fighting called the War of the Roses, that allowed Henry to come to the fore.

A body would think the dowager queen would be in

sympathy with Henry, Ross mused, as she was not from a titled family. More, her own marriage to Edward IV had been declared invalid by his brother, Richard, and her children therefore illegitimate. Edward, it seemed, had signed a betrothal contract, a legally binding instrument of marriage, with another lady prior to his marriage to Elizabeth Woodville.

The cynical claimed the dowager queen's partiality to the York cause had more to do with greed than loyalty. She, along with her sons from a previous marriage, her brothers and any number of other blood relatives, had held vast estates and rich offices while Edward was king. Richard had confiscated most of it on his brother's death, but a return to a Yorkist regime might well set it all back in place again.

Whatever Trilborn was about in company with the royal lady, it seemed unlikely to be to Henry VII's benefit. It might well be a matter of treason.

"Ross? Are you not going to the mass?"

So great was his concentration on the closed door that he'd failed to see Lady Catherine sweeping toward him. His frown as he spun at the sound of her voice must have been fearsome; she, her sister and their serving woman just behind them, all stopped as if they had run into a stone wall.

"Aye," he said, keeping his voice a low rumble, "I'll join you in a minute or two."

"You will have to stand if you delay," Marguerite informed him.

"On my own head be it," he said shortly.

Cate studied him, her gaze intent. "You are so recently

come from your bed, and you look flushed. What are you—"

"Not now." He made a swift gesture with one hand. "Later."

She was not pleased. Her gaze went to the closed door that was his target. When Marguerite would have said something more, however, Cate put out a hand to stop her. "Yes," she said as she moved away. "Later."

It sounded more a threat than a promise. Ross allowed a wry smile to quirk a corner of his mouth before he turned back to the business at hand.

Skulking in dark corners and eavesdropping on private conversations was not his idea of proper conduct for the next laird of the Clan Dunbar. Some things had to be done, however. Moving with purpose, he continued on across the larger chamber that gave access to the room that interested him. Making every effort to appear as if he had serious business within, he opened the door and stepped inside.

No convenient lamp burned here, not even a candle. It was, Ross realized, simply an antechamber where those who waited for an audience with the king could confer, dictate to a scribe or speak in private to a member of Henry's council. Ross paused a moment to allow his eyes to adjust to the darkness, noting a bench under the single window, a writing table, a chair, a stool. Of greater interest was yet another door to one side, narrow in width, half concealed by draping curtains, and with a sliver of light beneath it.

Easing forward with soundless footsteps on one of Henry's Saracen carpets, he reached the door. He turned to place his shoulders against the wall beside it and leaned his head back.

The wall felt substantial, comfortingly firm behind him, for he was suddenly weary beyond all reason. Yet his purpose was to make sense of the low mutter of voices he could hear in the next room, filtering around the door. He closed his eyes, the better to hear.

"Margaret…Burgundy…tidings…"

"…Yorkist…"

"…by spring's end, early…"

"…boy prince…puppet…"

"…thousand…German, well-armed…"

"…payment for…"

It was maddening to be unable to hear clearly. Ross could only guess the subject under discussion, and therefore its trend. Still, the pertinent fact appeared to be that Trilborn and the dowager queen were in league with those who sought to oust Henry VII from his throne.

It seemed that he and the English king had a common enemy, Ross thought with grim amusement. It was almost enough to put him in charity with the monarch.

Still, what arrogance, to penetrate to the very heart of Henry's favorite palace to thrash out their plan. Even given that the entire court would be at mass, it was still breathtaking in its daring. Was it Trilborn's choice, or the artful cunning of the dowager queen? She had a knack for intrigue, or so said the stories.

Trilborn had almost surely thrown in his lot with the Yorkist faction. He was part of the scheme to remove Henry, one that involved Margaret, Elizabeth Woodville's daughter who was also the dowager duchess of

Burgundy, and an army of mercenaries that would land somewhere in England in late spring or early summer. Their purpose was to place a child king on the throne. No doubt Elizabeth Woodville expected to be named queen regnant until he came of age, a position with only slightly less pomp and authority than being queen in her own right. The boy's supporters would then reap rewards beyond their most avaricious dreams.

Did the woman really believe she would be putting her own child on the throne in the person of the boy? Or was this the most cynical of power grabs, made in full expectation that the young boy mentioned in whispers was an imposter who would eventually be deposed? Or did that matter when, as with Henry himself, might of arms instead of birthright would dictate the outcome? Did God decide on the battlefield who would or would not be king as some suggested, so that whoever was the victor could claim to rule by divine right?

The stability of the throne of England was not his concern, Ross told himself with scathing disdain. If Henry died in the clash of foreign armies, it meant a likely end to Ross's own enforced stay on English soil. He could go home to Scotland, take his place in his father's keep and among his uncles and his cousins on their midnight cattle raids.

It would mean an end to any pretence of a betrothal to Lady Catherine Milton of Graydon, accursed Grace that she was. No more singing, dancing, arguments or quick, laughing comments; no more sweet, untutored kisses.

What to do with these bits he had learned? This was something requiring careful deliberation, a minute weighing of consequences, Ross thought. Mayhap he should take himself to mass and see if guidance came to him there.

9

"The king has sent for you, Cate! What can it mean?"

It was Marguerite who brought the news to where Cate was walking with Gwynne in the cloister between the palace and the king's chapel, breathing in the fresh moist air that came with the rain falling beyond its long colonnade. Her sister's eyes were wide and dark and her veil was askew. Behind her, looking none too comfortable with their errand, were two yeoman guards sent to escort Cate to wherever Henry was closeted at the moment.

How very like his regal male majesty to command her presence when she was wearing her oldest gown and had bundled her braided hair into a length of dull netting topped by a squat hennin of no great style. To change would be impossible, of course; Henry did not care to be kept waiting. Reaching up to tuck in a few tendrils of hair made unruly by the damp weather, she refused to think of the last time she had been summoned before the king, or what had been the result.

Marguerite came closer, twining her arm with Cate's. "Do you think it's about your betrothal? What if he insists you sign the contract?"

"My dependence is upon Ross. Well, and his father." The instant she signed her name, she would be considered both officially betrothed and legally wed to the Scotsman. That act must put him at greater risk from the curse. "But mayhap that isn't what Henry wants at all."

"What else could it be? You've done nothing you should not."

"Certainly not," she answered, with what firmness she could muster.

A small shiver ran over Cate as her midnight scurrying through the maze of the palace on the way to and from Ross's chamber ran through her mind. There had been no more of that in the handful of days since Christmas; she had not even been present when Gwynne removed the stitches from his wound. Still, news of the escapade might merely have been delayed in reaching the king.

Marguerite squeezed her arm. "You aren't nervous, are you? I know Henry seems stern, but the weight of his responsibilities would make any man so."

"You are dear to be concerned, as well as for coming to find me," Cate said with a bright smile, "but I will be quite all right."

Fine words, but she wished she could take them back before she was halfway to Henry's apartments. The progression of rooms and doors seemed never-ending; the number of people she had to pass with her royal escort was so great she feared every soul in the palace must know her destination. The measured thud of booted heels behind her made such thunder in her ears that she felt a little faint. It was a great relief when she was finally ushered into a long gallery, where rain pecked at the mullioned panes of window glass in arched openings that displayed the gray day outside.

Henry sat at a large table with sheets of vellum spread over its surface, tall floor candelabras at each end, and a courier standing at attention beside him. As she entered, a man turned from where he stood staring out at the falling rain. Ross faced her, his features set in grim lines and his eyes darkly blue and unreadable. Setting his feet in a wide and ready stance, he clasped his hands behind him.

Cate's breath caught in her chest as her gaze meshed with that of the Scotsman. She could not think for a long instant, barely remembered to drop into the required curtsy for the royal presence.

Henry raised her from it with a negligent gesture, though his head remained bent over his work. For long moments, the murmur of the rain and scratch of Henry's quill were the only sounds.

At last he put down the pen, read over the page he had finished, then sanded it and poured the excess grains back into their sifter. Rolling the vellum with care, he put it into a leather tube. Giving it into the keeping of the courier, he dismissed him. Only when the door had closed behind the man did he turn his attention to Cate.

"We bid you good day, Lady Catherine, and trust we see you well."

"And you, Your Majesty," she murmured.

"Yes, yes." He made a swift gesture, as if pressed for time. "We regret that this matter of your betrothal to

Dunbar has gone unsettled for so long, as we feel sure the outcome concerns you."

"Indeed, sire." Her voice was dust-dry.

Henry's eyelids flickered at the irony, but he chose to ignore it. "News of moment reached London this morning from across the Irish Channel. It seems a priest, Father Symonds by name, has presented to a gathering in Dublin a young boy whom he swears to be the earl of Warwick."

"Warwick," she repeated with a pleat forming between her brows, "not one of the vanished princes." Warwick would be the son of George, duke of Clarence and brother to Edward IV. In one of the more vicious turns of Edward's reign, George had been imprisoned in the Tower for treason, and subsequently drowned in a butt of malmsey wine. Some said the terrors of that time, and young Warwick's imprisonment afterward by his other uncle, Richard III, had addled his wits, making him an unlikely candidate for the crown.

"A patent lie, as we shall soon prove," Henry said with a dismissive gesture. "Warwick has been sequestered in the Tower for some time. There will be no difficulty in showing him to the people of London, a fair number of whom may recognize him from other years, other sightings. No, this is merely the symptom of a deeper rot."

Cate glanced at Ross, but he was watching Henry. If he knew what the king intended by telling her of this latest intelligence, nothing of it showed on his face.

"I am sorry to hear it," she said.

"It was unrealistic to expect the Yorkists to give over so easily," Henry continued with a brooding expression on his long face. "They have been used to bending all to their will for far too long, their leaders accustomed to meeting behind closed doors to arrange matters to suit themselves. They think of us as an outsider, barely English at all."

He stopped, looked away, mayhap thinking on his fifteen years of exile before landing on English soil with an invasion force. From some nearby chamber came the sound of a crying babe, a reminder that Henry had a three-month-old son somewhere in the palace, though the child seldom appeared in public. Cate wondered if he ever thought of the fate of Edward's vanished sons and considered what might happen to his own if he should be defeated while fighting for his crown.

She also spared a moment to think of this Yorkist pretender, the young boy caught up in the ambitions of powerful men who wanted to be yet more powerful. He must be at that awkward age between eleven and fifteen if he was to be taken as the son of Edward IV or his brother George. Did he understand the implications of what was happening? Did he realize he was committing treason, however unwittingly, and might die for it?

The baby stopped crying. Henry rose from the chair behind the table and moved to the window where Ross stood. Bracing a hand on its frame, he gazed out at the drear scene beyond, with its sheep-cropped tan grass, its skeletal trees and drooping, rain-wet hedges. Speaking almost as if to himself, he said, "We have need of allies who can be trusted."

"There are those who will rally to you," Cate said, driven to offer solace by the air of loneliness about him.

"Lancastrians, yes, those who gather round for what they can gain from it, or to be certain old enemies are kept from power. Also, those who shared our years in Brittany, hunted by Edward and Richard, or remember us from childhood as the duke of Richmond, or remain faithful to the duchess of Richmond and Derby."

The last named was, of course, his mother who had been so instrumental in seeing he had his chance at the throne. She was often a part of his councils, but not on this day. She had been given a Thames-side mansion no great distance away, Cate knew, and was seeing to its renovation.

"It's not enough," Henry went on after a moment. "Your sister's husband, Braesford, is our most trusted baron in the border marches, but what he may do there is limited, particularly as he is troubled by raiders from Scotland. He would be more effective if he had not that worry."

The outline of what he intended formed swiftly in Cate's mind. She recognized his magnanimity in attempting to explain it to her, but that did nothing to make it more acceptable. "If Your Majesty intends a role for—"

"We do. The alliance between you and Dunbar will add much-needed stability to the region. We desire that the marriage be celebrated forthwith. In return, as I have proposed, an estate no different in size to the lands of Braesford Hall shall be settled upon your bridegroom, along with its keep and all attendant villages."

She looked again toward Ross. He was scowling at the king, his lips pressed together in a hard line. She swallowed on bile, while stiffening her spine to keep from weaving where she stood. "But…but he has not gained the permission of the laird."

"Dunbar is well past his majority, thus able to choose for himself. While permission from the leader of his clan would be a boon, it is hardly necessary." The king turned to the Scotsman. "What say you, Dunbar?"

Ross appeared unmoved, though his accent was as thick as river fog when he answered. "To wed an English lass is nay what I intended."

"Three years ago we had no idea of wedding a princess royal, yet sometimes needs must," Henry said austerely.

"What manner of husband have you in mind for Lady Catherine should I refuse?"

"That need not concern you."

"Nay, but if it does?"

Cate, watching the byplay between the two men, could hardly breathe for the tightness in her chest. What was Ross doing? Why was he not declaring he would not marry her for all the jewels of Araby?

A judicious expression settled on the king's face. "A certain noble has applied for her hand. He may be encouraged to remain loyal to us if favored in his suit."

"If you give her to him as a bribe, you mean, along with her inherited lands and the northern estate you offer to me."

"Just so."

"Crafty devil," Ross said, his gaze hard as he met the eyes of the king.

Henry allowed himself a crooked smile. "We like to think so."

The king permitted this familiarity, Cate thought, because they were speaking in private, and possibly because he appreciated Ross's blunt way, which was so different from the fawning sycophancy that surrounded him. It might also be because he was glad to have matters out in the open. Henry knew Ross and Trilborn were enemies, and was deliberately fanning the flames of their feud to gain the end he sought.

That did not mean he would not follow through on his threat, she realized with a shudder of dismay. The words had been spoken and would not be retracted.

Yet something more seemed to hover between the two men. Was Henry playing a deeper game? Had he some doubt of Trilborn's loyalty, that he thought giving her to the man might sway him? Or did he, just possibly, want to bring the quarrel between Trilborn and the Scotsman to a boil in hope Ross would do away with a possible traitor?

He could not know of Ross's injury in that case, must not be aware that the outcome of a fight between the two men would be in doubt. Or mayhap he knew and didn't care.

"Yon Trilborn is no fit husband for a gently bred lady," Ross said with a look of hard disfavor. "He takes his pleasure by rough wooing."

"A fine reason to see Lady Catherine does not become his wife."

"As you say, and yet…"

"Surely, you lend no credence to this wild talk of a curse," Henry said in high impatience.

"Nay, but my father will curse me twice over if I agree.

I'll have neither clan nor country, and I'd never a notion of becoming an Englishman."

Henry turned his head to meet his gaze, his own ice-cold. "If the alternative is to take up residence in the White Tower, what say you?"

Ross tipped his head as his eyes narrowed. "'Tis a fair dwelling, one where kings and queens await their coronations."

"One they sometimes fail to leave."

The words, grim with warning, hung in the cool air. Beyond the window, the rain increased to a hissing downpour. A candle guttered in a stray draft, its wick popping. Distant voices grew louder, as if coming closer, and then receded again.

The White Tower mentioned was part of the complex known as the Tower of London. It was there the vanished princes had once been sequestered. It was also there, so some said, the old and sainted madman known as Henry VI had been murdered by his nephews, Edward IV and Richard III. The nearby Bell Tower was where Braesford, husband to Cate's sister, had been imprisoned for a time on a charge of child murder. Would the king really shut Ross away in either place merely for refusing to be married?

Yes, of course he would. What was the point of being king if a man was reluctant to use royal power to bend others to his will?

Ross seemed to have little doubt of it. A vein throbbed in his forehead as he stared at Henry, and a white line appeared around his mouth. He put a hand to his side where his dirk should have been, though the scabbard that usually held it was empty.

"Well?" Henry, grim and unbending, waited for his answer.

"Why then," Ross drawled, his eyes darkly blue as he turned his head to meet Cate's gaze at last, "post the banns and prepare the wedding meats. I shall be as blithe a bridegroom as was ever seen between here and Solway."

The curses that thundered through Ross's head matched the heavy tread of his boots on the corridor's stone floor. Tower or marriage? He hardly knew which threat enraged him more. It had been years since he'd bowed to any will other than his own. Even the old laird, his father, had never threatened to shut him away in prison to insure obedience.

By all the saints, but he'd longed to tell Henry to do his worst. If not for the lady who marched at his side, Ross would have opted for prison, and England's king bedamned. It would have been a pleasure to see the look on Henry's long face when he said it.

Aye, that it would.

Impossible.

If he refused to marry Lady Catherine, she'd be handed over to Trilborn. That mangy son of Satan would have her in his bed before the ink was dry on the betrothal contract. He'd strip her naked and ram into her without mercy, making her pay for every injury to his pride, every insult to his manhood caused by her refusal to be seduced, every instant of pain inflicted when Ross had pulled him off her. The thought of it was so sickening that Ross could never allow it, not and live with himself.

"Why?"

That question, so reasonable in Cate's quiet voice, enraged him anew. He should have known she would not leave it alone, but would insist on an explanation. The two of them had lost their escort on leaving the area of the king's apartments, after passing through the antechambers where courtiers stood talking in corners and their ladies strolled about to show off their finery. The part of the palace he and Cate traversed now was little occupied. Soon they would reach the great hall, and all chance of a private exchange would be ended.

"Why what?" he demanded. "You expected me to choose prison over being a husband? You thought I might enjoy keeping company with the Tower's ghosts?"

"You might have explained that you'd given your word."

"And you might have absolved me, so I'd not have to go back on it."

Her eyes flashed blue lightning at him. "I can't imagine how you can say that when you know how little I wish to be wed!"

"I didn't hear you calling for a wimple and crucifix as an escape."

"Henry was in no mood to listen if I had. He barely had time for anything except the matter at hand."

Ross grunted his opinion of that excuse. "He'd plenty of time to sign a prison order."

"You would rather die than face that possibility, I suppose," she snapped, "since that's what it will amount to now that we have signed the betrothal documents."

"Not that again." He'd no more patience with her portents of doom than he did with remembering how they had set their names to the various vellum scrolls while Henry watched. The king, leaving nothing to chance, had seen these were prepared and ready. Thinking of that point also irked Ross beyond bearing.

"It won't go away merely because you refuse to acknowledge it," she declared with a fulminating look.

"What I can't prevent, I must endure."

"Meaning?"

"Meaning your so-called curse may do its worst, for I've other things on my mind. My father has sworn to cast me from the clan, hearth and homeland, and so he will."

"But it didn't stop you from agreeing to be wed."

"Nay, that it did not."

"Which shows plainly that vengeance means more to you than any of those things."

"Oh, aye, I'd rather lose those things than see Trilborn claim you."

"A dog in the manger stance if ever there was one! Such a stupendous compliment, knowing I'm to be taken to wife as a blow in a feud."

"If that's the way you want it," Ross said shortly.

"How else, pray?"

He came to an abrupt halt. Reaching to catch her arm, he swung her hard against him. "It will be the greatest pleasure to snatch the bride Trilborn wanted from under his nose," he said with the roughness of unadorned need in his voice. "Yes, and to take you into my bed."

Her eyes widened, the pupils growing darker as she gazed up at him. Her lips were parted and as tempting as sweet summer cherries. The quick breaths that lifted her chest also pressed her warm curves against him, and the juncture where the curves of her thighs came together brushed his hard heat with tantalizing softness.

"No," she whispered.

"Aye," he said, his gaze on her mouth while his body hardened like tempered steel.

Wild rose color suffused her features as she searched his eyes. "You can't."

"I can. I will."

Her mouth, as he set his own to it, was as sweet as it looked. He tasted it in full, plundering its warmth and moisture with ravening force. He set his feet and shifted his grasp, sliding his hand under her arm to cup the soft resilience of her breast. The nipple nudged his palm, a tight bud of provocation. He brushed over it, drew in her soft moan of response as if it offered perfect sustenance. Mayhap it did, for he deepened the kiss with mindless hunger. Twining his tongue with hers, he abraded its silken surface, sought the tender recess underneath, intruded deeper and withdrew in a parody of his most urgent need. His breath burned in his chest. His brain simmered in the cauldron of his skull. He ached with such throbbing pain that the back of his neck seemed to scorch his shirt and red-hot coals burn his boot soles.

Cate shuddered, drawing a breath that sobbed in her

throat. The sound vibrated through him, found a touch spring of strained reason.

He released her with abrupt, muscle-wrenching reluctance. Stepping back, he turned so fast that his plaid flared around his knees, billowed behind his shoulder. He stalked away then, leaving her standing behind him.

It was either that or take her there in that drafty corridor with all the ungentle force that Trilborn had intended when he set upon her in nearly the same place. And Ross was not sure which stunned him most, that desperate need or the fact that he managed to subdue it.

Was she to be bedded to spite an old foe, or in payment for the loss of patrimony?

Neither alternative appealed to Cate, though her toes curled in her slippers at the mere thought of them as she watched the Scotsman stalk away from her. Soon he would be her husband, with all the rights and privileges that entailed. He could do whatever he liked to her, and none would gainsay him. And what might he not do, if he came to hate her for all he had lost?

She didn't want to think of it, nor did she care to envision the raw, physical act, how it would feel or how she would endure it. She had seen firsthand the hostility visited upon her mother by her stepfather. That Cate might have to abide with the same violent treatment, the slurs, insults, blows and worse that took place behind closed doors, was a horror in the mind. Better that the curse intervene than to suffer it.

Still, she could not picture Ross Dunbar as such a malignant husband. Her vision of him was quite otherwise.

She should not think of him at all in that guise; this she knew well. Yet how could she not? Nothing else was quite so important in a woman's life. And if the intimations of future pleasure brought by his kiss were more vivid than her memories of childhood fears, if she wished mightily in her weaker moments that he could be immune to the curse, what did that say of her?

Arrogant, shortsighted, thickheaded man! She had no desire to be the cause of a rift between him and his father. Nor did she wish to curtail Ross's freedom or tie him to England. She wanted only to save his life, if the fool would but let her.

Her hands trembled as she touched her veil to be sure it was in place, ran her hands down the front of her gown to remove any wrinkles. How very off balance she felt, as if she had come safely through some unexpected storm but could not be sure it was over. Moving with deliberate steps to allow her breathing to return to normal, she followed in the direction Ross had disappeared.

The entrance to the great hall was in sight when she heard someone approaching from behind her. A quick glance over her shoulder confirmed what she feared already. Her defenses closed in like window shutters slamming into place.

"I give you good day, Lady Catherine," Trilborn said, his voice even, as if nothing untoward had ever passed between them.

She sent him a cutting glance, but made no reply.

"You've just come from the king, I think. I heard you had been summoned, saw you and Dunbar pass through just now as I stood with friends."

"How convenient for you." He had been loitering, waiting to follow her again, she was sure. Regardless, he had delayed until she was alone. Had he seen what passed between her and Ross? She didn't care if he had. In fact, she hoped for it, if it would discourage him.

"You appear less than overjoyed at the tidings received from our good King Henry," he went on.

"Do I?" The heavy door to the hall lay ahead of her. She measured the distance with her eyes while increasing her pace a fraction.

"Shall I guess what has you in such upset? Henry the Grim has seen fit to end your maidenly shrinking. He has commanded you to the altar."

Maidenly shrinking, indeed! "If you must have it, yes. Ross and I are to be wed."

"My disappointment knows no bounds."

"You should be delighted," she snapped. "You have escaped the curse."

Ahead of her, the heavy door into the great hall swung open and two gentlemen emerged. Seeing her, the one in the lead held it while inclining his head. She almost ran the few steps that would allow her to pass through, escaping the private exchange with Trilborn.

He sprang after her with a muttered oath, sliding through the opening just before the door closed again. Cate did not look back as she paused to seek Ross among those scattered over the vast, echoing space. He was not there. The benighted man must have walked straight through the hall on his way out of the palace. Nor was her sister to be seen.

"Ross, is it?" Trilborn asked, frowning as he arrived at her side. "You use his given name?"

"We are to be wed, after all."

"Or not," he answered, his voice silken with menace.

She met his gaze then, while a small headache began to pulse at her temples, throbbing with each beat of her heart. She feared to probe his meaning, but was equally afraid to refrain. "What are you saying?"

"If his death is now decreed by this curse of the Graces, the thing can be arranged."

A cold tremor moved down her back like river ice sliding out to sea. "Don't!"

"But I had the impression you would be glad to be free."

"Well, but…"

"Have no fear. It shall be as you desire."

He set a fist on his hip as he bowed, then swung away with his short cape draped over his bent arm like a wing, flapping as he walked away. He thrust his legs forward in long steps, his head up, staring around. It was hard to say whether it was vanity that moved him, or if he watched to see those he would avoid before they saw him.

It shall be as you desire….

And how was that, pray? What did she want? What would she ask if she could have her desire?

Cate wanted to know what it was to be loved, wanted that above all else. If it must be denied her, then she longed to know what took place between a man and a woman in the dark of night, that upheaval of feeling that could make the more daring ladies of the court smile and toss their heads, and the serving women sigh. Was it too much to ask?

Ross could give her that much, at least. He was ready to bed her, for he'd said so in plain words. The betrothal contracts they had signed had all the legality of marriage. Few would say a word if she gave birth to his child nine month hence, and the babe would be his heir. If the curse killed him before a priest could hear their vows, he would not die without issue.

It was three weeks before the wedding could be solemnized. That length of time was required for the banns to be read, for news to travel near and far, so the old laird or anyone else could object to the wedding. The wedding feast must be prepared, her trousseau aired and made ready, and preparations made for traveling northward to take up the lands provided by the king. Three weeks were left during which Trilborn and the curse might vie to rid Ross of life.

What did she really want?

She had a mere three weeks to make up her mind.

10

The king removed from Greenwich to Shene Palace before the first of January. The shift in residence was, in part, to allow a different segment of his subjects access to the king's justice, but also to allow the vacated palace to recover from housing several hundred courtiers, their servants and animals.

Henry presented fine new raiment to his household in token of the New Year, a fresh beginning. Cate, not being a designated lady-in-waiting to the queen, was left out of that largesse. She received, instead, a fine costume of different fabric and design in honor of her coming marriage, and was assured Ross received the same.

The gift was no great surprise. Henry stood as guardian to her and her sisters, and Isabel had received something similar on her marriage to Braesford. Still, the richness of it startled Cate. The gown was of lustrous silk-velvet in an evergreen hue, as befitted the winter season, with slashed sleeves that exposed the gold-embroidered cream silk sleeves of the under shift. More gold lace edged the neckline and the inverted wedge of the split skirt that swept back to reveal the embroidered

underskirt. The girdle that accompanied the gown was
of gold mesh set with hundreds of small emerald beads,
while larger gems dangled at the ends of its cords, hanging nearly to the floor. A fine cloak in white velvet was
supplied to ward off the winter chill. Its attached cape-
let was of ermine, with a hood to cover her hair, which
would be worn loose on her special day.

Cate was delighted with the costume, though she'd
have selected a more blue-green shade of velvet, given
a choice. There was no chance of that, of course. White
and green were the colors designated by Henry for his
Tudor reign, so were a mark of his favor. She must be
content.

Watching Gwynne brush the velvet, fluff the fur and
twitch at the wrinkles in the silk, Cate felt a sinking sensation in her chest. The ceremonial presentation of the
attire the evening before made the wedding seem more
real. The days were slipping past one by one. Soon they
would be gone.

She had not slept for the past three nights. A part of
her waited, staring into the darkness, listening for the
thud of feet, the whisper of another serving woman outside or tromp of a sentry come to tell her that Ross was
dead. The dawning of every day was a reprieve. The first
sight of him in the great hall, breaking his fast with other
men downing their beef, bread and ale, lifted her spirits
like the rising of the sun.

The two of them had exchanged New Year's gifts,
more because it was expected, she thought, than from
sentiment. She had sewn a pair of gloves for him of the
softest deerskin, embroidered with the thistle of Scotland.

He had presented her with a silver pomander filled with the dried and spiced leaves of Saracen roses.

It was the only time in these past few days that they had spoken to each other with civility. The strain of their forced marriage, and the exchange between them after the documents were signed, left them uncomfortable in one another's company.

The thought of Ross's face as he'd proclaimed his right to bed her seldom left Cate. She could not erase from her mind the possessive promise in the depths of his eyes. Every time she brought it to mind, a tremor streaked through her, straight to the lower part of her belly.

She had half feared he would take Henry's edict as permission to be as intimate as he pleased with her. She also feared he would not.

Her mind was in such turmoil during these days, so awash in dread and longing, shrinking and anticipation, that she hardly knew what she was about. Eating was impossible, sleep uncertain. She was such poor company that Marguerite deserted her for whatever companionship she could find in the great hall. Left alone, Cate sat gazing at nothing, with her embroidery lying untouched in her lap, or else stared out some high window at the passing horsemen, searching for a familiar figure in plaid.

She should have more pride, she told herself. She was no serving maid, sighing after a pair of broad shoulders. No, she was Lady Catherine Milton, a lady of independent thought and considered decisions. What she should be doing was persuading the stubborn Scotsman to fly for the border while he was still able. Failing that, she should be petitioning the king's mother for her aid in entering a nunnery, just as she had threatened.

Cate could not make up her mind which action was best. Both were so very final.

They had been ensconced at Shene some days when a messenger arrived from Braesford Hall. He brought with him a bundle of New Year's gifts that had been long delayed due to a series of snowstorms. He also delivered a letter from Cate's sister Isabel.

As pleased as she was by gifts she had given up seeing until Braesford and Isabel next came to court, Cate valued the letter more. She waited until she was alone to read it, unwrapping it, breaking the seal and unrolling it with care.

Isabel's contentment was written into every word. She was growing huge with the child inside her, she wrote, so suspected it was a boy. She prayed it was, as she was certain that would please Braesford, though he assured her in divers satisfactory ways that he cared not at all. Little Madeleine, Henry's babe, was teething, though thriving otherwise. She was quite the chatelaine of the manse, betimes, providing for landholders, villeins and a full complement of men-at-arms, seeing to their needs like a ewe with her lambs. All that was lacking for her to be completely happy was to have her dear sisters with her. And that brought her to a message she had received from Marguerite. According to their youngest sister, a marriage had been arranged for Cate. Isabel would be pleased beyond words to hear of it, if only she knew her middle sister was pleased, as well.

Cate frowned as she wondered how the news had

reached the far north so quickly. A moment later, she realized Isabel must refer to the first time Henry had suggested a betrothal, that she could not know of his latest royal command. Cate began to read again:

> Marguerite believes you may think to escape this marriage by appealing to the archbishop, possibly through the duchess, for permission to take the veil. I know not your mind in this matter, but would caution you to think carefully upon it. A life of prayer and good works may not suffice for you, sweet Cate. I fear you are too volatile for such a vocation, that it may chafe you beyond bearing. I would also have you understand the sacrifice you would make. I can summon no words to describe how precious the closeness between husband and wife can be, how very powerful the moments when they are alone behind the bed curtains. These times are magical, the very essence of life, leading to this most glorious of states that I now embrace, the creation of a child. Moreover, to stand at a man's side as his helpmate, friend and lover, one whom he will protect with his very life, is a boon beyond compare. Do not deprive yourself of these things, I pray you, dear Cate. Or if you must, be certain you have excellent reason.
>
> I am, ever and always, your loving sister,
> Isabel

Cate sat staring into the fire with the piece of vellum clutched in her hand for an endless time. Her thoughts and impulses leaped and danced like the flames, flaring and subsiding, only to flare up again. They crackled and spat and spiraled into smoke, but in their center was a glowing red heat that did not die.

How weary she was of other people deciding her life for her.

She must do something.

Yes, she must do something, but what?

Life in a nunnery had little appeal. In all truth, she had no real vocation. Regardless, she could not continue at court if she refused to accede to the king's wishes.

She might go to Isabel and Braesford, but it would be unfair to force them to defend her, and unkind to set them at odds with Henry on her account.

It was impossible for her to take up residence at any of the properties received as her share of her father's estate. As a woman alone, unprotected by father, brother or husband, she would be besieged, subject to abduction and exactly the sort of forced marriage she wished to avoid. That, or else kept as a prisoner under Henry's guard until such time as she felt dutiful.

She could not allow Ross to die from the effect of the curse. Nor could she bear to let him risk it

All in all, it seemed the nunnery was the only sensible choice.

If she must give up her freedom, her fortune and all joy of the flesh to become a bride of Christ, so be it, but first she would have at least a taste of the closeness to a man that Isabel described. Surely God would not begrudge her that much.

When the afternoon was far gone, and evening drawing in, Cate got to her feet and crossed the chamber to step into the hall. Stopping a scurrying maidservant, she sent for Gwynne. When her serving woman arrived, Cate bade her arrange water for bathing, and also a light meal of wine, meat pie and fruit to be served in her room. Shutting herself inside, then, she began to remove the veil from her hair.

In the midnight hour, when the palace had settled for the night, Cate left her chamber. She stole like a wraith through the vast, high-ceiling chambers, once more wearing Gwynne's plain cloak of gray furze and wool servant's slippers that whispered over the flooring. A faint trembling seemed to come from deep inside her, and she clenched her teeth to prevent their chattering. She was doing what she most desired, yet it felt as if she watched from a great distance as some other woman moved in and out of the shadows cast by lanterns in niches, paused to allow the patrolling palace guards to pass, swept noiselessly away behind their backs.

Her pulse was hammering in her ears, her heart battering her rib cage, by the time she reached Ross's chamber. She lifted a hand to scratch upon the door, but barely touched it. To tarry, waiting for an answer, might mean being seen. In any case, she was in no mood to be denied. With a hand on the latch, she pushed her way inside.

The faint, whispering rustle of a footstep on floor rushes was her only warning. Hard upon it, a tall, black shape swooped down upon her. She was thrust backward against the door so fast her breath left her in a rush. Before she could get it back, something rigid and straight compressed her throat. A body as hard and warm as sun-heated armor pressed against her from shoulders to ankles.

For an instant, there was only stunned silence.

A curse, lewd, inventive and rasping with Gaelic, fanned the tendrils of hair at Cate's temple. The forearm across her neck was released so quickly that air returned to her lungs with a choking, whistling gasp.

"Have you no more sense than to come to a man's room in the middle of the night?" Ross demanded against her ear.

"I thought," she began, before swallowing against the dry constriction and trying again. "I thought you would be asleep."

"So I was, until I heard your kitten scratching. I bid fair to warn you, sweet Cate, if you've come to soothe my fevered brow this time, 'tis not what's needful."

"And what is?"

She could almost think she felt the same shudder run over him that shook her. Or it could be he shivered with cold. The chamber was chill and damp, with no hint of a fire, and he was quite, quite naked as he held her against him.

"Nothing you would be ready to supply," he said after a moment.

"How can you say so when you…when you don't know why I came?"

"If this is a game—"

"No! No, I only want what other women are allowed."

"And that would be?"

"To be loved."

"Loved." That single word sounded strangled in his throat.

"There is so little time before the wedding. You said…" She paused to moisten dry lips. "You said you could, and would."

"And it must be now, given that you are here? Now, before the wedding?"

Tears drained down the back of her throat and she had to swallow again before she could speak. "So it seems, else it may not be done at all. If you won't…"

"Oh, I will," he said, his voice thick as he pressed closer against her so she felt the firm, hot length of him through her skirts. "But you understand this is nothing you can set aside if you change your mind? Once done, why, 'tis done."

"I know that well," she said simply. "Do it now, while you can."

The words had scarce left her lips before he took them. His mouth was warm and questing, slightly open so he tasted her like sipping new wine, taking her flavor, giving her his. He pushed back the hood of her cloak, threaded his fingers into her hair and tilted her head to gain deeper access.

The surfaces of her lips tingled; she caught his sweetness as she inhaled in intense gratification. He swept the inside of her mouth again and again in vital possession, feathering the fine and sensitive inner lining of her cheeks, grazing the edges of her teeth, touching her tongue and retreating. As she advanced to meet him, he shifted so his thigh was between hers, and shoved a hand inside her cloak to draw her closer.

His scent of hot, aroused male surrounded her. The curling hair that mantled his chest was soft and springing under her hands. She flatted her palms against it, enjoying the feel of it between her spread fingers. Her breasts swelled, straining against her gown, while a moan vibrated in her throat.

He slid his mouth away, bent his neck to rest his forehead against hers. "Stop me, Cate," he said in both plea and warning. "Stop me now, or it will be too late."

"It was too late when I opened your door."

"Aye," he said in gruff acceptance. "Aye."

He bent to slide one hard arm under her knees and the other behind her back. The darkness swooped and spun behind her closed eyelids as she was lifted against his chest. The effect made her so giddy that it was a moment before she realized he had set her on the edge of his bed and was stripping away her cloak.

His movements were sure even in the dark. A man's cloak was very like a woman's, no doubt, yet she could not but wonder how many women he had undressed that he went about it so easily. Her gown, borrowed from Gwynne along with the cloak, was loose and without a girdle. He caught the hem, pushed his hands beneath it. Shoving the fabric upward so it gathered on his forearms, he slid his palms and spread fingers over her knees and then up her thighs. His thumbs met at the juncture, where they tangled in fine curls. He spread delicate folds and played among them.

The sensation was so startling, so exquisite, that she swayed toward him, clinging to his arms. He drew her up with his hands still under her gown, caressed her hips, clasping the rounded flesh like a miser clasping handfuls of gold. Then, in an abrupt move, he shoved the gown up, and her shift with it, stripping both off over her head. Before she could catch her breath or do more than gasp at the cold, he pressed her back onto the bed and followed after her, hot skin against her coolness, stonelike muscle and sinew against her softness, heated hardness against her soft curves and moist hollows. He reached for a coverlet padded with feathers, lofting it so it settled over them. Then he shifted over on the feather mattress and pulled her beneath him.

"Are you cold?" he asked, while nuzzling her neck, dragging handfuls of her hair from under her shoulders so its pull on her scalp was lessened.

"Not…not really." How could she be, when his heat enclosed her where she was half submerged in the softness of the feather mattress, and his hard body, faintly rough with hair on his chest, thighs and legs, pressed upon her with delicious friction?

"You're shivering, but never fear. I'll warm you."

Oh, yes, she knew he would, as he slid lower in the bed, his head disappearing beneath the coverlet while he tracked a line of moist, hot kisses down her neck, to the hollow between her collarbones, and between the twin hills of her breasts. He made a wet path between them, climbed in a spiral to the peak of one and then down again, began on the other. He flicked her nipples with his tongue, back and forth, while they contracted to near painful tightness, and then, only then, did he take one into the heated suction of his mouth.

She arched beneath him with a shrill cry, pressing

her heels into the mattress in the need to be closer. She wanted him inside her, needed him to fill the empty ache there.

He was not ready, not done. It seemed he had only begun.

He moved lower, rasping across the flat surface of her belly with his beard stubble, soothing the scrape with mouth and tongue before the sting began. He inhaled her, blew upon her with his hot breath. With his tongue gently lapping, he delved into the fine curls at the juncture of her thighs, then spread her legs wide to lie between them while he concentrated his caresses, feasting, applying suction, endlessly tasting.

She writhed, the breath sobbing in her chest, while he learned her inside and out, or so it seemed. In her extremity, she trailed her fingers through his hair, spanned his shoulders with feverish hands and explored the width of his back. She was captivated by the hard planes of his body, so different from her own, by the sinuous muscles that seemed to enwrap him like a living shield, by the lethal power of him. He was silk over steel, dominant yet supplicating as he whispered commands, guided her movements, placed her as he wanted her. His mastery was complete as the fury of her need burgeoned inside, bursting upon her in pulsing wonder, leaving her panting and breathless.

Rising over her again, he offered his mouth. Mindless, mindless, she took it, drew his tongue into the depths of her own, wanting more of him, all of him, needing something that hovered unrecognized, just beyond her grasp. She was on fire, melting inside, so heated at the very core that it seemed nothing could soothe the burning ache of it.

He could. He did.

At the very zenith of her most virulent need, he pressed into her moist heat, taking yet giving in slow incursions, withdrawing so she could release the breath she held, doing it again and again until she grasped his hips and dragged him to her again, urging him deeper against the burning sting of it. She sobbed aloud as he broke through the deep internal barrier of her maidenhead and filled her, made her whole.

He set a gentle pace then, a slow friction that made her turn her head from side to side, crying out, wanting more, wanting the wonder yet again. The coverlet slipped away unnoticed while they strained together in elemental need. And when she reached for him again, he pressed her knees wide and gave her everything, sinking so deep that the hardness of bone rubbed against the soft mound of her. He drew back, and then gave himself to her again, and yet again.

It was perfect, a tumultuous pummeling, ever increasing in speed and strength. They moved together with soft thuds that set the bed to rocking on its leather straps, and swayed the bed curtains until they fanned their heated bodies. Every plunge sent waves of pleasure rolling through her, taking away all strain and fear. She met him with stringent effort while seeking for the promise she had been shown, longing for it in simple lust, giving infinitely in order to receive it. And he brought it to her with tireless strength, gave it to her in boundless generosity and sweating effort, as gift and glory.

Afterward, she clung to him with tears sliding from under her eyelids. She tasted the salt of his skin at his neck with a private kiss, pressed her face against his warm skin while she inhaled the raw scent of him, his essential maleness. She absorbed the feel of him into her skin, her bones, the center of her being. She memorized him, this man who had given her such pleasure as she thought never to know again.

She said goodbye.

Ross lay half stunned with satiation, hovering on the edge of an urge for sleep so strong it almost dragged him down into it. The only thing that prevented it was his perplexed amazement. If not for holding Cate's warm and naked body to his side, he'd have thought the past space of time an unusually fervid dream.

She had come to him.

Against all hope or reason, she had appeared in his chamber with the same thing on her mind that had scarce left his for days on end. She had asked to be loved, and he had obliged her with hardly a coherent thought, because there was nothing else on earth he had ever wanted so much.

Not that it meant anything of great moment. Nay, of course not. They had been thrown into each other's company, each other's arms. The prospect of a bedding—the assumption that it would happen—had been there from the first. Some at court were sure it had occurred during the dark and cold of a night spent in the forest. That it had finally come to pass now was a simple matter of two people taking their pleasure, as would soon be their right and duty as husband and wife. No unruly passion came into it, no heart-burning adoration as depicted by poets.

Still, a swift wedding seemed a thing greatly to be wished.

The lady lying so close against him jerked a little as she drew breath. Concern rose inside Ross as he felt wet heat where her cheek rested on his collarbone. Could she be crying? It was not the reaction he usually inspired in the women he took into his bed.

"Are you all right?" He reached to draw up the coverlet as he asked it, covering them and tucking the excess behind her back.

She gave a quick nod but didn't speak. The conviction grew upon him that she could not without betraying her distress. As carefully as he was able, he brushed tangled strands of hair away from her face. "I never meant to hurt you. I should have gone easier with you this first time."

"How...how do you know it was my first?" she asked, the words choked as she stiffened in his hold.

"There are ways." He continued to comb her hair with his fingers. "You were very...tight."

"I can't help that!"

"Nay," he said, his voice grave, though laughter threatened to invade it, "and I'm not complaining, I promise you."

"Oh."

"'Twill be easier next time."

"If there is a next time."

He paused in his movements while his heart gave a heavy thud. "If?"

"Never mind. I'm sure it will be quite all right."

It was that damnable curse of the Graces again, he was sure of it. She believed he would not live to see another time. He was not given to auguries and portents, but her certainty made him just a bit uneasy.

Was that why she had come to his chamber—because she meant to have this time with him before he died, because she thought he was due it? The notion was even less welcome.

Not that he had any right to complain. He had taken her up on her request for reasons that went beyond mere lust. He'd longed for her, longed to prevent a brutal initiation from Trilborn. Ross was glad beyond reason that he had been the first with her. And it had little to do with the feud, though awareness of it was always at the back of his mind. He loathed the thought of Trilborn forcing himself on her, causing her more pain and injury. That the bastard would have was certain; to take his enemy's bride-to-be would give Trilborn a twisted satisfaction.

How was Ross to explain that to Cate? He could not even try. He would wind up sounding as if excusing his weakness, or worse, accusing Trilborn of intending no more than he had just done himself.

At least he knew a way to take her mind from thoughts of death. It was not entirely selfless, but that could not be helped; he did not pretend to sainthood. She had been so sweetly responsive that his body stirred to the point of pain at the mere thought of his aim. She was every soft and tender thing that had been absent from his life for so long, every honeyed joy he had ever tasted. More than that, she was here beside him, warm under the coverlet, sublimely naked in his arms.

"Ah, well," he drawled as he turned more fully toward her, nudged his knee between her legs the better to press his heated hardness against her while enjoying her wet softness, "if I am to pass away before—"

"Don't say that!" she said, her voice thick and her fingers clenching in the springing hair on his chest.

He winced and reached to take her hand, placing it on his flank. With it out of the way, he cupped her breast, bent his head to wet the nipple and then blow upon it, smiling as it budded for him. "If I am to pass away," he repeated, with his lips brushing the peachlike treasure he held, "I may as well taste again the one pleasure I will most sorely miss."

11

Cake woke in her own bed, in the chamber she shared with Marguerite. It seemed wrong. Lying there, staring at the ceiling, she could not remember making her way back through the sleeping palace.

Ah, yes. That was because she had not.

In a wash of sudden heat, she recalled Ross sliding from his bed the night before and padding to a basin, returning with a cloth. He had cleansed her with such thorough care that she'd almost moaned with the arousing nature of it except she feared he would think her in pain. Afterward, he had found her shift and straightened it before putting it over her head. That process had taken some time, as he seemed reluctant to actually cover any important portion of her body. He had dressed her completely once, only to strip everything away again and pull her into his arms.

They had slept the sleep of exhaustion afterward, slept until cockcrow. In the gray dawn, he had thrown on his own clothes, then tossed her shift and gown over her head, flung her cloak around her in haste and carried her back to her chamber. He'd kissed her and left her there, left her to slip into bed beside Marguerite where she belonged.

Where she belonged? It did not seem so, not any longer.

Cate stretched in the bed, easing muscles she had not known could become strained. She felt exquisitely tender in myriad places, sore inside yet replete. She should feel some shame for what she had done, or so the nuns would surely tell her, but she could not. She was fiercely glad she had gone to Ross. She knew now what passed between a man and a woman.

Yes, she knew, and the thought that she might never have it again was so painful she turned to her side, drew up her knees and pulled the coverlet over her head. Tears burned behind her nose, but did not seep under her tightly shut eyelids. What prevented them was the sudden realization that she could be with child. As with Isabel, a new life could be quickening inside her.

Ah, no, not like Isabel. In contrast to her sister with Rand Braesford, Cate did not love Ross, nor did he love her. What lay between them was lust of the kind the priests railed against. It was a thing of the flesh rather than the spirit, of bodies aflame and hands touching and grasping; of kisses so deep they were an exchange of life's breath, and of purest animal coupling. There was nothing of the distant worship of the knight for his lady as was described in the annals of courtly love.

No, indeed not. They were neither of them in love.

"Are you still abed, Cate?"

Marguerite banged into the chamber as she made that inquiry, bringing with her a rush of cold air that smelled of the fresh outdoors. Cate moaned a little at such rude energy.

Quick footsteps approached the bed, and the curtains were flung open. "The morning is half-gone, and a fine one it is, with promise of sunshine. You will miss it if you don't bestir yourself. You've already neglected to wave farewell to one of your favorites."

Cate sat up, moving with more speed than grace. She was naked under the coverlet, but Marguerite would not mind, as she slept in the same state of nature. "Which favorite would that be?"

"Trilborn, my dear," her sister answered with laughing irony. "Are you not pleased?"

Cate sighed with relief as she reached to push a pillow behind her back. For a moment she had feared that Ross…but it was not so. "Dare we hope he will be away for some time?"

"We may, indeed." Marguerite went on to give the latest palace tittle-tattle, which said Henry had been closeted with the nobleman for some little time the evening before, and his departure was the result.

"What passed between them, I wonder."

"It's said Lord Trilborn is to visit every manse and castle between here and the northern marches, letting them know the number of men and arms Henry expects to have supplied to him in the event of rebellion. It's this business of the pretender. Many claim it's naught but a farce, while others predict armies upon the roads come summer."

A shiver feathered down Cate's spine. "Surely not."

Her sister looked grave, as well she might after a childhood made terrible by reports of battles where men were slaughtered like cattle, followed by grisly executions of traitors. "I tell you only what I've heard. And there is more."

"More?" Cate pushed a hand through her hair, trying to free it of what appeared to be a rats' nest of tangles. How it had gotten that way, she preferred not to think.

"Word is, Lord Trilborn is to send back reports from everywhere he goes, lists of the men and supplies pledged to Henry's army."

"Showing proof of his industry?"

"Or his willingness to aid Henry's cause. The mission was decided upon, they say, during a private meeting between the king and your future husband."

"But that was about our marriage," Cate said in protest.

"Was it?" Marguerite asked with her most secretive smile. "Or was the marriage about the mission that has taken Trilborn from among us?"

It was a question for which there was no answer. In truth, it did not matter. It was enough that Winston Dangerfield, Lord Trilborn, was truly gone.

He was gone, which meant the danger from the feud had been removed. If Ross was going to die before the wedding, which was fast approaching, it would have to be from some other cause.

And if he did not die, if he lived, what would that mean? Cate refused to think of it. Her chest ached at the knowledge of just how unlikely that would be.

"What will you do tonight?"

Cate jerked her head up to stare at her sister. "What do you mean?"

"Will you go to Ross or not?"

"How do you—"

"I am a light sleeper, so saw you return this morning. Moreover, I'm no longer a child, have known about the act of procreation for some time."

"Please, not so loud," Cate said with a wince.

"Don't think I blame you, for I don't. It was brave of you to venture out for what you wanted." Her sister frowned, lifting a corner of her veil to her mouth, biting on the edge of it. "I don't know if I'd have had the courage."

"Courage?"

Marguerite gave her a dark look. "For the bedding, also what comes after it. Suppose you fall desperately in love with your future husband, but the sentiment is not returned. What if he dies, anyway? You will have nothing but heartache to show for your nights in his arms. Even if you have his child, they will take it from you."

"Never!"

"Of course they will, if you go into a convent as you've sworn. If not, it will be the same. They'll take the babe and banish you to some faraway keep, hold you under guard till you molder away. I would join you either place if allowed, but will it be?"

"You cheer me so, dear sister. I don't know where I would be without you." Cate should have seen the pitfalls herself, might have except for all else that was on her mind.

Her younger sister scowled at her. "Watching you and

Isabel, I've quite made up my mind. I shall avoid being betrothed again at all costs."

"The choice may not be yours."

"I'll run away before agreeing, I will. If I find a man who suits me, I shall live in sin with him, without need of vows between us."

"But if he loves you…"

"How are we to be certain of that, you and I? Any man can say he loves us, but the only way we will know is to wait and see if he dies before the wedding. What kind of person does it make us that we can allow a man to risk his life that way?"

"It's horrible, I agree," Cate said, her voice not quite even, "yet what else are we to do?"

"You could go to Ross tonight and ask him to take you away."

Cate gave a short laugh. "I did ask him to go for himself. He refused as a matter of honor, and I can't believe he would consider it any different if he took me with him. He would probably think it a worse abuse of Henry's trust."

"Of course he would," Marguerite muttered, "the great Scots numbskull." She looked up. "I don't know what is to be done, then, except wait. Well, and take what joy you can of him."

Cate could find no way to argue with such logic. She thought, in truth, that it had much to recommend it.

She failed to allow for the whims of the king.

At midmorning, Henry gathered a group of friends and rode out from the palace. The all-male hunting party would be gone several days. Naturally, Ross was obliged to go with them.

The news, when Cate heard it, sent horror through her in a blind rush. Ross had seemed reasonably safe from the dangers of the curse while he remained within the palace walls. That was now at an end. Accidents happened with alarming frequency on royal hunts. Men competed with bow and lance to prove their prowess or win favor by providing the most meat for the royal table. Competition led to recklessness.

Beyond the dangers of galloping over uneven ground, crossing streams running high with snow melt or cornering stags and boars that might turn on their pursuers, there were arrows that went astray. All such hunting deaths were not accidental. William Rufus, son and heir to William the Conqueror, had been killed that way. It was claimed his younger brother, Henry I Beauclerc, arranged it to take the crown. If a king could fall, how much easier might it not be for someone less protected?

Nor did it help her fears to know Trilborn was not with the hunt. He could be lingering close by to make certain the wedding did not take place.

Yes, and what of Henry's purpose? The palace larder might need replenishing before the wedding feast. It was possible he thought the Scotsman should help provide venison and pork for it. Nevertheless, she could not but wonder if Henry knew what had passed between the two of them. He might prefer to remove any suggestion that Ross had been seduced away from loyalty to his native land.

Time dragged past. The palace was unnaturally quiet

without the king's presence or his guard. Messengers galloped back and forth between the hunt and the palace. Wagons loaded with every manner of game trundled into the kitchen yard each evening, proving the outing a success. No news of disaster arrived from the hunting party. No message arrived to say when they would return. As the wedding loomed ever nearer, it began to seem that Henry meant to keep Ross away until it was past.

Then on the wedding eve, shortly before vespers, a mighty salute of trumpets was heard. Cries echoed through the palace. To the sound of shouts and full-throated cheers, the cavalcade of returning huntsmen clattered through the palace gates.

Cate, hearing the firestorm of welcome that swept through the old pile of stone and wood, ran in haste to a window overlooking the stable yard. She leaned out, watching the men dismount as stable hands came running. For long moments, she could make no sense of the confusion there in the gathering dusk.

Then she saw him.

There was Ross, swinging from his mount in a swirl of plaid, tossing the reins to a stable lad with a smile and a coin. He was safe, unharmed, moving with less saddle stiffness than most as he turned from the milling group of riders and dogs.

Abruptly, he halted and stared up at the palace. He searched the windows as if he felt her presence, knew she watched him.

Cate drew back inside, away from the window, with her heart pounding in her throat. What was she doing? She wasn't supposed to care about her betrothed. It would be fatal to fall into that trap, for only pain could come of it.

But of course she didn't care for Ross Dunbar beyond appreciation for him as an attractive man and breathtaking lover. His life or death meant no more to her than that of any man in whose company she had whiled away a few hours. She would always remember him because of the gift of caring initiation he had given her, but she would not be devastated by his passing. Her most fierce pang would be from guilt that he had become embroiled in the curse that followed her and her sisters.

Yes, that was it. Guilt alone caused the odd choking feeling in her chest. Well, and mayhap dread for what might yet take place between this moment and the hour of her wedding.

The figure of a woman glimpsed at a window set Ross on fire. It had been Cate standing there; he knew it as surely as he knew his name and lineage. He had hunted like a madman these past few days, chasing red deer as if trying to outdistance the gut-wrenching longings that plagued him. It was as if he had drunk some witch's brew designed to put him in thrall. He could not get Cate out of his head. She rode with him, talked to him in the thunder of his horse's hooves, appeared in the heart of the fire as he sat beside it, and visited him in his dreams.

Lust, he told himself. His body, denied these many months, had rediscovered the pounding joy of carnal surcease and wanted more of it. His thoughts were centered on his bride-to-be because he had tasted her honeyed sweetness but not had his surfeit. The talons of need that raked him would be routed by a few hours behind bed curtains.

Striding toward the nearest entrance to the palace, he made swift plans to visit the common bathing stew at the laundry room to remove the sweat, mud, horse and animal stench of the hunt, followed by a meal to quiet the clamor in his belly. He'd then find some way to convey the message that he'd be elated to have Lady Catherine lie with him this night.

The room set aside for bathing was warm from a constantly burning fire, and steamy from the cauldrons of water that hung above the flames. The bath was hot, herb-scented and deep. Its canopy of mildewed linen on a wooden framework closed off drafts on three sides, leaving the fourth open to the fire. The maidservant sent to tend him was saucy, plump and clean. The look she gave him from under her lashes held blatant invitation.

Ross was not tempted. He had a finer quarry in mind.

Dismissing the woman with a few curt words, he rubbed a handful of soft soap through his hair, lathered and rinsed. He scrubbed the rest of him and then lay back with his arms draped around the edges of the wooden tub, which were covered by its linen liner. The warmth of the water took the soreness from his muscles and routed the last chill of the long day. The night was deepening, the candles flickering on their stands, leaving the corners of the room in shadow. He closed his eyes while his chest rose and fell in a luxurious sigh.

He could make an assignation with Lady Catherine over their evening meal, but that required the rather chancy assumption that she would be willing to risk coming to him again. He could walk with her after they ate, and entice her into his chamber, but such a ploy would expose her to censure if they were seen. He could prowl the palace in search of some corner where they could be private, rather than expect her to be closeted with him, though any place he could think of would be subject to discovery. Or he could simply appear at her small nun's cell of a chamber and hope that Marguerite would be both complaisant and discreet enough to allow them privacy.

Somehow, the drawbacks of these possibilities loomed larger than they had as he lay trying to sleep while the king's men snored around him. None of the ploys suited him, yet the alternative pleased him even less. Abstinence was no doubt suitable for a bridegroom on the eve of his wedding, but Ross could see no benefit in it.

A soft sound, like the creak of a hinge, scattered his musings. With it came a draft that gently wafted the canopy above him and brought the rise of goose bumps across the tops of his shoulders. No one spoke, however, and no footsteps sounded.

This was not the entry of another hunter bent on cleanliness, nor was it a serving woman with towels, more water to replenish the cauldrons or a more personal offer. Ross lay perfectly still, barely breathing as he listened to the whisper of fabric against fabric caused by a stealthy advance. Man or woman, he could not tell. Not until he caught the acrid whiff of male sweat and belched ale.

Above him, on the canvas tent that enclosed the tub, a shadow crept forward, cast by the light of a bowllike lamp on its corner stand. The silhouette moved higher, wider, turned into the shape of a man with something short and pointed clutched in his raised fist. The intruder eased forward, lifted his arm higher.

Linen ripped with a dull scream. Ross thrust up a hand to catch the thick hairy wrist that appeared above him. He twisted with such force that the knife the intruder held dropped, splattering into the tub between Ross's spread knees. Surging upward with hard power and a sluicing cascade of sudsy water, he brought the arm down across his bent knee with a hard crack.

The man screamed, jerking, flailing backward so he dragged the split bath canopy half off its supports. Ross gave him a hard push to send him farther. The attacker landed so hard he rolled, halting just short of the fireplace. Eyes wild, he scrambled to his feet.

Ross leaped from the tub to plunge after him, but his foot caught in the dragging canopy, skidded in the soap scum spreading over the floor. He staggered, lunging enough that his hand closed on a filthy doublet, but the man grunted and tore free.

Thrown off balance, Ross hit the stone floor full length, sprawling in dirty suds, jarring his half healed knife wound to a vicious ache. As his attacker lurched toward the open doorway and fled through, Ross leaped up again, swearing in blistering phrases as he sprinted after him.

Naked, wet and raging, he halted in the antechamber outside, holding his side. A door stood open along the way. He sprinted toward it, emerging in the palace's laundry yard. The space was a maze of wooden troughs and sagging drying lines, deserted at this time of evening, made hazardous by gathering darkness.

He could go floundering after the bastard, but the chances of running him down were not good. The fellow seemed to know the palace, and had the additional advantage of being clothed. With a curse at every step, Ross turned and retraced the path made by his wet footprints, closed himself back into the bathing chamber.

He was dirty again, his skin coated with grit. Stepping back into the lukewarm tub, he splashed mightily to clear it away. As he scooped deep, he knocked against the knife dropped by his assailant. Ross groped for it, curled his fingers around the hilt to bring it up into the light.

His breath left him in a soundless grunt.

The blade in his hand was a dainty thing, a ladies' knife of the kind that usually nestled in a scabbard swinging from a chatelaine. Lethally sharp, it was a poniard with a chased silver blade and a hilt of ebony worked with silver filigree. It was the knife used at meals by Lady Catherine Milton of Graydon.

Ross felt a sharp pain in his chest, as if the thing had struck his vitals, after all. The wedding was nigh, and he had not yet died the convenient death that would leave the lady free. He had survived whatever accidents and disease usually carried off the suitors of the Three Graces.

The lady had no wish to be his wife. What was she to do if she was not to be wed on the morrow?

Why, take matters into her own hands, of course.

Cate had meant to see that she was spared. She had,

so it appeared, decided to invoke the curse herself with the aid of a paid assassin.

It had not worked, as she would soon discover. What would she do now, with the wedding almost upon them? Might she attempt the job herself?

His hand closed slowly around hilt and blade, tightening until he felt the sting of a cut and seep of warm blood winding down his wrist. The Cate he had come to know was willful, determined and fearless, yes; she did not bow meekly to her fate as was expected of a lady in her position. Still, he had not judged her to be a murderess.

What if she wasn't? What if the point had been a mere reminder of his vow not to be wed? If he withdrew as a bridegroom, might the curse not be nullified?

But no, that would not serve. She must know he was not so craven. Ross had signed the contracts, which meant he was her husband even if their union was never blessed by the church. The only way to be rid of him was to see him dead.

Well, then, let her try. Let her, though he would not provide his future bride with so convenient an opportunity as his bed this night.

Closing his eyes, he whispered a curse more virulent than all the rest.

Cate's heartbeat raced as she entered the great hall. Though it was thronged with people, she saw no one except Ross, in his seat against one wall. He lounged in his chair with a wine cup in his hand and brooding intensity in his eyes. His saffron linen shirt stretched across his wide shoulders, with the end of his plaid thrown over his left, but the new jerkin he wore was of blue-dyed leather that made his eyes appear as dark as a northern storm. His hair was furrowed, as if he'd combed it with his fingers before it dried, yet glinted with health and cleanliness in the torch light. He was every inch the Scots nobleman, easily the most handsome man present, and he was hers.

She paused, aghast at that instant of possessive pride. Of course, it might have been occasioned by the two ladies who sat at a table not far away, whispering as they batted their lashes in Ross's direction. How dare they ogle him when tomorrow he would be wed to Cate?

Skimming forward with the long back hem of her gown sweeping the rushes, she headed toward her bride-groom. Halfway there, she saw him turn his head in her direction.

He gave no sign of welcome. His features were calm, his gaze as appraising as if she had been a stranger.

Tightness seized her throat. She had expected a smile, or at least some small acknowledgment of the intimacy they had shared. The lack seemed damning in some way she could not grasp. She did not falter, however, but lifted her chin, meeting his eyes with all the boldness at her command.

He rose to his feet, inclined his upper body in a bow. It was shallow and far from deferential. Still, he waved her to a seat at his side and pulled out the bench for her convenience.

"Good day, my lady," he said, his voice even. "I pray I see you well."

"Full well." She swept her skirt aside and seated herself, though dismay crowded her chest, making it hard to breathe. Such a formal greeting, as if he barely knew her, as if they had not strained together skin to skin, or tangled tongues and breaths. The insult was almost as hurtful as the injury of it.

He regained his seat, leaned toward her so her view of the room was blotted out. "I rejoice to see you. I had thought I must wait until after midnight."

"Why, when you could have sought me out?"

"Did you expect it, fair Cate? Were you waiting for it?"

Alarm shifted inside her, though more from the look in his eyes than anything he was saying. "It would have been natural, surely."

"Because of what we did together, you mean to say."

His voice was deep and layered with suggestion. He searched her face, gazing into her eyes as if he weighed her every expression, every word. She could feel the heat of a flush rise from her breasts to her neck and sweep upward into her face, not all of it from embarrassment. She opened her lips to speak, but could find only a single curt word in reply.

"Yes."

"You were not expecting me to return your property?"

"I...don't know what you mean." Had she left something behind in his chamber? She could not think what it might be.

"This, mayhap." He reached into his sporran and drew something out, placing it carefully on the table in front of her. With a single finger, he gave it a spin. It whirled, catching the light again and again, until he stopped it suddenly, with its sharp tip pointing directly at her heart.

A poniard. Her poniard.

"Oh," she exclaimed, reaching for the hilt, "where did you find it? I've been looking everywhere."

He caught her wrist, gripping hard. "When did you last see it?"

She blinked at that stern demand, but answered readily enough. "Two evenings ago. I thought I must have lost it beneath the trestle while I ate, though the servants who break them down had not seen it. How did you come by it?" Her fingers were growing numb, but she refused to acknowledge it, just as she refused to give him the satisfaction of struggling in his grip.

"Why, I found it in my bath."

"Your bath," she repeated in blank incomprehension.

"After it was dropped there by the assassin who tried to bury it in my back."

She inhaled with a sharp gasp. "And you think that I…"

"It would be one way of making certain you need not marry. These deaths that left you and your sisters free so long have been opportune. Could it be that doing away with unwanted suitors is a family habit?"

Anger and alarm flickered like lightning in her brain. He was her husband, in all but the final vow. If he accused her of trying to murder him, the knife might be enough to prove her guilt. The penalty would be hanging, though some wives who did away with their husbands were burned at the stake.

She moistened lips gone suddenly dry. "You can't believe I would be stupid enough to hand an assassin my personal knife?"

"You might, had he no weapon of his own. It would have a certain justice about it, I will admit."

"Never would I have parted with it!"

He tipped his head. "You value it more than most then."

"It was a gift," she answered through stiff lips.

"From?"

Her fingers were turning bluish-purple. He glanced at them but did not release her.

"A friend met at court."

"A friend you see no longer, else we would have met. Allow me to guess then. The Frenchman, Henry's master of revels?"

She stared at him, surprised out of her hauteur. "How did you know?"

"The design, for one thing. Though in the Italian style, the workmanship is French. For the rest, I've heard of how familiar he was with you and your sisters, and even with Elizabeth of York."

"Leon was never familiar, not in the way you suggest," Cate corrected, her voice not quite steady. "His manner was always most respectful."

"What, even in the throes of passion?"

She met Ross's dark gaze while anguish rose inside her. "There was nothing like that. You know that, know I had never—"

Abruptly he released her, closing his fist on the knife's hilt instead. He kept his gaze on it as he answered. "You were a virgin. That much I'll give you."

"How kind of you," she said in trembling scorn as she rubbed her wrist and hand, which tingled with a thousand pinpricks as the feeling returned. "You might also give me my knife."

"And have its blade rammed between my ribs? I think not." He spun the poniard again, his gaze on the glittering show it made. "What was this Leon to you, then?"

"I hardly see that it matters if there is to be no wedding."

Ross looked up, his pupils so wide his eyes looked black. "Who said not?"

"You can hardly wish to marry a woman you think tried to kill you. But no doubt that was Trilborn's intention. If his man did his job, then well and good. If not, it would be all the same."

"Trilborn is no longer with us," Ross said evenly.

Her smile was bleak. "But he is not long gone, and he did say, before he left, that he would see you dead."

"Though you failed to warn me of it."

"What need, when his family and yours have been threatening each other for years? I might have mentioned it, however, if I'd known you would be hunting again. I did fear that something might befall you there."

"Because of this threat?"

"And the curse, though whether it was that or Trilborn's doing, the end would have been the same," she said impatiently. "You would have been gone."

He opened his mouth to speak, but then closed it again, so tightly his lips made a straight line. Spinning the knife in an idle gesture, he asked finally, "This Frenchman, tell me about him."

"He befriended us, my sisters and I, when we came to court," she said with a resigned shrug. "Our reputation for broken betrothals preceded us, as you may imagine, and Leon was unusual enough, elegant enough, power-ful enough in his way, that others followed his lead." She looked up briefly. "That was secondary to the lead and the fashion set by the king, of course."

"Of course," Ross said dryly.

"That Leon accepted us meant the rest did the same. Afterward, there was a matter of treason, also a threat against Henry and his queen. He was forced to leave England."

"You loved him." The words were quiet, but had not an iota of softness in them. They demanded an answer, though she could imagine only one reason for it. While unlikely to be jealous, Ross might be inclined to guard against any threat to his property. A wife was chattel, after all.

"He was different from my stepfather and stepbrother, not so crude or loud or quick with his fists. He was a mu-sician and a poet who sang of love and joy and spring. He teased and smiled instead of frowning, shouting or demanding his proper homage every instant of the day."

"And you loved him," Ross said again, his tone im-placable.

"I...may have, in a way. Most young girls lose their hearts to unsuitable men at least once or twice. It meant nothing."

"Unsuitable."

"He was an agent for Louis XII, commanded to join Henry during his last weeks in exile so he might send back private reports after Henry came to the throne. If Leon had lands or title, or even a surname, he never said so, though he had a gentleman's knowledge of letters and writing."

"You still look upon the knife he gave you as a treasure."

She disregarded that comment as inspiration struck her. "If you see that's so, then you must also see I would never let it out of my sight."

"But you did."

"I didn't! At least not…not intentionally. I had it at the noon meal, but missed it some time later."

"So it could have been taken from your chamber?"

"It isn't always locked, there being little worth stealing." She gave a quick shake of her head. "It's possible I dropped it from its scabbard while kneeling in the chapel or walking in the cloister. All I know is that it was gone, until now."

"A weak explanation."

"What else can I say? I don't know how the man who attacked you came to have it. I only know I am not your enemy."

Ross snorted. "So we are back to Trilborn."

Cate met his gaze, angry that she must defend herself, yet willing him to believe her. "Which is more likely? He did attack you with a knife before."

Ross watched her while dark currents of conjecture shifted in the blue depths of his eyes. Then he pushed the poniard toward her.

Slowly, she put out her hand, wrapped her fingers around the hilt. He seemed relaxed, accepting. That did not mean he was unguarded. Cate knew beyond doubt that his strength was merely held in restraint while he waited to see what she would do. The least gesture toward him with the blade would earn swift and painful retribution.

Not that she intended such a thing. Though it was both maddening and curiously painful to have him think her capable of such a deed.

"You believe me?" she asked, her throat tight.

"Mayhap."

"And the wedding?"

"Ah, well," he said as he watched her slide the poniard into the scabbard that dangled from her girdle, "nothing like a bit of danger to whet a man's appetite for bed sport with his wife."

12

The wedding was not the ordeal Ross expected. It took place at the chapel doors, a simple ceremony with Cate's sister and a handful of her friends present, as well as a few men he had hunted with or sparred with in the tilt-yard. The king, with a courtier or two and several of his yeoman guard, put in a brief appearance to make certain all transpired as he had commanded. Henry's frown of impatience no more encouraged an extended homily from the priest than did the blustery wind laden with a hint of snow that whipped cloaks and capes around them.

Cate huddled beside Ross with her hands thrust into the wide, flapping sleeves of her gown. He put an arm across her back, clasping her waist to steady her. The priest who stood before them wavered in the wind that lifted the graying fringe of hair around his tonsure and burrowed under his robes. The exhortations to godly and fruitful married life were as hurried as the vows he mumbled. The instant they were repeated, the good father blessed them and all who stood with them, and retreated into his sanctuary.

The wedding feast awaited them in the great hall. It

was a sumptuous repast as befitted a ward of the king, with oysters steamed in almond milk, roast venison and sanglier, or boar. Also partridges and turtledoves basted with honey and herbs, gilded calves' heads, mutton in divers dishes, stewed cabbage, bread flavored with herbs, and tarts and custards, all washed down with spice-infused mulled wine and new-brewed ale.

No one was in a hurry to end it, for the evening had turned a forbidding gray and the wind shrieked and howled around the palace towers. The minstrels strolled and sang, acrobats leaped and tumbled, and dancers whirled. A fine bit of mummery was presented, after which a grizzled old bard gave them a legendary tale with many a lascivious twist and dramatic turn. The king made Ross and Cate a pleasant toast, afterward sending them choice pieces of meat from his own plate as a mark of favor. The ribald jests usually offered a newly married couple rained down upon them, but were no worse than might have been expected. The fires leaped and smoke hazed the air as wind gusts forced gray clouds of it into the great hall. Voices grew louder and ever more raucous as servants moved up and down the tables with their flagons, refilling tankards, beakers and the goblets of the high table.

Ross ate with hearty appetite, but the same could not be said for Cate. She sipped her matrimonial wine, but merely crumbled the bread he gave her, nibbled at the roast pork he offered, ate only a mouthful of the apple slice he put on her salver. Dark circles lay beneath her eyes, like stains on her pale face. Her mouth had little color. If she heard the vulgar jokes at her expense, she gave no indication of it.

Even so, she was beautiful beyond telling in her dark green velvet, with her unbound hair lying upon it in unfair competition with its embroidery in golden thread. His gaze was drawn to the tender turn of her neck, the pale skin of her throat and the delicate hint of her breasts at the line of her bodice. The need to soothe her fears, warm her, protect her from all that fate might bring, warred inside him with the hot urge to have her naked and trembling beneath him. He knew she wanted nothing of him, that she dread what was soon to come, due to his temper. Knave that he was, he could not find it in himself to spare her.

She was the prize he was owed for being inveigled into this marriage, and he would not be denied it. That he had tasted it once already was a fine boon, but not enough, not nearly enough. He meant to take her by candlelight, without defenses, weapons or artifice. He intended to explore every inch of her delectable body, to imprint it upon his mind past forgetting. He wanted to make her press against him, moving, pleading to be taken.

He wanted her to want him. Whether he would have that much from her was more than he could guess. How could he, when he suspected she preferred a dead husband to a live one?

Henry appeared bored and restless, as if he would rather be elsewhere. Now and then Ross felt the cool royal gaze resting upon him. It was no great surprise when, two hours into the meal, he was summoned to Henry's side.

"What is it?" Cate asked as she put a hand on his arm to detain him. "Have you any idea?"

"Not a one, but I suppose we shall see."

"Yes," she whispered, more to herself than to him.

Uneasiness shadowed her eyes. She still expected some last minute end to their marriage, he realized with a taut feeling at the back of his neck. She might well be right.

Regardless, it behooved him to play the doting bridegroom for their audience. Lifting her chilled, almost bloodless fingers from his arm, he carried them to his lips. "Never fear," he said. "Nothing will interfere with the wedding night before us."

Anger brought color to the elegant planes of her face. "That is not my concern."

"No," he drawled with a curl to his lips, "but 'tis mine."

"There are other things more important."

"Mayhap, but they are not on my mind at the moment. If they are on yours, it will not be for long."

He didn't wait for a reply, not because he thought she wouldn't have one but because he was sure she would. He was in no mood for more prophesies of doom.

Henry had pushed back from the table and angled his canopied throne chair, Ross saw as he approached. He moved closer at a gesture, going to one knee close enough for quiet converse.

It was nearer to the king than he had been in days. Though he had hunted with him, eaten with him, lounged with him in rough hunting manses, they had spoken so little Ross had begun to think it deliberate, a quiet threat.

"So you are wed and have lived to tell the tale," Henry said in sardonic amusement.

"As you say, sire. At least to this point."

The king's lids lowered over his deep-set eyes, hiding his expression. "You do not wear the complete set of wedding garments that was our gift. Did the remainder not please you?"

"Verily, Your Majesty, how could they not? I am grateful for your generosity. Still, I am a Scotsman, and no manner of embroidered silk and fur trimming can disguise or change that." He had donned the velvet doublet that was a mate for Cate's gown, along with his shirt and his plaid, but that was all.

"You are stubborn, as with most of your kind."

Ross merely inclined his head. There was no point in denying the obvious.

"Chance favors you, however, or so we are told. You escaped being knifed in your bath last evening."

"As you say."

"Fair fortune is often a better quality to possess than expertise in combat, though you must have that, as well, that you fended off this attack. So. You have vanquished the curse of the Graces to take the lady. We are pleased."

"No more than I, Your Majesty."

The ghost of a smile slid over Henry's face, then was gone. He sat forward in the chair, resting his elbows on its arms as he lowered his voice. "We extend every wish for future happiness to you and Lady Catherine. Toward that end, we have made certain arrangements."

"Sire?"

"As indicated when the marriage was broached, a sizable estate known as Grimes Hall has been made over to you in token of our approval. It is our desire that you occupy this holding without delay. You will depart in the morning."

Ross could not help the frown that settled upon his face at this arbitrary command. However, it seemed best to be clear about it before he protested. "Alone, sire?"

"By no means. Lady Catherine will travel with you in company with her sister and their serving woman, and with ample knights and men-at-arms to ensure your safe passage. You will proceed to Braesford with all haste. There you will present our compliments to your newly acquired brother-in-law and give him our order to man the pele tower of his manse until further notice, that we may not be surprised by invasion from the east. Afterward, you may journey to Grimes Hall at your leisure, there to make survey of its men, discovering their fitness for our need."

In other words, Ross thought, he was to ride northward into the teeth of a snowstorm while surrounded by three females and their baggage, plus a sizable escort and the supply horses required to serve their needs. He was to become a good Englishman, inspecting his estates and seeing to it that Henry had access to whatever men and supplies he might demand from this demesne he had given away.

It was not how Ross had intended to spend the days following his wedding. Regardless, he had no fear of cold or snow, and at least the journey would be in the right direction, northward toward the border.

"As you command."

"Excellent." Henry allowed himself a smile. "And now I daresay you would be grateful if we took our queen and retired."

No one was permitted to leave table or hall while the king remained, not even an eager bridegroom. "It would be a boon, sire," Ross answered in wry acknowledgment.

"It shall be soon, when some small time has passed so it need not appear a result of our discussion."

Ross inclined his head, suddenly glad he was no anointed king who must consider every word and action in light of how it might reflect upon all else. He was grateful he had not been required to marry for reasons of state, would not be seeking a marriage bed made chilly by duty and politics.

Or would he?

Cate had been amazingly responsive when she came to him in his chamber. Who would have guessed it when she appeared so cool on the surface, as if little affected by common passion?

Some men preferred their wives to be submissive and unmoved in the marriage bed, as if that lack of desire guaranteed purity and fidelity. He'd overheard a man marveling at his luck because his bride prayed all the while he enjoyed himself between her legs. Ross thought the idiot must have married either a poor, affrighted female or else a clever lady who intended to rule the braggart with her more tender parts.

Cate was not like that. Never had he been so beguiled by a woman's kisses, her touch, the generous way she opened herself to him. It was almost worth the risk of death to have known it. Yet would it ever be that way again? Could it be, when a question of attempted murder lay between them?

He didn't care if she did try to kill him in his sleep. He wanted her, had dreamed of little else while sleeping rough among men who smelled as rank as the stags they hunted. Nothing under God's heaven would prevent him from having her this night.

Cracked nuts and pears stewed in wine and spices were still on the trestles when Henry finally rose and gave his hand to his queen. The two of them made their good-nights, and then turned away toward the solar that opened from the dais. The company saw them out. They then remained on their feet as Ross immediately took Lady Catherine's hand and led her from the hall. Laughter, ribald suggestions and shouted encouragement followed after them.

"What are you doing?" Cate demanded in a whisper. "I should have been taken away and prepared for bed, then left to wait for you."

He gave her a dry look. "And who was to prepare you?"

"Marguerite, of course, as she is my only family present, though naturally Gwynne will be waiting to serve me."

"Your sister seemed little inclined. All she has done these hours past is scowl at me while chewing on her veil, as if she expected me to keel over in front of her."

"I'm sure you're wrong."

"And I'm convinced she thought all along her services would be unnecessary. As, in all truth, they are," Ross said, leaning close, inhaling his lady wife's intoxicating scent—of roses and warm female—as he spoke against her ear. "If you are to be placed naked in my bed, I prefer to attend to it myself."

She gave him a glance of dawning comprehension. "You have no friends or family to escort you to the chamber when the time comes."

"A number of men offered. I discouraged it."

"You did?"

"It was unnecessary. Also unwanted."

Her lashes swept down to conceal her expression. "You would have no public disrobing, no one to see us closed inside the bed curtains."

"No."

Her chest lifted in a deep breath that she released in the softest of sighs. "I'm glad. It's heaven's sweet mercy, for which I must say a prayer of thankfulness."

Ross rather thought she should thank him, as he had seen to it. Though he'd assumed she would prefer to avoid the ordeal, the arrangement had been made for his own satisfaction. Common though it might be to have a dozen witnesses trooping along with him to his marriage chamber, seeing to it he and his bride were left together in the same state as Adam and Eve, he had no wish to share the sight of Cate's tender white body with his hunting companions. Nakedness was no particular mystery, but he preferred to reserve her sweet secrets for his eyes alone.

And if she drew her knife against him, he wanted no witnesses who might drag her away for summary justice. That, too, was something he meant to keep for himself.

Gwynne waited in the chamber they were to share,

just as Cate had said. It was a fair-size room that had
been extended to him on his return from the hunt. He'd
had scant opportunity to make use of its fireplace and
glazed window, the large carved bed and heavy chest
that sat at its foot, the carpet in Turkey red and the table
with matching benches. It appeared he would have even
less now, if they were to leave with the dawn. As there
was little time to waste, Ross merely stood at the door,
holding it while Cate walked into the chamber. He gave
the serving woman a straight glance and tilted his head
toward the hall outside.

Gwynne curtsied with bowed head, though she darted
a look to her mistress. Cate nodded in dismissal. The
woman did not tarry, but went quickly from the room.
Ross closed the door behind her, then turned to face his
wife.

He might have been somewhat hasty, he thought, as
he ran his gaze down her comely shape, noting the intricate fastening of the golden girdle that draped her hips.
It looked to be fiendishly complicated to remove. No
matter. He would manage.

Deliberately, he secured the latch and then leaned
against the door. He crossed his arms over his chest and
waited.

Cate swallowed, a swift movement in the smooth line
of her throat, while watching him as a sparrow watches a
hawk. Long seconds passed while the fire on the hearth
danced, throwing shadows on the walls, and the candle
flames trembled on their wicks. Then she placed her
own hands to the catch of the girdle and slowly released
it. She set it on the table, piling the chains and other ac-

coutrements it carried next to it, including her poniard. She turned to him then with a dazed look on her face and tears rimming her eyelids.

He lowered his arms, took a quick step toward her. "What is it?"

"I can't…" She stopped with a helpless gesture, unable to speak.

"What?" he asked, in hard certainty that she meant to deny him this night. It seemed, now he thought about it, that something like a bright shimmer of anger lay in her eyes, like fire in water.

She swallowed, tried again. "I can hardly believe we're here, that you are here."

"That damnable curse again," he said, moving to take her shoulders in his hands. "Have I not told you it's nothing more than superstition?"

"Yes, but so many others died." She met his gaze a scant second before looking away again. "Are you sure you don't…don't care for me, that it hasn't taken you?"

"Cate."

"That is known to make it harmless. It would explain why you…why you escaped not only Trilborn's attack but the dangers of the hunt and an assassin's skill."

She had not used the word *love,* yet it hung there between them. Did he love her? Was it possible?

Suppose he did—and he was by no means sure of it—how could he say so when her bewilderment might be caused by his escape from her scheme to see him dead? By all the saints, he had no wish to believe it. And yet he'd seen her slash the outlaw leader in the forest, had recognized the lethal anger that drove her blade then, the fiery resolve that she could summon at will. She wanted no husband, had thought never to have one. How could he believe she had changed her mind? Was he to be fooled by the age-old female lure, her smile, her taste, her soft yielding to his need?

Ah, yes, his need. He wanted her, and everything else was shadows and darkness. None of it mattered. Another time it might, but not here, not now.

"I escaped because of luck and a cautious nature," he said with deliberation. "What matters is that I am here, as you pointed out, and so are you. You are my wedded wife and I want you in my bed. Take off your clothes."

The order snapped her out of her odd bemusement, as it was meant to do. She stiffened in his hold, lifting her head. "Just like that?"

"How else?" he asked, his voice tight in his throat. "Unless you'd like me to do it for you?"

"You will have to," she said with precision, "as you sent Gwynne away."

So he had, and a fine arrangement it was, too, now that she was free of her girdle. To strip her naked was his most perfect wish. In fact, he had never wanted anything so desperately in his life.

He loosened his hold, sliding his open hands from her shoulders down to her breasts, which rose and fell with the quickness of her breathing. He skimmed the twin mounds, molding them briefly with his fingers. Her bodice of embroidered green velvet was laced with silk cord held by gold hooks. He gazed into her wide eyes as he freed each one with precision so the bodice edges spread open, then fell away, along with the overskirt attached to it. Her heavy oversleeves had been sewn to the edges of her gown, but the long stitches gave under his quick tugs. He slid them down her arms and tossed them aside. Quickly then, he unbuttoned the two large rounds of gold that held her skirt, and shoved the heavy folds of velvet down over her hips so they made a puddle around their feet. And there she was in her embroidered shift, slender and pale and vulnerable to his every wish.

He spanned her waist through the fabric, drew her closer and smoothed his palm down her spine and over the swell of her backside. He pressed against her, almost groaning at the feel of her, then nudged her with slow and deliberate movements, watching her face turn rose-red with her recognition of what rubbed against her soft belly. Gathering warm linen in his hands, he drew up her shift in back, higher and higher, until his hands encompassed bare flesh, and he smiled a little, deep inside, at her shivering gasp. Releasing one deliciously full sphere with reluctance, Ross tangled his hand in her hair, drew her head back and took her mouth.

Dear God, but she was sweet and fresh and warm, so warm. Though the corners of her lips trembled, she took him in, twining her tongue with his with such delicate acceptance that he was nearly undone. The need to push her down onto the bed and fill her was so strong it was an agony. So virulent was the impulse that he barely noticed as, one-handed, he jerked her shift up until it was caught under her armpits.

He broke the kiss in order to draw the garment over her head and down her arms. It joined her skirt on the floor as he set his hands on her rib cage, holding her away a few inches while he stared down at the sculpted perfection of gently molded shoulders, high, tip-tilted breasts, not overlarge but beautifully formed and delectably pink at the nipples; also a sweetly curved waist and hips that blended into sculpted thighs and calves to rival those of a marble goddess.

"You are mine," he said with a growl as he lifted his gaze to her face again. "My wife. Mine."

"So I vowed before the priest," she answered, her eyes richly blue and her voice a strained whisper. "But you are also my husband, and mine alone."

The words were like a brand, and yet he didn't mind. Nor did he mind when she lifted her hands to his belt and unfastened it and his sporran, so his plaid fell free. More nimble than he by far, she opened the braided edges of his doublet and shoved it from him, slid his shirt up his torso and brushed his arms upward with a quick gesture so she could strip it away.

When he turned back, they were naked together in the firelight, unprotected by the trappings of modesty and pretence. And she looked at him as if she could not quite tear her gaze away, as if she'd never seen the like.

Mayhap she had not. Surely she had not.

It stirred Ross far too much, forced him to movement, so he caught her up in his arms and turned with her to the bed. He laid her upon it and joined her on the mattress. Though goose bumps pebbled her skin, he did not cover her, but lay on his side with his head propped on the heel of his palm as he skimmed his hand over her from knees to her waist to her throat and back down again, sliding over breasts and belly and the silken curls at the meeting of her legs, enjoying the satin smoothness of the skin at the tops of her thighs. Yes, and between them.

While he busied himself below her waist, she put her hand on his chest, trailing her fingertips through the hair that veiled it, touching the flat brown circles of his nipples while watching from under her lashes as they tightened. She brushed her palm over his shoulder, down his biceps and along his elbow. Dropping her hand to his hip bone, she smoothed the backs of her fingers over the flat surface of his abdomen, again and again as if that unremarkable hardness enthralled her. Then slowly, she inched toward the jutting hardness of him until her knuckles grazed his fevered flesh. She uncurled her fingers, fastened them around it.

He covered her small, sweet mound with his hand and pressed a long finger into her folds.

Her fingers flew open and she inhaled sharply, snatching her hand away from its prize. He shook his head, probing deeper. "Take it," he said, "if you want it."

She was innocent as yet, but not without imagination. She caught the implication that he had in hand what he most desired. As lightly as a butterfly then, she reached to grasp him, holding carefully as he jerked in that gentle imprisonment.

His vision blurred and his breath whistled in his throat with the sudden need to be clasped tighter, more firmly, with movement. She was learning him, however, tracing strutted veins, thumbing the smooth tip. Mindlessly, he plundered what he held, circled the silken nub at the apex of her soft folds with his thumb until she moaned. He leaned to lick a pink nipple as if tasting a berry, took it between his teeth, suckled in rhythm to her discovery of the gliding motion of skin over skin where she held him.

She was moist and molten hot, and he was blind with the restraint he clamped upon his responses. Until, suddenly, his control was at an end.

Catching her close, he leaned over her and then rolled to his back, pulling her with him so she lay full upon him, stretched out atop his long form. Her legs were spread open and he nestled against her, so close, yet not where he belonged.

"As you will, my lady," he said against her hair, "when you will."

She put a hand flat on his chest, raised herself enough to drag her other arm up and brace it upon his shoulder. Her hair twined around her, around them both, like fine gold wires binding them together. She moistened her lips, the look in her eyes intrigued yet determined, poised yet uncertain. "You mean…"

"Exactly," he answered, pressing a little against her warm and open wetness to make his meaning clearer.

She was still for long seconds, measuring his will, mayhap, for he felt it stretch to its utmost reach. Then, with a hesitant dip of her head, she hitched higher and pressed her lips to his.

It was sweet, that kiss, but so far from what his body clamored for that he nearly devoured her with his mouth. His heart thundered in his chest, so fiercely she must surely feel it. His brain felt on fire, and his lungs strained for air.

She lifted her head, squirming upon him in a way that

put a catch in her breath and caused his arms to tighten around her of their own accord. "I'm too heavy," she said in breathless protest. "Let me off."

"Nay, never. You're a mere feather. Only take me inside you, if you have any mercy. Take me inside you now."

She stilled an instant, and then moved down to allow a bare inch of penetration. "You mean…like this?"

"Exactly, only…" She was killing him. Was it, could it be, deliberate?

"This?" she said, wriggling lower.

"Aye," he breathed, and would have begged for more, except she shifted to brace her hands upon his shoulders and raise herself, getting her knees under her and adjusting her weight until she sank home, so fully that he shuddered with the piercing gratification of it.

She was vise-tight, but relaxed by slow degrees so he was seated even more deeply inside her. She altered the angle a degree to accommodate him, dragging a hissing breath from her lungs that he echoed in full.

"I'm hurting you," she insisted, lifting as if she would dismount.

"Nay, don't move. Don't stop," he commanded, catching her hips and holding her in place while he pressed upward.

"Don't stop what? I'm not doing anything. I don't know what to do."

He liked the frustration in her voice. In fact, he adored it. "Do whatever pleases you."

"This?" she asked, easing forward and then back again.

"Aye, God, aye," he managed to say.

She took him at his word, clutching his shoulders as she began to ride him. And her efforts set her hair to flailing him like a thousand tiny whips. She flung it behind her shoulders, leaning her head back with her eyes closed. Her breasts jounced in a most enticing fashion and she panted, her rose-red lips parted.

Ross watched her with fierce wonder and a curious ache in his chest. He aided her with a firm grip, forced her onward when she would have faltered, grasping her so tightly he feared he'd leave bruises, though he could not let her go. And when at last he felt her internal muscles clench around him, pulsating, he raised his head and took a nipple into his mouth, suckling strongly while he bucked under her.

She cried out, went rigid as her body surrendered to infinite pleasure. He released her breast, burying his face between the twin mounds as he thrust upward with hard power, again, again and yet again, until his world dissolved and the bursting brightness behind his eyes was like a small and glorious death in the midst of perfect life.

13

"Up, milady! The bell for prime has rung, and we must be gone. You'll not want to keep the horses standing, for 'tis cold as a witch's teat, and snowing besides."

Cate moaned at the sound of Gwynne's voice, for it seemed she had only just fallen into sleep. The night past was a hodgepodge of images and sensations in her mind, most so incredible she blushed to recall them. She had never dreamed there were so many ways to make love, most of them sinful, according to the holy fathers who condoned one position only and that with as little touching as possible. Ross surely had pagan leanings, for he brushed aside all such prohibitions. Any way of seeking such joy was good, he said, and priests who preached otherwise merely begrudged their parishioners the pleasures denied to them.

Turning with a grimace due to soreness in muscles she'd never dreamed she might use, Cate opened a single eye. Her voice husky with sleep, she asked, "What horses?"

"Those readied for your travel, of course. We leave the instant you are dressed."

"Leave?" she asked in confusion.

"For Braesford Hall? Did yon Dunbar not tell you?"

Cate gave a slow shake of her head.

"Just like a man, to leave the telling to someone else. Doubtless he'd no wish to hear you moan."

That was not true at all, Cate thought, closing her eye. Ross had seen to it that she moaned and cried his name any number of times in the night. He had encouraged it, reveled in it, from what she remembered.

Abruptly, the sense of what Gwynne was saying penetrated her fog of satiation and weariness. "Braesford? We're going to Braesford and Isabel?"

"Have I not been telling you? Come now, there's no time to waste. Up with you, wash your face and let me dress you. Lady Marguerite is already waiting in the great hall."

The day was a wretched one for a journey, just as Gwynne had said. Cate discovered exactly how miserable it was the instant their cavalcade emerged from the protection of the palace and the snow-ladened wind struck them. By the time they were beyond the town, they were chilled to the bone in spite of fur-lined mantles of boiled wool with layers of padded clothing underneath.

Holding the hood of her cloak over the lower portion of her face, squinting into the white pall, she envied the armor worn by their escorts, and even the cuirass worn by Ross, for the breastplate must surely ward off the wind and hold body heat inside it. She was also certain Gwynne, riding pillion with her arms around the waist of a man-at-arm, was better off for the extra warmth of her companion, not to mention for his broad bulk as protection from the sheets of blowing snow. Cate, mounted on Rosie, had no such shield, nor did Marguerite on her own palfrey.

They stopped often to rest the horses and heat cauldrons of ale and wine over the fires lighted to warm them. It was little comfort. No sooner were they back on the road than the chill found them again. It was an excellent thing the Great North Road was well marked or they might have lost it in the swirling whiteness.

"What can be the king's purpose in commanding our travel in the teeth of a winter storm?" It was Marguerite who posed that question in disgruntled complaint during the third rest of the day, standing with her back to both the wind and the fire. Smoke swirled around her until she appeared like some witch being burned at the stake, but she did not seem to regard it.

"Quietly, my dear," Cate said, with a quick glance toward the men-at-arms around their separate fire.

"Why, because I may be taken up for treason? What odds, when we're being sent to our deaths, anyway?"

"'Tis a matter of security," Ross answered.

He stood near Cate. Accident or not, his wide shoulders blocked the worst of the wind and smoke from reaching her. His fur-lined cloak was a gift from Henry, a part of his wedding raiment he had scorned to wear until driven to it by the biting cold. He had even donned hose under his plaid.

The additions gave him more the look of an Englishman. Oddly enough, she was not sure she approved.

"His royal majesty's security, I'll be bound, for it cannot be ours," Marguerite muttered.

"What else? It's the first priority of kings, protecting their realms." Irony laced Ross's voice, though his gaze was on the men-at-arms who were melting snow at a separate fire, using it to water the horses. "Though the fewer who know of our journey, the better our chance of getting through with his orders."

Cate glanced up at Ross. When she spoke, she kept her voice to a murmur. "Orders for Braesford?"

"Aye." Her husband answered just as quietly.

"Henry suspects a threat from the sea?"

"So it would seem. The order is that Braesford man the pele tower attached to his manse, ready to kindle the fire atop it that will warn of invaders."

At least he did not scorn to answer her, or tell her to hold her tongue and leave such matters to men. "Sent by the Yorkists, I suppose, but I fail to see..."

"The dowager duchess of Burgundy despises Henry, views him as the Antichrist himself. She froths at the mouth to see him dead."

Such talk concerning the lady, once a princess of the house of York, had been current at court for months, but Cate was too grateful for Ross's protection just now to point that out. "So she has provided recognition of the pretender. Can she really believe he is her nephew?"

"Who can say? She stirs this particular pot with a long spoon, as she is still in Burgundy. Whoever the poor little sod being made much of in Ireland turns out to be, he's still no more than an excuse for toppling Henry. True prince or not, he'll serve as a cat's paw for those who would snatch the crown when he falls."

"Such as John de la Poole, once Richard's appointed heir?"

Ross inclined his head. "A noble malcontent who feels he was done out of his due when Henry took the crown at Bosworth."

"There will be fighting," Cate whispered, as the realization struck her.

"Oh, aye."

"And you are now expected to aid Henry."

Ross tipped his head with its Scots bonnet in assent. "I'm to begin gathering men and arms."

"So you'll do it?" She searched the hard lines of his face, shivering a little at the implacable look in his eyes.

"So long as Scotland stays out of it." His accent was stronger, a sign of his disturbance of mind.

"And if King James does intervene?"

"We'll see when it comes to it." Turning away, Ross called for the fires to be doused, and set the troop back on the road again.

Toward midafternoon, the snow began to thin. It soon ceased altogether. The sky remained gray and heavy, however, and the wind picked up the snow disturbed by their passage, and scattered it like fairy dust behind them. The land lay white and near silent, an endless sea of snow with the tops of hedgerows winding through it, and rounded humps where brambles and old haystacks were covered over. Nothing moved other than their thudding, jangling column with Henry's official banner fluttering above it. The houses of the few villages they passed were closed up tight, with wisps of smoke drifting over snow-smothered rooftops, and barking dogs the only signs of life.

Their party lost their way due to a marker buried in the snow, so had to backtrack for several leagues. The extra effort sapped their endurance and strained tempers. Some small distance ahead was the monastery where they could expect to find shelter for the night. As the early winter dusk began to draw in, they listened for the vesper bells that would lead them to it.

They still had not heard them when they approached a ford. It was a gray-purple and steep-sided runnel, overhung by leafless trees with ice-coated limbs that clacked and rattled like dice played on a marble floor. The stream at the bottom was almost certainly frozen, under snow that appeared deep enough to touch the bellies of the horses.

Ross led the way down the bank. Half the complement of men-at-arms followed close behind him, with Cate and Marguerite among them. The remaining men-at-arms, including the man with whom Gwynne rode pillion, brought up the rear. The footing was slippery, and Cate gave close attention to Rosie as the palfrey picked her way over the unseen ice.

A shout rang out as she started up the opposite slope. Mounted men charged from right and left. All was confusion as yells and curses rang out and snow was thrown up by flying hooves.

Ross and the men-at-arms with him swung to form a protective cordon around Cate and Marguerite. Their swords whined as they drew them. Hoarse calls and grunts echoed around them.

The horses, wall-eyed with terror, screamed and reared, slamming into friend and foe alike as they fought for purchase in the slippery ford. Swords whistled, clanging on metal like an insane, cracked-bell dirge.

An armored man, a dark shape in the boiling fury of snow and ice, flailing blades and struggling horses, reared his mount and forced his way through the tumult. He shouldered Rosie away from the others and leaned to grab for Cate's bridle.

Her poniard was in her hand, though she had no memory of drawing it. A quick stab at the gloved hand that held Rosie's head, and she was free again. She jerked the palfrey back inside the protection created for her and Marguerite, and then gave her attention to making certain she remained there. Ross and the others could not fight so mightily if they had to watch that she wasn't caught up in the melee, or worse, snatched away beyond it.

Swinging her head to search for Ross, she saw he was looking in her direction. His eyes blazed through narrowed lids and his mouth was set in a grim line, but he gave her a hard nod of approval. Her heart throbbed and her breath was hot as she jockeyed and backed her mount, yet wild exhilaration sang in her veins. Meeting the gaze of the warrior who was her husband, she tipped her head in return.

A bloody gash opened on the flank of Marguerite's horse. Maddened with pain, the beast leaped and curveted. Cate feared her sister would be thrown, but she managed to control her mount. In that same moment, a man reached as if to snatch her to him. Marguerite whirled on him with a shriek, using her rein ends as a whip across his face. The man drew back sharply. Then he wheeled to stare toward Cate.

Ross thrust his destrier between them. The man was forced outside the cordon once more.

By all the saints, was that what this was about? Could it be another try at abduction?

Cate, her mind afire with white-hot logic, could see no better explanation. It seemed no mere robbery attempt; the assailants were too many and too well armed. And who would dare such a thing other than Trilborn?

Yes, but to what purpose? Why, what else except rapine to spite the Scotsman, to sully his bride and so sting his pride? Or was the purpose to force Ross to come after her, the better to kill him?

She would not be taken. She would not.

But suppose that was not it at all? Trilborn's first aim could be to slay Ross in this vile ambush. Then he could ride away with her to some isolated keep, there to make sure she rued her rejection of him.

Marguerite and Gwynne could not be left alive to tell the tale, nor could a single man of their escort. Cate's heart constricted in her chest as that obvious fact came home to her.

Rosie pitched and shrieked, and Cate fought with strength she scarce knew she possessed to control her. A man-at-arms went down, his blood splattering bright red against the pure white of the snow. Ross slashed at the attacker who slew him, connecting with a body blow that sent the man reeling over his charger's neck as the horse bolted for the upper bank.

Three of their assailants converged on Ross. He gave

battle like a demon, his eyes narrowed upon the blades
that came at him as he swung his mighty sword, so
much longer and heavier than those used against him. It
shrieked with vicious purpose as it bit into metal, clanged
against armor, thudded into the side of one man with the
sound of breaking bone.

Abruptly, the way before him was clear. "Cate!" he
shouted, and whirled his mount to find her. "To me! To
me!"

She was beside him in an instant. He collected her
sister and the man who had Gwynne with a single commanding glance. And then they were plunging ahead,
thrusting their way up the slope toward the open track
that lay beyond.

They reached it and kicked their horses into a run.
The other men-at-arms of their party fought free, stream-
ing out behind them. Their pursuers followed like dark,
thundering shadows.

The galloping column plunged through rolling yet
open country as the day closed in around them. Lavender and purple shadows smudged the snow, turning dark
gray in the hollows.

Then it came, the sound they most longed to hear. For
somewhere just ahead, over the brow of the next hill,
rang out the melodious and infinitely welcome chimes
of vesper bells.

The monastery came into view, a low building of
yellow-brown stone attached to a modest chapel and protected by stout stone walls. The instant it was sighted,
their pursuers fell away. Ross did not slacken the pace,
however, but led Cate and the others on. They breasted

drifts of snow, driving through until they reached the great wooden gate, which swung open to receive them.

Pigeons flew up from the monastery eaves, wheeling against the darkening sky, as they clattered inside and pulled up in the cobblestoned court. Dim light shone through cracks in the shutters of a long chamber that ran along one side of the ancient structure. There was no brick here, no glazing, no stained glass in the chapel windows. Norman arches in the squat structures suggested the place had been protecting travelers since the time of William the Conqueror, however. The gate that crashed shut behind them, closing out their enemies, was as thick as a man, and strapped and studded with iron.

They were safe.

Cate slewed around in her saddle to stare at Ross. His face was streaked with blood, his cloak spattered with it, and his gloved fist red to the elbow. Worse, his knee was covered in gore where it was protected only by hose.

"You are injured," she exclaimed. "Where? Get down, and let me—"

"Nay, sweet wife. The blood is that of other men. And you?" He rode close and removed his glove, leaning to take her chin in his hand and rub his thumb over an itchy spot on her cheek. "Were you cut?"

She shook her head, warmed, unaccountably, by his touch and the look of concern on his hard features. "As you say, the blood of others."

He glanced behind her to Marguerite, who shook her head though she breathed heavily through her mouth, holding her palfrey's mane. Gwynne sobbed against the back of the man-at-arms who had her up behind him, but seemed to have suffered only a minor cut down one leg and a fair-size rent in the back of her mantle.

Others among their escort were not so lucky. One reeled from a blow that had dented his helmet, and two more had slashes to arms and legs that needed immediate attention. That seemed forthcoming, for the man at the gate was ringing an alarm. Men in the plain brown garb of their calling poured from the lighted room at one side of the court. They surrounded the wounded, assisting them from their saddles with care. In no time, they were borne away inside.

Ross swung from his destrier and came to help Cate down. She clung to his arms while she shook with tremors. It was not fear, she thought, but glad relief and the awakening from some strange, cold savagery.

"You are certain you are unhurt?" Ross asked, bracing his feet as he held her, his cloak blowing around them both.

"Yes, but…I wish I'd had a sword out there. I was so… I wanted to run them through for what they did, to kill every one."

A laugh shook him. "And would have, I expect. It's just battle madness, my apple, my sweeting. It will pass."

"I would that I might have aided you." She rather liked those curious endearments spoken in his quiet Scots burr.

"You did, by staying behind me."

She grimaced. "Hardly a brave showing."

"But a wise one that proved your trust, for which I am grateful." He glanced over his shoulder in the direction the injured had been taken. "And now…"

"And now you must see to your men," she said, straightening her shoulders. "Go. Marguerite and I must look after Gwynne, as well."

"Later, then," he answered, and swung away.

She did not ask what he meant, though she watched him until he passed into the doorway of what must be the infirmary, and was lost to sight.

Gwynne's cut was not deep, but it was long and painful. Marguerite dosed the serving woman with several cups of new wine while Cate bound the wound. Afterward, they left her, snoring from the libation and exhaustion, in the small cell with its two benchlike beds of stone that Marguerite was to share with her.

The chamber allotted to Cate and Ross was no larger, nor was it more luxurious. The stone bed was softened only by a thin mattress stuffed with straw, and had a single wool blanket for cover. The room had no window, no fireplace or fire pit, not even a brazier. A few rushes scented with rosemary served to ward off the chill of the stone floor. A tallow candle illuminated the three-legged stool, narrow table holding a wooden basin and crude prie-dieu that completed the meager furnishings. In short, there was nothing to encourage overstaying their welcome with the good brothers of the order.

Cate and Marguerite, being female, were forbidden the communal hall, so were served their evening meal in this small chamber. The repast was no more sumptuous than the accommodations, being watered wine, cold bread and a few bits of meat drowned in lukewarm broth. It was brought by a monk so elderly he was past all chance of sensual temptation, though he had a singularly gentle and pleasant smile.

"Well?" Marguerite asked, when the stooped brother had shuffled away with the front hem of his robe dragging in the dust that coated the stone floor.

"Well, what?" Cate, cold to the marrow of her bones, warmed one hand on the pottery bowl that held the broth, while dipping her bread into it with the other.

"You know very well what I mean! What is it like to be a wedded wife?"

"It is well enough."

"You seem all right, but you barely moved when I looked in at dawn before sending Gwynne to you."

"How should I look?"

"As if you had been properly bedded by a loving spouse?"

"Really, Marguerite," she said, without quite meeting her eyes. "It's not as if it was the first time, after all."

Her sister watched her with an intrigued air. "So what passed between you? How did—"

"Never mind!" Cate interrupted in haste. "It's enough to know that all is as it should be."

"Yes, but did your Scotsman say nothing concerning the curse? Has he sworn to love you forever, that he's still able to walk among us?"

"Ross has no belief in curses." Cate huddled on one end of the hard bed, as she had allowed Marguerite the stool. Why her husband's lack of belief in the curse should make her feel colder than she was already was more than she could say.

Marguerite lifted a brow. "Pray, what has that to do with it? Come, Cate, he must know how he escaped the fate that removed all your suitors who came before him.

He has had full many an opportunity to die, you know. He might even have done so this day."

"Don't, please don't say such a thing," Cate begged her with a shudder.

Her sister sat back, staring at her. She lifted a corner of her veil of plain linen, nibbling on it. After a moment, she lowered it. "So that's it."

Disquiet assailed Cate at something she saw in her sister's penetrating gaze. She returned her attention to her broth.

"*You're* in love with *him*."

"Don't be foolish." It could not be. She was too sensible, too wary. Surely it was impossible?

"Wouldn't it be interesting if that is also a key to vanquishing the curse—if our love for a man worked as well as his for us?"

"You would like to think so, I'm sure," Cate said. "Then all you need do is persuade Henry to choose a man you can adore."

Marguerite shrugged. "Oh, Henry. As I've said before, I shall not heed his command to wed."

"I should like to know how you will avoid it," Cate said in sisterly annoyance. "But I've no idea why Ross still lives. Mayhap it's because he was born Scots."

"Instead of English? Being foreign born didn't save your betrothed from Bruges." Marguerite put a corner of her veil between her teeth for an instant, her gaze intent. "But we could ask Isabel. She may know, being eldest."

"I suppose," Cate said, though she could not see how having a husband some few months longer gave their older sister any additional expertise.

"She may also know if the curse can carry off a man once we are wed."

"Marguerite!" The very idea gave Cate a choking sensation, as if her leaping heart had clogged her throat.

"It must be considered." Her sister reached for her bowl of broth.

Cate didn't want to consider it. That very reluctance made her wonder if her younger sister could be right, at least in part. Cate might be somewhat attached to the Scotsman who was her husband.

Oh, but that wasn't love. Was it?

No, of course it wasn't, she thought, wrapping an arm about her waist under her mantle. Love was more than admiring a handsome face and manly form, more than being awed by his prowess with a sword. It had nothing to do with the pleasure she enjoyed in his arms. Love was warm affection that grew from years of living side by side, of sharing the joy of bearing children and the sadness at the inevitable loss of a few. It was respect and appreciation for a man's protection. It was working together to build a life.

No, she wasn't in love with Ross. How could she be in love with a man who thought she just might have tried to have him killed?

Marguerite went away to check on Gwynne and retire for the night in the bed next to her. Cate wrapped her mantle and the threadbare wool blanket around her shoulders, and braced her back in the corner where the bed was placed in the angles of two walls. She was still there when Ross finally made his way to the chamber.

The candle had burned down to a flickering, malodorous stub. Her husband was hardly more than a shadow as he stepped inside and pushed the door shut behind him.

"Still awake?" he asked. "I thought you would be abed long since."

"I am abed, but…" She shook her head.

He glanced around, located his sword which he had sent to the chamber earlier, as he could not appear with it in the hall. Assured it was near, he swept off his cloak, removed his jerkin and began to loosen the belt that held his plaid. "You are troubled by the deaths this day?"

"I…suppose so."

"Your teeth are chattering. You're cold."

She tried to control the small sound to little avail. "Who…would not be?"

He tossed the plaid onto the bed, where it fell across her feet. Even through the blanket that covered them, she could feel the body heat that lingered in its folds.

"You were cold that first night, there in the forest," he said with gravel in his voice. Nimble of finger, he freed the points that held his shirt to his hose.

Her glance was exasperated. "It was snowing."

"I could hear your teeth chattering then, too." He shook his head before ducking to pull his shirt off over it.

"You built up the fire." She almost lost track of what she was saying as the dying candlelight gilded the hard ridges of muscle that wrapped his chest and upper arms.

"It wasn't what I wanted to do." He sat on the opposite bench to strip away his boots and the hose he was not used to wearing, though he watched her instead of what he was doing.

"No?" The single word came out in breathless anticipation as he rose and came toward her in hard and naked splendor.

"No," he answered. Kneeling on the thin, narrow mattress, he began to unwrap her blanket with ruthless efficiency.

"What did you prefer?" She helped him, the saints forgive her. At least she stripped off her mantle and allowed him to unlace her bodice.

"To lie with you, to warm you, hold you."

"I wish you had," she said, her voice not quite even.

"To be warmed by you." He pushed up her gown and shift, and then drew her up to kneel with him so he could rid her of them.

His hands were cold, as was his nose, his forehead and everywhere else that had not been covered. Shivering, she twined her arms around him, drawing him to her as she pressed her body with its rash of goose bumps to the wondrous heat and strength of his torso and what was below. "Lie with me now," she whispered against his neck, "and we will warm each other."

14

God's toes, but this monk's bed was hard, doubtless the better to mortify the flesh and therefore the soul. Ross swore silently, certain he'd slept on rocky ground more comfortable. He would give thought to getting up and joining the men-at-arms in the stable, except Cate had finally fallen asleep. She seemed to have discovered a mattress to her liking, as she was lying more on him than on the miserable excuse for a bed.

Not that he minded. Her weight and soft curves satisfied him in some curious way. Odd, that, when she might be a murderess.

The attack this evening was no random incident by a roving outlaw band. The men had been disciplined, well mounted and protected by chain mail. They had chosen their trap well, and waited for the perfect time to spring it. He'd wager his firstborn son that Trilborn was behind it. Ross's only question was whether Cate had known it was coming.

Conceited though it might be, he found it difficult to believe she would prefer Trilborn to him. Still, who knew the mind of a woman? It was possible she felt an

Englishman would be easier to understand, less difficult to manage.

Even with his doubts, Ross could not resist coming to her, bedding her. He must be bewitched. Could be there was something to this curse, after all. Could be it made fools of the men it did not kill.

He had not told her they would be leaving on the morn after their wedding night. It was no oversight, but a deliberate ploy. How could she have known to send a message then, and when could she have sent it, when he had taken her straight to their chamber? The chance that she had slipped from their bed afterward was minuscule. He had kept her too busy, had left her too wearied for it. That was more desperate need than plan, but the results were surely the same.

Her wild concern as she sought his location during the skirmish, her wifely dread that he might be injured, had seemed real enough. Her need of him just now had been extreme, her generosity marked, almost humbling. What was he to think of that, except that she wanted him? It could be feigned, a woman's ruse to cloud his judgment. If so, it had been successful. He was more ready to make excuses for her now than he had been the night before.

Most men would not dare. Fearful for their life and immortal soul against such magic, they would repudiate her forthwith. What man wanted a wife who might smile and open herself to him one moment and attempt to see him dead the next?

Ross did.

Against all caution and common sense, he desired this woman and no other. The last thing he could allow was for her to know it, however. That was a weakness he could not afford.

She felt his lack of trust, he thought. She was more reserved, more closed against him. She might give her body to him, might take pleasure in his caresses and give pleasure in return, but she allowed nothing else. It annoyed him, that determined self-possession. For all his suspicion, he wanted to see once more the acceptance he had glimpsed once or twice in the heaven's blue of her eyes, back before they were commanded to wed.

As if sensing the disturbance of his thoughts, Cate murmured in her sleep, settling closer against him, drawing up one knee across his thigh. He reached to tuck the blanket, his plaid and her mantle closer around her. Sighing, he closed his eyes. Here in this safe place, with Cate in his arms, sleep came with the sudden force of a headsman's ax.

"Is it safe, going on with fewer men-at-arms?"

Cate asked the question of her husband where he lounged on the bed, watching while Gwynne, favoring the cut leg, braided Cate's hair. She could not imagine what Ross found so entrancing in the sight, yet he sat with his back to the stone wall and one wrist resting on his bent knee, hardly looking away. Surely he had more important tasks, such as checking on the injured men they would be leaving behind, and seeing all was ready for their departure. Of course, he might have done that already, as he had left their small chamber while it was still dark, and was only just returned to it.

"We have to go," he answered, "or risk being trapped here."

"What if those who set upon us are waiting outside, or somewhere farther along the road?"

"The reason we leave at once, before Trilborn can gather a larger complement around him."

"You are certain he was behind it then." She risked a glance in Ross's direction, but his set features told her nothing. It was beyond her understanding how a man could hold her so tenderly, touch her with such magic, then look at her as if nothing had happened between them.

"Who else?"

The words were so short and laden with scorn that she frowned. "How am I to know? He is your enemy."

"So he is."

"Bend your head, milady." Gwynne, done with braiding, stood ready to add her veil.

Cate did not make the mistake of thinking the serving woman paid no attention because she kept her gaze lowered. Cate gave her an ironic glance as she allowed her to set in place a flat cap to which the square of linen was attached, tying it under her braid.

"At least we survived the attack," Cate said. "That must mean something."

"Oh, aye. It means a close watch was kept for trouble and, all praise to Henry, we had a larger escort than might have been expected."

"Agreed, on both counts. Still, you allow nothing for the terms of the curse?"

He snorted. "Nay, but I've a question about this curse of yours."

"Yes?" She stood still while Gwynne put her into a padded tunic that fastened under each arm.

"Is there no provision for *your* feelings? Can you not reverse the effects if you fall in love with the man chosen as your husband?"

That was the same question that had troubled her since Marguerite had hinted at it earlier. It had never occurred to Cate before, because she and her sisters had never known their previous grooms in advance of the betrothals.

"I have no idea," she said with a small shake of her head.

"When you decide," he said, pushing himself to his feet and striding toward the door, "you might let me know."

Infuriating man, to leave in the middle of such a discussion. Her first impulse was to stride after him to continue.

No, it might be better left alone. If he cared only for his skin, she did not want to know it. And if he wished to inquire if she loved him, she would not have him think the question held any particular importance to her. Not that it did, of course. How could it, when it was quite clear that Ross Dunbar might enjoy having her in his bed, but had little care for her outside it?

He didn't love her.

Why, then, was he still alive? Why?

They rode out long before dawn, covering considerable ground before the sunrise tinted the snow-white world with pink and rose-red, lavender and gold. Every tangled briar and tree branch sparkled with diamond fire. The air was like some icy elixir. The sun, in its climb heavenward, touched them with vagrant warmth.

They made good time, pushed by threat and Ross's exhortations. A dozen times during that long day, he rode ahead to scan the countryside and then galloped back to harry their column from the rear. They rested less often and kindled no fires. On edge, watchful and weary of the endless, jarring ride, they endured in silence. By day's end, they were glad beyond words to reach a priory, even though the prioress required men and women coming under her jurisdiction to sleep apart, in separate buildings.

It rained during the night, a solid downpour that was still falling when they set out again the next morning. The mood among them was as grim as the weather. Ross seemed particularly ill-tempered, his commands sharp-edged. Only part of it was caused by the wet ride and quagmire of a road they were following, at least according to Gwynne. The rest, she said, could be laid to his being forced to sleep alone. Cate wished she could believe her.

Nothing was seen of Trilborn or any other danger on this third day. All they encountered were a covey of wool merchants with their wares, pilgrims traveling together for protection, a troupe of players in a gaily painted wagon and a Scots messenger riding along with a ragtag company of knights bound for a tourney.

The last wore a plaid Ross seemed to recognize, for he hailed him in sharp query. On closer viewing, even

Cate could see that the swath of wool cloth the man had around him had a weave in colors very similar to Ross's blue, gray and red. The two of them drew aside, speaking in the rapid burr of Scots Gaelic. The man handed Ross a leather pouch he carried. Almost immediately, Ross ordered a halt in the protection of a copse of beech trees, and allowed fires to be lit.

While a meal was prepared, Ross remained in conversation with his countryman, standing at some small distance from both the women and the men-at-arms. Cate did her best to ignore them, though she and Marguerite waited with scant patience to learn what this chance meeting portended. That it signified something seemed plain from the grim lines of her husband's face.

The newly met Scotsman warmed himself and shared their meal of bread and beef, drinking from the wineskin that was passed from one man to another. When done, he and Ross clasped each other's arms above the wrist in the double grip of kinship. The messenger mounted up then, and made ready to join their column until he must split away back toward Scotland.

Ross walked apart, opened the messenger bag and took a leather-wrapped bundle from it. Opening it, he stood perfectly still as he read the contents. The wind, damp with the rain and mist, tossed his plaid about his knees, ruffled his hair and swung the sporran dangling below his waist. He appeared not to notice. After a moment, he crammed the message back inside, turned and shouted the order to mount up.

Cate made no move to obey. Instead, she walked to

where he stood with the messenger bag trailing from its strap in his hand.

"What is it?" she asked in quiet concern.

"Nothing."

"Has someone died? Is it your father?"

"Nay, he's well enough."

"And the rest of your family?"

"Lost to me."

An odd ache settled in her heart for the pain she saw behind the hard mask of his face. "You are disowned. It's official then."

"Banished, denied, no longer of the Dunbar clan nor welcome on Dunbar lands. You, my lady, are married to a man without kith or kin, or prospects beyond those conferred by an English king he should not despise."

She caught her bottom lip between her teeth, hesitating before she spoke. "It isn't unexpected."

"No. What I didn't expect was that Henry would send to my father, saying that my days as a hostage were done and I was free to return home."

"Is that not a good thing?"

Ross turned his dark blue gaze upon her. "Not when the old laird declares that Henry might as well have killed me and been done with it, since I am dead to him and all who ever knew me, and have been since the banns were first read."

"You expected no less," she said, placing her fingers on his arm in a gesture of compassion.

"That isn't the same as receiving the notice." He shook his head. "Dead to him. Mayhap there is something to your curse, after all."

She gained no satisfaction from hearing Ross admit it. His loss, and his pain because of it, were too much her fault. Because of her, so many had turned against him. Like some strong and noble stag with the dogs on his heels, he seemed too close to defeat. She could not bear it.

"You have a family," she said through the tightness in her throat. "You have me, my sisters and all who make Braesford their home. You have land, and can build a home and a clan of your own."

His brief smile held recognition for her attempt at comfort, but little more. "It isn't the same."

"I'm so sorry." The words were a whisper in the wind, a cry of the heart.

"So am I," he answered, "so am I."

In due course, they reached journey's end. Topping a hill, they saw before them the manse known as Braesford Hall upon its high eminence, its battlemented pele tower topped by a straining blue-and-white pennant, and the straggling village like mud on the hem of its skirting of high stone walls.

There was no need to hail the gate. They had been seen long before, so it stood open to their arrival with the portcullis raised, showing a hint of mellow red brick in the manse walls beyond. A chorus of trumpets sounded, echoing away over the hills. Hounds poured out of the doorway in the base of the tower. And there was Braesford and Isabel following after them, the baron cradling small Madeleine who chewed happily on her thumb, coming forward to welcome them to their home.

What followed was a confusion of laughter and tears

as sisters embraced, exclaimed and cooed over baby Madeleine's fine red-gold curls, talking so fast they tripped over their words, holding on to each other as if they had been parted for years instead of mere months. Cate and Marguerite made much over Isabel's condition, which showed as a nicely rounded hump under her accommodating gown. A little shorter than Cate, more blonde than Marguerite, Isabel bloomed in her prospective motherhood. Rand, tall and forbidding in repose, with his hair shining like a raven's wing in the sun, grinned as they teased him about being a father. His gaze seldom strayed from Isabel for long, however, and his gray eyes shone silver with love as they rested on his wife.

The curse had tested the two of them, Cate told herself as she looked from one to the other. Yet it had finally allowed them to be together. Might it not do the same again?

Through it all, Ross stood apart, his gaze watchful. That was until Cate turned to him, drawing him forward. She was astonished at the sudden swell of pride inside her as she began, "Allow me to present my husband."

Rand, Baron Braesford, took charge then, directing the men-at-arms to where they would be billeted, also assigning men to help Gwynne see to their female baggage. Immediately afterward, he swept them from the public court where laundry women and kitchen maids, blacksmiths, cobblers and lounging men-at-arms were being entertained by the reunion. With unconscious command, he ushered them up the tower's curving stair and into the vast comfort of his great hall.

Ale and wine were pressed upon them, though little

else, since it was not long until the main meal of the day. This small hiatus gave time for baths to be prepared, to remove the dirt of travel before they ate. While they satisfied their thirst, Ross and Braesford spoke of the situation along the Scots border, though Braesford's young squire, David, a blond gentleman with sapphire eyes and the face of a Botticelli angel, spent his time gazing at Marguerite. Cate and Isabel indulged in a fine gossip about the latest scandals, to which Marguerite contributed from time to time—when not slanting her brown eyes in David's direction. In due course, the sisters were shown to their sleeping quarters.

Ross remained in the hall with Braesford, saying he would avail himself of the bathing tub when Cate was done. She was just as happy to be away from him for a short while, in all truth. They had been constantly in each other's company during the journey, which was enough of a trial in their present circumstances. But he had been like a bear with a sore paw. Nothing had pleased him during this last stage of their travel, not the state of the road, the slant of the sun, the queries from the patrols of the noblemen through whose territory they crossed, or requests for necessary halts. More than once, Cate had been forced to bite her tongue to keep from lashing out at him. All that kept her from it was knowledge of the responsibility that sat upon his shoulders.

To undermine his authority for the sake of venting her temper would have been the height of stupidity, yet it had cost her. She needed a few minutes to herself to soothe her frazzled spirits.

They had reached Braesford with no further sign

of Trilborn. The relief of it was intense; she could feel
the knots of strain melting from her neck and shoulders. Closing her eyes, she leaned her head back against
the edge of the linen-lined tub. She was so tired that
she could almost go to sleep here. She might have, too,
except the water was rapidly cooling and her stomach
rumbling with hunger. Gwynne would be returning soon,
as well, bearing clothing that was deliciously clean for
a change. She would expect to bathe her, and Cate was
in no mood for it, could not think of being touched just
now by anyone except Ross. Since he was unlikely to
return for the task, she took up the cloth and hard cake
of Spanish soap and began to bathe herself.

Ross owed it to his host to apprise him of the situation
with respect to Trilborn. Not that he thought the Englishman foolish enough to attempt an assault upon Braesford Hall; Trilborn preferred weaker, less well-guarded
targets. Still, after his attempt to take Cate, it might be
dangerous for Braesford's good lady to ride without a
heavy guard. Lady Isabel was so similar in coloring and
size that she could easily be mistaken for her. More than
that, she had value as a hostage. It might take Ross's and
Braesford's combined efforts to prevent Cate from riding
out to exchange herself for her sister under such circumstances, particularly as Isabel was with child.

The fire had been built up in the great hall, with its
gridded and painted ceiling high above a stone floor
laid with fresh rushes. The walls were hung with arras
depicting a hunt of mythical beasts, as well as with ancient banners, swords and helms. The solid table on the

dais was being set and trestles put together. The baron paid no attention, but sat with his feet stretched out to the fire while he played with the silky ears of the hound lying beside him. A keen look glimmered in his eyes as he glanced at his guest, but he made no effort to draw him out.

Ross spent some small amount of time lauding the holdings of his host and asking if there was aught he could tell him of Grimes Hall, Henry's gift. Braesford knew the property well, as it happened. His own lands had come from the king after the battle of Bosworth placed Henry on the throne, so he had some idea of the questions in Ross's mind. Without prompting, he gave him a fair notion of the size and value of his new holdings, and offered good counsel on a number of issues.

In due course, a small silence settled between them. Ross drained his tankard and sat turning it in his hands, his gaze on the leaping orange flames under the heavy mantel. "You'll be wondering, I expect, how I came to wed Lady Catherine," he said finally.

Braesford lifted a brow. "If you think I stand as guardian in any sense to Isabel's sister, banish the notion."

"Nay, not that. I know well she is a ward to Henry. But you may be of a mind to know how I came into it."

"As to that, my lady and her sisters were convent educated. All read English, French and Latin, and write a hand far fairer than any I can produce. Cate has kept us apprised of events at Greenwich and Shene."

The dry note in his host's voice sent a tingle down the back of Ross's neck. "All of them?"

"I take leave to doubt that, but enough." Braesford allowed himself a smile. "We know the command to the altar came of a sudden. What we don't know is what has brought you here so soon after it."

Ross frowned. "If it isn't convenient to have us, you have only to say—"

"Peace, brother, no Scots touchiness is required. You are more than welcome, as Isabel has been longing to see Cate and Marguerite. I'm glad to leave off finding excuses for why she must not ride to London in her present condition."

Brother. Ross supposed they were that, in a way, being related now by marriage. The idea was not unpleasing. If he had been blessed with a brother a year or two older, it would have been fine to have one like Braesford. Emboldened by the exchange, he set out the adventure of their journey.

"So there is substance to the rumors of rebellion," Braesford said with a frown when he was done.

"Aye, according to the reports of Henry's agents. He plans to present the young duke of Warwick to prove the boy being touted as a lost prince is an imposter, for all the good it may do."

"As he may face invasion whether the boy brought forth is Plantagenet or pretender."

"And so I was sent in haste to ask that you man the beacon that tops your pele tower, and send to your neighbors to do the same."

"I stand ready to comply, of course," Braesford replied with some irony, "though I daresay it was a command."

Ross tipped his head in mute agreement.

"As was your marriage. What say you to it now?"

"Needs must."

"The Tower having no appeal? I do understand."

Ross gave him a straight glance. "You endured it, so I've heard."

"Oh, aye, though not because I objected to taking Isabel to wife. Never was there anything I wanted more, then or now."

It was a strong man who could admit such weakness for a woman. The contentment in Braesford's voice was unmistakable, however.

"You were in love with her before..." Ross stumbled to a halt. "Nay, I should not ask. 'Tis none of my affair."

Cate's brother-in-law chuckled. "I was. I am. But you have the curse in mind, I'll warrant. You've survived it, so need not worry."

"I'm not worried," Ross answered, then lifted a shoulder. "Well, but what think you? Is it a true threat?"

"They believe it so, Isabel and her sisters."

"That's nay the same thing, is it now?"

Braesford eased lower in the chair, crossing his long legs. "A man's mind can play strange tricks. Thinking a thing can sometimes make it so. Have you not seen the like?"

"Aye, I suppose." His own certainty that he was meant to die in his bath by an assassin's knife touched Ross for an instant. "A prophecy can also be made to come true."

Braesford turned a pointed look upon him. "Meaning?"

"An unsuitable groom could be removed," he continued in dogged determination.

"You think Cate wanted you dead?"

Put in such blunt words, it seemed unlikely, yet there was still the image of her poniard, gleaming as it fell into the bath. Ross explained in a few blunt phrases.

"What of Trilborn?"

"I don't discount his fine hand in it, though he had been sent away from Shene Palace."

"At least you have that much sense," his brother-in-law said with a growl in his voice.

Ross refused to back down. "I am tied to a woman who expected me to die from the moment the king decreed the wedding. No one would have been surprised if I did. What could be easier than giving the curse a helping hand?"

"Yet you live. You are wed."

"By luck and vigilance."

"Think you Cate preferred another, and that's her reason for having you killed?"

The specter of Leon, the French master of revels, flitted through Ross's mind. It took an effort to unclench his teeth enough to make an answer. "I know not."

"It can't be Trilborn. I know him of old, though his holdings are more to the west." Braesford sent Ross an assessing glance. "She must needs be a fool to take him over you, and Cate is no fool."

"By the saints, no! She despises him, and with good reason." Ross was sure of this much after her trembling relief at not falling into his hands on the night spent at the monastery.

"He would have her, regardless."

"Oh, aye, and enjoy it for that reason," Ross answered with contempt. "Though he claims to be besotted."

"Is he?"

"Could be it's her Graydon inheritance that enthralls him. Though you will know this, as your wife has a third of it."

Braesford let that pass as he continued his thought. "So Trilborn must kill you now to get to it, and abduct Cate so the king may see fit to hand her and her inheritance over to him. Naturally, he will rape her to make it more likely."

Ross's hand curled into fists so tight his knuckles ached. Such forced alliances were by no means uncommon. "As you say."

"For some men, passions such as avarice and rapine are enough. What of you? Have you no feelings for Cate? Did you have none before your vows were spoken?"

Ross gave him a hard stare.

A low laugh sounded in Braesford's chest. "Oh, aye, not my affair."

Quiet descended that was really not quiet at all, but carried an undercurrent of the whining wind that whipped around the battlements, the quiet crackle of the fire at their feet, low murmurs from the butlery and pantry where the meal was being prepared, and muted thumping where trestles were being laid with trenchers somewhere behind them.

The two men stared into the flames until finally Braesford stirred, spoke in low consideration. "As I see it, you have two choices."

"And they would be?" Ross could not forebear to ask, though he was wary of the answer.

"You can leave your bride behind here at Braesford

while you take up your new lands without encumbrance, or you can see to it she would rather have you alive than dead."

Ross considered it. He thought with immense concentration of being free of Cate as his wife, of leaving her with her sister and never holding her, never taking her into his arms and his bed again. He thought of it for the span of an entire breath.

"With your permission, I will leave her here while I inspect this Grimes Hall, as I know not what I will find there." The place might be a ruin for all he knew of it, fit only for vermin. It might be overrun with men-at-arms awaiting his arrival. It might have no bed worthy of the name, much less of Lady Catherine.

"And then?" Braesford said in soft inquiry.

"And then I will keep her close beside me, the better to know her every move."

Amusement gleamed silver bright in Braesford's eyes. "I see."

Ross feared that he did see, and all too well. He was married to the eldest of the Three Graces, after all.

15

Ross left her behind at Braesford. It should not have mattered, but it did.

Cate knew the reasons well enough. Her husband had laid them out for her in brusque yet ample detail on the evening before. He knew not what he might find when he reached Grimes Hall, he said. Trilborn could be lying in wait if he had learned what manse had been Henry's gift. It might still be occupied by its former owner, some attainted Yorkist who refused to acknowledge Henry's right to transfer ownership, and so must be removed by force. Villagers could have taken shelter there while it remained empty, might have used it to pen their cattle or else half demolished the walls for building stones. The well that supplied the castle with water might be tainted or poisoned. Certainly, it was unlikely there would be anything edible in the larder, or a stick of furniture left unbroken.

So it had gone, a litany of possible disasters. She would be far better at Braesford, where it was safe and comfortable, according to her husband.

Ross had not looked at her as he spoke, however, nor

had he expressed regret that she was not to see her new home. She was expected to be patient until he decided it was both safe and worthy of her.

The last thing she felt was patient.

She was no pampered female incapable of dealing with inconvenience. She had been taught by the nuns to achieve order in a household, to make certain a kitchen was scrubbed and well supplied with victuals, and that nothing offensive was allowed to remain in the entrance court. After years of being restricted in her activities while a dependent at Graydon and at Henry's court, she had looked forward to ordering everything as she wished in her own realm. To be prevented was a bitter disappointment.

She might have insisted on going if not for the obvious fact that her husband did not want her with him. It was possible he was as ready to be free of her company as she had been to escape his. Her need had been momentary, however, not a matter of days or even long weeks.

"Men," she said under her breath, where she stood with Isabel on the battlements, watching as Ross and his men-at-arms grew smaller in the distance.

"Just so," her elder sister answered. "If he could, Rand would have me lie abed from now until our babe is born."

Braesford had ridden out with Ross for some small distance before turning aside to attend to some problem concerning a flock of sheep. He also meant to ride along the blue line of the sea in the distance, on his way to visit neighbors with pele towers like his own. Isabel had wanted to join him, but been dissuaded. She and Cate were to remain within the walls until they were certain Trilborn was not in the neighborhood. The last thing he wanted, Braesford had said, was to risk injury to his wife and their unborn child in a clash of arms, or while making a wild dash to safety.

"At least he cares," Cate said with a sigh.

"And Ross does not?" Isabel turned to frown at her.

"How can he when the match was forced upon him?"

"But then…"

"I know, I know. By what means has he escaped the curse? I wish I knew."

Her sister's face cleared. "How a man may feel and what he may admit of it can be two different things."

Was it possible? Cate would like to think so. The way Ross touched her, the tender care he lavished upon her, felt as if it were directed by more than mere desire. He had been most ardent the night before, and early this morning, as well, making love to her in ways that stirred her blood now to remember. It was as if the bonding of their bodies must last him for some time, maybe even forever.

"Cate, my sweet, you are blushing. Pray tell from what cause."

"Nothing," she said, lifting her face to the wind to cool it. To prevent further questions, she went on. "Should we go inside? You must not become chilled."

"Don't you start fretting over me! I am as healthy as any peasant woman who gives birth one day and winnows the fields for grain the next."

She appeared so, Cate had to admit. "Have you any idea when your babe will be born?"

"In May, by my reckoning." Isabel made a wry grimace. "It seems I caught the first time Rand and I made love."

Cate gave her a swift glance. "Does it often happen that way?"

"When both bride and groom are young and healthy and take pleasure in the act, so the old wives say, though less often when the man is older. Why? Do you think—but no, there's hardly been time to know?"

Cate gave a mute shake of her head.

"No." Isabel sighed. "I wish I might have been there for your wedding."

Hearing the regret in her sister's voice, Cate stepped closer to give her a swift hug. As the eldest of the three, Isabel had always felt responsible for her and Marguerite, always tried to protect them. It was she who had created the special bond between them.

Soon, now, she would face childbirth. It was a dangerous time for a woman. Cate prayed all would go well. For it to turn out otherwise would be unbearable.

Would she be fearful in Isabel's place? Would she dread bringing Ross's child into the world? She hardly knew, yet the thought of a child gave her a warm feeling around her heart. A baby, a son with his father's black hair and fathomless blue eyes. He would grow tall and sturdy and brave.

Yes, and he would ride off to war with a shield on his arm and his sword by his side, while she ached with dread for what might happen to him. Just as she ached now, thinking of what Ross might find when he reached Grimes Hall, his prize from Henry.

And how she had come to that thought, she had

no idea. It wasn't at all what she wished to feel as she watched him disappear from sight.

"Do you think he will return?" she asked in stark doubt.

"Rand? But of course he will."

"Ross, I meant. And there is no 'of course' about it. He may have left me here with no idea of coming back for me."

"Surely not."

"No, but how can I know?"

Isabel studied her a long moment. "What you are really asking, I think, is how you can be sure he cares about you."

"Or if he may in the future," she whispered.

"Because you love him?"

Her smile was crooked. "I must, or it would not hurt so much to be left behind."

Isabel twined her arm around Cate's waist, holding her closer. "There is only one way I know to persuade him to it, and that is to be loving yourself. Men are sometimes like the mirrors made by silversmiths. They can be hard and cold, even the best of them, but if kept well polished, will reflect back what they are shown."

"And the worst of them?"

"Are to be guarded against, for they are not worth the tears they cause a woman to shed."

Best or worst—which was Ross? Cate thought she knew, but how could she be certain?

Time closed in upon Braesford Hall. Days slid past, becoming weeks, a month, then two, with little to set them apart. Winter loosened its grip and spring crept over the hills. The guards who kept watch near the iron basket of wood that topped the pele tower came and went, with never a need to kindle it into flame. The men who patrolled the walls had nothing to report. An occasional neighbor rode up to pass the time of day or share a meal, but no strange riders were seen and Trilborn did not appear. Little was heard from Ross, though he did send word that he had arrived. He had met with no opposition, but the hall was a shambles and required much work to put all in order.

Cate was spinning, with her wheel set up in a corner of the great hall, on the day fresh news from London reached them. It came by way of the earl of Peverell, who stopped with them for a night while on his way north. He and Braesford seemed not to notice her presence as they sat talking soon after the earl arrived, or else Rand thought she should hear. At least he made no effort to send her away or even lower his voice.

The rebellion had ceased to be a matter of rumor alone. The priest who claimed to have discovered the Plantagenet princeling, the young earl of Warwick, had appeared with him in Ireland. The boy was presented to the Yorkist faction in Dublin, and by early April, received promise of their backing. This group included the powerful earl of Kildare and his brother, who had no love for Lancaster kings.

With this solid support in the offing, there were rumblings of sedition in Devon and Cornwall. Henry had paraded the true Warwick through London in an effort to calm the situation, but it seemed to make little difference. He then held a council at Shene to form a strategy to deal with the crisis. One result of this meeting was a general pardon for all offenses against the crown resulting from Bosworth, including high treason. The point was obviously to persuade those who might be at odds with his reign to avoid joining the forces against him. Afterward, he had embarked upon an extensive progress through the countryside in hope of quieting the unrest.

The threat of war stalked the land again, so it seemed as it had so often in the past years of conflict between York and Lancaster. It gave Cate a sick feeling in the pit of her stomach to think about it. What manner of pride and lust for power caused men to fight so easily? What made them hack and slice at each other, then hunt down the defeated like vermin when the battle was done, chopping off heads as if ridding a harvest field of rats? It was blood madness of the most pernicious kind, a peculiar lust that fed on the fear of other men.

Did Ross know what was taking place, there where he was resetting stones and cleaning cow byres, or whatever he was doing that he had not returned for her? If so, what did he make of it? Yes, and what did he intend to do?

It was not his quarrel, this business between those who followed the white rose or the red. He was not English, so had little concern for who might or might not be king. Yet Henry had settled lands upon him that he might aid in holding the northern border. He would also expect Ross to take the field when and where he commanded.

And what would happen if Ross refused? Henry would no doubt strip him of his honors. He might be imprisoned as a traitor, or even executed if the king decided he had sided with Scotland to attempt his downfall.

James III had been silent so far on this business, but how long would he remain so? Any weakness in England's defenses could be seen as an opportunity.

Ross would be damned if he fought for England, and damned if he fought for his homeland. What could he do?

It was tempting to see this promise of war as the work of the curse, the means by which Ross would be finally removed as her husband. Cate shuddered at the thought, but it would not leave her.

She looked up as Isabel swept into the hall, followed by a manservant bearing a tray set with mulled wine, nutmeats, cheeses and marzipan candies. She moved with the grace of a ship with full sails, her features serene, her manner brisk yet kindly. Her sister was noticeably larger now than when she and Ross had first come, Cate thought. Was it possible her babe was due earlier than she expected? Or was she, by chance, to be delivered of twins? One possibility seemed as likely as the other.

Cate need not concern herself with such calculations. Her courses had come and gone, proving she was not with child.

Isabel's arrival provided a good excuse to pause in her work, leave the hall to the men. Cate set her spinning wheel aside and stood, brushing bits of cream-colored wool from the front of her skirt. As she looked up, ready to say something about duties elsewhere, she caught the glance that passed between her sister and her husband. As warm and intimate as a caress, it was a message of loving appreciation from Braesford to Isabel for her care of him and his guest.

Such a small thing, yet Cate felt painful anger rise up from deep inside her. She should be doing things of a like nature for her own husband, as chatelaine of his keep. She should be ordering her servants while tending the needs of his villagers, his guests and his friends. She should be working beside him to make the place he had been given livable, comfortable, a home. She should be receiving his smiles, yes, and his caresses.

But no, she was denied these, her rightful tasks, and her due as a wife. She was a charge upon her sister and her husband, as if she had never married. Cate was forced to fill her days with spinning and embroidery, and the occasional task Isabel was too large or clumsy to complete.

It was ridiculous.

It was not to be borne. She would bear it no longer.

Cate was forced to hold her peace through the remainder of the day and another night, however. She had need of Braesford's aid if she was to leave his hall, and he had no time to attend to her request while a guest was with them.

Early on the morning after Peverell finally left, Cate went in search of her brother-in-law. He was not in the great hall, but neither had he ridden out that day, according to his seneschal. She thought he might be in the solar, the fine chamber he shared with Isabel, and where she sat embroidering before the fire when not about other tasks.

Neither of them was there. Cate turned away, thinking the chamber was empty. At the last second, her attention was caught by a small movement near the window that overlooked the courtyard. It was Marguerite who stood there, her attention so concentrated on whatever was taking place below that she was oblivious of all else.

"Have you seen Braesford?" Cate asked as she walked closer, curious to see what held her sister's attention.

Marguerite jumped a little, and then waved toward the window. Cate, stepping to her side, leaned to peer through the distortion of the glass.

Two men were sparring with sword and shield in the court below. One was Braesford, she saw, while the other was a stripling whose blond hair shone silver-gold in the spring sunshine.

"But that's…" she began.

"David, yes," Marguerite finished in strained distress.

Cate turned back to watch Braesford and his young squire have at each other as if mortal enemies, with blades that clanged and chimed and dripped sparks as they scraped edge to edge. The men had stripped to shirts, braises and hose, and the fabric clung to heavy musculature that was usually concealed by the fullness of doublets and tunics or swinging capes. Raw power was manifest in every hard stroke that squealed against metal or thundered upon the shields on their left arms, in every swift advance and controlled retreat. The combatants gave no quarter and asked none as they slashed and grunted, attacked and parried, cursed and defended.

Braesford was magnificent, Cate had to admit, a marvelous figure of a man and an excellent swordsman. David was holding his own against him, however, an indication of how much he had progressed since becoming Rand's squire. His shoulders had broadened, and hard muscle encased his arms, outlined by his damp linen. He would be a formidable man one day.

She glanced at her sister, wondering at her rigidity. Marguerite's gaze was fastened upon the squire. Her face was pale, her breathing uneven, and a fine dew of perspiration shone on her upper lip.

"Marguerite?" Cate touched her arm as concern burgeoned inside her.

Despair shadowed the dark brown of her sister's eyes. "He'll kill him. I know he will."

"You must not worry so. I'm sure Braesford is more than a match—"

"Must he maim David in order to make a knight of him?"

Marguerite's concern was for the squire. He had been injured: Cate saw it now, though she had not noticed the patch of red on his arm until that moment. It was not a fatal cut by any means, yet such things were always dangerous. Blood poisoning carried off more men after a feat of arms than ever fell in battle.

"It's the way of these things," she said with a helpless gesture. "How else is he to learn to use a sword? He must grow so accustomed to the cut and thrust of it that it becomes second nature. As you saw with Ross, when we were set up at the ford, there is no time to think when you are attacked."

"I know, but it's terrible to watch." Marguerite's face was set in lines of tragedy.

"Come away then." When she didn't move or even appear to hear, Cate gave her a speculative look. "You fear that much for him?"

"Who would not?" Her sister finally glanced away. "At this rate, he'll die before he can win his spurs."

"Is that what he wants, to be a knight?"

"It's all he's ever dreamed of. He's so serious about it, thinks of little else. He was a foundling, you know, brought up in a convent after being left at the gate."

"It happens all too often."

"Now he has this grand plan to win a fortune and great renown in the tournaments of Europe, and nothing can be allowed to stand in his way."

"An admirable goal, surely?"

"Not if that's all there is for him."

It was unlike Marguerite to notice such things. Or was that unfair? Her younger sister had always been quiet, ethereal, preferring to keep to herself. They had grown used to leaving her alone, she and Isabel and most everyone else. How could they know what might occupy her thoughts?

It seemed she thought a great deal about Braesford's young squire. It was something to keep in mind.

The contest below came to an end as Braesford, with abrupt power, disarmed David. He bent to pick up the squire's sword as it clanged and slid, coming to rest against his boot toe. Holding both that weapon and his own in his hand, he slung an arm over David's shoulders, shook him a little and said something that made the young man laugh. The two of them turned and walked away in the direction of the stables.

"At least it's over for now," Cate said in encouragement.

Marguerite sighed. "Yes, for now."

Her hope of speaking to Braesford was over, as well, at least for the moment. He and David would require a bath, by which time the main meal of the day would be ready. Afterward, the master of the hall usually rode out from the keep, galloping away in the direction of the sea to make certain all was well on his lands. She would be lucky if she saw him again before dark.

In the event, it was the next morning before she was able to capture his attention. She came upon him as he started down the stairs to the hall.

"Sir Rand!" she called out, running the last few steps to catch up with him.

"Lady Catherine," he said with a polite bow, though wariness slid across his features as he turned to face her. "How may I serve you?"

"I would ask if you had thought of paying a visit to the property Ross received from the king."

Irony rose in the gray of his eyes for that artful suggestion. "Nay, milady, not without invitation."

"But have you no curiosity to see what he's done with Grimes Hall?"

"Very little. And you?"

"Much," she said succinctly. "I wondered if I might prevail upon you to act as my escort, should I decide to inspect it."

His eyes narrowed a fraction. "It appears to me you have already decided."

"And if I have?"

"I regret that I am unable to accommodate you. Isabel must be my first consideration just now. I could not risk being away when the babe is born. Above that, I am pledged to stand ready to warn of any invasion. It would be worth my head if Henry should be surprised by an enemy landing while I was absent from my post."

Both points were valid; still, she hated to admit defeat. "The distance isn't that great, only a day's ride if we don't dawdle."

"Also a night there and another day for the return. My deepest regrets, Lady Catherine, but I dare not."

He would dare without a backward glance, she thought with a certain cynicism, if the need was his or even Isabel's. "Given the short distance, a few men-at-arms should be sufficient protection. Could you not so order them, with mayhap the added guard of your squire?"

He tilted his head, his features unreadable. "David, is it?"

"I noticed just yesterday that he has gained considerable skill with a sword."

"His talent is God-given. What he has gained is the power to use it."

She smiled, seeing he had added to her argument. "Without a doubt."

"Nevertheless, the danger is great. Bands of men are everywhere, gathering for York, for Lancaster or for their own gain."

"I feel sure David is competent enough to see me there and back again in safety."

Rand watched her while swift consideration darkened his eyes. "You do intend to return then?" he asked finally.

"Unless my presence is required permanently."

He hesitated, then shook his head. "If Dunbar had required your presence, he would have sent for you. Meanwhile, I am entrusted with your security. I am persuaded your husband would not be pleased if I sent you to him without his leave."

Annoyance flashed over her, particularly as she had thought he was softening. "I could grow old and gray waiting for that!"

He lifted a velvet clad shoulder. "I would not come to blows with my brother-in-law and nearest neighbor because I allowed you to overrule my doubts and his wishes. This is between you and Dunbar."

"And he is a stubborn Scotsman too stiff-necked to admit I am more useful there than here! I appreciate your concern, sir, and am grateful for your care, but cannot permit myself to be governed by your fears for me."

"Can you not?" he inquired, the words edged in steel.

Apprehension slid down Cate's backbone. How did her sister deal with this man? He was as immovable as the stone steps nearby, almost as immovable as her husband. "I must go," she said in desperation. "The longer I stay away, the harder it will be to…to take him as my husband again."

"Never fear, milady," Rand, Baron Braesford, said with the ghost of a smile. "I misdoubt Dunbar will have any difficulty whatever taking you to wife."

If that observation was meant to reassure her, it missed its mark. She was not reassured at all.

Since Braesford refused to escort her or direct David to undertake the duty, then she would have to make other arrangements. All she had to do was put her mind to the problem.

Difficulties abounded, however, as she discovered

after discreet inquiries here and there. No man-at-arms would dare take her in charge without an order from Braesford; the mere idea was enough to make them blanch. Not a single stable hand would choose a mount for her, much less saddle it. With the current unrest, the gates were opened only at need, and a watch patrolled the battlements day and night.

If she had not spoken to Braesford, she might have convinced him of a sudden desire to go hawking, now that the weather had turned warmer and a green haze lay over the land. She could have ridden out with a groom and a pair or two of men-at-arms, and then persuaded them to accompany her by swearing to take full blame. As it was, she had little hope that her brother-in-law would be fooled, was certain her escort would be given strict orders to keep her close.

It was surely possible for her to saddle a mount without aid, lead it from the stables and let herself out of the keep through the postern gate. She would first have to slip past the hands who slept in the stable, however, and then elude the watch. Those men would all be punished if she managed it, a burden for her conscience. More than that, she was far from certain of the wisdom of going alone. Much of the way would be through open country. A woman riding through it without escort would stand out like a pimple on a courtesan's nose. That she would become instant prey for any outlaw or errant soldier who saw her was a given. To be caught and held for ransom was the very least of what she could expect.

The risk in going was not small, she saw that clearly.

Yet she could not bear to remain where she was, doing nothing while others decided her life for her.

She would go, and soon.

16

Cate put on a show of cheerful resignation. It seemed best if Braesford thought she had taken his refusal to heart and given up her intention. Meanwhile, she began her preparations.

Her first act was to stroll through the stables and discover the stall where Rosie was kept, also where she might find the saddle and other accoutrements. She took notice of the posts of the battlement guards, and the times of least activity around the postern gate. Food and drink had to be secured for her journey. This was a slow process, to make certain the provisions were not missed.

She could have asked Gwynne to see to these things, but preferred to do them herself. It was not that she didn't trust the serving woman, but rather feared she might let something slip to Marguerite or Isabel. Her sisters were discretion itself, but Isabel could decide the danger was too great to be allowed, and so go to Braesford.

Several times every day, Cate mounted to the battlements to stare in the direction Ross had taken. Her heartbeat increased as she reached that height, in her hope that she might see him returning, so her preparations would be for naught. The land remained empty, however, rolling in green waves to the slate-blue mountains.

On the day she had appointed, nearly two weeks after her talk with Braesford, Cate slid from her bed before dawn and dressed in the dark. Taking her cloth sack of provisions from its hiding place deep in the chest at the foot of the bed, she eased her door open and peered out into the empty corridor. Dim light shone from the staircase that led down to the hall, a reflection from the smoldering coals in the cavernous fireplace on one wall. Though she listened with care, the only sounds she heard were snores from the small chamber Gwynne shared with the serving women who looked after Isabel, and a few from the men-at-arms who slept in the great hall. She stepped out, closing the door soundlessly behind her in hope of discouraging too early notice that she was missing.

Her footsteps barely whispered along the stone floor as she made her way down the short corridor. Every sense was painfully alert, her pulse leaping under the skin, her heart shuddering in her throat. The head of the stairs appeared in front of her. She shifted her burden to her left hand, reaching for the heavy railing as she put her foot on the first step.

The cry came the instant her toes touched the tread. It was faint and oddly disembodied, echoing like the hollow moan of a ghost.

Cate ceased to breathe. Her every muscle seized.

Another moan followed the first. It seemed to come from the far end of the corridor, where it ended at the garderobe set into the wall, with its latrine in one corner.

Cate thought it had a familiar timbre. She turned toward the sound, listening with painful intensity.

It came again.

Isabel!

Cate whirled and ran toward the garderobe. Pushing through the door that stood half-open, she almost stumbled over her sister. Isabel was slumped on the floor, one shoulder against the wall for support. As she slowly raised her head to look at Cate, the faint light from the hall showed her face pale and sweating and her eyes glazed with pain.

"What is it?" Cate demanded, dropping her sack as she flung herself to her knees beside her sister. "Did you fall? Are you hurt?"

"The baby," Isabel gasped. "My stomach was cramping. I thought... My water broke. The baby is coming."

Cate saw then that Isabel sat in a widening puddle of liquid tinted red with blood. A strangled gasp caught in her throat. It was too early by almost a month for her sister to go into labor.

"Gwynne! To me!" she shouted in terror, an unconscious echo of a battle cry. "Braesford! To me! To me!"

What followed was a nightmare of flaring torches, curses, running servants and moans. Braesford, barely decent in hastily donned braises, slammed into the garderobe and lifted Isabel in his arms, carrying her at a run to their bed, which was raised on a dais in the solar. He stripped away the quilted coverlet and laid her upon the mattress, roaring out orders in a hoarse voice while fear darkened his eyes. It was Gwynne who pushed him away, shoving him out the door while instructing one serving woman to build up the fire, another to bring old linen set aside for the event, another to set water to boiling and Cate to bring her a bag of simples.

They stripped Isabel, washed her and wrapped her in soft, worn linen. Gwynne mixed a weak tincture of honey, herbs and warm, watered wine, and bade Isabel drink it. The birthing chair was brought from a storehouse. Then they prepared to wait.

The pains grew regular as dawn rose and daylight glowed beyond the shutters that covered the glazed windows. They came closer together near noon. As the day waned and still they continued, Braesford cursed at Gwynne and pushed her aside when she would have kept him from the solar. His presence seemed to give Isabel strength. A mere half hour after he joined her, she gave a final gut-wrenching push while gripping her husband's hands so tightly her nails cut him to the bone. Her child slithered from her body, a perfectly formed boy. He was small but mighty; his voice raised in raging protest at his entry into the world was enough to frighten the rooks from their tower perches.

Cate could not prevent tears from seeping down her face as she saw her sister's joy and Braesford's pride and fervent relief that the ordeal was done. An ache throbbed in Cate's abdomen, as well, an odd sympathetic emptiness. It was impossible not to imagine what it would be like to present Ross with so fine and lusty a son. Would her husband be glad or sorry? Would he care? Yes, and would it affect him at all to think she might have died while giving birth?

A short time later, when Isabel finally slept with her babe in her arms and Braesford watching over her, Cate slipped away. She retrieved her sack of supplies from the garderobe. Returning it to the chest where it had been hidden, she closed the lid upon it.

She could not leave now, not while Isabel had need of her. Even if it were possible, she would not trouble her sister with worries over what might happen to her on her journey. The joy Isabel held was precious. It could end soon enough if the Yorkist faction forced Henry to fight. Nothing must mar this time with her husband and new son, nothing at all.

Weary beyond description, Cate bathed and ate a light meal in her room while darkness deepened in the courtyard beyond. A light spring rain had begun, pattering against the window. She lay listening to it, staring into the darkness, wondering if it fell wherever Ross might be sleeping. Finally exhaustion crept over her and she closed her eyes.

The dream was exhilarating, a beguilement of the senses that was disturbingly real. The scent of rain-washed, herbal freshness surrounded her. Caresses more vivid than mere memory sent heated pleasure from the tips of her breasts to the furrow between her thighs. Bare flesh, roughened with hair, glided against her so she murmured in her sleep, rolling closer. Her blood poured through her veins with the intoxication of strong mead. She was deliciously warm, in spite of the cool, hard surface she pressed against. It seemed natural to lift her knee, to rest it on a hard flank. She shivered, moaning with incredible gratification as hard heat entered her, and callused hands caught her hips and pulled her close until she surrounded it, clenched upon it as she came suddenly awake.

Ross inhaled with a hissing oath that was like a prayer. Cate tried to push away from him, but he gripped her with such uncontrollable need that he feared he left bruises. Her body held him, her internal muscles so tight around him that he ached, yet the completion was too perfect to relinquish. "Don't," he whispered against her hair, with its faint scent of roses. "Just...don't."

"What are you doing?"

"If you don't know," he said with a tired laugh, "then Braesford was right, and I've neglected you far too long."

She stilled in his arms, though the sharp breath she took drove the small, tight buds of her nipples into his chest. "Braesford?"

"Aye. He said I'd best come to you or he feared you would try to come to me. Knowing the determination of your sister, he feared you might succeed in escaping his guard."

"Did he indeed?"

"You needn't sound so surprised. He can't be everywhere, and he does have a few other things on his mind." Ross hardly knew what he said, for his attention was on the soft skin under his hand as he smoothed upward from her hip to her back in soothing circles. She relaxed a degree, so he was able to ease from her an inch or two and slide back again.

"Other more important things...I suppose," she said with a definite hitch in her voice.

"Different, that's all."

"He is a father. Isabel had her babe today."

"So he said, after he signaled the guard to open the gate for me."

Cate clutched at his arm with a small sound deep in her throat as he twisted his hips, gently circling, abrading the small nub of her greatest desire. "You were abroad late."

"I rode hard," he said, plunging a little, "and fast," he added with a short, swift pumping, "as I could not let you ride out alone. Would you have come to me, sweet Cate?"

She allowed her fingertips to roam over his chest, threading through the hair that grew there. Finding one flat, hard nipple, she ducked her head to lick it. Her breath warm against him, she said, "I meant to see your hall, to turn it into a decent place to live."

His disappointment was like a knife thrust. Heaving up, he flipped her to her back, shoving his hips between her thighs and spreading her legs wide so he filled her to the hilt. "And that's all?"

She sucked in a breath, tilting her head back. He thought she closed her eyes tight, though it was too dark to see. "Should...should there be more?"

"This," he said, and set a rhythm that sent the blood thundering through his veins, racing away from his brain and heart to his nether parts so fast he felt light-headed, delirious with the pounding, shuddering bliss. He plumbed her, learning anew the enthralling silken heat and depths of her, absorbing every surge she made toward him, taking it, taking her, having her as he had dreamed, had planned with every weary mile he rode in these past hellish hours.

He couldn't go deep enough, couldn't have enough of the feel of her against him, her thighs, the smooth surface of her belly, the tender yet firm globes of her breasts. He took her mouth in the extremity of his need, an additional possession, as if he could consume her in that manner if in no other. She was his, and no small corner of her would be unknown to him. He held the hard pressure of his need in unrelenting constraint, even as he felt the small contraction, the liquid heat of her release. It was too soon, too soon. Not enough, never enough. And even as his own release escaped him, as he felt the fierce explosion of pleasure beyond limit, he was still hungry for her, still longing, still afraid he might never have her again, as he had been afraid every second since he had received Braesford's message in hand.

No, it was not enough, and so he waited until her breathing slowed, until she was boneless in her relaxation against him. Then he began again. This time he was slow, thorough, tasting her essence in every hollow, suckling her breasts, licking, teasing and tempting until she writhed under him, moaning and calling his name in plea and demand. When he pushed into her, he went deep, hovering until he felt the hard throb of her heart deep inside, could count its beats against his own tender skin. He drove into her with carefully measured force, testing her depths again and again, until he saw red behind his eyes and his scalp felt on fire, until every muscle burned and his teeth ached from the effort of containment.

He let go then, but did not let her go. No, he was seated

inside her still when sleep took him. He would have stayed there until dawn except he shifted in his sleep, or she moved, and he slipped free.

He groaned in the depths of his dreams as he felt it.

Three days later, the drilling in preparation for war began.

Ross had brought with him the men Henry required from the lands given him, along with the horses, arms and supplies to support them. Well, he had actually ridden ahead in his impatience and fear that Cate might be riding into danger, had left his men to follow behind. His haste had caused no end of ribald comment among them, he was certain. He could ignore it as long as no one dared say anything to his face, or in front of Cate.

Gathering the company of cowherds, shepherds, field laborers, poachers, an itinerant knight or two and a few hill outlaws had been no easy task. He'd first had to estimate the number of men of fighting age in each village, and then decide who could be spared and who could not. At least they were no longer as green as when they'd first lined up for inspection.

The past three months had been spent putting them through their paces, trying to give them some familiarity with weapons and following orders. He'd no stomach for herding them onto the king's battlefield to be slaughtered without at least some idea of defense. For one thing, he had need of them to see to his lands in the years to come. For another, facing the mothers and wives of those who did not return was not his favorite part of a homecoming from raid or battle. Winning a degree of acceptance as their new lord from them, and the cooperation that went with it, had also seemed better than riding with a sullen company at his back.

Marching and countermarching, following the orders of Ross's captain of the guard, could only be beneficial to them. He should have brought them sooner, should have come sooner himself. That he had not was...

He wouldn't think of that.

Surveying Braesford's keep, his several villages near and far, the animals that grazed his field, his various craftsmen and the lands that were beginning to be cultivated for crops, Ross felt a new respect for the man Cate's sister had married. All was order, energetic activity and harmony. Every person in sight seemed to know what to do and be doing it without complaint. No one shirked or slouched about with a dullard, uncooperative mien, as had the villagers at Grimes Hall.

Things had started to improve by the time he left. Pray God he could return there before his labor was completely undone.

This time, he would take Cate with him, the consequences be damned.

"You've heard the king is on the move?"

Ross woke from his reverie, swinging toward Braesford where they sat their horses while overseeing their combined men at their drill. "A few tinkers' tales only."

"Word is he showed himself in the eastern counties during Lent, that being where rebellion seemed most likely to break out. At Easter he made a pilgrimage to Walsingham, for whatever blessing that might convey."

"Pious Henry," Ross said with a wry smile.

"God's truth. He apparently sent for papal bulls some time back, for they were duly read while he was in Coventry for the Feast of Saint George. Now all who rise up to resist his rule are cursed with bell, book and candle."

"A canny move, that."

Braesford dipped his head in assent. "It won't hurt to have the head of the church on his side. And he may need divine intervention. Margaret of Burgundy's German mercenaries have landed in Ireland. Some put the number at five thousand or more, though others say only two thousand."

"We did hear that," Ross said. "It seems a clear signal for war."

"The Germans arrived in good time to guard against interference while this boy they call a prince is crowned. He's to be Edward VI, with a new coin struck carrying his image."

"Sure of themselves, aren't they?"

"Or making every effort to appear that way."

Ross frowned as he considered the implications. "And Henry has made no effort to prevent all this?"

"None that I've heard, though that makes no odds. Henry, like Richard before him, and many another king of this isle, will doubtless wait for invasion."

"It will come," Ross said with conviction.

"Oh, aye. It's proved too successful in the past for it to be otherwise."

"Surely Henry will call up his forces beforehand."

"So he will, and I will go," Braesford said, his gaze assessing. "The question is, will you?"

Ross gave him a straight look. "I've done as Henry commanded so far."

"But will you fight?"

That was plain speaking. It was also a question Ross had answered for Cate, as well as asking it of himself a hundred times since leaving Shene Palace. England's wars were no concern of his. The more Sassenachs that killed each other, the better for his countrymen. Henry had threatened him with prison and forced him to the altar. What reason had he to aid the man?

And yet he liked Henry, with his constant labor for the crown and lack of regal airs. He had given him Cate and a fair and valuable property. He had played square, also, for a king. That was more than his own father, high-handed, hot-tempered old curmudgeonly laird that he was, had done. With Scotland and his patrimony lost to Ross, what was left? This new boy-king, Edward VI, and those who advised him were hardly likely to honor the pledges made by Henry VII. Ross could well lose what he held now by the king's grace.

"I'll fight for Cate," he said.

"Well spoken," Braesford said with a low laugh, and reached out to offer his hand in the pact of friendship.

It felt like a benediction. It felt as if he had come home.

Ross was not so in charity with his brother-in-law that afternoon, when they had a small set-to with swords and dirks. It was practice only, a fine bout of cut and thrust to keep them in fighting trim and with their reflexes well-oiled. Their weapons were not blunted, however, nor were their intentions.

Ross was no stranger to the game. He and his cousins had often indulged in such swordplay, and he had the scars to prove it—nothing like sundry slices here and there to teach a man to keep up his guard. He had faced off against Henry's yeoman guards now and then at court, as well, though he chose his opponents with care. Nick the wrong man, and it could become a killing affair; kill the wrong man, and it could mean the scaffold.

Braesford was more than a match for him. His skill was so lethal, in fact, that Ross's heart pounded against his breastbone in high exhilaration every second that they strove together. He fought with scant thought, advancing, retreating, attacking, parrying by instinct alone. Isabel's husband had a few tricks he'd not met with before, while he himself had a handful culled from an Italian who had wintered at his father's table and taught them in return for the hospitality. They exchanged these in mutual respect, circling, attacking, defending, while their muscles burned and sweat ran into their eyes and dripped from the ends of their hair. Their swords clanged like a pair of blacksmiths hammering at their anvils. They scraped and slithered, singing, clanking, glittering in the sunlight.

A crowd gathered to cheer them on, among them Braesford's squire, David, who stood with his hands on his hips and a frown on his handsome young face. Around him, the others placed bets, yelled encouragement. Insults were also exchanged as Braesford's men ranged themselves on the side of their champion and Ross's did the same.

It was David who put a stop to it. He said not a word,

but only stepped close and then jerked his thumb toward the battlements that rose above them.

Braesford followed his gaze with a fraction of his attention. Ross, catching his brother-in-law's blade on a cross made of dirk and sword, did the same.

Lady Isabel stood there, with Cate on one side holding her sister's newborn babe, and Marguerite on the other. Their veils blew around them in the late spring wind, and their skirts flew back behind them. The sun poured its pale gold light over them until they seemed to glow with it. Though they were too far away for the men to see their expressions, their very stillness, the set of their heads and stiffness of their shoulders, told its own tale. The ladies, unlike some, were not entertained by the prospect of imminent bloodshed, nor were they amused by the air of joyous mayhem.

A strong shudder ran down the back of Ross's neck. In that moment, he would have sworn the three females on the battlements had a touch of the divine about them, some sublime protection beyond the kin of mortal men. He'd have accepted without question that a curse had them in its keeping.

He slewed his head around to stare at his opponent, half fearful of a fatal blow coming at him during that instant of distraction. Braesford seemed as shaken as he, however.

They pushed away from each other with a single hard shove, downed their swords, whipped a salute and stepped back. Turning together, they walked in the direction of the tower that sheltered their wives.

"If you had killed Braesford," Cate said some time

later, speaking in conversational tones as she sat beside him at the evening meal, "Isabel would have spitted you herself, I do believe, and served your gizzard to you as a delicacy."

Ross slanted a glance at his wife, watching her between his lashes. "And you, my sweeting, what would you have done if he had dispatched me?"

"Applauded."

He had asked for it, yet the answer pained him more than he expected. "I might have guessed."

She looked away an instant, and then back again. "No, but truly, it was not well done by either of you when Isabel has just risen from childbed. Isn't it enough to fear you'll fall on the field of battle without having you try to annihilate each other?"

"It was because of the coming battle," Ross said shortly.

"Deliver me from the logic of men. It was bad enough watching David and Braesford hack at each other, though at least one of them had the sense to end it. You and Braesford seemed ready to carry it to the death."

Her cheeks were pink with her fury, her eyes like twin blue flames, and her breasts heaved in a way that hardened him to a state not unlike his sword blade. His lips twisted for an instant before he spoke. "Why such outrage, as you care so little?"

"A fine question," she answered, taking him up at once, "and here's another of like nature. Why such fervor in returning to my bed when you could not be bothered to send for me to join you?"

"That's a sore spot, is it?"

"I am your wife, so chatelaine of whatever keep you are pleased to call your base. It's my duty and privilege to set it to rights."

He shook his head. "Not this one."

"What do you mean?"

"It was a shambles, Cate. The walls were falling down, the bailey one huge dung heap and the great hall a den for wild animals. There was not a tapestry that was not rotted or ripped to tatters, or a bed mattress that had not been pissed upon, if not worse. I could not ask you to live there."

She stared at him for a long moment while the heat died out of her eyes. "You lived in it."

"Only after I had made a fire in the bailey and thrown everything in it that would burn. Cate…"

She gave a small shake of her head. "It was a bad bargain then."

"Nay. The land is there, grand open stretches of it, as are the villages and the people. The wall has been mended, cottages repaired, the bailey and keep made wholesome again. The rest can be replaced in time."

"I can do that," she said, her eyes darkly blue as they rested upon him. "It would be my pleasure."

"Nay, that won't be necessary," he said with finality.

"I have the means, and it will be my home, too."

He could feel his anger like a hot coal in his chest. "I'll not be dipping into your money chest, heavy though it may be."

"Why not? Every other man in Christendom would feel it his right."

"Call me a stiff-necked Scot, but I'd rather place every

stone with my bare hands than be beholden for so much as a bread crust."

She narrowed her eyes at him. "Beholden to me, you mean."

"Aye."

"Pride is an excellent thing, but meanwhile I'm to have no part of it, no say in how things are to be arranged. You will decide all, while I remain here upon the charity of my sister and her husband."

Put like that, it did sound more than a little overbearing. That could not be helped. "Mayhap Isabel and Braesford will take your coin, but I can't. I won't."

"I can be your bedmate, possibly even the mother of your child, but not a helpmate."

His heart stopped. "You think you may be with child?" he asked, the words coming out in abrupt demand.

She shook her head so her veil shifted around her shoulders. "No, but continue as we are and—"

"Aye," he interrupted, more aware than he wanted to be of the bleak disappointment inside him. The thought of Cate carrying his babe had been with him since he caught sight of her on the battlement with Isabel's little one in her arms. It had seemed so natural, so right. He had wanted, with desperation more painful than a sword slice, to know she had his get under her heart when the call to war came.

It wasn't too late.

Heat rose inside him along with a fierce, stinging pressure that coalesced, throbbing, between his legs. He drank down his wine, set the glass back on the high table with a thump. "Mayhap we should."

"Should what?"

She met his gaze with a look of inquiry in her eyes, yet soft, wild rose color slowly tinted her cheeks. Something in his face must have given him away, for she knew, oh yes, she knew.

"Continue," he said around the knot in his throat. Pushing back his chair, he stood and held out his hand. Never had he been so glad of his plaid and sporran, which hid his rampant state.

The hot color in her face deepened. She sent a quick glance around the hall, as if to see if anyone paid attention to them. Then the smallest of smiles tipped her mouth. She gave him her hand.

It felt like a victory. Ross drew a breath so deep it hurt the back of his throat. Turning, he led her carefully from the hall.

17

Henry's call to arms came on a morning of sublime beauty, when the sun spread its mellow light upon the land, the tender green of new grass clover and bracken lay like velvet upon the hills, and birds swooped in delirious flight, singing on the wind. The herald lingered only long enough to present his message and wolf down bread, beef and ale. Then he raced away to the next keep.

At least the village women had sense enough to dread the news, Cate thought in despair. The young men seemed to view it as a holiday from labor, swaggering and boasting as they gathered under the command of their leaders. Ross and Braesford, by contrast, were methodical and grimly accepting. They also seemed to be everywhere, checking supplies and the carts that would transport them, assigning weapons, sending messengers here and there, deciding the order of placement between green recruits and veteran men-at-arms, and a thousand other details.

Soon, too soon, the line of march was ready. Mothers hugged their sons and men kissed their wives goodbye. Orders were shouted, and the column of soldiers levied by the king began to move. Dogs barked, running back and forth. Young boys trotted alongside the marching men. The villagers gathered along the road, calling, waving, while some few wiped their eyes or clasped their hands in prayer. The first rank began to gain distance along the road, tramping away to reach the king, who was at Kenilworth, where he had been joined by the queen and his mother.

They were going, and Ross had not said goodbye. Cate had lain abed while he dressed, watching as he pleated his plaid around him, strapped on his sporran and slapped his bonnet on his head, pulling it down on one side to make it snug. To distract herself from what he meant to do, she had wondered if he would ever fully adopt English dress, and thought it would be a loss if he did. She liked the view of his sun-bronzed knees she caught now and then, and the hard muscles of his calves.

She also liked the ease with which he could take her when the mood struck him, without any awkward fumbling with hose and points. It was a benefit she had discovered in these past days since he had returned.

He had kissed her, a brief brush of the lips, before he strapped on his sword and whirled out of the room. Pausing at the door, he had thrown her a tight smile, then was gone. She had not known it was for the last time before he went to war. She had thought surely he would come to her once more before he left.

Or was it possible he was waiting for her to come to him? From the battlement where she stood she could see a few horsemen pacing along with the marching men, but Ross was not among them, nor was Braesford or his

squire, David. She could not see into the court directly
below, in front of the pele tower, though she thought she
heard restless hooves on the cobblestones. Mayhap these
leaders lingered there for their goodbyes.

Turning in a swirl of skirts, Cate ran down the stone
steps, one hand against the rough wall for balance, then
raced along the corridors. The door of Isabel's solar stood
open as she passed. She glimpsed her sister inside, held
fast in the arms of her husband, along with their new
babe and young Madeleine, as he bent to her lips. Cate
did not pause.

She did break stride in the great hall. Marguerite sat
there on a bench. David was on one knee before her. He
held her hand in his while he bowed, pressing it to
his forehead in reverent intensity. Marguerite, a look of
stunned bemusement on her face, used her free hand to
touch his well-shaped, golden head with gentle fingers.

It was a farewell too private to be interrupted or even
witnessed. Cate turned away, running a few steps again
as she made toward the tower stairs that gave onto the
court. Then she stopped, dragging breath into her burning lungs.

Ross was emerging from the shadowed staircase. He
was coming toward her.

He reached her in a few strides, bringing with him
the scents of fresh air and leather, warm wool, heather
and horse. His eyes burned darkly blue, and his face was
hard with determination. His gaze rested on her mouth
as he caught her shoulders in his hands.

"Ah, Cate," he said, his voice rough, "I'd not go if I
need not."

"No," she whispered.

He stared down at her as if memorizing her face. His hands caressed her arms. Then his lips tightened. Abruptly, he bent and scooped her up in his arms. His strides long and swift, he carried her to the stairs, mounting them without pause. At their chamber, he strode inside and kicked the door shut, then stepped to place her on the side of the bed.

"Forgive me, sweet, but I must…"

"Yes," she said in breathless haste, reaching for his belt.

He caught her hands, stilling them, and then leaned to take the hem of her skirts and flip them into her lap. Pressing her back onto the mattress, he spread her legs and lifted his plaid.

He took her then in fast, hard possession, with a look on his face that was like pain. And Cate took him, as well, wrapping her legs around him as he pressed into her again and again as if trying to reach her very core. It was a furious joining, a mating both animalistic and divine. It was an affirmation of life, the defiance of fate and of death. And in the midst of it, as she felt the sweet internal shift, the sudden giving of her being at the apogee of desire, she knew she loved him, had loved him for weeks. She would love him forever, even if he never returned.

"Ross," she whispered.

"Ah, my Cate," he said, his breath warm in her hair.

Then it was over. He stepped back, adjusted his plaid, caught her to him for a last hard, deep kiss. He turned toward the door.

"Stay safe!" she called, the words almost strangled in the tears that clogged her throat.

He made no answer. Mayhap he did not hear.

In the space of a drawn breath, he was gone.

And it seemed to Cate, in that moment of aching loss, that now must be when the curse would finally strike, now when she could least bear it. Henry's battles in defense of his crown would be the instrument that must take Ross from her. What could be more likely?

What, indeed?

The days crept past, spring moved forward into early summer, the year turned with its cycle of plowing and planting, herding and shearing, carding, spinning and weaving. Flowers bloomed in the blowing grass, birds nested and berries ripened. All was as it should be, and yet nothing was right.

Isabel, as Braesford's wife, had been left in command of the keep. She was slow in regaining her strength after the early childbirth, however. As a result, much of the responsibility came to rest on Cate's shoulders. She formed the habit of riding out as Braesford had done, surveying the coast, overseeing the workers that remained to till the fields, and hearing the complaints of the villagers. The difference, of course, was that she never rode alone, had always a quartet or more of men-at-arms at her back, part of the complement left on guard duty.

It was while returning from one such circuit that her guard suddenly spurred forward to surround her. The captain, a grizzled, one-eyed veteran of tournaments and sundry wars on the Continent, flung out his arm as he drew even, pointing southward.

"Horsemen, milady," he said in his gruff way. "There, coming fast."

So it was, a mounted troop small with distance, riding beneath a drifting pall of dust. The sunlight glinted on mail, helmets and the tips of lances. It was possible they were friends, but were just as likely to be foes.

Braesford Hall stood on its prominence, a bastion of safety. The gates were open, however, allowing villagers to pass in and out. Cate stared from it to the approaching troop while her heart jarred against her lungs with a sudden hard beat, leaving her breathless.

"Ride!" she called out in a firm order, and set heel to her palfrey, leaning forward over its neck as she turned Rosie's head toward home.

The race was headlong, thunderous with the dull thudding of hooves, deafening with the rush of the wind. Sheep fled from their path. Clods were thrown high behind them. A cowherd's dog ran after them, snapping at their heels. Ahead of them, the guards at watch on the battlement gathered, pointing away behind them. As they drew near the keep, Cate saw men running to man the gate, to don armor, to snatch up weapons. Women flew after their children, bundling them out of harm's way, while dogs leaped, barking in excitement, and pigs ran squealing for cover.

Then Cate and her guard were sweeping over the drawbridge, under the portcullis and through the gate, rattling to a halt in the courtyard. The heavy barrier slammed shut behind them and the portcullis rumbled down, its teeth clanging into place. The babble and cries that greeted them died away, and all was quiet within Braesford's walls.

Hoofbeats pounded closer outside. They slowed to a halt. A shout rang out.

"Hallo the keep! Lord Trilborn begs leave to enter. He would hold converse with Lady Catherine and her sisters, the Three Graces of Graydon!"

Trilborn.

Cate heard the name with disbelief. Trilborn here, while Braesford and Ross were away.

"What does he want?"

It was Isabel who asked, coming from the tower door as Cate stepped off her palfrey at the mounting block. Her sister's features were set in lines of distaste. Trilborn had never been a favorite of hers, and hearing from Cate of how he had attempted to force marriage upon her had made him even less so.

"I've no idea," Cate answered. "He should be with the king's forces."

Isabel's face lost even more color. Her voice was tight as she spoke. "Do you suppose he has news?"

It was a pertinent question. Anything could have taken place since the men of Braesford and Grimes Hall had departed: an accident on the road, an attack by stray York forces, even a pitched battle. The only way they would learn of it was if someone sent to let them know.

"Hallo the keep!"

At this second call, Cate spun from where she stood and ran to the open stone staircase that led to the top of the keep's curtain wall. Her foot was on the first tread when she realized Isabel was behind her. Retreating, she allowed her sister to go first, not only because she was true chatelaine at Braesford, but also to make certain Isabel did not grow dizzy and fall. Before they reached the top, Marguerite came running from the tower entrance and pounded up behind them. Together, the three of them followed the walk, passing behind the men-at-arms who stood armed and ready, and stopped above the milling horsemen beyond the drawbridge.

Trilborn spied them before they could speak. Removing his helm, pushing back his mailed hood so it gathered around his neck, he swept them a bow from the saddle. "Lady Catherine, Lady Isabel, Lady Marguerite, I give you good day," he called up. "Pray open to weary travelers who have need of your kind hospitality!"

Isabel, every inch the mistress of the Braesford hall, stared down at him in cool hauteur. "What is your business, sir?"

"Why, nothing, fair lady, except to visit with old friends and mayhap bring news you would wish to hear."

"What news?" Cate demanded. "Has there been a battle?"

"Not yet, Lady Catherine, but soon."

"You have word from my husband?" Isabel asked tightly.

"Nay, milady. Why would you think so?"

Isabel turned to Cate, her eyes wide. Braesford might have no more use for Trilborn than the rest of them, but would never have let him ride north without sending a written message. That was, of course, if they had been with the same army.

"It's a trick," Marguerite murmured, with the certainty of an oracle in her voice.

It seemed all too likely.

"We are puzzled, milord," Cate said, clenching her hands on the stones of the wall as she looked over it. "Why are you not with the king's forces?"

"At Henry's command, I journey far and wide to gather more to his standard. It is thirsty work, Lady Catherine."

Such a thing could be true, for Henry had sent him on a similar errand while they were at Shene. But was it?

"Don't let him in," Marguerite whispered to Isabel.

"At least, not with his men," Cate added, so quietly only her sisters could hear.

"Fair ladies, I beg you!"

Isabel turned back to the supplicant below. "We would hear your news, Lord Trilborn, my sisters and I. We invite you to sup with us, if you will leave your men outside."

"Have mercy, Lady Isabel," Trilborn said, a scowl drawing his brows together as he stared up at them. "They have been long on the road, and crave those comforts to be found within your fine walls."

"And we are desolated to withhold them, but what would you?" Cate said in mournful tones. "The best we can do is lower ale, beef and bread. The country is unsettled, and we are three females alone. You must allow for our womanly fears if you wish to join us within our walls."

Trilborn didn't like it; that much was clear. Still, he agreed in the end. Sending his men to camp in a nearby hollow, he entered upon his destrier and surrendered himself to their hospitality.

Cate dressed with care for the repast that was to come, selecting her wedding gown of green velvet, as it was the most sumptuous in her possession. She allowed Gwynne to tint her cheekbones with color and add berry-redness to her lips. Deliberately, she pulled her girdle tight, while bending from the waist to encourage a deeper valley between her breasts at the neckline of her bodice.

She thought of these preparations as similar to donning battle armor. Trilborn was at Braesford Hall for a purpose, and she meant to engage him in verbal skirmishing until she discovered what it might be.

That was all, however. Trilborn had been accorded the honor of having a bath prepared for him. By rights, Isabel should have attended him, but used her weakness after childbed as an excuse to avoid it. Cate might have offered to take the duty, but sent a serving woman instead. No matter how much she longed to know why Trilborn was here, she was not so big a fool as to be closeted alone with him while he was unclothed. Letting him into the keep was dangerous enough.

Shortly thereafter, Cate and her sisters were seated at the high table with their guest. Florid compliments tripped off his tongue without letup. All three ladies came in for their share, while Trilborn preened in the manner of a lone rooster among a flock of hens. With Marguerite on his left, Isabel on his right and Cate beyond her, he smoothed his chin, played with a lock of his hair and stretched his shoulders back to display his chest under a doublet of wine velvet embroidered in silver.

Cate, watching the expression that flitted over Isabel's face, was not surprised at the curl of distaste that formed at the corner of her mouth. Nor was she amazed when her sister went on the attack.

"What brings you here, sir? You can't think we have men to send to Henry's aid. My husband has joined him with his complement, as has Cate's bridegroom."

"Oh, I am come to see Lady Catherine," he answered at once, "as it was no great distance out of my way. There is a matter left unfinished between us."

Isabel gave him a frown. "I believe not. My sister is married, and that's an end of it."

"Not if her husband dies," he said in silken suggestion.

"Sir!"

"But let us not quibble over details. I am still in need of a bride, and have a taste for the Graces of Graydon. Now that I see your younger sister, I am inclined to pay her my addresses."

Marguerite, just taking a sip of her wine, choked and coughed. Before she could prevent it, a spray of wine bejeweled the doublet of their guest, lying like droplets of blood on the purple-red velvet.

"Forgive me!" she said in a croak. Her ale-brown eyes were wide with horror, though whether for Trilborn's suggestion or the desecration of his clothing, it was difficult to say.

Cold displeasure sat on their guest's brow. He used

the tablecloth pooled in his lap to wipe at the wine with quick, hard strokes.

"Marguerite has sworn not to wed," Cate said quickly, in hope of diverting his attention, "a most solemn vow."

"So I have," Marguerite seconded with vigor as she blotted her mouth on the hem of her veil. "I am also under the protection of a most dedicated knight."

"You are?" It was Cate's turn to be amazed, while Isabel blinked at their younger sister.

"David has sworn a most solemn oath to be my shield and buckler," she answered, having raised the young squire to knighthood with a fine disregard for reality. "His love for me is pure and true, a perfect example of a knight bound to the service of his lady."

"Service." Trilborn's laugh had a salacious edge, and he licked his moist lips. "I'm sure of that."

"So you may be," Marguerite answered, lifting her firm chin. "He has sworn to protect me from all things, asking only that I allow him the honor."

So that was the meaning of the tender scene she had glimpsed, with David on one knee before her younger sister, Cate thought. How very gallant it sounded, but also how young and idealistic. In keeping with the tenets of devotion handed down from the Courts of Love of ancient Aquitaine, a knight might attend his ladylove in all ways, but the relationship must be of the spirit rather than the flesh.

"And you return his ardor?" Trilborn inquired.

Marguerite arched a brow. "That is for me to know. The point is that there is no bride for you here."

"A noble fool," Trilborn said, lowering his eyelids so

they shielded his expression. "Loyal, too, no doubt." It was clear he gave no credence to her protests.

"You disdain loyalty, sir?" Isabel inquired, drawing back a little in her chair.

"That depends on the object of it, milady."

"And the man?" Cate took up the question, partly to spare Marguerite, but also out of curiosity. "Surely you are loyal to the king?"

Trilborn glanced at the remaining Braesford men-at-arms who lined the table below them, eating with rough haste and a low mutter of male badinage. Pitching his voice so it could not be heard above the melodious tune of the minstrel's harp, he said, "Since you ask, I will admit I lack a proper sense of fealty toward our Lancaster sovereign. I was promised the defunct title of earl of Graydon, along with you and the property that went it. Henry snatched these from my grasp at the last minute for the sake of a deeper game. What allegiance do I owe someone who played me false, a usurper with only the weakest claim to the throne, based on a union between a long dead prince and his concubine?"

"If you mean Henry's ancestor, John of Gaunt, he married his ladylove when he was able, and legitimized his children. Yes, and Henry won his crown on the field of battle, a sign of divine will." It was clear Trilborn felt free to admit his fault because he considered her and her sisters of trifling importance, Cate thought, three women far from the arena of important events and helpless to effect them. The arrogance of it fired such anger inside her that she felt scorched by it.

Their guest made a dismissive gesture. "So he likes to claim."

"You might live to regret it, should you join those allied against him," Isabel suggested, the scraping sound of her voice suggesting a similar rage behind her cool demeanor.

"Think you so? I am not impressed by the army he gathers around him. Mercenaries from the best armies of Europe will support the young king crowned under York's white rose. They are a tough, disciplined force that will cut through Henry's men like a scythe through wheat stalks."

"But they are in Ireland." Cate spoke in calculated derision.

"On the contrary, they have embarked for Piel Island off the west coast near Furness. Once on the mainland, they will march with Edward VI and the earl of Lincoln at their head. They will be upon Henry before he knows what is happening."

"You are sure of it?"

Trilborn laughed. "Oh, yes, very sure."

"Yet you tarry here, instead of riding with the news."

"A man must look at all sides before he acts."

Marguerite leaned forward, snaring his attention as she spoke. "You almost sound inclined to turn your coat."

The man's smile was superior as he directed it at her. "It's a possibility."

"It's treason!"

Cate was surprised at the heat in her younger sister's voice, though she blessed her for engaging Trilborn's attention. Her own thoughts were barely coherent. Invasion was imminent, and Henry did not realize it, had no idea of the quarter from which it would come.

Trilborn knew, but had no apparent intention of informing the king.

"Treason is no more than a word if the rightful king wins," their guest said easily.

"You mean the right king," Isabel said with a frown, the distinction being a question of legitimacy versus mere preference.

"Do I? Of course, it will be all the same if the wrong king dies. These things happen on the battlefield."

Cate lifted a brow at that. "I doubt Henry will make the same mistake as Richard III. He'll not be so rash as to mount a personal attack against the pretender."

"Probably not, as he is cautious to a fault. The attack will have to come to him."

"York forces will first have to breach the wall of his defenders," Isabel said in sharp disdain, no doubt because she was thinking of Braesford, who might well be charged with protecting the king.

Something malevolent flickered in Trilborn's eyes and was gone. "Or not."

A frisson of chill foreboding slid down Cate's spine. It almost sounded as if he... But no, she would not put it into solid thought. "La, sir, 'tis fine to talk of betrayal, but I feel sure you will be rejoining Henry as soon as possible."

"In good time, milady, in good time."

When Marguerite opened her mouth with fiery condemnation in her eyes, Cate put out a hand beneath the drape of the tablecloth, clasping her sister's knee in silent caution. Marguerite closed her lips with a snap, though she trembled with indignation.

Isabel, following the byplay with close attention, spoke in soothing tones. "It will assuredly turn out as God wills, and there is little we poor females can do about it." She rose to her feet, continuing with scarcely a pause, "Meanwhile, I believe my husband has a butt of rare malmsey put by for guests. How could I have forgotten? Excuse me, if you please, while I have it properly decanted for you."

"Surely a manservant can see to it," Trilborn began with a frown.

"Your indulgence, sir," Cate said at once, leaning close with a confiding air. "My sister has endured a difficult labor not that long since, and is still far from strong." Let him think Isabel was leaving the table to check on her babe, or that she had need of the garderobe, if he would. She was certain the mistress of Braesford had other things on her mind. It might have been the straight glance Isabel gave her over Trilborn's head, or merely the silent communication that sometimes happened with the three of them, but she felt her elder sister's hard purpose as if it were her own.

She prayed for it, as some manner of diversion was needed. Someone must ride to inform the king of the invasion force approaching the west coast, and where they intended to land. Advance knowledge would allow the army to meet the invaders before it became entrenched. Still, who could be trusted with such a vital message?

Braesford had taken the most steadfast of his men-at-arms with him. The captain of the guard was the ex-

ception, but he was required here to safeguard the keep
and those within it. The other men were mere soldiers.
Though loyal enough in their fashion, they had little of
the cunning it might take to reach Ross or Braesford,
who could then take the message to the king.

What could be done to stop Trilborn from interfering
with such a messenger? Their guest might be seized and
bound, but how long could he be held? Yes, and what
reprisal might he not visit upon them for the indignity?
Someone might slip away from the keep, but how far
could he get with Trilborn's men encamped just beyond
the front gate?

Isabel, so it proved in good time, had the matter in
hand. She returned with a serving man bearing the
malmsey. She poured it herself, all the while lamenting
its sweetness and asking with every sign of concern for
Trilborn's opinion. Watching him taste it, she neglected
to serve Cate and Marguerite. When Marguerite picked
up her glass as a reminder, their older sister made a tiny
negative movement of her head. Taking that as her cue,
Cate beckoned a serving woman and had her glass, and
that of her younger sister, filled with a common vintage
diluted with water.

The next half hour was a severe strain on Cate's
nerves. Uncertain what to expect, she followed Isabel's
conversational lead on court scandals, summer fairs and
the difficulty of maintaining clothing of suitable elegance
while immured in a remote hall. Trilborn's eyes soon
began to glaze, as well they might, given the inanity of
what was being said around him. He lolled in his chair,
leaning heavily on the table.

Cate, eyes wide, stared at Isabel, who moved her gaze to the wineglass in his fist and gave a slight nod. All solicitude then, Cate filled their guest's glass once more, urging him to revive his flagging spirits with the malmsey. When his eyes finally closed and he keeled forward in his chair, it was all she could do not to leap to her feet in triumph.

Marguerite whisked away their guest's silver plate just before his face could land in it. Isabel gave an artificial trill of laughter. "Dear me, I do believe Lord Trilborn is in his cups."

Those men-at-arms who had looked up at the oddity of a man passing out at the head table, went back to their cheese and nutmeats. It was nothing so unusual for those below the salt, after all, nor was it any of their affair.

"I believe it's as well that we leave Lord Trilborn here," Isabel said, rising and shaking out her skirts with a decided air. "He'll wake soon enough, and won't thank us for witnessing his overindulgence."

"No doubt his long and weary ride today is to be blamed," Cate said in kindly tones. Waiting for Marguerite to rise and follow Isabel, she trailed after her sisters as if bored by the prospect of an early evening.

None of them spoke again until they had climbed the stairs and the door of the solar was tightly shut behind them.

"You must go, Cate," Isabel said at once as she swung to face her and Marguerite. "The stable hands are used to saddling your mare and will think little of you riding out, particularly if you mention one of the village women heavy with child. The guard who usually goes with you may think an evening outing unusual, but I feel sure you can handle their questions."

"Yes," she said in swift comprehension, though she felt light-headed from the sudden acceleration of her heart. It did make sense, though she suspected it would not be as simple as Isabel made it sound. "We can leave by stealth from the postern gate."

"Yes, as you must avoid Trilborn's camp. It will be necessary to circle wide to prevent raising the alarm."

Marguerite frowned as she looked from one to the other of them. "The journey will be fearsome."

It would indeed. But at the end, she would see Ross again, Cate thought. Was that what she wanted? Was it?

"Gwynne must gather what's needed for you and your escort," Isabel said, still forming plans.

"She can't go with me."

"No, that would be too arduous for her and somewhat obvious, as well. She should be on hand when Trilborn wakes in the morning, or mayhap toward midday. If she tells him you have gone to the village, he will believe her, as he might not a mere sister."

"So will waste time awaiting my return." Cate shook her head. "He will be in a rage when he discovers I've gone. I would not leave you to become the target of it."

"I shall not meet him alone," Isabel said.

"I will be there," Marguerite stated with a decided nod, "and armed guards, as well. With any luck at all, the devil of a man will tear away to seek you in the village, giving us a chance to close him outside the gates."

Isabel gave a nod of agreement. "Besides, the fate of England may ride with you, Cate. Without the knowledge you must carry, Henry may be defeated. The lives of those who have supported him will not be worth a shilling, including those of our men. Everything Braesford has gained, everything he's worked so hard to build, will be forfeit. Ross will lose what he was given. You do this for all of us."

It was a huge responsibility.

What if she failed?

If she did so, Ross might die fighting alongside Braesford and the king, or else be hanged by Yorkist victors as a traitor.

She would not fail, she thought with a lift of her chin. Not as long as she had breath in her body.

They lingered for several minutes longer, planning details. But time was more important than perfection. Every minute lost might spell life or death for those they loved.

"Cate?" Marguerite said, gliding into the chamber where she stood pulling on her gloves.

"My love?"

"When you see David…"

Cate's distracted counting off of items needed for the ride ceased at once. She met her sister's eyes, which were dark with concern. "Yes?"

"Tell him…oh, tell him…"

"What?"

Her sister put a corner of her veil between her teeth, tugged on it an instant, then dropped it. "Never mind."

Sympathy rose in Cate, filling her chest with hard pressure. "Are you sure?"

Marguerite nodded. "It will be all right."

She wasn't so certain, but refrained from saying so. With a swift hug for her younger sister, she went quickly from the chamber and down the corridor.

Cate looked in on Isabel. She was feeding her baby, as she scorned to use a wet nurse for so important a small personage as Braesford's young son. Little Madeleine sat at her skirt hem, playing with wooden blocks. Leaning over her, Cate placed a kiss on her older sister's forehead, bent to touch Madeleine's soft, red-gold ringlets, and trailed her fingertips over the fine black hair that covered the babe's small head. Her throat ached, suddenly, with unshed tears.

Would she ever hold Ross's child to her breast? It seemed possible, for her courses had not appeared since his return to Grimes Hall, and other signs were there. She could not dwell upon it now, however, not and do what she must.

Smiling with an effort, she met her sister's eyes, seeing there all the trepidation she felt, as well as the shimmer of welling moisture.

"God go with you," Isabel whispered.

"And leave his angels to watch over all here," Cate answered.

Another strained smile, and then she turned in a swirl of skirt and cloak hems to leave the solar. Quickly, she made her way down a back servants' stair to the kitchens. From there, she let herself out into the dark back court. Soon, soon, she was on the opposite side of the postern gate, where her guard waited with their mounts behind them.

"Milady," the one-eyed captain who had been put in

charge of the expedition said as he stepped forward, "is this wise?"

Her laugh was soft and tinged with irony there in the dark. "By no means."

"If we refuse to go…"

"If you refuse," she said simply, "Baron Braesford may die, as well as many of those who went from here with him."

"And your Scotsman, too."

It was a daring thing to suggest. He had the right, however, as he would be putting his life on the line to protect her over the next few days. In truth, it was her most virulent fear, the one that made her heart race, fretting at this delay, demanding she ride like the wind.

"Yes, and him."

The night breeze drifted around them, shifting their cloaks. A horse stamped and blew through its nostrils.

Abruptly, the captain nodded and swung around to confront the five men gathered behind him. "Why do you delay?" he demanded. "Follow Lady Catherine."

An eternity later, they skirted the camp where Trilborn's men slept, walking their horses far beyond its perimeters. Leaving it behind, they reached the main road, a dusty ribbon glowing dully in the light of a half-moon. Mounting up, they began the long journey southward.

18

Ross lifted the tent flap and stepped inside with acidic rage burning in his chest and a red haze rising behind his eyes. There she was, by all the saints, just as he had been told.

Cate, his wife, stood like an apparition in the middle of the space he shared with Braesford. Pale and resolute, she had her hands clasped in front of her. Her face was smudged with dirt, her clothing carried dust in its folds and mud at the hem, and she was as redolent of sweat and horse as he was himself. He wanted to beat her for the risk she had taken, the danger she had passed through to reach him. That was after he took her down to the tent's earthen floor and buried himself inside her.

"Are you mad?" he demanded in a low growl as he paced forward, slinging the helm he carried aside so it bounced off the stretched canvas of the cot and rolled to a stop against the tent wall. "What in God's holy name possessed you that you are here?"

Apprehension sprang into her clear blue eyes as she met his gaze, and well it should. Never had he felt such sick, roiling fury and terror. Anything could have happened to her between Braesford Hall and here, anything at all. She had no idea of the brutality of men primed for war, no notion whatever of the things they were capable of doing. She could be lying dead in a ditch somewhere, raped, strangled, maimed, mutilated, stripped of all her lovely pride and dignity. Lost to him, lost forever.

God...

"I came because I had to," she said, her lips trembling, tears shimmering along her eyelids. "I came because..."

She was swaying, almost dead on her feet with weariness and strained nerves; he saw that finally as he came within reach. With a groan, he caught her shoulders and drew her to him, closing her against him with desperate strength. He felt her shudder then, and burrow into him as if trying to crawl inside his clothes, into his body, into his heart.

"Tell me," he whispered into the dusty veil that covered her hair, while sudden hot tears burned behind his eyes. "Tell me."

The news she brought was difficult to understand at first. Trilborn had been at Braesford Hall, had let fall information about Yorkist movements. He had almost certainly gone over to the cause of the pretender. An injury for an injury was the code of the border, whether Scots or Sassenach. Betrayal was the least of what they should have expected from him.

If Trilborn intended to rejoin the army Henry was gathering, then there was a reason for it. Could be it was only to keep a foot in both camps, ready to jump toward the winning side. The reason could also be more sinis-

ter. A king who fell in battle by the hand of a supposed
friend was as dead as one killed by a foe.

Anger still scourged his veins, but with it ran hot
pride. Cate, his Cate, had brought this news that might
change the course of the battle to come. She had served
Henry a fine turn, had served them all well.

"Come," he said in rough command, "you must speak
to Henry. Then you may rest."

She drew a breath that lifted her breasts against him so
he felt their firmness, their soft resilience even through
his chain mail. "Yes."

He hardened like steel in a forge, his need fiery, tempered and lethal. "But first…"

She drew back to look at him. Her lips were chapped
by wind and weather, yet had never looked so sweet.
He took them in rough possession, branding them with
his heat, thrusting inside as if she were a spring and he
dying of thirst. His hands plundered her curves, molding
them, remembering. He pushed her veil aside, tangled
his fingers in her hair in an agony of need. He wanted
her beneath him, surrounding him, panting as she clung.
He needed her as he had needed nothing in his life, and
in spite of men passing, laughing, shouting oaths and
profane ribaldry just beyond the flimsy walls.

He wanted her, but couldn't have her. Not yet, not yet.

Drawing away with a wrench, he turned his back,
clung to the center tent pole with a vicious grip while ex-
erting every ounce of control he possessed. She touched
his shoulder, and he shuddered, tried beyond bearing.
Then he shook himself, turned to help her adjust her veil,
and led her out to find the king.

Events moved then with the speed of a diving hawk. Henry and his commanders, headed by the duke of Bedford and his companion from his exile years, John de Vere, earl of Oxford, met in hurried conference. Within moments, the order to march swept through the encampment. An hour more, and they were tramping toward Nottingham.

Ross, riding in the vanguard, cursed with every inch of the road that fell away behind them. Cate was somewhere far back in the baggage train. If she had arrived only a few days earlier, while the king was at Kenilworth, she could have been left in safety there with Henry's queen and the duchess, his mother. Instead, she had found them at Leicester. Ross could have left her there, but did not trust the town not to be overrun if the Yorkists prevailed. So now she was riding with the laundresses, prostitutes and wives of common soldiers, probably learning a goodly amount more than a lady should know about an army on the move and the needs of men about to face battle.

It could not be helped.

She was where he wanted her to be, where he could protect her at need.

Protect her. Now wasn't that a fine word for it?

He had promised rest for her, but there had been no time. Mayhap tonight.

How was she faring? He would ride back down the line to check on her in a few minutes, when his need to see was not so obvious. He would not have her made the butt of coarse suggestions because he could not stay away. It would not aid Henry in the least if Ross was forced to kill a few dozen of his men for their insults.

He could, just possibly, arrange a covered cart for her use, he thought, one that might keep most of the sun and dust from her. If she was able to sleep a short while, then he need not feel such a selfish bastard if he made love to her when they finally halted for the night. Though at the unrelenting pace set by the earl of Oxford, that might come late, if at all.

It was near dusk when Ross heard the thud of hoof-beats coming up fast behind him. He turned in the saddle to see Trilborn overtaking him. Contempt gathered inside him and he put his hand on his dirk. That the man had not been arrested on sight amazed him, but the decision rested with the king. No doubt he had his reasons for letting him go free. He often played a deep game, did Henry VII.

"Well, Dunbar," Trilborn said as he drew even, "I see your lovely lady wife has joined you."

Something raw and dangerous moved inside Ross. He resented Trilborn even knowing Cate, much less speaking of her with such familiarity. "She has."

"If I had known she would be so inspired by my talk of Henry's movements that she'd set off to war, I'd have made certain to ride with her."

"I'm sure you would," Ross answered with a snort.

"I followed as quickly as I could, of course." Trilborn drew his mount to a walk beside him. "Females are wonderful creatures, but notorious for confusing details, particularly on places and directions."

"Is that what you told the king?"

"Oh, he knew it already. Henry has a fine appreciation for the ladies, but trusts only his sainted mother."

Was it possible Henry had discounted the news Cate had brought him? Ross's hand tightened on his reins at the thought, so his mount curveted, leaping a few steps ahead of Trilborn, before he brought the strong black destrier under control again.

"Lady Catherine is uncommonly canny," he said as he returned to the Englishman's side.

Trilborn gave a hard laugh. "It goes with some members of the breed, don't you find? I do admire your sangfroid in dealing with the charming witch you married."

"Witch?" he said in soft inquiry, his eyes narrowed.

"Oh, I'll not name her that where others may hear," Trilborn answered with a shrug. "She's far too winsome to burn. Yet a lady who pays to have her betrothed dispatched so she need not wed is hardly in the common way."

"Take care," Ross said with menace in his voice. "You are speaking of my wife."

"Better yours than mine! I pay no heed to a few scratches while bedding a woman, but prefer not to be sliced to ribbons. The poniard carried by Lady Catherine is a pretty trifle, but damnably sharp."

Hard on the words, he kicked his horse into a lope and drew away. Circling, he rode back down the line of marching men to a place near the center. Ross watched him go while virulent curses formed in his head.

What did Trilborn know of Cate's knife? Yes, and what made him think Cate had paid an assassin to try to kill him? Only he, Cate and possibly her sisters knew

of the attempt, as far as he was aware. Well, and the assassin.

It was lunacy, the ravings of a man who could not bear
to be bested, especially by a woman. If Trilborn could
not separate her from his enemy one way, he would do it
another. If he could not punish her for making him look
foolish, he would persuade her husband to do it for him.

Cate would never deal with such a dastard; she despised Trilborn for the way he had hounded her and hurt
her. She knew him for a traitor, had ridden through count-
less dangers to bring news of it.

Ross knew these things with his head, but his heart
pounded in his chest and he felt sick to his stomach. It
was what happened when a man married a woman who
wanted none of him. It had to be considered when the
bride was protected by an ancient curse.

Cate lay full-length on the cot with her hands behind
her head. By the light of a single candle in its pierced
tin lantern, she stared at the tent above her as it billowed
in the night wind. Now and then the blue-white flash
of lightning filled the space with its spectral glow. She
flinched each time, frowned at the far grumble of thunder that followed. Her nerves were tied in knots and her
mind in turmoil. Where was Ross and what was he doing
with a storm bearing down upon the encampment?

She was tired and on edge. They had marched until
late. When they halted, she had alighted from the cart
found for her, and walked down to the river where they
had camped, along with two of the laundresses she
had become acquainted with during the day. They had

washed a few things by lantern light, standing ankle-deep in the flowing current, then had bathed away the dust and sweat of the march. Cate had not lingered, however, thinking Ross might have come to the tent during her absence.

He had not, nor had she seen him since.

The two men, apparently assigned to Ross, who put up the tent, had ushered her inside and brought food and drink. She had eaten alone, and then sat down to wait.

She still waited.

Ross had duties and responsibilities; his time was not his own. It wasn't his fault she had nothing to do and the passing hours weighed heavily upon her. She should try to sleep, for morning and more riding would come all too soon. She had napped during the afternoon, however, and was not at all sleepy now. She was too keyed up, too fearful of what was going to happen. Soon, too soon, they would meet with the invading force led by the earl of Lincoln. The two armies would clash in battle; it could be no other way.

Had they landed yet, the Yorkist contingent with its Irishmen and German mercenaries? Were their numbers greater than those that would fight for the king? Where were they marching? Was the boy being touted as Edward VI with them? Were men flocking to his standard? Where would the two forces face off against each other?

Where would Ross be when they did? Yes, and how would he be killed?

No, no, she refused to think of it. He was too strong,

too skilled with a sword, too experienced. He could not die. He must not.

The candle flared, even behind its protective tin, as the tent flap was thrust open. Ross ducked inside and straightened to his full height, so the shadow that slid over the canvas walls appeared that of a giant. His hair was damp and wind-tossed, and he carried his mailed shirt and coif over his arm. A black scowl sat upon his features.

Alarm skittered down her spine, but she refused to let him see it. Pushing up to one elbow, she fixed him with a frown as deep as his own. "Where have you been?"

"Seeing to my men," he said shortly. Tossing the mail toward a stool, he paid no attention as it slid to the floor with a metallic rattle. It was followed by his bonnet, which had been tucked into his belt. He put his hand to the lashing that held his shirt.

Strained tension hung between them. She sought for something that might break it as she ran her tongue over her bottom lip. "Is it raining yet?"

"Not yet. Soon."

Not only was his hair wet, but his shirt was damp, pulling across his wide shoulders and upper arms as he stripped it off over his head. He had bathed then, as she had, and probably for the same reason. She could not seem to look away from what he was doing. Heated fullness gathered inside her and the muscles of her inner thighs tightened in sudden spasm.

"I saw...I thought I saw Trilborn today."

"You did." Ross levered off his boots and kicked them aside.

"Has he been arrested?" She sat up straighter.

"It appears Henry is not convinced of his betrayal."

"You mean...I suppose Trilborn persuaded him otherwise. It's my word against his, and Henry believes him."

"Or prefers to see evidence, one way or the other."

"But...but we marched based on the information I brought."

"Which may have been received from other sources, so was confirmed."

She gave a dazed shake of her head. "Trilborn is up to something. The man is a devil."

"Funny." Ross gave her a mirthless smile. "He says the same of you, or as near as makes no difference, since he named you a witch."

Ross unfastened his belt with its sporran, whipped away his plaid and sent it flying. The move plainly exposed how ready he was for her. She looked at that rampant male hardness, glanced up to meet his eyes, then looked back down again in fascination. Her voice hardly more than a whisper, she asked, "And what do you think?"

"I think," he said, stalking forward the two steps it took him to reach the cot, then dragging her up against his hard frame so she was melded to him from breast to knees, "that you are *my* witch."

He took her mouth, setting his own to it at a slant, pushing deep. The stubble of his beard abraded the tender edges. The hot thrust of his tongue was an invasion that mocked what he meant to do to her. She took it, twined around it, applied suction while sliding her hands from his shoulders to his hair, fisting them in its long length.

She cradled the hot iron of him against the softness of her belly, moving against it in instinctive pleasure. He cupped her bottom, aiding the slide, clasping, squeezing the two half spheres with his fingertips grazing their cleft.

Clenching her hands in his hair in an abrupt reflex, she drew his head back, spoke against his lips. "If I am a witch, I want to ride."

A choked sound left him, while his grip tightened upon her. "Aye, my sweeting, and so you shall, so you shall."

Hard on the words, he stripped off her shift, then caught her to him while he straddled the cot. He dropped down upon it so hard it creaked, still holding her belly to his as he lay back upon it. Lifting his legs, he stretched out, seating her so that his hard rod was at the apex of her thighs, nudging at her hot, damp softness.

She needed no more. Levering upward, she settled upon him, sliding to take him deep. She rode him then with wild abandon while he fingered their joining, circling the small peak of flesh at her arched opening with his thumb. She rode him until she was mindless, heedless of everything except the magical flight. She rode him while he bucked beneath her, rode him until her chest ached, her muscles were on fire and her mind burned with longing; until there was nothing, nothing except the two of them and the night. And when the storm broke, so did she, arching above him like a pulled bow, flooding him with her very essence as she took his deep inside. Boneless, then, she collapsed upon his chest while their hearts shuddered, thundering together.

Well before the dawn, the march continued.

It picked up speed as the royal heralds came and went, lashing their horses as if the hounds of hell were after them, or mayhap the dogs of war. Their news, delivered to Henry from his spies within the rebel camp, and his patrols that put ungentle questions to stragglers and looters from it, filtered down in a matter of hours to the trailing end of the column where Cate rode. The earl of Lincoln had not only landed at Piel Island and crossed to Furness, but had led his forces into Yorkshire, stronghold of the Yorkist faction, where he hoped for a groundswell of support.

Though many joined his cause, it was not in the strength he had anticipated. The peace and fair-handed governance Henry had brought to England seemed to have found favor even in Yorkshire. The end of the thirty-year conflict between the white rose of York and red rose of Lancaster that he had brought about was something few wanted to see undone. Fewer still cared to set off another round of bloodletting by countenancing an upstart who might or might not be a true Plantagenet. Nor did it sit well that he was being brought to them on the shoulders of Irish and German soldiery.

Henry, by contrast, arrived at Nottingham to the cheers of the populace. He was joined by a force of men far larger than expected, making his army some fifteen thousand strong in contrast to the eight thousand credited to the Yorkists under Lincoln. They lay there for a few days to rest and replenish supplies, while Henry and his commanders held council to decide on strategy before moving on toward Newark.

This last advance was enlivened by a pernicious report that the two forces had met and Henry been defeated. Spread by the enemy to prevent more men from flocking to Henry's standard, it had to be countered by a flurry of heralds sent in all directions.

On the move again, the king's army paused for the night at the village of Radcliffe, some eight miles out from Newark. It was there, an hour or two after midnight, that news came of the rebel army. It was encamped on a ridge above the Trent Valley, near the village of East Stoke.

What followed was controlled chaos. Henry intended to prevent the earl of Lincoln from supplying his army in Newark, it seemed, as well as mounting a surprise attack. His officers and men would move fast, leaving the supply carts, provisions, cooks, bakers, laundresses and all other followers behind.

Ross, summoned from their bed by the discreet call of a sentry outside the tent flap, threw on his clothes, accepted Cate's help with his mail and armor, and then buckled on his sword. With his helm under one arm, he swept her to him for a long, hard kiss. When he lifted his head, he stood staring down at her, raking her face with his dark blue eyes. For an instant, she thought he would speak. Instead, he kissed her once more and was gone.

She wanted to run after him, to call out to him, to tell him…what? What was there to say?

Nothing could change what was between them, nothing stay what was to come. She would not burden him with her doubts and fears, the news that she could be with child or a declaration he might not care to hear. Closing her eyes, she prayed in less than coherent phrases while tears squeezed between her lashes.

When the men began to move out, she wrapped her cloak around her and stepped outside the tent to watch them go. Some swung along, grinning, as if heading to a fair. Many seemed half-asleep, and others stared ahead with grim-faced acceptance. The tramping of their feet raised so much dust it was almost impossible to identify the mounted knights that rode up and down their line, shouting encouragement, harrying stragglers. Still, she knew Ross beyond doubt by his plaid, which billowed around him. She followed him with her gaze, turning to keep him in view, straining to see the last of him as he grew smaller in the distance.

The horseman came out of the dust, so armored he would have been unrecognizable but for the device on the tunic that covered his breastplate. He drew up with such abruptness that his destrier reared, raking the air with its hooves. Staring down at her with his visage distorted by the metal crosspiece that covered his nose, Trilborn drawled, "Well, Lady Catherine, will you wish me God-speed?"

"No." The word was brittle with disdain.

"Come, have you no concern for what I go toward?"

"None whatever."

He laughed with a hollow echo inside his helm. "You should, you know."

Foreboding trickled down her backbone in icy rivulets, but she answered with bravado. "I fail to see why. It's nothing to me."

He reined in his restive mount with a hard jerk. "Not even if I am sworn to cut down the king?"

Her heart smote her lungs as it jolted into a harder beat. "You would not dare. You would be cut down in your turn."

"You think so? Much is possible in the thick of battle."

"Ross knows what you are about," she said with a lift of her chin. "He will stop you."

"Oh, I depend upon his trying. 'Twas my whole point in letting you guess my intention, so you would pass it to Dunbar. The only honor I crave more than ridding England of Henry Tudor is that of making you a widow."

19

The battle was finally joined on a cloudless summer's morning, in a meadow where larks had saluted the heavens only moments before, and the grass was so verdant a green it hurt the eyes to look at it. The rebel army poured down a gully from their height, trampling the heath and bracken of the moorland. They met Henry's vanguard upon the open meadowlands and newly planted fields beyond.

The collision was vicious, the ensuing fight a bloody melee. The earl of Oxford led the vanguard, taking the brunt of it in the center, while the remaining force divided to either side. Braesford charged on the left with his company, including David, who was outfitted as a knight this day, while Ross was on the right.

The noise was deafening, an endless confusion of shouts, curses, groans and shrieks amid screaming horses, clashing steel, blows crashing on shields and the whistling of darts used by the Irish. The sun shone down, bouncing off helms and sword blades with blinding force. Half-deaf, squinting against the bright light and dust, boiling hot under his mail, Ross fought with the fury of some infernal machine. He acted on instinct, with rote moves practiced so many thousands of times that he could follow them in his sleep. Time ceased to have meaning. Minutes became hours. He seemed to neither advance nor retreat, but to cleave to the position he must hold or die.

Somewhere on the edge of his field of vision, he was aware of the king. As with most royal commanders, he sat his destrier on a hillock where he followed the action, sending heralds flying here and there with orders. Ross knew his duty. He must not stray far from his place as guard for the English sovereign.

As the center faltered and began to fall back, Henry sent his yeoman guard flying to support Oxford. The king was suddenly alone, virtually without protection.

It was then that a knight, backed by a half dozen more with the same colors, detached himself from the main body. He charged Henry's hill, lance leveled and steady, shouting something that was lost in the dusty din. Ross glimpsed the knight's device as it flashed past him, felt the hair stand up on the back of his neck.

Trilborn.

Trilborn charged the king, who had no guard. It was just as Cate had said, after all. If he killed Henry, the battle would be over.

Ross dispatched a German mercenary armed with an ax, then wrenched his mount around while shouting to Braesford and David. The young squire swung toward him, but Braesford did not hear as he slashed his way toward a knot of soldiery protecting the Yorkist earl of Lincoln and the boy-king for whom the battle was being waged. The wind whistled through Ross's helm as he leaned forward along the huge destrier's neck, red-stained sword at the ready. His blood beat high and wild and his brain was on fire. Rising inside his chest was that ancient shout, a Scotsman's call to battle in blood feud. It scraped his throat, filled his ears and rang in his mind with ghostly echoes of a hundred raids with his kinsmen beside him.

Ahead of him, he saw the king slam his visor shut and bring up his sword, saw the royal blade flash as Henry defended himself against the onslaught with fierce and steady strength. His standard bearer, all the protection he had left, received a blow across the chest and dropped from sight. Now the king was surrounded. He could not hold out for long.

Ross's great-hearted destrier, whinnying in triumph, crashed into the fray. Trilborn's mount was shunted aside, while one of the other knights lost his balance and toppled from the saddle. Cursing, the English lord disengaged and kicked his way free. Yanking his mount around, Trilborn trampled his own man as he rode upon Ross again.

Ross met the attack with savage power, felt the reverberation of the blow shudder through his arm and down his spine. He spared a glance to where a fierce-eyed horseman with a raven device had come to the king's aid. David, he saw with an edge of despair, only a stripling instead of a war-hardened veteran.

He and Trilborn settled into a clanking, ringing exchange. Sweat poured into Ross's eyes. His teeth ached far up into his skull from clenching them. His sword arm burned, yet furious energy powered his every blow, and he waited in low cunning for his opponent to make a mistake. He wanted him dead, this Sassenach bastard, enemy of his clan who had dared to strike Cate, dared to lust after her, threaten her and name her a liar. He would see him dead here, at last.

The man who had engaged the king was down, struck from the saddle and laid low by David. The boy wheeled to face the next who might try to take him.

In that instant, a cry went up. Lincoln had fallen! The false king was captured!

The earl of Lincoln, Yorkist commander, was dead. Young Edward VI, so-called king, had been taken. Braesford had the boy, carrying him up before him as much for his safety, belike, as for a captive of war.

Trilborn cursed and reared his destrier, letting the flashing hooves fend off Ross's slashing advance. With a howl of hatred, he swung free. He wheeled around and galloped away, fighting through and beyond what had suddenly become a bloody rout.

From where Ross sat upon his destrier, it was clear the battle was ended. The field before him was littered with the fallen, exposed as their comrades ran. Henry's army had been not only superior in numbers, but better armed and outfitted against primarily Irish troops without swords or bucklers, and protected only by leather jerkins. With something like half their number slain, the rebels had broken and were running away, with the Lancaster forces in pursuit. Henry could plant his standard here at the top of this hill and call himself victor whenever he chose.

Yet Ross could not ride after Trilborn, not yet. Henry was protected only by his own sword and that of one lone squire, David.

Ross stared over his shoulder to where his enemy had disappeared, even as he leaned from the saddle to flick the royal standard upward with his sword point. He watched while David, Henry's new standard bearer, took it from him and let it unfurl in the warm summer wind.

Trilborn was running away. He was leaving the field, deserting both Yorkists and Lancastrians, riding back the way they had come. He was heading south toward Radcliffe, where Cate waited.

The battle was over and Henry defeated. Both Ross and the king were dead.

Cate shook her head, staring up at Trilborn where he sat his destrier, while her heart stalled in her chest at the news he had brought. "No," she whispered.

"Come," he said, shoving up the visor of his helm as he made his appeal. "You must leave here. The camp will be overrun shortly by Lincoln's army."

"How…how did it happen?" She could not make herself accept it. Ross was too vital, too strong within himself for such a fate.

"What does it matter? If you stay here, you'll be forced to spread your legs for every foot soldier in Lincoln's army. I would save you from that fate. Come with me, before it's too late."

It was the curse of the Graces. It had triumphed at last.

Or had it?

Doubt moved through her in a sickening spiral. Faced with the final effect, her mind refused to grasp it.

"Where were you when he fell?" she asked, shading her eyes with her hand against the midafternoon sun. "Were you nearby?"

"God's blood! What does it matter?" Trilborn demanded, with hot choler rising in his face.

"You swore to kill him, and the king."

"A stupid jibe only. Cate…Lady Catherine, we must make haste. If you are caught here, I may be unable to save you."

"Braesford? And David? Are they dead, as well?"

"I know not." His face darkened with his rage. "Come with me now, unless you plan to be a whore trailing after the Yorkist army. Can you really prefer that to my bed?"

She did. She would rather by far take her chances with the laundresses who had befriended her. To lie beneath Trilborn, to accept him inside her, would sicken her to her very soul.

Was Ross truly dead? She wouldn't believe it, could not. She would surely feel it in her heart if it were so.

"No," she said, over the ache that threatened to close her throat. She lifted her skirts as she backed away. "No, I can't go with you."

"I insist." He kicked his huge mount into movement, following after her.

He meant to force her. Eyes wide with the discovery, Cate glanced around her. The nearby tents seemed deserted, though movement could be glimpsed far down the row. She could hear a babble of voices somewhere, thought another rider must have come from the battlefield. No one was paying the least attention to what was happening with her.

Abruptly, the distant shouts took on meaning. "Lancaster! Lancaster! Henry was victor! God save King Henry!"

"You lost," she said in sudden discovery, even as she skipped backward from the destrier's steady advance. "You changed sides, and now must run or be hanged as a traitor."

"They'll not catch me unless they can reach across the Irish Sea."

"Flying like a coward. I might have guessed!"

He gave a barking laugh. "But alive, unlike some."

Had he really killed Ross in the heat of battle as he had sworn? The raw ache of that possibility fueled her rage. "They'll hunt you down. You'll never get away."

"Could be, but I'll have you first," he said, and set spurs to his stallion.

The destrier surged forward. Cate broke and ran. She could hear the heavy thud of hooves behind her, smell hot horseflesh and feel the whiff of the huge animal's breath on the top of her head.

Abruptly, her flying veil was caught, and her hair in its long braid beneath it. She cried out as she was lifted high. Reaching back, she grasped Trilborn's gloved wrist even as he hauled her against him, crushing her to the hot steel of his armor.

She fought him, twisting, clawing, kicking and shrieking like a madwoman. She almost wrenched from his grasp, almost fell.

He grabbed her again, cursing, dropping his reins. She

glimpsed his face, his lips twisted in a snarl as he drew back a gloved fist.

It slammed into the side of her head. Pain burst inside her skull. She reeled away over the neck of the destrier, plunging into swirling gray-black mist. She felt herself caught, jerked upright in a hold so tight she couldn't breathe. Then merciful darkness took her.

Agony jolted her awake. Dazed, drifting, she remained still with the ancient intuition of the hunted.

The movement beneath her told her she was held upon horseback. She thought the big destrier must have leaped a ditch or low wall, coming down hard with its double burden. Cate sat unmoving, eyes closed. The pain in her head was so fierce she feared she was about to be sick.

Slowly, she recognized her position in front of Trilborn, recognized his scent of acrid sweat and cloves. The armhole edge of his cuirass dug into her shoulder, the big saddle's cantle pressed into her hip, and she was far too snug against the juncture of his spread thighs. A moan pressed against her throat, and she swallowed it down.

Where were they? How long since they had left the camp? She opened her eyes in the barest of slits, but clenched them shut at once as bile surged into the back of her throat. It had been shortly after midday when Trilborn approached her, and now the shadows were long under the trees, stretching over the field they were crossing.

She had seen no sign of a road in her brief survey. Trilborn must be traveling crosscountry. How far had they come? Where were they headed?

Oh, but yes, the Irish Sea, he had said. He meant to

escape to Ireland, and then perchance to Burgundy or some other country beyond Henry's reach.

Had anyone witnessed her abduction?

The king's men would be hunting down those who fled from the battlefield. Mayhap someone would be coming after Trilborn. They could be gaining on him even now.

Henry was alive. He must be, if he was the victor. If Henry, then why not Ross?

Tears forced their way from the corners of Cate's eyes. She could feel their wetness, but would not move to wipe them away.

Her mind was far from clear, yet she had not been raped while out of her senses; she ached in many places but not there. That threat from Trilborn had hovered over her so long it seemed the only thing that could have stopped him was fear of being overtaken while in the act. What if that fear sprang from knowing Ross might be somewhere behind them?

He would come after them, if only because she was his wife. It was a matter of honor, never mind the bad blood between him and his old enemy. If no one had seen them go, Ross might still guess the direction of Trilborn's flight from simple logic: where else was safety to be found except Ireland? He could be following on their trail even now.

Delay...she must delay him. Yet what could she do to stay their progress to the coast? Surely something would come to her, if she could only think.

Trilborn shifted, turning in the saddle as if to look back. Cate's head throbbed so viciously with the movement that a moan of protest sounded in her throat before she could stop it.

"'Tis time and more," Trilborn said, his voice rumbling from behind the visor of his helm that he dropped back in place. "I'd about resolved to leave you behind."

She breathed deep to help settle her stomach before she spoke. "Would that you had."

"Not bloody likely, not without having you in every way possible."

He went on to tell her the many ways that would be. The crude descriptions were as much from the need to cow her as from lust, she thought, as if her helplessness and dread must excite him. It was part and parcel with the way he had struck out at her before.

"I don't believe these acts possible," she said, putting a hand to her head, willing the glassy edge of her vision to clear before lowering it to her belly in a protective gesture. "Not on horseback."

"We won't always be on horseback," he snapped.

He was annoyed that she wasn't shaking with fear. Might that cause him to call a halt, to be certain she had reason to be afraid? It seemed best to curb her wayward tongue.

Still, wasn't a halt what was required? She could surely find a reason for it that would not involve rapine.

What if he used it for that purpose, anyway? Could she endure it? Would he really leave her behind afterward? And if he did, would she be dead or alive?

The risk was great, but what was the alternative? Once free of England's shores, Trilborn would make her his doxy, regardless. He would take his pleasure of her in all the degrading and painful ways he had described. She would bear the brunt of his rage, be at the mercy of his fists. She might as well be dead.

If she succeeded, and if Ross or the king's men were indeed somewhere behind them, then it was Trilborn who would die. That possibility was worth the sacrifice.

Quickly, before she could change her mind, she put out her hand to clasp his wrist. "Stop, stop now. I need...I am going to be ill."

"Endure it. We've no time."

She lifted a hand to her mouth, speaking through her fingers. "I promise you, I cannot. If you prefer that I spew all over you..."

Trilborn snorted in anger, but altered his course toward the nearest trees. Reaching their shade, he walked the destrier a little deeper among them. He dismounted, then dragged her down beside him.

Cate stumbled, almost fell, with no play-acting whatsoever. Her legs felt like mop rags, and her stomach heaved. Clamping a hand to her mouth, she pushed away from his hold, took a few wobbling steps. With her back to him, she put one hand on the trunk of a large oak and bent forward, quickly thrusting a finger down her throat.

The effort was almost unnecessary. She was violently sick, gasping and choking, while tears streamed down her face. She heaved again and again, until her stomach was empty. Spent at last, she wiped her mouth with her hand, straightened, and then closed her eyes and leaned back against the tree trunk.

Something swung against her thigh with that move-

ment. She was so accustomed to that light weight that it
was a moment before she recognized the source.

Her poniard. It was still attached to her girdle, the
scabbard hidden among the folds of her gown. Through
carelessness, ignorance or similar familiarity, Trilborn
had not taken it from her.

"Come, we must make haste," he commanded. He
reached to put a hand on her arm.

She shook him off. Staggering a little, she moved
away, walking deeper into the woodland.

"Where are you going?"

"Where do you suppose?" she demanded over her
shoulder. She walked on until a screen of shrubbery stood
between them.

He allowed that defiance, which seemed miraculous
until she realized from the sound that he was availing
himself of the opportunity, as well. She caught up her
skirts and crouched, watching his shape through a screen
of leaves as she did what she must. At the same time, she
eased her small knife free of its scabbard. She pushed it
into her long sleeve, against the underside of her wrist.
With that done, she straightened and moved into the open
again.

The urge to run was strong, so strong. Another time,
she might have tried it, but not now. Her head felt too
large for her body, yet too small to contain the swelling
pain inside it. Her vision was so hazy that distant objects
wavered, taking on fantastical shapes. A goat on a far hill
became a dragon, a rabbit turned into a giant toad and a
sapling took on the form of a dark figure on horseback.
She blinked, and the sapling wavered, developed two

heads. Looking down, she saw she had two right hands, as well. She was seeing double.

Stepping with slow care, she wandered back toward where the destrier stood, though allowing her footsteps to take her to the open edge of the wood. Trilborn, cursing, strode toward her. He had removed his helm, the better to see to his needs. With it under his arm, he wrapped his fingers around her wrist, dragging her along as he turned back toward his mount.

"Wait, wait," she gasped, covering her eyes with her hand as sickness assailed her again. "Shouldn't we rest a little longer? Your destrier can't go on forever, carrying both of us."

"My worry, not yours." He shoved her ahead of him. She stumbled and almost fell, would have if he hadn't dragged her upright, hauling her against him. She could feel the heat of him through her skirts, and the threatening hardness at his groin. He stared down at her mouth, bent his head.

The smell of him surrounded her, sweaty, randy, with his acrid hint of cloves. A dry heave seized her. Moaning with more art than necessity, she let it convulse her body.

His oath was savage as he took a fast step back. It was followed by every scurrilous name for a female he could voice. Snatching her arm again, he shoved her toward the destrier.

She stopped beside the huge stallion, clinging to the saddle leathers with her back to her captor. "I can't," she said, hiding her face against the stirrup. "I can't go on."

"You can. You will."

"No." She moved her head from side to side.

"You prefer to die?" Trilborn demanded. Hard on the words, she heard the slither of metal on metal, the sound of a sword being drawn from its scabbard.

She slid the poniard from her sleeve. Where to strike? His neck? Too easily defended. Between the cuirass that covered his chest and his lower protection? He was wearing a long hauberk that would deflect all but the sharpest point. To merely prick him would invite a retaliation she might not survive.

Abruptly, she knew. His hand and wrist had been bare when he held her arm just now. In relieving himself, he had removed his glove.

Had she a chance?

Did it matter?

She could never submit to Trilborn. She could never give herself, never be taken by any man other than Ross Dunbar.

Cate lowered her arm and turned slowly to face her abductor. She kept the small, sharp knife hidden against her thigh, and her gaze focused somewhere beyond his shoulder so he would not see the purpose in her eyes.

He was scowling at her, though his face changed when it seemed she would obey him. With satisfaction flaring in his eyes, he seated his sword back in its scabbard with a decisive click.

Cate saw these things on the edge of her vision, but her attention was snagged on something beyond the wood's edge, across the field. The sapling she had noticed just now was closer, larger. It was moving, shimmering in the slanting sunlight. A horseman, after all. A mounted knight with a nimbus of light around his armor.

Trilborn must not see, not yet, not yet. She snapped her eyes shut, moistened her lips. Tears blurred her vision as she lifted her lashes again to focus upon the man in front of her.

"Why?" she asked in hoarse demand. "Why me, why now, when I am married to someone else?"

"You were meant to be mine from the first. Fine looking, of rank, an accursed Grace of Graydon whom a suitor must court death to claim? What man could resist such a challenge?"

"Almost any other, I should think."

His snort was derisive. "Superstitious fools. You were also an heiress and my purse was empty."

"That I can accept," she said with a twist of her lips, "though I think your interest grew sharper when I was given to Ross."

"That was never supposed to happen, damn his eyes. Never!"

"No, he wasn't supposed to follow me when I fell behind the hunt, was he? You meant to carry me off then, just as you're doing now."

"You figured that out, did you? Oh, yes, I was to play the lovesick gallant who must have you by any means, offering marriage after your rape. You'd have been grateful in your humiliation."

"Ross was caught in the scheme instead, and you hated him for it."

"A Dunbar, whoreson border reiver that he is? How could I not? Henry was to award you to me, not him!"

"So you attempted to remove him by vicious attack, expecting him to come to my aid when you turned your ire in my direction."

"Oh, I was ready to lay hands on you, as well, being you were stupid enough to prefer him."

"But Ross recovered from his wound."

"So he did, devil's spawn, just as he survived an assassin's knife and my attack upon him and the king this day."

Survived...

She had known it must be so. Still the joy that rose inside her at this confirmation was strengthening beyond anything she'd ever felt. Her heart swelled with it, and the image of a knight on horseback, galloping, galloping, was engraved on her mind's eye, though she would not, dared not, turn her gaze again to the field behind Trilborn.

"He's alive," she whispered.

Trilborn gave a rough laugh. "No doubt his royal majesty will present him with a barony after this day's work. More spoils for Dunbar, as he was lucky enough to stop me from dispatching Henry. But he'll not have you to go with it."

Her captor's eyes burned in his flushed face. The recital of his grievances had roused him again. He was crowding her, easing closer. He reached to seize her arm.

The poniard was in her hand, its silver metalwork over ebony smooth against her palm. She lashed out without conscious thought, striking across the inside of his wrist.

He howled. Incredulity leaped into his eyes as he looked at her, though it turned rapidly to murderous rage.

His helm dropped from his grasp. He clamped his free hand on the wound while bright scarlet droplets squeezed between his fingers.

Cate did not wait for more. Dodging around him, she staggered into a run. Her head jarred, the pain blinding her more with every pounding step. Her breath came in harsh gasps. Her knees seemed unhinged, and she felt as if she moved through a bowl of custard as she broke from the cover of the trees.

Behind her, she heard Trilborn cursing, grunting as he hauled himself into the saddle, screaming at his destrier. The enormous beast leaped into a run. Its hooves struck the ground with a hollow drumming. She could feel the earth shuddering beneath them.

The dark knight across the field veered toward her. He was coming fast, riding low. He reached to draw the sword that rode at his back, whipping it forward so the sunlight followed it in a glittering arc. He was faceless behind his closed helm, though the red dragon of Henry's guard marked the tabard he wore over his armor. The thunder of his horse's hooves blended with those behind her to make a dull roar.

Cate glanced back. Trilborn was gaining on her. His lips were drawn away from his teeth in a snarl. His sword hung from his fist as if dragged down by its weight, and blood made a dark line down the polished steel. As he pounded nearer, he swung it back, swept it up.

She flung herself to the ground. Steel whistled above her, ripping through her flying veil. And above that sound, soaring in rich and deadly threat through the ringing in her ears, came the Scots yell of the Clan Dunbar.

The two men came together with a screeching crash like a metal-clad battering ram against a metal-clad gate. The very earth shook with the power of it. Horses whinnied, stumbling under the impact before recovering. Cate rolled away from the tumult. An instant later, armor clanged and rattled as a body thudded to the ground.

She reared up in time to see Ross leap from his mount to stand above Trilborn, where he lay. Ross put a foot on the downed man's armored chest, leaned to rest the point of his sword at the hollow of his exposed neck.

"Strike," Trilborn croaked, his face twisted in a defiant sneer. "Go on, kill me."

20

Ross had not made his mad ride on Cate's trail alone. Braesford, who had endured it with him, came trotting up at a deliberate pace designed to support but not interfere. Dismounting, he moved to Ross's side. They stood gazing down at Trilborn.

The bastard was having trouble breathing. Ross made no move to help. He didn't give a tinker's damn if the man never drew breath again. In fact, he would prefer it.

For a single instant he had been greatly tempted to accept the dare, driving his blade through Trilborn's neck, ending his breathing forever. Such satisfaction would have been in it, such justice.

Chivalry and honor could be damned nuisances.

"I have him. See to Cate," Braesford said.

Ross dreaded going to where she had fallen. His brother-in-law, though concerned, did not seem alarmed, but it was difficult to tell with him; he carried sanguine temperament to unmatched heights. She might be bleeding beyond Ross's power to stop it, might be maimed, dead. Sword in hand, he turned slowly toward where he had seen his wife fall beneath Trilborn's sword.

She was sitting up in the waist-deep grass. She watched him approach, her gaze wide, even as she untangled her veil from her hair.

"He said you were dead."

Her greeting had an undertone of wrathful accusation to his ears, though tears rimmed her eyes. Where was her anger directed? He could not tell.

"A slight exaggeration." He stepped closer. A dark bruise spread from her left cheekbone to her temple. Her eye on that side, he saw, was bloodshot and swollen. His voice rattled like gravel in his throat as he said in a different tone, "He hurt you."

"He meant to take me to Ireland with him. I was of no mind to go."

"Preferring to stay and make certain I'd been killed."

Resentment flared in her eyes, along with something that looked like half-blind agony. "Ross…"

"Later," he said, and let his sword dangle from his wrist by its fighting cord as he reached to lift her to her feet. Alarm poured like acid along his veins as he saw she could barely stand. Curses roared through his mind. What had Trilborn done to her?

He should have killed the bastard while he had the chance.

Stabbing a glance toward the others, he saw that Braesford had helped his enemy to his feet. His breastplate had been removed, and Braesford was binding a pad of shirting to a nasty cut that pumped arterial blood from his wrist.

"Touching," Trilborn called out to where Ross stood holding Cate. "How would you treat a female who cared about you, given you're so tender toward one who tried to have you killed?"

Cate inhaled a sharp breath, swayed on her feet. Dismay at the accusation or guilt for a truth revealed? Ross could not tell, wasn't sure he wanted to know what she felt at this charge Trilborn had hinted at before.

"That little dagger of hers is a lethal toy, is it not? You found it in your bath after an attack. She tried to bleed me with it. Welladay, I'd have killed you if my sword arm had been in good form."

"I didn't," Cate whispered. "Well, I did cut his arm, but I had to do that."

"She did, else I'd have had her," Trilborn said lightly. "First she spewed like a fishwife, enough to turn any man's ardor limp. I do think she's breeding with your get. A dilemma, I will admit, but you can always shut her away until the babe is born."

Ross's hold on her tightened; he couldn't help it. Was Trilborn right? She had been through so much. What if she was with child and nigh to losing it?

"Cate?" he demanded.

Hot color washed over her features. "I think... mayhap."

Rage slammed into him, along with a fierce protective urge that turned his every muscle to stone. Trilborn had been at Braesford Hall, had somehow guessed Cate's condition. Had he meant to punish her, and him as her Dunbar husband, by seeing to it she miscarried? The threat to his unborn child was blighting, but worse still was the danger to its mother.

"How do you know where I found the knife?" Ross

demanded of Trilborn. "How could you know unless you were told of it by your hireling?"

"Mayhap she told me? No, I merely took the trinket when she offered it, and hired a man for her. I'd have found a more nimble assassin if the plot had been less hasty."

"I didn't offer it," Cate cried, "I didn't!"

"Careful, man," Braesford said. "You're confessing to attempted murder."

Trilborn laughed. "What odds, if I take her with me?"

"What odds indeed?" Ross said, turning with Cate in the circle of his arm, supporting her as he walked with her toward Trilborn. "That's been your purpose all along, to take Cate away from me. Why not confess to attempted murder? They can't cut off your head twice. Though the headsman will surely come for you for treason and your try at regicide, Cate could well burn for attempting to kill her husband. But you will never take her from me, not here and not in the hereafter. She is mine by duly consecrated ceremony. She is my wife, my hope and my future, and I'll hold her with the last breath in my body."

Manic rage twisted Trilborn's face. The grunt in his throat rose to a bellow. Wrenching his arm from Braesford's grasp, he bent to snatch up his sword from the grass at his feet. In the same move, he lunged in low attack, slashing at Ross's unprotected knees.

Ross spun Cate away, slinging her away from danger. Without looking to see where she fell, he swung up the blade that dangled from his wrist, parried with a hard twist of his body to stop the wild advance. The steel edges of the weapons scraped together, screeching metal on metal. Then the two settled to the fight.

It was not pretty, had no fine moves, no elegant strategy. It was cut and thrust and hard, laboring effort while the sun poured down upon them and sweat stung their eyes. It was kill or be killed.

Trilborn was crazed, advancing, always advancing, with savage daring in his blows and bloodlust in his eyes. Ross parried, watching, waiting, knowing the Englishman could not keep it up, knowing his wrist was weak, knowing he must tire. Yet the man seemed possessed of demonic strength. He had no fear, no caution and scant defense.

He wanted to die.

Trilborn meant to die by the sword rather than face the ax, had asked for it moments before. He wanted no trial with jeering nobles, no date with the headsman while the crowd laughed, bought pasties and threw slops. He meant to be a suicide.

Ross was of a mood to oblige him.

He did it then, and not just from fury, from ancient scorn or even for Cate, but from sudden, vital compassion. He used his strength and skill for a slicing cut as clean and true as he could make it. It took Trilborn in the neck, providing the exact sharp and sudden end as a headsman's blow. It was a merciful finish for an old enemy. It was what he might have wanted someone to do for him, had he been in Trilborn's shoes.

When it was done, when Ross could catch his breath, could bear to face the horror and condemnation in Cate's eyes, he turned to her. She lay where he had thrown her, sprawled in the grass. She did not move when he dropped to his knees beside her, didn't move when he called her name, didn't move when he gathered her close. She didn't move when he took her up with him upon his destrier and turned back toward Henry's camp.

She never stirred at all, not even when he whispered over and over into the braided silk of her hair, "Don't let her die. Pray God, don't let her die."

The messenger from Scotland arrived at Braesford a month to the day after the Battle of Stoke. The news came to Cate where she sat in the courtyard garden Isabel had created, reclining among cushions in a bower of roses while stock and lavender scented the air.

It was Ross who brought it, approaching her with quiet footsteps as if he feared to wake her. It was not so unreasonable, for she had slept much of the weary way from the battlefield, and dozed often since then. Concussion, Henry's physician had called it, though Gwynne swore it was because she was breeding. Mayhap she was right. Though close work with a needle and other such tasks still gave her a headache, she was tired of being treated like an invalid.

This deferential approach was not how she had once dreamed of being accosted in a garden by a handsome knight, as in the *Roman de la Rose.*

"Yes?" she asked, lifting her lashes, which she had let fall briefly against the brightness of the sun. "What is it?"

"Do I disturb you? I can return another time."

"No. Please." She moved her feet, gesturing toward the end of the bench. "I heard the trumpet for the gate. Is there word from the king?"

Ross accepted her invitation, turning to face her as he settled on the bench. "From Braesford, rather, under Henry's seal. All is well with him. The number of the fallen from the battle at Stoke has been set down as only two hundred killed for Lancaster, though several thousand for York. And the young pretender, born Lambert Simnel, is safe. Henry, unlike Richard before him, saw no need to have this boy done to death. He has been put to turning a spit, instead, earning his keep in Henry's kitchen. Even the priest who tried to turn him into a prince has been sentenced to prison instead of death."

"Judicious."

"Oh, aye, if that's another word for canny," Ross said. "He would distance himself from any hint of child murder, and who can blame him?"

Cate could only agree. After a moment, she said, "And was that all?"

"There was also a message from the old laird, sent first to London because he thought it would find me there."

"Not ill tidings, I trust."

Ross gave a small shake of his head that set the sunlight to shimmering in the dark waves of his hair. "All is forgiven. I am ordered home."

Home. He still considered Scotland as where he belonged. She looked at the rose blossom she had broken from the canes that arched above her, twirling it in her fingers. "A grand boon, but sudden. How does it come about?"

"Word reached my father that Trilborn was slain by my hand. The Englishman was the last of his line. The feud is over. Having brought this about, I am considered to be redeemed as a Dunbar."

"Being in charity with you, your father, the laird, is prepared to overlook a small thing like taking a Sassenach wife?"

Ross leaned forward, resting his wrists on his knees and meshing his fingers together. "As you say."

"Will you go then?" The words were light, almost without expression. She was proud of that, regardless of the effort required to make them so.

"I must."

It was on the tip of her tongue to ask if he would return, but she couldn't bring herself to form the words. "When?"

"At once. An escort was sent along with the message."

At once. He did not intend to wait for her to make ready, did not mean to ask her to go with him. A lump formed in her throat of such size it was impossible to speak.

He glanced at her, and then returned his gaze to his hands. "It's best if you don't travel just now," he said, as if in answer to her unspoken question. "You haven't been well, and there is the babe."

It made a fine excuse, just as it had excused him from sharing a chamber with her, or a bed, since their return. It was time that was ended. "I'm perfectly well now."

The gaze he turned on her was dark with doubt. "Are you? You were so... I thought you might die."

"Are you certain that's all?" She drew a deep breath, let it out with care. "Or can you possibly believe there was truth in what Trilborn said, that I sought your death to fulfill the curse of the Graces and be free of our marriage?"

"Cate, no."

"I wouldn't blame you." She went on with a quick shake of her head. "All those things I said about the curse, the evidence of the knife you retrieved, the confession of a man who expected to be executed—it must look damning."

"It looks impossible," Ross countered, his voice firm, his eyes clear. "You would never connive in a sneaking murder, Cate. If you wanted to be rid of me, it would be in so fine a rage you'd carve out my lights and liver with your own hand."

It was not a picture she could appreciate, but she let it pass. "Well then?"

He rubbed his hands together with a dry rasping of sword calluses. "I never deserved to take you to wife," he said to the ground at his feet. "You are Lady Catherine, daughter of a peer of the realm, while I'm naught but a border reiver. They'll call me laird one day, but 'tis an honorary title with little nobility about it. To think you might want me dead was naught but an excuse to keep me from homing to you like a hawk to the lure, to prevent me from turning into an Englishman for your sake."

"That could never happen," she said as a smile twisted her lips.

"More than that," he went on with a dogged air, "I kept you with me when I should have sent you away from danger. I left you unprotected at Henry's camp, and look how that turned out. I'm a selfish bastard and no courtly knight. Even yon David, Braesford's squire knighted by Henry, proved a better lover."

"No," she said plainly.

He seemed not to hear. Rising with the effortless flex of hard muscles, he moved away to stand with his back to her. "You would be better without me."

Was that truly what he meant, or was he saying he preferred to return to Scotland alone? He had been forced to marry her, had accepted Henry's charity because he had no home or homeland. That was changed now.

"What of Grimes Hall?"

"It was given for your sake. You must do with it what you will."

She opened her lips to ask if she was to bring up their child by her will only, and alone, but that smacked of whining. She would not make him a hostage again, tied to her by the babe they had created. Nor would she beg him to stay with her, to love her, though the words rang in her head with such force that the ache of concussion returned from the pressure.

"So this is farewell," she said to his broad back.

"If you will it so."

Her will. That word again.

"What has my will to say to anything?" she demanded in ire. "When have I been allowed any decision whatever in this affair?"

He swung back to face her. "You could have refused to be married."

"Oh, yes, and with what result? Being branded a harlot after spending a night alone with you, or being handed to Trilborn, instead, by Henry's decree? No, I thank you!"

Ross set his hands on his hips. "You preferred me."

"Of course I did, being possessed of my full wits," she fairly spat at him. "Not that it signifies in the least."

"Except you could have let me die of a putrid knife wound, but did not."

Her face flamed as she recalled sponging him to lower his fever, enjoying the glide of a cloth over his body, uncovering him to see how he was made. "I felt responsible. You were injured while coming to my aid."

"And later, when you came to my chamber?"

"I thought you might die before…that is, before the marriage could be consummated."

"Thoughtful of you," he drawled, his eyes narrowed.

"Wasn't it?" She glanced at him, then away again. "And all for nothing, because you were hale and hardy both before and after the wedding."

"And why is that, do you think?"

"I've no idea. Mayhap because you had no belief in the curse, or because it was Trilborn who first asked Henry for me, so the malice was directed at him."

Ross's eyebrows lifted. "Now there's a thought, though you did your part to bring his treasonous intentions to nothing."

"Not from malice," she said quickly.

"Nay, only for the king."

She lifted her chin. "And for you. Trilborn meant to kill you in the confusion of battle."

"In addition to dispatching Henry. An ambitious turncoat."

"But neither of you believed me when I told you." It

was a grievance that had troubled her then, and did so still.

Ross crossed his arms over the broad width of his chest. "We believed you, but it was necessary to convince Trilborn otherwise. We preferred that he strike as planned instead of getting cold feet."

"You might have let me know."

"So we might, except that it was you he was watching, you who could best convince him that it was safe to act."

"Oh, aye, but I was not safe."

"No," Ross agreed, his voice sober, "which is why I would leave you here, in Braesford's care."

She stared at him for long moments while the summer breeze tossed the roses above them, releasing their sweet scent along with a shower of pink petals. "Braesford is an excellent brother-in-law and fine husband," she said finally, rising to her feet and taking a step forward, "but not the one I married."

Ross set his jaw, though wariness came and went in his eyes. "He is better able to keep you safe."

"Did I ask to be safe?" she inquired with an edge to her voice. "Mayhap it's not my will. Besides, you came after me when Trilborn forced me to go with him. You named me your wife then. You prayed that I would not die. Over and over, you prayed it."

Dull color rose under the darkness of his skin. "You heard."

"As in my most fervent dreams."

"You had saved my life with your warning. To come after you was the least I could do."

"You said to me, 'later,'" she reminded him, moving toward him with footsteps that grew more certain as she came closer.

"Later?"

"When I would have told you how I felt about your death." He'd said it other times, as well, she remembered, especially when there was something he didn't wish to discuss.

"It wasn't the right time then."

"Because you came upon me with Trilborn and knew not what had passed between us, what he might have done to me?"

"That had nothing to say to it," he returned with a scowl. "'Twas because I was a bloody-handed Scotsman fresh from battle, and you an English lady. It's still true."

Relief brought a lump to her throat that she swallowed with difficulty. "But has even less to say to it now. I believe you are overnice in your ideas of English ladies, Ross Dunbar."

"You are one of the Graces of Graydon."

"And only a woman for all that. It means nothing—unless you fear me because of it?"

"Nay, never!"

"So I thought. I also think you claimed me after Stoke, prayed that I would live, because you love me. You've been unaffected by the curse because you loved me from that night in the New Forest, when you nearly set the world ablaze to keep me from freezing. You allowed me to come to you because you loved me. You married me for the same reason and no other. It's why you stayed away so long at Grimes Hall—because you dreaded that

I should see it. It's why you kept me with you, marching with the army."

"No," he said, his voice hard.

She jerked, as if that single word had been a blow. "No?" she whispered.

Slowly, he shook his head as he reached for her like a man in a dream who fears a vision will disappear. "I loved you from the moment I saw you face the outlaw leader with that puny poniard in your fist. The courage of it stunned my heart. It nearly killed me later to think, even for an instant, that you might have turned it against me. And then knowing you had been forced to use it against Trilborn, that I had failed to protect you, made me see I wasn't worthy, had never been worthy of the bride Henry gave me."

"I thought..." She had to pause to clear her throat before going on. "I thought I was not a fit bride for a Scotsman."

"Don't be daft. My father would be your slave within an hour of meeting you. Aye, as I was. As I am."

It was no doubt an exaggeration, but she would not hold that against him. "Then should we not make certain he does?"

"Should we?" Ross asked, his thumbs smoothing her upper arms through her silk sleeves. "When you may not stay?"

She drew back a little, the better to see his face. "Why would I not?"

"I claimed you as my wife. You have not claimed me as a husband."

"Of course I did," she said, frowning, "every time I came to you."

A smile, fleeting as a memory, came and went across his face. "Was that what you were doing? I rather thought it was something else."

"No," she whispered, stepping closer until her breasts brushed his chest.

"I don't suppose you would care to...nay. The priests say it's forbidden while you're carrying the baby, and after the birth. For two long years." He sighed.

"The priests," she said, running a finger along the opening of his shirt for the delight of touching him, "know little of breeding, having never carried a babe under their hearts."

"True."

"They've never given birth to one, either."

"No. Do you think..."

"That this is more of their perversity to prevent our pleasure? I do, yes."

"You're certain?"

"I am."

"Ah, Cate."

The heat that rose like blue flames in his eyes warmed her to her toes. She gave a small laugh, then a relieved sob as he swept her against him with sure strength. His mouth came down on hers in a kiss that devoured, but also cherished, possessed, bestowed trust, love and fidelity. When he released her for an instant, she rested her forehead against his chest.

"What of your father, the laird?" she asked with a sigh, "and the escort he sent for you?"

"They can wait. It was his idea to disown me. I see no hurry about returning to his good graces."

She glanced up, an anxious frown puckering her brow. "But you will go? I would not keep you from your family and friends."

"You would have me be a border reiver again?"

"If…if it pleases you," she said, though her distraction was caused by his thumb rubbing over the crest of her breast, rather than by the threat.

"I am an English baron like yon Braesford now, by Henry's grace, and own fine, wide lands. I have no time for reiving, even had I the urge. But there is a desire of mine that could be satisfied in Scotland."

Her eyes were heavy lidded as she met his. "What might that be?"

"To have you among the heather and bracken, with naught but the sky above us and my plaid beneath."

"So," she said with a catch in her breathing, "we will go soon?"

"Who can say?" he drawled, his gaze on the tight, tight bud of her nipple beneath the linen of her gown. "Mayhap when I am tired of making love to you on English soil, say in fifty years or so. Or it could be only after our babe is born."

"A long time for your poor escort to wait."

"Aye. He can return alone."

"I misdoubt he will want to face the laird of Dunbar without you."

"By God's teeth, no," Ross said, with a chuckle. Yet there was respect in his voice as well as humor.

"Such a fearsome man," she said, trailing her hand

along Ross's neck, tangling her fingers in his hair. "I believe I must meet him for myself before too long."

He smiled down at her with a quirk at one corner of his mouth. "If it pleases you."

"We leave today, then?"

"Nay, not today." He cupped her breast as if testing its perfect fit in his palm.

"Tomorrow?"

"I misdoubt I'll be ready."

"When do we ride?"

"Tonight, sweeting, and it be your desire."

"To Scotland?" she asked in all innocence, while wild heat rose in her face and dampness seeped between her thighs.

He whispered his answer against her hair.

Cate laughed, gasping, as she heard it, but did not gainsay him.

* * * * *

Acknowledgments

I'm grateful beyond words to the creators of Project Gutenberg and Google's Public Domain book online service for making it possible to access ancient volumes on the life and times of Henry VII and his contemporaries. To be able to read these books that actually reside in one-of-a-kind copies on the dusty shelves of far-flung libraries has been an incredible boon; to download them instantly and read them in the comfort of my office was nothing short of amazing. I am also indebted to the originators of the many websites dedicated to medieval history in general and the Tudors in particular. Their expertise and generosity is fantastic. These include, but are not limited to www.henryvii.org/; historymedren. about.com; luminarium.org; www.britannia.com/history; www.medievalhistory.com; www.tudorplace.com.ar; www.the-tudors.org.uk; tudorhistory.org; history.wise. edu/sommerville/361/361-04.htm.

To the various authors, ancient and modern, who have treated on these subjects, as well, my most heart-felt thanks for their labors, which have made mine easier: *Bacon's History of the Reign of King Henry VII*, Francis Bacon; *Famous Men of the Middle Ages,*

John Henry Jaaren and Addison B. Poland; *Henry VII,* S. B. Chrimes; *Henry VII,* Gladys Temperley; *Lives of the Princesses of England,* Mary Anne Everett Green; *Lives of the Queens of England from the Norman Conquest,* Agnes Strickland; *The Battle Abbey Roll* by Catherine Lucy Wilhelmina Powlett, Duchess of Cleveland; *The King's Mother,* James Underwood; *The Making of the Tudor Dynasty,* Ralph Griffiths and Roger S. Thomas; *The Reign of Henry VII from Contemporary Sources,* Albert Frederick Pollard; *A Source Book of Medieval History,* Frederick Austen Ogg; *Albion,* Jennifer Westwood; *Daily Life in the Middle Ages,* Paul. B. Newman; *Dictionary of British History,* J.P. Kenyon; *History of England,* James White; *Life in a Medieval Castle,* Frances and Joseph Gies; *Life in a Medieval City,* Frances and Joseph Gies; *Life in a Medieval Village,* Frances and Joseph Gies; *London and Westminster, City and Suburb,* John Tombs; *Marriage and Family in the Middle Ages,* Frances and Joseph Gies; *Medieval People,* Eileen Power; *The Cambridge Medieval History,* John Bagnell Bury; *The Castle Explorer's Guide,* Frank Bottomley; *The History of Normandy and England,* Sir Francis Palgrave; *The History of the Ancient Palace and Late House of Parliament at Westminster,* Edward Wedlake Brayley; *The Knight, The Lady and The Priest,* Georges Duby; *The Ordnance Survey Guide to Historic Houses in Britain,* various editors; *The Steel Bonnets, The Story of the Anglo-Scottish Border Reivers,* George MacDonald Fraser; *The Time Traveler's Guide to Medieval England,* Ian Mortimer; *The Waning of the Middle Ages,* J. Huizinga; and *Westminster,* Walter Besant.

I'm indebted to my editor, Susan Swinwood, and

her colleagues at MIRA Books for their expertise and superlative efforts on my behalf, and to my agents, Richard Curtis and Danny Baror, for advice and their continuing support. To my family, surely the most understanding people in the world—thanks for your forbearance and being there. And to my husband, Jerry, for his quiet and eternal support, plus cups of coffee when most needed, love and gratitude always.

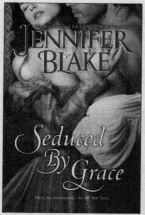

$7.99 U.S./$9.99 CAN.

$1.⁰⁰ OFF

**Look for the next book
in the brand-new trilogy from
New York Times and *USA TODAY*
bestselling author**

JENNIFER BLAKE

Seduced by Grace

*Available September 27, 2011,
wherever books are sold!*

HARLEQUIN®
www.Harlequin.com

$1.⁰⁰ OFF the purchase price of
SEDUCED BY GRACE by Jennifer Blake

Offer valid from September 27, 2011 to October 18, 2011.
Redeemable at participating retail outlets. Limit one coupon per purchase.
Valid in the U.S.A. and Canada only.

52609884

5 65373 00076 2   (8100)0 11750

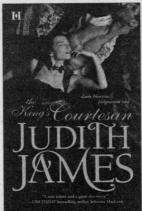

New York Times and *USA TODAY*
Bestselling Author

JENNIFER BLAKE

Once a starveling bootblack, Christien Lennoir has risen
to become the sword master known as *Faucon,* the Falcon.
When a desperate gambler stakes his plantation in a card
game, Christien antes up. He wants River's Edge—and the
tempestuous widow whose birthright it is.

Reine Cassard Pingre feels trapped: the only way to keep her
inheritance and her beloved home is to accept Christien's
proposal of marriage. Though she instantly despises him,
Reine cannot dissuade him from wedding—and bedding—her.
Their union is electrifying, but the honeymoon may be cut
short by the lurid secrets at the heart of River's Edge.

TRIUMPH IN ARMS

Available wherever books are sold.

MIRA®

www.MIRABooks.com

MJB2748

HARLEQUIN® HISTORICAL:
Where love is timeless

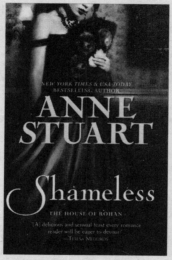

REQUEST YOUR
FREE BOOKS!

2 FREE NOVELS
FROM THE ROMANCE COLLECTION
PLUS 2 FREE GIFTS!

A LADY JULIA GREY NOVEL

A Lady Julia Grey novel from award-winning author

DEANNA RAYBOURN

THE SPIRITS SPEAK OF SECRETS....

Partners now in marriage and in trade, Lady Julia
and Nicholas Brisbane's private investigation service
is sought out by an unlikely client. Julia's very proper
brother, Lord Bellmont, needs their help.

An eerie enclave unfolds a lurid tangle of dark deeds
and they face myriad dangers born of dark secrets—
the kind men kill to keep....

The DARK ENQUIRY

JENNIFER BLAKE

32748	TRIUMPH IN ARMS	___ $7.99 U.S.	___ $9.99 CAN.
32454	GUARDED HEART	___ $6.99 U.S.	___ $8.50 CAN.
31254	BY GRACE POSSESSED	___ $7.99 U.S.	___ $9.99 CAN.
31243	BY HIS MAJESTY'S GRACE	___ $7.99 U.S.	___ $9.99 CAN.

(limited quantities available)

TOTAL AMOUNT	$	_____
POSTAGE & HANDLING	$	_____
($1.00 for 1 book, 50¢ for each additional)		
APPLICABLE TAXES*	$	_____
TOTAL PAYABLE	$	_____

(check or money order—please do not send cash)

To order, complete this form and send it, along with a check or money order for the total above, payable to MIRA Books, to: **In the U.S.:** 3010 Walden Avenue, P.O. Box 9077, Buffalo, NY 14269-9077; **In Canada:** P.O. Box 636, Fort Erie, Ontario, L2A 5X3.

Name: _____

Address: _____ City: _____

State/Prov.: _____ Zip/Postal Code: _____

Account Number (if applicable): _____

075 CSAS

*New York residents remit applicable sales taxes.
*Canadian residents remit applicable GST and provincial taxes.

MIRA™ HARLEQUIN®
™ www.Harlequin.com

MJB0911BL